Bottle and Glass

Bottle and Glass

Morgan Wade

First Edition

Hidden Brook Press
www.HiddenBrookPress.com
writers@HiddenBrookPress.com

Copyright © 2015 Hidden Brook Press
Copyright © 2015 Morgan Wade

All rights for story and characters revert to the author. All rights for book, layout and design remain with Hidden Brook Press. No part of this book may be reproduced except by a reviewer who may quote brief passages in a review. The use of any part of this publication reproduced, transmitted in any form or by any means, electronic, mechanical, photocopied, recorded or otherwise stored in a retrieval system without prior written consent of the publisher is an infringement of the copyright law.

This book is a work of fiction. Names, characters, places and events are either products of the author's imagination or are employed fictitiously. Any resemblance to actual events, locales or persons, living or dead, is entirely coincidental.

Bottle and Glass
by Morgan Wade

Editor – Helen Humphreys
Cover Image – Bernt Løve Nielsen
Cover Design – Richard M. Grove
Layout and Design – Richard M. Grove

Typeset in Garamond
Printed and bound in USA

Library and Archives Canada Cataloguing in Publication

Wade, Morgan, 1971-, author
    Bottle and glass / Morgan Wade.
ISBN 978-1-927725-19-1 (paperback)
    I. Title.
PS8645.A334B68 2015   C813'.6   C2015-904254-2

Cover image adapted from a photograph by Bernt Løve Nielsen. To see more of Nielsen's work please visit http://www.flickr.com/photos/berntln

Map adapted from an original map at the Library and Public Archive of Canada: "Plan of Kingston and its vicinity. The shores and measures by Lieutenant A.T.E. Vidal Royal N. Under the direction of Captain William Fitz William Owen R.N.: The town and works from a survey by Lieut. H.L. Renny, Royal Engineers, and the soundings, by Actg. Lieut. Wm. Bayfield Royal Navy. signed W.F.W. Owen Captain dated Kingston 14 June 1816. Copied by L. Pereira March 1908."

Acknowledgements

Many thanks to Richard Grove/Tai of Hidden Brook Press; to Bruce Geddes and Tom Hollenstein for being early readers; to Adam Davidson-Harden, Brett Christopher, and Rob Smith for their interest and support; to Heather Home of the Queen's University Archives for her research help; to Dr. Brian Osborne (Professor Emeritus of Geography - Queen's University) and Major John R. Grodzinski (Professor of History – RMC) for their invaluable historical critiques.

Thanks to Bernt Løve Nielsen for the use of his photo for the cover.

Thanks again to Helen Humphreys for her encouragement and her steady editorial hand.

And to Nancy, love and gratitude for continuing to be my first and last reader.

There is nothing which has yet been contrived by man, by which so much happiness is produced as by a good tavern.

Samuel Johnson

A tavern is a place where madness is sold by the bottle.

Jonathan Swift

Table of Contents

Prologue – *p.1*

Chapters:
1 – The Rode and Shackle – *p. 3*
2 – HMS Lancer – *p. 12*
3 – Franklin's Tavern – *p. 24*
4 – White Bear Tavern – *p. 36*
5 – Badgley's and Metcalf's, Blake's and Brown's – *p. 40*
6 – The Golden Ball – *p. 58*
7 – Ferguson's Tavern – *p. 77*
8 – Old King's Head – *p. 89*
9 – Walker's Hotel – *p. 95*
10 – Violin, Bottle, and Glass – *p. 101*
11 – King's Arms Inn – *p. 124*
12 – Mother Cook's – *p. 141*
13 – The Britannia Inn – *p. 152*
14 – The Royce Inn – *p. 165*
15 – The Black Bull – *p. 173*
16 – Old Sam's – *p. 184*
17 – Tête-du-Pont – *p. 202*
18 – Richmond Hotel – *p. 213*
19 – St. George and Dragon – *p. 223*
20 – Olcott's Tavern – *p. 228*
21 – The Rob Roy – *p. 235*
22 – Burnside's Tavern – *p. 239*
23 – Jim Beach's – *p. 254*
24 – Violin, Bottle, and Glass – *p. 265*
Epilogue – *p. 272*

Author Bio Note – *p. 277*
Author's Notes – *p. 279*

xii

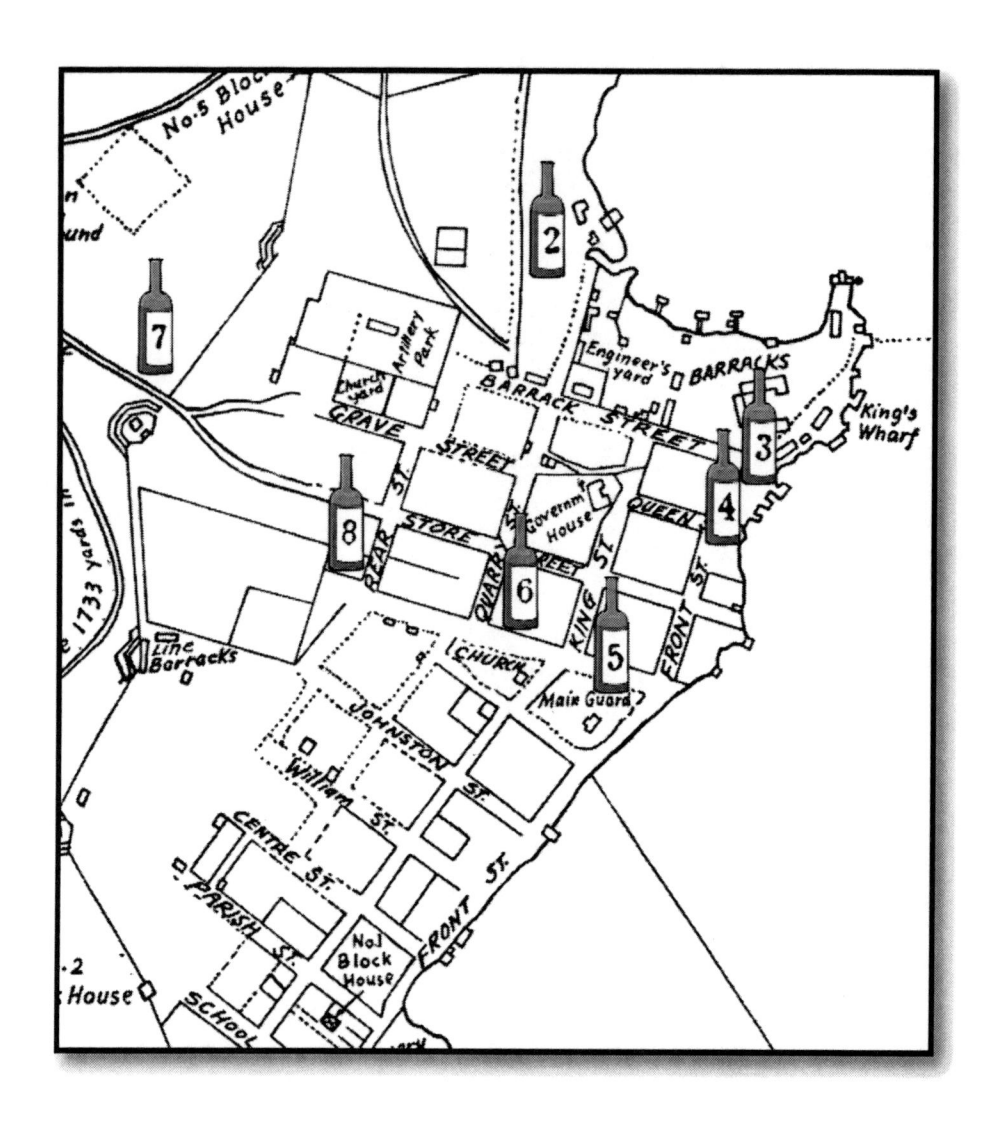

xiii

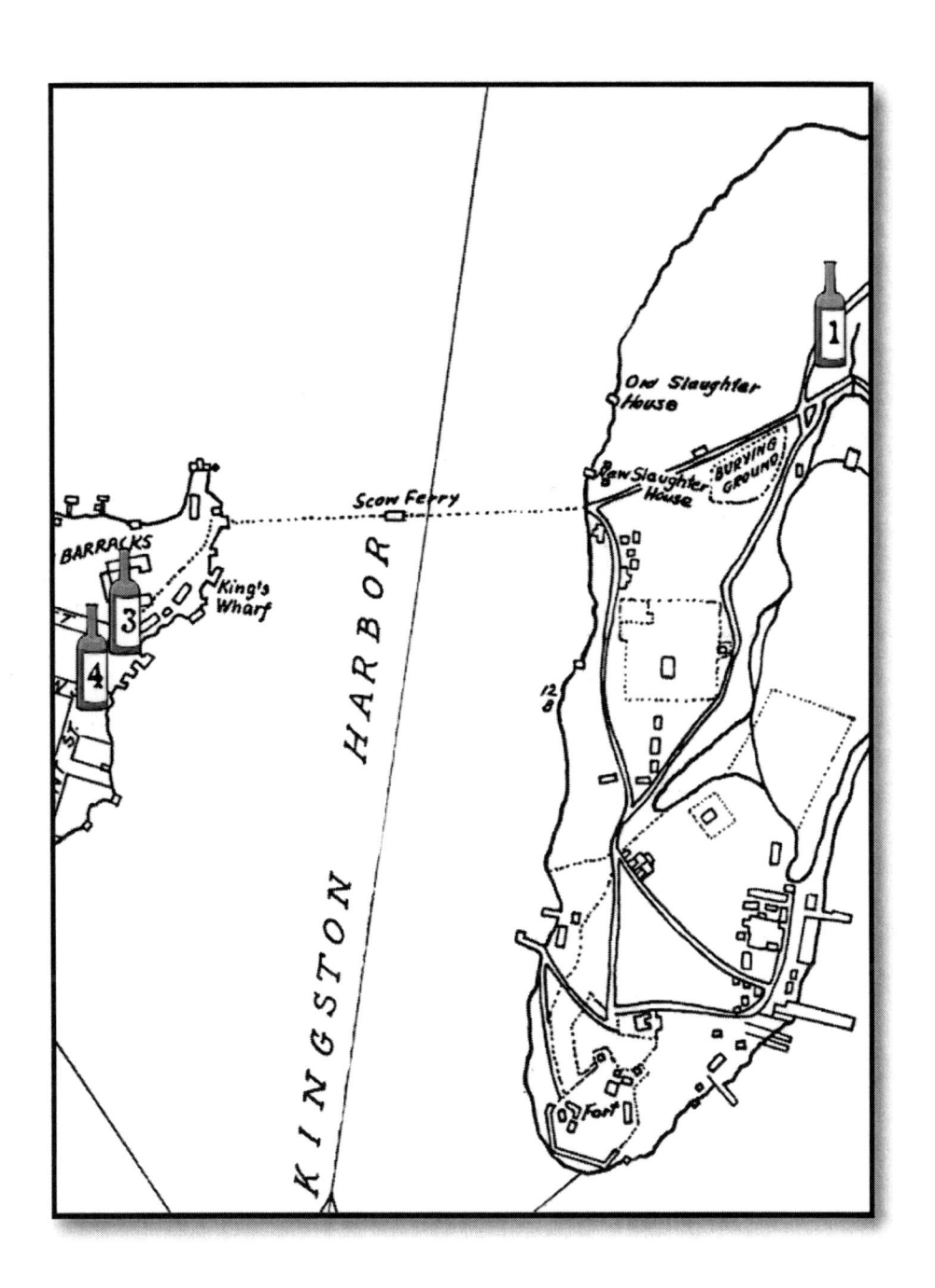

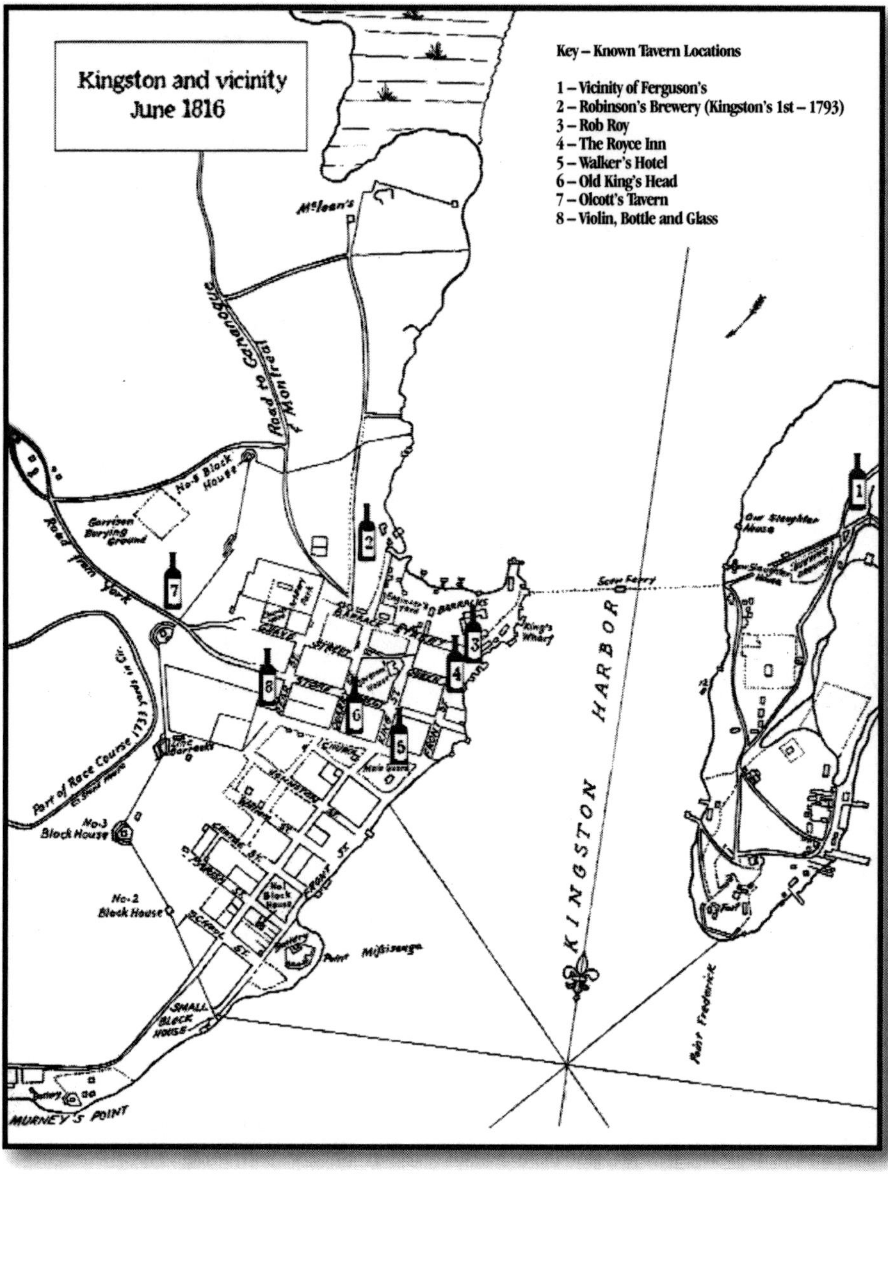

Kingston and vicinity
June 1816
Key – Known Tavern Locations
1 – Vicinity of Ferguson's
2 – Robinson's Brewery (Kingston's 1st – 1793)
3 – Rob Roy
4 – The Royce Inn
5 – Walker's Hotel
6 – Old King's Head
7 – Olcott's Tavern
8 – Violin, Bottle and Glass
KINGSTON HARBOR
Road to Gananoque & Montreal
Road from York
Garrison Burying Ground
No-3 Block House
No-2 Block House
SMALL BLOCK HOUSE
MURNEY'S POINT
Point Mississauga
Point Frederick
King's Wharf
Scow Ferry

Prologue

THE GLASSBLOWER TOILED, even as the auctioneer's men, under the watchful eye of the bailiff, packed up his shop. They tossed his battledores and borsellas into crates, noisily and without regard. His tongs and clappers were bundled into burlap and it was as though he himself was getting dismantled. Still, he kept his eye on the slender bulb at the end of the pipe, gauging its delicate progress. They carted away the charcoal and potash, muting the roar of the kiln, until even the bellows failed to rouse its snickering embers.

The glassblower waved away the bailiff's exhortations. He spun the embryonic vessel, maintaining its symmetry, bent on achieving the perfect form, as if everything might ride on it. He closed the furnace doors against the diminishing glow and brought his final issue into the glory hole. Trying to imagine himself alone, trying to ignore the clattering of the packers all around, he focused on the glimmer at the end of his pipe. He breathed life into it, gently, not so much it might burst, not so little it might collapse. Each piece a new beginning.

The glory hole, too, began its decay. He could have done more, he could have tweaked and twisted and tweezed. The proportion was just short of immaculate. He could have spent a lifetime, happily, cultivating that one last whimsey.

The bailiff rumbled again.

With the assurance of a midwife, the glassblower cut the shiny body from the pontil and put it into the annealer to cool and temper. He handed the last pair of tongs to one of the packers who threw them into a sack.

There was nothing left to say. From the annealer he pulled the whimsey, an amethyst-tinted ampoule, fragile and elegant and still very warm, and he swaddled it in rags, placing it carefully into a crate with the rest of the bottles and glass, inventory he'd been allowed to keep. He stepped outside. Before departing with the auctioneer's men, the bailiff closed the door and fastened a heavy padlock on it. The glassblower sat on a stump across the road and looked at his shuttered shop. When the wisp curling from the chimney finally gave out, he began the long walk back into town.

1

The Rode and Shackle
Late Summer, 1813

GLASSES AND BOTTLES TREMBLED.

Hobnails clattered against the broad rib of granite-porphyry shaping the moor, resonating through the inn's foundation, up dry-rotted posts, and along scuffed oak planks. Miniature cat's paws, a mariner's telltales, ruffled the surface of swanky-filled mugs.

Jeremy Castor launched the heavy boom of his right leg out from his stool and swiveled, looking for his cousin. Momentum caused him to lose his balance and he compensated by clapping his left hand down. His vessel capsized and the brew gathered in sweet, viscous pools around his fingers.

Merit Davey had just staked a guinea on the crude anchor etched into the table and he had his right arm raised above his head. His left hand stroked the lucky feather hidden in his pocket. A sunken, toothless man sitting across from him stared up at the fist, as though anticipating a blow. Merit held no weapon; he wielded a pair of pig's knuckles of his own fashioning, slightly weighted. They favoured the anchor; not the crown. Never the crown. They were moments from their maiden voyage, christened with a measure of swanky-infused spit. When Merit heard Jeremy slap the bar he turned abruptly, jouncing his blond curls.

The cousins held each other's gaze for an instant. From Jeremy's expression, Merit immediately understood that the pressers would soon be upon them. And Jeremy saw in Merit's face what amounted to an apology.

"Best be out the back, lads" said the innkeeper, as he calmly opened a narrow door behind the bar.

Merit turned back to the table and the gummy grin of the banker. Again, he raised his fist.

"Merit!"

Jeremy stood, overturning his stool. Merit squeezed his eyes, thrust the dice back into his trousers and ran toward the door. He was at the threshold when he remembered his stake.

"My guinea!"

Jeremy's hand, wide as a fluke, spread across Merit's back and propelled him through the opening. The banker wheezed as he salvaged the abandoned coin.

If he'd wanted to be spiteful, Jeremy would have reminded Merit that he'd been warned. How foolish it was to be out on a Saturday night, frolicking. Prime time for the trawling press gangs, with the saloons full of young merchant marines and fishermen in a pliable frame of mind.

We'll go to the Rode, Merit had said, no-one will look for us there.

The Rode and Shackle, a public house of weathered stone anchored in the middle of the Cornish countryside, two miles inland from Porthleven, had withstood six centuries of royal successions. It used to be called the Rode and Anchor. One night thieves made off with its namesake, a modest-sized anchor adorning the front stoop, securing the inn against the gales and horizontal rain slicing in from the Atlantic. They knocked the iron crown from the rotted wooden shank and left the rode and shackle, still chained to a ring jutting from the brick. The rusting crown likely went to outfit a Porthleven fishing ketch, to replace one that had been cut away. Rather than find and haul another anchor up from the harbour, the proprietor chose simply to change the name.

Only old men - arthritic fishermen, broken miners, lame soldiers – frequented the Rode. Even then, as a group, they were few and declining. Younger men preferred the atmosphere provided in Porthleven or Helston; livelier entertainments, higher stakes, regular fights, the occasional woman. Eighteen year-old Jeremy and twenty-two year old Merit wouldn't be expected at the Rode.

Still, Jeremy's mother implored them to stay out of the taverns. Brainless pilchards, Alice would say, rushing straight into their weirs. Keep to yourself, they won't bother with you. Do your job. Then straight home. Don't you leave me, Jem.

Jeremy's father and two brothers were on the continent, fighting Napoleon. There were only three things to do in their part of Cornwall: mine, fish, or fight. That's the way it had always been. But Alice had always hoped her youngest might attain a different station. Sporadically, since he was ten, Jeremy had attended school at St. Michael's in Helston. The curate accepted fifteen students a year, boys of exceptional promise, for a small tuition. Alice's unmarried aunt Gladys, the curate's housekeeper, used the extent of her meager influence, baking extra batches of Eccle's cakes, to convince the curate to take Jeremy as one of his students. Alice hoped he would continue to study and to even become a curate himself one day, or at least a deacon. To never leave the parish. You're all I've got, Jeremy, she would say. Like the other young men of Porthleven, Jeremy's future was confined; in a different, more maternal way.

Alice's other directive: keep an eye on Merit.

"He's kin," she'd say. "Distant, but relative. We're the only family he has left."

Merit's mother, a Parisienne, died when he was five, bearing his stillborn sister. His father, Alice's second cousin, lay beneath the crust of Spanish soil, shot through by a republican musket ball. Merit's brother, impressed by the Royal Navy, was likely dead or drunk, or both, in Singapore, Port Royal, Halifax or some other Godforsaken foreign port.

Hide him from trouble, Alice would say, he's rebellious like his mother, his heart pumps Jacobin blood. And he's single-minded, like that rooster his father.

On this occasion, as on so many others, her competing pleas were impossible to honour.

Merit had spent most of his free time in the last month crafting dice from a set of gleaming pig knuckles he'd obtained from the butcher. He was certain he'd devised a pair so subtle in their design and execution that they could not fail. He insisted that he would try them out that Saturday night.

We'll be safe at the Rode, he'd said. Jeremy, despite his misgivings, went along, only able to satisfy one of his mother's requests.

The cousins tumbled out from the back of the tavern onto the moor just as the press gang mobbed through the front. A newly backing wind high above the Rode had corralled the clouds, wrung them of their moonlight, and condensed them into a low ceiling of damp wool. Shafts of yellow from the tavern's windows reached into the gloaming.

Jeremy clutched at Merit's neck. "Nowhere to hide," he said, breathless. "What have you done to us?"

Merit raised his hand; he was thinking.

"Chough Tor," he said, and he was off north, toward the outcropping where the birds congregated, the choughs; black as stout, with beaks like bloodied marlin spikes. Jeremy loped behind Merit. A memory ghosted through his brain; he was five, struggling to keep up with his two older brothers as they marched to the pond, never looking back, his home-made rod slipping from his shoulder, his line catching and fouling in the gorse, restraining his progress.

Five men stamped across the granite lobby of the Rode, making their contribution to the scuff that had worn and polished it dismal black. These men were unemployed miners from the nearby villages of Gweek and Goonhusband. For one reason and another, they were no longer fit for the mines, no longer fit for much of anything beyond snaring other young men for the Royal Navy. They were squat, meaty, rooted to the ground; thick in every sense of the word, made confused and irritable by the lead that dusted their lungs and clotted their blood.

They scanned the lounge, passing dull eyes over the few customers: the fat one, snoring loudly, lantern light flickering against the globe of his bald head as it lay parallel to the table; the ancient one, barely visible behind the pewter mug that towered over him, a stinking puddle at his pigeon-toed feet; the two nestled in a blue cloud huffing on their slender, clay pipes, a shuffle of cards between them; the one sitting behind the crown and anchor table, grinning; the bartender mopping a rag at the sticky pool atop the bar. Even these five miners, rejected by the lead wheals at thirty and likely dead by forty five, found the scene pathetic.

"Even' to you Da," one of them said through a curled lip, "a fine sty you run here."

The bartender continued mopping.

"I's told two fishermen been by."

The miner called Biscuit scraped toward the bar. His colleagues spread out through the lounge. One of them picked up a mug from a table, took a long draught, and spewed it over the snoozer's bald head. The man woke, crying "You know I can't swim!" He toppled sideways from his chair. No-one laughed, not even the perpetrator.

"You seen em Da? You seen em?"

The bartender shook his head.

"Who's swanky you sponge Da?"

Biscuit had the innkeeper by his suspenders and was pulling them in left and right across his throat.

"May have been," the old man whispered, raising clouded eyes, "maybe it was they."

Disgusted, Biscuit excavated a wad from the lining of his tortured bronchials and launched it across the bar. If he could finish this task soon, receive his payment, he could be back in town by midnight, drinking himself painless before the headache returned. He jerked the old man's suspenders. For a moment, a smile threatened, as he imagined drawing the straps across each other as far as they could go and popping the tender's head from his neck like a daisy from a stem. He tightened. The fabric cut further into the man's windpipe and goggled his eyes.

"No, it t'aint, 'tis it?" Biscuit said out loud, to no-one but himself, releasing his grip. "T'aint worth the bother. Not t'all." The old man fell to the floor. Killing the man would only complicate the task. Biscuit spat again, this time in the direction of the fallen man, another futile attempt to rinse the taste of metal from his mouth.

He nodded to his colleagues and they proceeded to enter the remaining rooms of the inn, kicking open closets, tipping chests, overturning tables. When they were satisfied all that remained in the inn were old men and their residues, they spilled out the back and headed north.

It took about fifteen minutes for Jeremy and Merit to reach the tor. A whiff of ammonia told them it was near. Far off they could hear the rustle of feathers and the ticking of talons on rock, but could see nothing. Merit led, feeling his way around the outcropping until he stumbled behind a granite stack in the shape of a crow's nest. Jeremy followed and joined his cousin. They crouched down, shoulder to shoulder, panting, looking back in the direction they came. With the woolen sky absorbing the soft spill of moonlight, nothing could be discerned across the moor. Narrow slits, emanating from the windows of the distant Rode, stared back at them like a pair of beastly eyes.

For several minutes, there was only the sound of their breathing as they began, slowly, to uncoil. Still, they kept watch on the unblinking Rode. Merit was the first to break the silence.

"'Tis a pity about my guinea, though," he said softly.

"Mer?" Jeremy whispered, after a time.

"Aye."

"Where's your special die? Can I see it?"

"Why?"

"I'd like to grind it beneath my heel."

"You'll not have it. It'll lay a golden egg yet."

They were quiet again for several more minutes.

"I'm sorry Jem," Merit said, finally. "Truly I am. It was a hair short of prudent, I see that now."

Jeremy said nothing, so Merit pulled his luck charm from his pocket and ran an index finger down its filament ends. Marianne, his mother, had given him the feather just months before her death. "C'est une plume exceptionnelle mon petit lapin," she had said in her high, bright voice, gathering him in her arms. It had fallen from the sky, she had explained, as she and her friends had crossed the seventh arrondissement on their way to a parade and demonstration. It was all that Merit had left to connect himself to his mother.

"But you understand," Merit continued, encouraged by Jeremy's silence. "Them old hens at the Rode were overdue for a plucking. An enterprising man needs a project, needs keeping busy. He might go spare."

Jeremy watched as Merit held the quill by its nib and twirled it. Jeremy thought of his own mother, Alice, probably keeping vigil by the hearth, pouring another tepid cup of tea, imagining the worst. He thought of the cap, sitting half-finished on the side table.

I'm the fool, going along with Merit again, aren't I? More pleasant at home, knitting my cap, purling and casting by the blaze.

Part of him longed for the satisfying order and symmetry of a well-executed stitch. Still, he couldn't deny that the adrenaline-laden blood pumping at his temples and the briny air in his nose had left him invigorated. He couldn't help imagining himself one of those acrobatic birds whose rookery they'd squatted, out to sea within a couple of beats.

Free.

"I think we're out of the soup now Jem," Merit said. "It's looking all clear. I don't see a thing. Can't hear nothing but the choughs."

Jeremy wasn't fooled by his cousin's bravado. He'd witnessed the same performance many times. It wasn't the first near scrape that his cousin had inflicted on them both. And he knew on this occasion, like all the others, that despite his hopeful words, Merit's own heart palpitated and his breathing was fast. It was the same when he had grounded their employer's ketch, The Pelican, on a joy ride to Prussia Cove. And when he had enlisted Jeremy's help in trying to sell to The Seven Stars in Penryn a cask of port he'd salvaged from the beach. On that occasion, the proprietor nearly had them jailed. And when Merit had fleeced the patrons of The Turk's Head, with an unprecedented twelve straight rolls on anchor; they'd had to dash from the premises then too. Jeremy despised his cousin for his recklessness and lack of consideration, even while envying his spirit. Even so, Merit had always been more of a brother to Jeremy than his own, older biological brothers. Thomas and William dismissed him as a blouse-clutcher, rarely including him in their plans.

Jeremy reached over and engulfed Merit's knee in his palm, bringing the bouncing to a halt. His cousin, startled, looked back. He smiled, pried Jeremy's hand from his knee, and kissed the top of it.

And then he whooped. The lights at the Rode had been extinguished.

"They're gone! Packed in for the night."

He whooped again. "We're clear!"

Jeremy buried his enormous fist deep into Merit's ribs, pounding the air from his lungs. Merit convulsed and clutched at his side.

Jeremy peered around the granite crow's nest.

Nothing.

"Jackass," Jeremy said with a hot whisper.

He could no longer see The Rode. Night had foreshortened the overcast moor.

No shapes. No sounds.

Just a swishing of feathers.

And another.

And then a dozen.

Jeremy turned to see five stocky shadows emerge from the crags behind them.

"We was given up hope until we heard the hollerin'," one of them said, dully.

"Ain't it funny," another said, without a hint of amusement, "how wise the old owl seems until he opens his pecker and hoots?"

The last image Jeremy Castor recalled of that evening was the row of studs in the bottom of the miner's boot. Hard leather against the bridge of his nose.

Hobnails. Short tacks with thick heads.

2

HMS Lancer
– Captain's Cabin

DAWN'S FIRST LIGHT KNIFED INTO THE ROOM from a single porthole. On a table, before a tall, label-less bottle, stood two short jiggers. A man with a laurel of pearly hair, a matching silk scarf, and a bloom of rosacea on each cheek laid his pipe down. He twisted the cork from the bottle's neck and poured. It treacled out; liquor black as a Carib.

"Welcome aboard ducklings," he said, "*HMS Lancer.*"

At his shoulder stood a well turned out man as tall as Jeremy. The moustache decorating his lean face was the shape of a swan's wingspread and almost as wide. His hands were held crisply behind his back. A number of other lieutenants, mates, and midshipmen crowded into the captain's cabin, leaning over the engraved teak table, getting a good look at the new recruits.

Jeremy dabbed at his nose, inexpertly set by the ship's doctor, still dribbling blood. Through his sniffing, he detected a trace of molasses perfuming the cabin. He cast a sideways glance at Merit and the plum-coloured band encircling his cousin's left eye. Their abductor, Biscuit, the glowering miner, slouched into a corner making cradles from a loop of string.

"She's a 50-gun, fourth rate, Portland. A proper harpy. But we love her, we worship her, don't we?"

The men murmured their consent.

"It is our custom on the *Lancer* to spirit aboard a new man. This here, what I've poured, is some of the finest, and by finest I mean most heinous, blackstrapped rumbustion that's ever been swilled. Made by appointment at the hands of a wraith from King's Town known only as Scratch. We are delivered a case each year, and that's about eleven bottles too much."

"See that?" the captain said, showing them the pontil mark on the bottom of the bottle. "AB inside an acorn. The Scratch mark."

"Kewsel Kernewek," whispered Jeremy, urging Merit to speak Cornish, and make like they were simple farmers. "Ni tiek."

The captain pretended not to notice.

"Of course, you'll get your daily ration of Nelson's blood here on the *Lancer*, one gill morning and night, smoothed over with small beer, leavened with lime. And your regulation gallon of curdled brew. But only new recruits and condemned men get to sip this venom."

"Na marner Mer," Jeremy coughed, "na marner."

Merit remained motionless.

"You have the great privilege of serving his majesty when he needs you most. We won't be paying Bonaparte any visits this time I'm afraid, but we'll have plenty to say to Brother Jonathan. Won't we?"

"Aye!" and "Bully!" rang through the cabin.

"I'm somewhat disappointed that Biscuit couldn't flush a few more of you from the heather. He was so insistent that we stop at Porthleven. Plenty of sailors to nab, he said. But there you have it."

Biscuit continued to study the patterns made by the string between his thick fingers.

"Among press masters, he has no equal. 'Tis why I fished him from the mines and insisted on his pardon. So, we have to assume, if there was a prize worth catching, you're it."

The captain waited for some reaction, from the impressed men, from his officers, from Biscuit. It was quiet save for the sea breaking against the hull and the cackling of distant gannets.

"Enough dallying, duties await. Sign the articles of agreement, drink your toast to daft George, and I'll give you a shilling each on his behalf."

The captain pushed a bound ledger across the table. Another man came forward with a quill and a pot of ink.

"An X will do. Tell us your names and we'll scuff them in for you."

Merit still had not moved. The *Lancer* see-sawed gently through the swells and Jeremy wanted to retch. Their only chance, he decided, was to convince the captain that they weren't fit for duty.

"Na marner Mer," Jeremy whispered again, hoping Merit would know to present himself as a landsman. "Tyr-denyon, tyr-denyon."

"Enough with the Welsh, or Breton, or whatever it is. Biscuit here is from Cornwall himself and understands every muttered word. If you've got something to say, now's the time. In King's English, if you please, Mr…"

Jeremy stepped forward a quarter-step, his one hand pulling at the bloody kerchief in his other hand, and bowed his head slightly.

"Castor. Jeremy Castor, Sir, thank you."

"Captain. Captain Rowton."

"Thank you captain. Please, I think there has been a terrible mistake."

"That's so?"

"Aye, a bad confusion. We are no sailors. I work on the wharves, helping with equipment and storing the catch."

The captain was unmoved.

"I'm studying at Helston," Jeremy added. "Perhaps to one day become deacon."

Rowton nodded.

"It is my understanding," Jeremy continued, "only seamen and merchantmen are eligible for the press. I don't think we'd be any use to you, simple country folk such as we."

The captain pushed the ledger further across the table.

"Simple country folk often make good marines, do they not Major Stokes?"

"Aye captain, they do at that," the man at his shoulder replied.

"I implore you. Our mother lives all alone in her cottage. She has no idea where we are. She depends upon us. She's infirm. We're all she's got."

"Oh my," Rowton said, "poor sainted woman. None have mentioned their mother before."

"She is likely sick with worry at this very moment."

"Very likely. Don't worry, we'll make sure you get a letter to her on the first packet we cross."

"Captain, sir, I'm a deacon's apprentice, not a sailor."

"Have you proof? Protection papers?"

"I have nothing, I…"

"You need not raise your voice, sir."

Jeremy swallowed hard.

"Your mastiff forced us aboard, sir," he continued, "against our will, bearing nothing but our tunics. If you would return to Porthleven I could produce proof. I will take you to my employer, Mr. Pringle, owner of the Pelican."

Rowton gestured over his shoulder.

"Can you see through the porthole? Has the fog lifted? You might just be able to make out the outline of Land's End and beyond that Penzance. We are already two leagues closer to Newfoundland. There's no turning."

"We're apprentices. We can't be impressed. It isn't right."

"Don't presume to teach me maritime law, Mr. Castor. It is your duty and honour to serve your king. There wouldn't be a Royal Navy without the press. And without the Royal Navy, there wouldn't be an England."

"Your dear mother might this day be serving gazpacho to fat, garlicky señoras," sniffed Lieutenant Coulson, one of the gathered officers, "if it weren't for the recruitment of brave young lads such as yourselves."

"Just so. Sign our articles and we'll call you volunteers. Thirty shillings a month, with a three pound sign-up bonus."

"Articles? We don't even know what we're signing."

"Would you like me to read them to you?"

"I can read."

"I'm sorry Mr. Castor, we haven't time. The gist: we're bound for the colonies, to teach Brother Jonathan some manners. You and your mate agree to give us five years or until the commission is over. Four hot meals a day and lodging. Drink allowance, I covered that. A fair divvy of prize money. I've already discussed the pay rate. That is, if you sign now, without further delay. Otherwise, we'll consider you conscripted – twenty shillings a month, no bonus."

"But we're landsmen!"

Rowton stood abruptly from behind the table.

"I can outrig any topsman," Merit said, finally.

Biscuit looked up from the tangle of string at his fingers.

"Abarth Dúw," Jeremy stepped back, hanging his head.

"Choose your best rigger," Merit continued, "and set us a task. I'll do it faster and tidier every time. My cousin Jeremy here, it's as he says, he's no sailor. And his ma is too a saint, a lady who deserves better in this life. If I beat your man, which I'll do, you take Jeremy back to Porthleven and relieve him."

"A gambler. Naturellement. One hundred percent a seaman. If your clothing and deportment don't give you away, a penchant for wagering surely does. And, if you lose? I already have you both."

"If, hypothetically, I should lose, which I won't, we'll sign your articles, drink your toast, and promise not to desert at the earliest opportunity."

Rowton was quiet a moment, thinking. As he tugged at the white tuft of his eyebrow the officers leaned in closer.

"Mr. Coulson," he said finally, smiling again, "please fetch four equal lengths of line and the bosun's mate, Mr…"

"LeSaux, captain," said Coulson, stepping forward.

"Yes, Mr. LeSaux, if you'd be so good."

As Coulson went in search of lines and LeSaux, Rowton brought his chair around so its ladder-back faced Merit. He gestured for Jeremy to sit, which he did, folding his large frame awkwardly onto the chair.

"You should know that ordinarily we frown upon ship-board wagering. Too many nippers parted from hard-earned pay. Sows discord."

Rowton picked up the two full tumblers and handed one to the seated Jeremy and one to Merit, still standing.

"I think we can make an exception in this case," he said. "It may prove to be instructive. We'll stage a knot-tying competition. What's your name son?"

"Merit. Merit Davey."

"Mr. Davey against our Mr. LeSaux. But let's make it more sporting. For every knot correctly tied first by Mr. LeSaux, you Mr. Davey will take a dram. For every knot LeSaux gets first, Mr. Castor will take a dram."

"Me?" Jeremy attempted to turn in the chair but Rowton held him at the shoulder. "But what about Mr. LeSaux?"

"We can't have a man on active duty intoxicated. Tell me," the captain said, turning again to Merit, "have you ever been aboard a Royal Navy vessel."

Merit shook his head. "Not 'til today."

"What sailing have you done?"

"I work aboard the Pelican, for Captain Pringle. Netting pilchards mostly."

"And what sort of boat is the Pelican?"

"She's a fishing ketch. Double masted, main and mizzen."

"I know what a ketch is, Mr. Davey."

Coulson arrived with four coils of line and LeSaux, a slender reed with a face full of freckles and down, looking not older than fourteen.

"Ah, the bosun's mate. The challenge is this," Rowton said as he took the coils from Coulson and gave two each to Merit and LeSaux. "I will call out a knot, you each will tie it, and call out 'done' when it is completed. Lieutenant Coulson will verify the quality of the knot. The man with the fastest, verified knot wins the round."

Rowton grabbed the knobby ends of the back of the chair. "These will serve as bitts. Questions?"

Merit held out the rum tumbler in his left hand.

"Down the hatch eh? Unless you are so marvelous you can tie one-handed."

Merit hesitated a moment or two before tilting back the liquid ebony. He grimaced, coughed, and stamped his foot several times before handing the empty jigger to the captain. Laughter filled the cabin as he wiped his eyes.

"All right gentlemen, a master class in knot tying. Let's warm up. A clove hitch please."

Merit let one coil of line fall to the crook of his elbow while he twisted an end of the second line in one half loop around the knob of the chair-back and then another half loop twisted in reverse and pulled tight.

"Done," he cried, a fraction of a second before LeSaux yelled the same.

"One for Davey, just. Try our punch Mr. Castor, your turn."

All eyes were on Jeremy as he raised the rum to his mouth, the lip of the glass lingering near his own.

"Best to do it quickly," Rowton said. "To the King."

Jeremy closed his nostrils and tipped the jigger. The distillation of burnt molasses scorched his throat like lava and threatened to bounce back immediately. Once, when he was ten, Jeremy had got a mouthful of paraffin when trying to retrieve a fallen wick from an oil lamp. The paraffin had been milder.

"Not your mother's gin lemonade is it?" Rowton took the empty jiggers and handed them to Stokes. "Mr. Stokes, please repour."

Stokes wiped out each jigger with a handkerchief and refilled them neatly.

"Leave your knot," Rowton bawled at Merit, who was untying his hitch in preparation for the next one. "As you must know, ability to untie is just as important as the tying. An inherent quality of the first rate knot is the ease with which it can be undone. Re-tighten please. A one-armed imbecile with his hat down over his eyes could tie a clove. Let me see a round turn and two-half hitches."

Merit unfastened his hitch, made a long loop around the makeshift bitt, encircling it one and a half times, brought the tail end under the standing line, snaked it through, once, twice, and tightened.

"Done." Once more, Merit was a shade quicker than LeSaux.

"Buntline hitch."

Merit's hands fluttered, the previous knot melted away, and a buntline hitch replaced it.

"Done."

"Carrick bend."

Undoing the first line from the chair with one hand, Merit took the tail of the other coil with his other, and looped the two ends together into the symbol for infinity and pulled.

"Done."

"Bowline."

"Done!"

"That's some handsome knottery for a so-called landsman," Rowton said, looking pointedly at Jeremy, who was struggling to down another pouring. "But, you understand, running the lines of a fishing ketch is one thing. Rigging a Royal Navy warship is a task of an entirely different order. Biscuit, your assistance please."

Biscuit stuffed the jumble of string in his hands into a pocket and grunted out of the bulkhead.

"An able seaman of the King's employ must execute flawless hitches in all species of weather and under all kinds of duress. Hurricane gales. Murderous swells. Between the teeth of a dozen carronades, a hail of splinter and shot. Biscuit, if you will."

The press master took a truncheon from his belt and prodded it hard into Merit's bruised ribs, where he'd kicked him the night before. Merit cried out and clutched at his side.

"Bowline on a bight," Rowton said.

Merit began to untie but Biscuit poked again. And then boxed an ear. Then kicked a shin. LeSaux had his bowline finished before Merit had his line free.

"Your toast," Rowton said, handing Merit another measure of rum.

"To Cornwall," Merit said, hoarsely, after draining the shot, "and liberty."

"Sheet bend."

Biscuit slapped and kneed and cudgeled and LeSaux won again. Merit drank.

Rolling hitch. Running bowline. Noose. Merit drank each time.

"Turk's head, three bights, five leads."

Merit's head was swimming. His fingers tripped and fumbled and he could not lace the line through the intricate weavings of the decorative knot. Biscuit's interference was no longer necessary. LeSaux called "done" just as Merit had restarted for the second time.

"Too challenging? Let's simplify."

"Stopper knot."

"Figure eight."

"Reef."

LeSaux finished and Merit drank three more drams. He swayed counter to the ship.

"Thank you Mr. LeSaux, well done, though you could stand a bit of bowline practice."

Mr. LeSaux saluted and left.

"Mr. Davey, what do you think, a final wager, all or nothing? One final hitch, if you can tie it in under a minute, you and Castor are free to go. If not, you sign my articles with no further complaint."

"I can tie any knot," Merit replied, enunciating each word deliberately, like a child.

"Are you ready sir?"

"Aye."

"The allfer knot."

Merit unfastened the two lines from their reef knot and began a loop, and then another. He uncoiled the loops and wound the tail around the bitt. He twisted and bent. And then he stopped. The officers snickered and whispered.

"Mr. Davey, a simple allfer knot, if you please. Your time is almost up."

Rowton strolled back to the other side of the table, retrieved his pipe, and opened the ledger to its latest page.

"All for naught!" he shouted. "This isn't negotiation, understand? All for naught! You're impressed. Now sign the God damned articles!"

Jeremy picked up the quill and jotted his name on the next available line. Merit scrawled his own, unsteadily, on the line below.

"Excellent. From what we've seen, I have no doubt you'll make an able seaman. And you," Rowton said, pointing his pipe stem at Jeremy, "have all the raw material of a first rate marine. Be good lads, follow your orders, and with any luck, this will be the last time we ever speak to each other. Biscuit, take these men to see the quartermaster to get their kit and show them their bunks. They'll want a wink or two before first watch. The rest of you to stations, let's get this crate under way."

~ ~ ~

An hour later, Jeremy lay cocooned in a hammock, his feet extending past the supporting ropes, his backside brushing the timbers of the floor. He was attempting, unsuccessfully, to still the eddies frothing his brain. Above him, swinging like a pendulum, Merit sobbed.

Jeremy had the urge to jump out of his hammock, pluck Merit from his canvas envelope, carry him top-side and pitch him over the gunwale into the Celtic Sea.

"Merit," he said, softly, despite himself.

Merit's arm fell disconsolately down from the hammock's edge as he shifted and his sobbing increased.

"I'll make it up to you, one day," he said finally. "And to Alice. I swear I will."

"Merit," Jeremy whispered again.

"I'm scared Jem."

Jeremy clasped his cousin's hand with his own, engulfing it.

"Aye. I am too. But we'll get through. We'll survive. As Cornishmen do."

"Where they from?" A voice from the gloom called out to another.

"Cornwall seems."

"Porthleven," Jeremy answered.

"Me uncle is from Penzance," the voice continued, "I'm from Brighton."

"Biscuit nabbed me in Hastings. Suppose t'be in the Indies."

"Cork. I miss me mam too."

"Cardiff," another voice said, with a lilt, "just before we shipped out on a freighter."

"Also Cardiff," said a third voice, distinctly female. "We'd just betrothed. They got me into the bargain."

"Don't believe a word. She volunteered. Came out on the bumboat, with t'other whores."

"Married now though, ain't I?"

"Of a fashion."

"Boston."

"Brest," another said, "merde le Biscuit."

"Aye, but don't let him hear you saying it."

"Why Biscuit?" Jeremy asked.

"Ship's biscuit," the original voice said.

"Hard."

"And unpalatable."

"I know him," Merit said, "from before."

"You do?" Jeremy asked, surprised.

"Shut your dribblers," a new voice growled, "let me sleep."

The murmuring faded and only Merit's sniffling could be heard. Jeremy drifted uneasily and slept until a boot end jabbed him awake.

"Let's go Castor, it's our watch. Let me show you the ropes."

Jeremy rubbed the damp from the corner of his mouth and stumbled after a marine into the harsh light of the afternoon. They arrived at a station just in front of the fo'c'sle.

"Finn Davies," the man said, grinning. "We stand here and keep an eye out."

Jeremy was painfully thirsty and his stomach leapt and fell with the motion of the ship. He tried to steady himself by holding onto a nearby railing and his eyes gradually accustomed themselves to the glare of the water. A squadron of fifty terns, oily black and efficient, sliced across the *Lancer*'s course, materializing from the fog to starboard. Hypnotized, he watched their silent progress, in perfect formation and maximum pace, so low that they left a string of ripples dissolving in the surf.

"Happens every spring," Finn said, appraising their effortless flight, "no-one knows why. They fly out to sea, low and fast. Now that's freedom, ain't it?"

Jeremy watched them disappear to port.

"It's called a dread."

Jeremy lurched to the gunwale and pitched himself half over, emptying himself of all that was left in his stomach, bile-black and just as bitter.

3

Franklin's Tavern
– Montreal Road
Late spring, 1814

THE WAGON RIDE FROM THE FARMSTEAD HAD BEEN UNPLEASANT, taking four and a half hours instead of the usual two. Though the sun was strong and unimpeded, spring rains had made Montreal Road impassable in many places, adding at least an hour. On six separate occasions, Dorephus and Dunbar had to get out to push and pry and cajole the wagon from one mud-slicked slough to another while Amelia pulled at the reins. Jude, the nag, had to stop frequently for watering. Where the road wasn't dissolved into muck, where it opened into a clearing and was hardened by the sun, it was pitted and pocked, causing the wagon to jolt violently every few yards. Repeatedly, Amelia would find herself suspended in the air, an exhilarating instant of weightlessness followed by the unyielding pine bench snapping back, spanking into the thin seat of her petticoat, sending a sharp pain up her tailbone. Very often she walked behind, taking care to avoid the mud. Even so, her only pair of leather boots, lace-ups with twelve clasps on either side, were spattered. Midge and blackfly carcasses speckled her face and hair.

Amelia would have faced the mud, the bugs, and the bone-jarring potholes with good humour if it weren't for the other travelers. Not many were met, but the majority of those were at some level or another of inebriation. All manner of men: young and old, handsome and ugly, healthy and diseased. Farmers, labourers, loggers, carters, couriers, trappers, fishers, soldiers, militiamen, deserters, vagrants, and criminals. Five in six would be drunk, any time of day or night, toting a demijohn, squeezing a wineskin, sucking from a flask, coming from or going to the tavern. She was unnerved by the gush of their menace; the undisguised aggression, the impertinence, the air of grievance – behaviour that, ordinarily, soberly, would have been repressed, corked by decorum.

There were four crucifixion scenes on the route from farm to town and Dorephus had insisted that they stop at each one. They now arrived at the most elaborate, a thick beam of cedar standing at least twenty feet tall with another beam lap-jointed against it, lashed with coils of rough hemp, decorated with a giant wreath of briars. It stood at the intersection of Montreal and Loughborough Road, erected by the King's Mill Methodists on a rise in the centre of a circle scythed from the sedges, and it was visible from at least a mile away. Dorephus brought Jude to a halt and he and Dunbar unfastened his harness so that Jude could nibble.

Amelia crossed the clearing to the cross. Cricket sopranos and bullfrog bassos filled the space with their repetitious hymn. Wild geranium, lupine, and trillium bouquets entwined a rough ladder leaning against the beam. At its foot, there was a wooden figurine with a crudely painted scarlet coat, a piece of silvered glass, a chipped pipe with a small pouch of tobacco, and a tablet painted with the words: *Lord Jesus Christ, Son of God, have mercy on me, a sinner.*

She wondered what child had left his toy soldier and why. A votive offering? Was the father at war, marching on Plattsburgh or Fort Erie? She looked across the dell at her own father, Dorephus, patting Jude's nose, offering him a fat carrot.

"Pilgrims!"

A voice, loud and sharp, rose over the diminuendo of the thicket choir. A man and a teen-aged boy stumbled into the clearing. Instinctively, Amelia backed away, behind a young hemlock.

"Pilgrims," the man took a long, dramatic bow, forcing his companion to bow as well by clutching his neck and pushing downward. "Delighted. First souls since we set out."

He crossed the clearing, nearly sprawling to the ground when he tripped on a root, and he dropped himself to a stump, directly midway between the wagon and the cross. He swabbed a rag across his forehead and directed his speech to Dorephus and Dunbar.

"It's been a hot morn and God-damn we're thirsty..."

The man noticed Dorephus' frown. And the giant crucifix.

"Oh, beg pardon." He drew his thumb across his chest, kissed it and aimed it at the wreath of briars. "Say," he continued, "mightn't you have a drink to share with your fellow sinner?"

Dorephus nodded to Dunbar and the Irishman pulled a water skin from a bag in the wagon, filled a tin cup, and brought it to the man.

"Praise be," the man said before taking a long swig. He passed the cup to the boy and then he clapped both his knees. "That is a most pleasant draught, refreshing and all. But I wonder about something a little more spirituous? Our only bottle is now tragically hollow and forsaken along the way. Have you anything with which we might make communion."

"Where are you from sir?" Dorephus asked, coolly.

"Originally, sir? Albany, sir."

"Loyalist then?"

"Loyalish, yes." It was unclear whether the man had slurred.

"What is your trade, sir?"

"Ploughman, sir. Carmichael Jones. And," he gestured to the boy, who looked on dully and said nothing, "apprentice."

"Then, Mr. Jones," Dorephus said, pausing, "should you not be ploughing?"

"Day off," the man said, with a hint of resentment. He puffed breath through slack lips and then seemed lost in thought. Finally, he said, with new conviction, "Actually, we're free lances, you see. Seeking our next engagement."

"Maybe you could volunteer your services to the King. I understand General Prévost could use all hands against Brother Jonathan."

"Aye, I'm sure he could, but we're not in that line of work, see? Still and all, we'll happily drink the good King's health if you supply the toast."

Dorephus stiffened.

"You'll find," he said, "a good, clear spring a mile and a half north, fifty paces from the road. There is a red, painted blaze that marks it. Plenty of water, most salubrious."

Dorephus began to put away Jude's oats. The ploughman stood and stared. "I see," he said, "that is it then, is it? No breaking bread? No water into wine?"

"Come Amelia," Dorephus said. The ploughmen stood between her and her father. She started on a circumscribed path back to the wagon, walking on the balls of her feet as if to not make noise.

"Stop!" the ploughman cried. Amelia halted and Dorephus looked up from the harness he was resetting.

The ploughman approached Amelia, slightly hunched with his head cocked to the side.

"Samuel, behold. A vision."

He pinched her cold, sweating hand between his thumb and forefinger and raised her arm, as though inviting her to a quadrille. As he scanned her length her neck blushed above the tight collar of her dress. "Ma'am, your beauty strikes me nearly blind. You can't be more than sixteen, seventeen? Samuel's age." He turned to Dorephus. "Your wife?"

"Daughter. Come Amelia."

"Daughter! Praises. Not married?"

Amelia, stared at the ground and shook her head.

"Hoseanna! We could have the ceremony right here – a perfect place. Samuel, good Sam, me best man." He gestured to the garlands ringing the ladder. "Blooms for your tresses. We've not much time to get acquainted, but no matter. It's providence."

Amelia tried to withdraw her hand but the ploughman pinched tighter.

"Honeymoon in the King's Town. Would you like that, sweet clover? Many a swish hotel for newlyweds."

"Dunbar," Dorephus said, "retrieve the cup. And please escort Ms. Barrett to the wagon."

Dunbar pulled his watch from its pocket, opened the glass, blew on the hands, shut the glass, tapped it, and put it back. He walked slowly toward the ploughman, palms upraised.

"Oh mister! Mr. Barrett is it? We's just funning ain't we Samsie?"

Still the boy was silent, his eyes locked on Amelia.

"A little trick in exchange for lack of drink. We mean nothing by it. What happened to Christian charity? Appalling times we live in. Appalling."

Dunbar faced the two men.

"Lay off the old man," he said quietly, "and you'll get your drink. Mr. Barrett runs a farm on the Spafford grant, to the north of here. This Saturday he holds a work bee – we are collecting the supplies this day. Be gracious now and you can quench your thirst then."

The ploughman released his grip on Amelia's hand and she walked quickly back to the wagon and her father.

"And the cup," Dunbar said. Samuel finished it and handed it back.

"Very good," the ploughman said. "Safe travels. No harm done. We'll see you then. Pleasure." He swept an imaginary hat in a bow so deep he nearly toppled. "We'll spread the good word."

Dunbar returned to the wagon, pulled himself into the bed and sat with his back against the sideboard. Amelia stepped up to join her father on the front seat and Dorephus got Jude moving with a gentle cluck. As they left the clearing Amelia turned to see the ploughman ascend the ladder of the cross, crushing the trilliums under his boot heel. At the top, he lay back with his arms extended and he thrust out his livid tongue. The toy soldier with the scarlet coat protruded from between the buttons of his trousers.

"Eyes front," Dorephus said. "Satan makes tools of idle hands."

Amelia looked down at Dunbar who met her gaze with a wet grin and a wink.

She turned and shuddered. Dorephus had hired Dunbar on Colonel Spafford's recommendation and she believed her father to be altogether too trusting. Amelia suspected that Dunbar remained loyal to Spafford and reported back to him on his days off, not to her father's advantage. They had their Irish connection.

Amelia detested how little Dunbar was grinning all the time, licking his lips, like some old world gargoyle. There was a perpetual dampness about him. His crow-black hair hung heavy over his face and was always slick. He was forever tamping a shirt cuff into the corners of his watering eyes. His mouth was always open and he would often suck back the saliva that threatened to break the levee of his bottom lip. When he spoke, his brogue percolated through the reservoir, the words made slushy with spit.

"Father," Amelia said, quietly, "it's not too late to change our minds. We can just turn back. When the war is over, and Freddie and Archie return…"

Amelia and her mother had questioned Dorephus about the necessity of a work bee. Amelia's older brothers would have helped with the farm. They would have worked with their father to erect a new barn, to clear acreage, to produce and collect the potash, to break the earth. But they'd enlisted and were in Prescott, preparing to march on Plattsburgh. Surely the war would end soon. Surely they could wait another season and store the hay in one of Colonel Spafford's extra barns.

"It's been discussed," Dorephus said, snapping the reins.

"Aye missus," Dunbar slurped, "it's how it's done, hereabouts. It's as the Colonel says. He knows."

"Thank you Dunbar. As I say, it's been discussed."

Amelia could tell herself she'd accompanied her father for his own sake. Dorephus had asked her to come. Joseph Franklin and his wife had long seen her as a favourable match to their eldest son, Stanley. They always asked after her, hoping she would visit. If she put in a polite appearance it would improve their bargaining position with the Franklins. She was glad to help her father, but it wasn't the only reason she'd come. If she'd stayed home, she'd have spent the whole day with her mother cleaning and cooking and preparing, trapped within those same few monotonous acres she never seemed to leave, talking to herself, seeing no-one. She had read every volume in Dorephus' small library, some of them several times over: Defoe, The Arabian Nights, The Odyssey, tales of high adventure, of spirited women and daring men, of exotic lands and wine dark seas. By comparison, her life seemed to be one of melancholy exile, behind the drab bars of cow parsnip and burdock. She'd come on this trip for a bit of excitement, a feeling of freedom.

They rode in silence, except for the cacophony of the trundling wagon, each of its corners jolting violently in a different direction than the other, up or down.

"But, it's true," Dorephus said, after a few minutes, as though voicing an internal conversation. "Many 'steaders have held successful bees. There is no quicker way of clearing a field or raising a barn. Or of building community spirit. 'Tis neighbourly, isn't it?"

"Aye," Dunbar answered.

"I'm already indebted to Colonel Spafford, both personally and materially. We need a substantial crop that we can store and bring to market and sell for a good price, this season. Then I can start to repay his generosity. If the Colonel thinks it's a good idea, it must be. He can only want me to make good on my debt."

"Aye."

"Don't worry Moonie," Dorephus said, smiling at his daughter, "it will all work out."

One night when Amelia was ten she and her father stayed up late to trace the progress of an impossibly swollen September moon. They'd wrapped themselves on the porch in a wool blanket, with a pot full of popped corn, salted and buttered, and a jug of cold, hard cider. Dorephus told stories of his youth, in Yorkshire, describing Amelia's grandparents and her extended family. "Just fifteen minutes papa," Amelia would say, every fifteen minutes, when Dorephus suggested they turn in. The sudden call of a rooster had shocked them both. When they dragged themselves from the warmth of their observatory into the chilled sheets of their beds the moon was low and pale. Every year since, after the hard work of the harvest was done, they would keep a vigil for the last full moon of the season. Dorephus took to calling his only daughter 'Moonie'.

Amelia brightened when they crested a hill and saw the tavern, a boxy, two-story, frame building with a clapboard shell and a broad chimney at each roof end, sitting next to the road like a giant treasure chest. It was fronted with apple trees and a fence of close pickets. In the yard, two boys played fetch with a collie.

"You see," Dorephus said, putting his hand on his daughter's knee, "I told you it wouldn't be long. We'll get ourselves some sparkly and rinse the filth clean away."

Joseph Franklin met them at the door.

"Mr. Barrett!" he said, "'tis a pleasure. We expected you hours ago. No trouble on the road, I hope?"

The two men shook hands.

"Nothing to speak of. Some muck, here and there."

"Come inside, refresh yourselves. Mrs. Franklin has made meat pies. And a bowl of early greens." He signaled his sons to help Dunbar take Jude to the stables for watering and feed.

"And who is this lovely lady?" Franklin asked, as they stepped across the threshold into the foyer of the tavern. Inside it was warm and musty like the inside of an ale-filled mash tun. A simmering aroma of stew and browning pastry permeated the dining room.

Amelia told him her name.

"Your daughter?" Franklin asked Dorephus, an exaggerated look of incredulity on his face. Dorephus nodded, smiling.

"My goodness, Mrs. Franklin," he cried, "come quick. Come see young Amelia Barrett. Once in a while the fruit rolls far from the tree, eh Mr. Barrett? Sometimes you get a real peach!"

Mrs. Franklin emerged from the kitchen wiping her hands on a corner of her apron. She was tall and thin with a wedged-shaped face and large, shallow-set eyes, like a walleye. A triangle of the striped kerchief she wore on her head lifted like a dorsal fin.

"What a darling," she said, taking Amelia's hand. "I wish we knew you were coming. Stanley is away in town, looking at a horse. He'd have so wanted to see you again. You must be completely tuckered. Come, there is a basin of fresh water in this room. You'll want to bathe."

Amelia thanked Mrs. Franklin and stepped into a room with a day bed, dry sink, ceramic basin and pitcher of water. On a nearby table there was a chunk of yellow soap and a stack of towels. Amelia poured water into the basin, cupped it into hands and gratefully rinsed her face of road accumulations. She held her face in the centre of a towel, relishing its plush capacity to scrape away grime. Looking at herself in the hanging mirror she tried to restore order to her hair, confused as it was from wind, gnats, and perspiration. As she returned to the door, she overheard Franklin speaking with her father. She stopped to listen.

"We appreciate your custom Dorephus. It's been difficult."

It was only then that Amelia noticed the inn was empty, except for them. No carriages out front, no-one in the sitting rooms or dining rooms.

"You've always been decent to us. I trust you."

"I moved here ten years ago. Of my own accord. As a businessman. Surely they must know where my allegiance lies. I'd have moved back to New Hampshire, otherwise."

"That's so."

"Damn war. Bloody useless. Bad for business."

"Depends on the business."

"Suppose. But I'm for Canada now. They don't believe it. Once a Yankee, always a Yankee. Even your Colonel Spafford."

"Spafford? He was here?"

"Aye, he guaranteed your order."

"Did he?" Dorephus was thoughtful a moment.

"Aye, with reservations. After thoroughly dunking me in the stock pot, so to speak. Wanted to know who my suppliers were, whether they could be trusted to deliver quality. Whether I'd have everything in time. Whether I wasn't going to pack up and join my so-called countrymen. What a lot of strawberry fool stuffed into a scarlet coatee, if you don't mind me saying so."

Joseph stopped when he realized Dorephus wasn't listening.

"Did he not discuss it with you?"

"Eh?" Dorephus returned from his thoughts.

"You and the Colonel. Did you discuss payment?"

"Oh, yes, maybe we did. Of course we did. My apologies, Joseph, it was a long haul."

"I understand."

"Of course, I can't make any payments to you now. It must be on credit. But I will settle with you in the fall."

"Perfectly fine. Your Colonel Spafford has guaranteed everything. Not to worry."

"Yes, quite right."

"Come, let's fortify you for the trip home. After, you can look over the stock."

Mrs. Franklin put out venison pie, stewed rutabaga, roast parsnips and dandelion greens with vinaigrette. To wash it down, they drank cider from sweating, earthenware jugs, that had been chilled in a nearby stream. The conversation was dominated by Mr. and Mrs. Franklin asking about Amelia's prospects, of which there were none. They marveled that she wasn't already engaged. Were there any young men from good families she had her eye on? When would she like to return and meet again their son, Stanley? She was glad that Dunbar was taking his lunch in the kitchen with the help and wasn't within earshot.

Amelia bore the interrogations politely, demurely, but inwardly she now hoped the lunch would end and they would soon return home. She would never say so out loud, but Amelia often wondered what all the fuss was about. Sure, there was Bartholomew Case, the miller's boy, who always sat close to her at church and who had shyly offered to give her a tour of the mill. And there was her brothers' friend, Eldon Sturridge. She enjoyed Eldon's company; he did side-splitting impressions of the parson, his mother, Colonel Spafford, and there was something about his skewed grin with a mouthful of straight, milky teeth that stirred something inside of her. But the truth was she'd given little thought to questions of boys and men, love and marriage. There was hardly an opportunity to meet friends and socialize. With her brothers gone, she was far too busy helping her parents with farm chores. Dorephus and Millie seemed similarly unperturbed. It would happen when it happened and Amelia was in no rush. She had little enough freedom as it was. To give her life, which seemed like it hadn't yet begun, to some other farmer to tend his house and garden, seemed an additional sentence.

"I hope, when you do find your lucky Stan," Mrs. Franklin started.

"Man," Joseph corrected her.

"Pardon?"

"Man," Joseph said, chuckling, "you said Stan."

"I didn't. Nevermind. I do hope you will consider our inn for your honeymoon. Many folk stay in town. They go straight from getting the licence, to the service, to the celebration. But there's something about a nice, country inn. The tranquility. Natural beauty. The romance. We'd be sure to make it special for you."

"That's very kind," Dorephus said, before draining his mug of cider. "But first we must get through the work bee. Thanks so much for your hospitality Mrs. Franklin, superlative as always. We must harness up again, to make it home before dark. Joseph, we should look to loading those supplies."

They made the trip home in five hours, Jude straining under the additional load: a wheel of cheddar, three cured hams, three barrels of ale, one barrel of port wine, one barrel of claret, a cask of rye whiskey, and a case of Franklin's own applejack. It was one wheel, one cask, and three barrels less than what Spafford had set aside. Dorephus wasn't comfortable with the added debt.

"I hope it's enough," Dunbar said, running his fingers over the arc of the oak staves, dabbing the corner of his mouth with his sleeve.

On the way, they encountered another half dozen itinerant drinkers. All were cheerful and well-supplied. One, sprawled across the road wearing nothing but a nightshirt, snoring loudly, they nearly bisected under the wheel of the wagon. Two others walked with them for three miles, serenading. When the wagon got stuck and could not be budged by Dorephus and Dunbar alone, the two singers leant their shoulders and helped push it free – a good deed which netted them a bottle of applejack.

When they reached their own fifty acres, they unloaded their cargo, had supper and Amelia fell into bed exhausted. She spent the next two days with her mother cooking and baking, cleaning and drawing water. Early Saturday morning would bring, they hoped, twenty-five hungry, thirsty men, a large new barn and ten more acres cleared.

4

White Bear Tavern

THE SINGLE-ROOM SALOON OF THE WHITE BEAR was stale and close. Heavy wood shutters had been barred against the street. Inside, sweat and tobacco mixed with the spent paraffin exhaled by a few grimy lamps. The creaking floorboards and the broad, oak rafters that absorbed every sour breath and every slopped beer defined the place. The din that prevailed earlier, over games of faro and hotly contested shuffleboard, had faded to a murmur.

Carmichael let the last shard of ice cascade from the beaded glass into his tilted, waiting mouth. He sucked on it and looked around. Samuel, next to him in a chair propped on two legs, his back against the wall, was asleep. The man across from him tapped a nest of tobacco from his clay pipe onto the table, spread it out, pinched it up, and tamped it back into the bowl. Another man, to his left, argued half-heartedly, refusing to accept that last winter Tusker McTavish had caught a two hundred pound sturgeon just by cutting a hole in the ice and spearing it. A confusion of cards lay forgotten between them.

Carmichael studied the drops on the outside of his glass. One sparkling bead let go and streaked down the side. Then, another. And another. Like shooting stars.

Every evening started with such promise. Hilarity. Bravado. Lust. A sense that anything could happen. Then, the climax, which always seemed to pass him by. A waning. His acquaintances, the other patrons, melted away, one by one, until only the desperate remained.

A Punch and Judy show, always the same ending, night after night. Always bottled, always stoppered.

Carmichael gripped the glass until it shattered in his hand. The men near him whooped.

"Tam," he said, not looking up from his hand, marveling at how no blood had been drawn. "Another."

"All done, Carm." Tam Grant had spent the last half hour putting away chairs and tables, bottles and glasses. He picked up a corn broom and shuffled toward the latest mess. "And you'll not be getting another glass here. Next time, bring your own."

"What about last orders?"

"Called 'em."

"When?"

"Three times. Before each of your last three drinks."

"Tam. What's wrong? The White Bear used to have claws. It used to crackle and growl."

"Damn it," Tam said, laughing as he swept the glass pieces into a dust pan, "you talk sometimes."

Carmichael let out a primal roar that caught in his throat and sputtered. Samuel woke with a start and slid awkwardly to the floor.

"You're alive," Carmichael continued, after the coughing subsided. "More than I can say for the rest of them."

"You've had enough," Tam said. "You're full up."

"One final sling."

"No ice."

"Fine. Just whiskey."

"Glasses packed away."

"Skip the glass," Carmichael said, looking at his bloodless hand again.

"You have no money."

Carmichael pulled a sheaf of papers from inside of his jacket.

"I have notes." He squinted at the top note. "Farmer's Bank."

"Not accepted here."

"Credit."

"The last two were added to an already substantial tab. Plus cost of broken tumbler."

"So what's a third?"

"We're closed."

Tam poured the glass pieces into a bin and began to extinguish the lamps. The few men left in the tavern began to collect themselves.

"Hold it!" Carmichael shouted. "We ain't beaten yet. Or is we?"

The men shuffled to a stop and turned to listen.

"I know a place," Carmichael continued behind his hand, shouting his whisper, "a place of unlimited food and drink for men like us." He looked over his shoulder at Tam, flipping chairs onto tables. "Free of charge."

"Yeah Carm," one of them laughed, "and what kind of bribe to St. Peter."

"'Tis no jest. 'Tis a work bee. A plump flock, tastefully presented, awaiting wolves such as we."

Tam was shepherding them gently out the door, but they stopped again.

"A work bee?"

"Come on lads, best be on your way."

When the last was on the street Tam Grant barred the door.

"Aye, a bee," Carmichael continued outside. "Brandy and beer. Perry and applejack. Port and champagne. Roast beef, good cheddar, rye bread, mash and hash, chains of fat sausage, apple tarts, raisin pudding with sauce. Are you hearing me?"

"Mash and hash?"

"Aye, mash and hash. Maybe even dead man's arm."

"Jam roly poly?"

"Aye, all free."

"In exchange for labour."

Carmichael turned to face the man, dipped his head, and peered at him through his eyebrows.

"Where is it?" the man asked.

"Up Montreal Road."

"How far."

"Two hours."

The men, half-lidded and heavy-limbed, groaned.

"Champagne?" one of them asked as they headed north from the White Bear.

"Aye, free flowing, I guarantee it. And the old man has a daughter. The finest you've seen west of Montreal. My God! She's like a crock of butter, just churned, she's so fresh and creamy. Ain't she Samsie? Samsie seen her. Oh, how I'd like to dip my paddle and spread her far and wide."

5

Badgley's and Metcalf's, Blake's and Brown's

MORNING STRETCHED WESTWARD OVER THE BARRETT FIFTY. A few of the local volunteers had already arrived and were sitting under the shagbark, some chatting quietly or snoozing. Amelia and her mother were arranging muslin over the loaves of bread, pots of butter, jars of preserves, and dishes of double cream spread out on a rough board between two stumps. Underneath, staying cool, lay the barrel of beer. Nearby, a cast iron cauldron over a fire simmered roasted chicory.

Dorephus stood in front of the log cabin where his family lived and chewed at a fringe hanging from one of his cowhide work gloves. He wished his sons Arch and Freddie were home from Prescott. He wished he had one or two more men he could trust. A man who knew how to handle a bee. The only one he'd ever attended had ended early due to inclement weather. The men he could trust, the ones that hadn't enlisted, were busy with their own homesteads this time of year. Case, the miller, had sent his boy. Sturridge, Freddie's friend, had arrived, but he was not much more than a boy himself. George McNair, their direct neighbour, also a tenant on the Spafford grant, had assured him he'd be there. But McNair was a notorious drunk, and Dorephus wasn't sure he even wanted him to show. Dalgleish, his neighbour to the other side, said he would attend, with two of his sons, but he'd also said that about the well-digging and the fence-mending and the road-clearing.

There was Noble Spafford himself, corpulent veteran Marine Colonel, absentee landlord, owner of 800 acres of impregnable Canadian shield, granted to him upon semi-retirement by King George. "You'd think that the Colonel might attend," Dorephus said to Millie and Amelia, "The work bee was his idea afterall, he practically insisted upon it. What good is it to him if we fail?" But Spafford didn't even put in the road that Dorephus, McNair and Dalgleish begged him for. He limited his involvement to owning the land and collecting the rent.

"We won't fail," Millie insisted.

There was dim, drooling Dunbar, Spafford's man. He was mostly incompetent, but at least he could be trusted. The rest were the indigent and unemployed; layabouts with empty bellies, powerful thirsts, and nothing better to do. Dorephus studied the men lazing under the hickory. They waited sullenly for the liquor and grub, resenting every hurdle. Oxen, he thought. There's no alternative, only one way forward – to yoke them, switch them, drive them, and hope for the best. With a bee, we stand a chance of a decent harvest, to pay some debts; to live to work another year. Without, we die a slow death.

Amelia, too, stole furtive glances at the assembling men as she sawed through the bread and pasted the slices with butter and preserves. There must have been eighteen or nineteen now, milling about the grass, grumbling. She despised them; cluttering her front yard, trampling the lilies, terrorizing the finches. She looked from one to the other and made a silent inventory. Perforated sennit hats. Mismatched boots. Poorly darned tunics. Exhausted suspenders pulling at patchy trousers. In each face there was a mixture of hunger and disappointment. To Amelia they were a band of jackals, stretching and yawning and panting, kept at bay only by the presence of her father.

A palpable gust of desire puffed outward from the knot of men.

One of them, a beefy man in overalls with reddened eyes and a profusion of black whiskers, caught Amelia's gaze. He retracted his thin lips and ran his tongue along checkerboard teeth. She looked down at the tranche of bread she held, with its smear of raspberry, and blushed deeply. Her mother Millie, made a "whist" sound and flicked her shoulder. Amelia tilted her eyes even lower, renewed her slicing and pasting, and wished again that the day would soon be over.

It was an hour past dawn. About twenty men had assembled. Dorephus was pleased; there was potential for real accomplishment. It seemed like a good time to start. Stragglers could be assigned while work was underway. He stepped forward.

Gentlemen. The word caught in his throat.

"Gentlemen," he tried again.

The diggers and cutters quit their murmuring and turned to listen.

"Thank you all for coming. We are very appreciative. And please know that I, and Archie and Freddie when they are back, will happily return the favour."

There was no noise of reply, either approval or otherwise, so Dorephus continued, as he gestured toward a field of fallen timber.

"There are two main objectives today. One, to clear as much acreage here to the north as we can in one day. My goal is four acres, but I'll settle for as many as we can manage before dusk. We'll assign a team to sawing, another to hauling, and a third to burning for the salts. Great care must be taken to keeping the fires under control and away from the building and underbrush. Eldon Sturridge will captain this team, but I will look in frequently."

"Sturridge?" asked Overalls, pointing at Eldon. "Him? Downy chin 'n all?"

"Last year, he ran his father's farm for four months while Sturridge was away. And it is his father's team of oxen. He has my every confidence."

"Four months? That all?"

"Sturridge is captain," Dorephus said. "I'll set up the operation and be by regularly to monitor. The second objective is to raise a small barn, so this year we can move the hay and animals from our house. I will captain this project. Bartholomew Case will be my deputy. And McNair too, if he arrives. He has fair carpentry skills. Dunbar?"

The Irishman loped from the porch into the sun.

"This is Dunbar. Grog boss. Keep your cups handy. Water breaks every hour."

"And grog every half?" asked the man in overalls.

"For those men who require a stronger refreshment, it will be available hourly, at Dunbar's discretion."

Overalls grumbled to the man standing next to him.

"We will have breakfast now. And a toast to success. Please line up at the table."

The men roused themselves, languidly, and stalked toward the table as a pack.

"A line please!" Dorephus cried.

They ordered themselves, reluctantly. They received their bread and jam and Dunbar stood at the end of the line dispensing applejack into each man's cup. None refused. Three bottles were emptied.

Dorephus raised his cup.

"Thank you gentlemen, here's to a successful day. Recall. All hard work brings a profit; mere talk leads only to poverty."

Dorephus took a draught. Most of the men had already finished and had returned to the line for more bread. He began counting the men out and assigning them to one or another of the work crews.

Mid-morning the clearing droned with the *zhug-zhug* of two man saws and the regular reports of mallets on posts. A pair of men switched and cursed at the oxen stumbling through the hummocks, gouging the earth with their heavy loads. Others heaved the thick columns of elm and ash they brought onto a great fire set in the middle of the clearing. The smoke, sweet and damp, hung unperturbed in the still air above them, blotting the sun. More than half of the men who had showed actually applied themselves to their assigned tasks. The rest contented themselves with cajoling Amelia and her mother for an extra morsel of food, to lean on their axe handles and gossip, or to sit under a tree and watch the effort of their fellows. Not one passed up their fair measure of applejack or rye or beer when Dunbar came around with the grog bucket, often convincing him of their need for a second and a third.

Still, it was a promising start and as good as other bees Dorephus had heard about. The men who were working, were working hard. They had already cleared three acres of timber and the frame of the small barn was nearly done. Most of the stumps were left in the ground but they could be planted around. The remainder could be pulled or burned out the following year.

Dorephus was envisioning a finished barn and a burgeoning crop when Carmichael Jones and his cohort emerged into the clearing, trampling through his imagined expanse of wheat. Carmichael's hair was wild, paradoxically slick and unruly at the same time. His face and neck were florid. One leg of his trousers was rolled up to his knee, exposing a raw calf. He strode toward the victuals like a man who was coming home.

"Hallelujah brothers," he cried, beckoning to the rest, "he shall supply all you need, if only you will believe. Never doubt Carmichael Jones."

"There she is," he said, when he reached the table, clutching at his chest, gasping. "My angel. My fiancée. It was your lovely, buttery face that kept me going, one foot falling in front of t'other, cross the miles."

He got down on a knee in front of Amelia.

"On your feet, sir." Dorephus stood behind him.

Carmichael rose stiffly.

"The father," he said to his companions. "Bit of a blister. Best behaviour now."

"Why are you here."

"To pitch in, of course."

"You're not invited."

"Not true. Your man invited me."

"Dunbar?" Dorephus looked across and Dunbar shrugged.

"Aye, the same. On the Loughborough Road. When you so courteously pointed Samsie and me in the direction of that natural spring, two miles away. And, you'll be pleased to note, I've informed every able-bodied man I've since met, who hasn't been otherwise engaged, that they might do the same."

"Which men?"

"Men of Badgley's and Metcalf's, Blake's and Brown's, of White Bear…"

"All taverns."

"Aye."

Dorephus paused. He raised a glove to his face and chewed fiercely on the leather fringe. The men who'd materialized from the bush, like malevolent spirits, Amelia and Millie, Dunbar, and a number of loafers lingering near the buffet; all had their eyes on him, waiting. He wanted to pry the axe from a nearby stump and lodge it between Carmichael's eyes.

"What's for suppah?" Carmichael asked, rubbing his hands together.

"Nowt."

Carmichael's expression changed. He put two fingers to his temple and looked as though he was trying to push them into his head.

"Must they hammer like that," he said, waving at the men on the frame.

"Don't let him stay," Amelia whispered hotly, now at Dorephus' side.

"Now, this is some welcome," Carmichael said. "Real warm. We been marching all night. Sleeping in ditches. Getting bit. Look at this!"

He was shouting now. Men at the fire and on the frame had stopped their work to watch. Carmichael pointed to his exposed calf and its streaks of red.

"Poison oak! I'm gonna scratch my buggery leg clean off. All God damn night we walked. Me mates and me, we haven't eaten a whole day. We ain't had a sip since yesterday. By the hair of Christ's ass, I wish they'd stop hammering!"

Dorephus, appalled that his wife and daughter should be within earshot, became aware that the clearing was now perfectly still. Carmichael took his hands from his head and looked toward the frame and the men staring back, mallets at their sides.

"Look," he said, quieter, "I'm a ploughman by trade. I can plough."

"Dor," Millie said, "it wouldn't hurt to give them a little food, would it?"

"We aren't doing any ploughing today," Dorephus said stonily.

"If not for me," Carmichael said, pulling at Samuel, gaunt with dark crescents under his eyes, "for Samsie. He's just a boy."

"Dor," Millie said.

Amelia clutched at her father's arm. Dorephus looked at all the men at the frame and in the bush, standing idle, watching.

"You can join the rest of the men, either raising the barn or clearing the field. We'll divide you up…"

"Eh?" Carmichael interrupted, incredulous. "We have marched all night sir. No sus'nance to get us started? No show of faith? Samuel will as soon fall over as pick up an axe."

"Dor," Millie said again, "there is plenty of bread. Let's give them something."

"Fine."

"Daddy."

"My wife will serve you bread and jam. Dunbar, bring some fresh water. Meet me in the bush when you are finished and I'll assign you to work groups." Dorephus strode toward the frame. "You men! Continue! We have reinforcements. Supper in two hours."

It took about ten minutes to reassemble the grumbling men and direct them to their tasks. From there, Dorephus moved back to the bush to help Eldon Sturridge marshal men and beasts to the timber clearing effort. Twenty minutes later, Amelia was again at his side.

"It's a mistake," she said. "Look." She pointed back to the clearing, under the shagbark, near the fire. Carmichael sat with his back against the trunk, a wedge of cheese in his left hand and a bottle of applejack in his right. He was surrounded by his companions, shouting and laughing.

Dorephus started briskly towards them not knowing what he would do when he got there. Then he slowed. He stopped.

"Dad?"

"Tell Dunbar to bring them two more bottles."

Amelia stared.

"They're too disruptive. It's safer that we keep them at a distance."

"Dad."

"Please Amelia."

Reluctantly she went to find Dunbar.

An hour later Dorephus was gratified to see Carmichael quiet and motionless under the shagbark, a bottle clutched to his chest. Samuel was curled up at his feet and the rest of his companions splayed about the mossy circle beneath the hickory's crown. With luck, they would sleep the rest of the day.

The sun was now past its peak and the rate of work began to slow. Volunteers took longer breaks, lingered longer by the food table, taking shade where they could find it. The men of Badgley's and Metcalf's, Blake's and Brown's continued to filter into the clearing through the day, few of them chafing their palms with axes and ropes, all of them stopping Dunbar for refreshment. Others melted away. The original count of twenty had swelled to forty, with at most a dozen actually working. Dorephus' throat burned with endless goading.

"Why ain't they working?" Overalls asked loudly, pointing at Carmichael snoozing serenely beneath the tree. "Why do we sweat, while they sleep?"

"They were unwell this morning," he said, "they'll work this afternoon."

"'Tis after noon. Let's wake 'em up."

"Let them lie," Dorephus said, wearily.

"Carmichael?"

A man with a friar's haircut and a pumpkin middle entered the clearing. He wore nothing but what looked like a night shirt. He advanced on the sleepers.

"Carmichael Jones," he cried, kicking the ploughman hard.

Carmichael jumped and scrambled like a badger. From the other side of the tree trunk, he looked back, bewildered.

"Corny," he said, finally. "Corny Harris! It's you. You old bull tit."

"It's me." The man picked up the empty bottle of applejack that had rolled to his feet and examined it. "I hope you saved me some, you greedy filcher."

"Dunbar!" Carmichael called, "A fresh bottle for me old mate, Cornelius Harris, knight of the White Bear, order of the gutter. And one for me."

The two men clasped each other's forearms and began to prance in a circle, a jerky parody of a waltz.

"Back to work," Dorephus said to Overalls, standing next to him. "We'll break for supper soon."

Again the men who were working had stopped, curious about the latest disruption. Dorephus hurried back to the bush. And then to the frame. Then to the fire. And back to the bush.

"I'm sorry Mr. Barrett," Eldon Sturridge said, holding a kerchief to his nose, tamping at the blood. "I told them to get back to it and that one started in on arguing, and I told him we got more to do, and that I'm the captain after all, and he clouted me."

"That's fine Eldon, feed and water the oxen, we'll take a break."

Dorephus could hear the clearing before he saw it. Most of the volunteers were now gathered around the tapped barrel of ale at the end of the buffet, braying. Carmichael and Cornelius Harris sang and danced, arm in arm, before Millie and Amelia. The men circled them, clapping and laughing. Dorephus watched from behind a tree, paralyzed.

"The Oak and the Ash," Carmichael cried and the men cheered.

Carmichael sang a verse and Cornelius sang a verse and all the men joined the chorus.

> *There once was a waitress from the Prince George Hotel*

Carmichael gestured to Amelia, and then to Millie.

> *Her mistress was a lady, her master a swell*
> *They knew she was a simple girl and lately from a farm*
> *And they watched her carefully to keep her from harm*

Amelia blushed and buried herself in her mother's arms. The men cheered and sang.

> *Singing an oak and an ash, leaves of maple too*
> *Let her rock the cradle like her momma used to do*

Cornelius stepped forward and raised his hand, his expression dramatic.

> *The 41st Regiment came marching into town*

He sang,

> *And with them came a complement of rapists of renown*
> *They busted every maidenhead that came within their spell*
> *But they never made the waitress from the Prince George Hotel*

All together they cried,

> *Singing an oak and an ash, leaves of maple too*
> *Let her lick the ladle like her momma used to do*
>
> *Next came a company of the Canadian Fencibles*

Carmichael had a mallet in his hands, handle outwards, thrusting it from his hips like a bayonet.

> *They piled into a whorehouse they packed along the bars*
> *Every maid and mistress and wife before them fell*
> *But they never made the waitress from the Prince George Hotel*
>
> *One day came a sailor just an ordinary bloke*
> *A bulging at the trousers, a heart of solid oak*

Amid riotous cheers, Cornelius lifted his tattered night shirt to reveal, underneath, he wore nothing at all.

> *At sea without a woman for seven years or more*
> *There wasn't any need to ask what he was looking for*
>
> *He asked her for a candlestick to light his way to bed*
> *He asked her for a pillow to rest his weary head*
> *And speaking to her gently as if he meant no harm*
> *He asked her to come to bed just so to keep him warm*

Carmichael acted out the next verse as he sang it.

> *He lifted up the blanket and a moment there he lie*
> *He was on her. He was in her, in a twinkling of an eye*
> *He was out again, and in again, and ploughing up a storm*
> *And the only word she said to him was "I hope you're keeping warm"*

The men were shouting, deliriously,

> *Singing an oak and an ash, leaves of maple too*
> *Let her lick the ladle like her momma used to do*

"Hold it," Carmichael said, raising his hands. "Hold it! This is my future wife you are singing about."

The men roared.

"I jest thee not! I'll not have her sung about in this manner. Her sensibilities are of a nature most delicate. And her father's a prig."

Cornelius padded toward Millie and Amelia, his nose twitching, his fingers outstretched ahead of him as though he was about to take washing off the line. They cowered. He took Millie by the shoulders and gently turned her around so her back was to him. He ran his finger down her back and tugged at her apron string until it was unfastened. Delicately, he lifted it over her head. He placed it over his own, tied it, and removed the muslin from the dishes of ham, cheese, and preserves on the table. He wrapped a piece of muslin around his bald pate.

"Supper's ready!" he cried, in a shrill voice. "Come and git!"

Millie and Amelia retreated to the front step of their cabin as the men descended on the table, ripping apart slabs of cheese, meat and bread. Dorephus walked past them, glassy-eyed.

"Go inside," he said.

"Dor."

"Go inside!"

They followed him into the cabin.

The barrel of ale was emptied. More was demanded. Dunbar gave them the cask of rye, the last of the supplies.

"A toast," Cornelius bellowed from atop the table, one foot in a loaf of bread.

> *My morals are sound, for they lie in my glass,*
> *My religion and faith are my bottle and lass;*
> *My church is the tavern, a vintner my priest;*
> *And thus I go on 'till the saint is deceased;*
> *And when I no longer can revel and roar,*
> *But must part with my bottle, my friend, and my whore,*
> *Embalm me in claret, pay rites at my shrine;*
> *Thus living I'm happy, when dead I'm divine*

The men cheered, drank from their cups of rye, and began to dance a frenzied quadrille, leaping and locking arms. Carmichael stood in the middle of them, croaking like a lunatic caller. He pointed his pewter toward the homestead.

> *There was an old woman lived in a cabin on a hill,*
> *And if she's not gone yet, why she's living there still.*
> *She had a daughter whom she lov'd the best,*
> *And she kept her at home to please each guest*

He gestured demurely to himself.

> *A ploughman by chance came riding by,*
> *And he called for a bottle because he was dry*

The whirlers hooted, jostling and smashing into one another.

> *He called for a second, and called for another,*
> *And then he did kiss her before her mother.*

Carmichael stuck out his arm and waggled his upraised fingers.

> *He put his fingers under her tucker,*
> *And whispered softly he wanted to...*

The quadrille shuddered to a halt and the pairs of men parted. Dorephus emerged from the gap. He held out before him a mottled flintlock, braced tightly to his chest. It was the old army-issue land pattern he'd purchased from Spafford, on the Colonel's recommendation. For the wolves. Dorephus had never done so much as load it. He walked to the centre of the assembly and stopped when the smooth bore muzzle was less than a yard from Carmichael's smirk, steadily dissolving.

"Leave," he said, quietly. Only Carmichael could hear him.

"Now Mister Barrett," Carmichael said, raising his hands, "there's no necessity in this."

The barrel jigged up and down like a piking rod.

"Just leave."

Cornelius called from atop the buffet table.

"I say, those are some manners. Tuck away your beard-splitter."

Dorephus, not taking his eye from Carmichael, fumbled at the cock and jerked it back, releasing the sear.

"Fully cocked and balled," Cornelius squawked from the table. "Cock and balls. Cock and balls."

"Corny," Carmichael said, "you'd be doing me a great favour if you would cease your natter. You do nothing but hinder."

"Leave!" cried Dorephus. "Get off my Goddamn land and don't come back."

"Capital. We'd just been considering it."

"Then, do."

"Aye. We're resolved."

"One more for the road," Cornelius said, diplomatically, "and we'll be off. Dunbar?"

"We're dry." Dunbar stood nearby holding the dribbling, upended cask of rye.

Dorephus squeezed and the flint plunged into the frizzen. Sparks found purchase in the fine powder and the pan flashed. Acrid smoke mustaschioed his face. He raised his head from the musket to get a better look. Carmichael remained, looking back, quizzically. Dorephus stared at the gun. Then, at Carmichael again. Misfire. The touch hole, gummed with decades of powder residue through long years of service in Spain and France, had failed to ignite the main charge in the breech.

Dorephus clutched at the hammer. It jammed. He struck at it with his palm. He bashed it until the flint shredded his thumb.

"Carm."

Cornelius pointed at the dark patch at Carmichael's crotch.

"You've pissed yourself."

Carmichael looked down at himself.

"Christmas! So I have."

He convulsed with juddering, hiccupping laughter.

"It's warm. I thought 'twere blood."

The men, some still frozen arm in arm, began to laugh. The spell was broken. The carousing continued. They nudged Dorephus aside and he retreated to the cabin, dazed, struggling with his musket.

"Dunbar, drink!" Cornelius waved majestically. "We celebrate! Another soul saved."

"We're dry," Dunbar said again.

"There must be something," Carmichael said, now angry. "I've just given a wink to my maker. I have the thirst of the reprieved."

Dunbar pulled his watch from its pocket, checked the time, tapped it, and put it back. Then he shrugged and backed away.

Carmichael crossed the clearing and rooted through Dunbar's stores on the porch of the cabin. Other men followed. Overalls found one bottle of applejack, still full. Carmichael ripped it from his hands.

"Oy," Carmichael said, before taking a long draught, "for me nerves."

Overalls wrenched the bottle from his lips. Another man to his right grabbed at it, as did another. Carmichael re-entered the fray and a scrum formed, lurching and roving across the clearing, men shouting and grunting, clutching and writhing. It stopped only when the bottle at the centre was smashed against a rock. A punch was thrown, a boot was kicked, and the men separated into brawling factions. Carmichael emerged from the snake ball, doubly soiled, with the applejack remnant, shards out, neck in fist.

"Pestiferous boil. Look what you made me do."

He advanced on Overalls.

"I'll gut you stem to stern."

Overalls backed away until he was at the giant potash kettle. He picked up a burning bough from the cool end and waved it like a flag. His partisans did the same. Now they advanced. All around them men threw and thumped and smashed. The buffet table collapsed in a clatter of broken plates. The chicory pot overturned and burned a man's leg. Saw horses were upset and another man, falling, gashed his hand on an adze. Carmichael and his supporters, retreating, backed toward the barn's partly finished timber frame. They swung and parried and fenced. Embers cascaded from smouldering limbs with each strike against posts and beams. The splinters and shavings tamped against the barn floor, dry as black powder, ignited. Within minutes the melee disintegrated as men became aware of the flames licking their necks.

"Pa," Amelia said, trying to get her father's attention. Dorephus continued to wrestle with the flintlock, emptying the breech, scouring the barrel, reloading.

"Pa!" She gripped his arm. He looked at her, eyes wild.

"Look!" She pointed at the fledgling barn and the fire slithering up the frame.

Dorephus raised his head and stared, not comprehending. Finally, he threw the old shooter to the floor and he charged toward the conflagration.

"You men!" he cried, "there are buckets at the well. Fetch water! Shovels. We need shovels. Smother it!"

None were listening. Most of the men, drunk and bewildered, some limping, some bleeding from the nose and lips, had already evaporated into the woods whence they came. They feared getting caught in the fire. They feared the repercussions of having started it. The casks and bottles were empty and they feared that most of all. Appraisals of their actions in the light of their own sobriety. They trickled away.

Only Sturridge, young Case, and a couple of others remained. This late in the day, they were already exhausted, their arms and legs leaden, their boots full of limestone. But they fought. They fetched, doused, stamped, and dug. Amelia and Millie labored alongside the men, their petticoats discarded, their bloomers hitched. Amelia drove her foot so ferociously along the brow of her spade that her boot split in two.

They were unable to save the barn. Papery bits of flaming birch bark, hoisted by the thermal gusts, alighted on the cedar shakes of the cabin's roof. They were unable to save the cabin but they salvaged most of its contents. Somehow, they were able to create a firewall of felled trees around the clearing and stop the flames from spreading to the woods. They were able to save their lives.

Noble Spafford arrived on horseback around sunset. The survivors, draped over stumps, backs against logs, dazed and silent, resembled a grotesque troupe in black-face.

"What in blazes? What in blazes?"

Spafford repeated the phrase over and over as his horse skittered about the wreckage.

Dorephus got wearily to his feet, leaning on Amelia at his elbow. Dunbar stood and crossed the clearing to Spafford, taking his horse by the reins. Slowly, the two men met in the middle.

"What in blazes," Spafford said again.

Dorephus and Amelia looked up at Spafford. Neither spoke.

"I think it is safe to say you will not be bringing in a harvest this season, Dorephus. Again."

Dorephus dropped his gaze to the horse's stamping hoof.

"Franklin told me you reduced the order I made for drink and victuals. Why?"

"It was not because of a lack of drink that we failed," Dorephus said.

Spafford snorted.

"You ran out though didn't you? Never run out. First rule."

Dorephus said nothing.

"Where will you live? How will you sow? How will you repay your considerable debts?"

Spafford caught Amelia's gaze.

"How will you provide for your wife? Your lovely daughter? Her future must be taken into account."

Dorephus nodded.

"You and your family may move, temporarily, into the guest house. Meet me a week hence, at the Old King's Head. We'll discuss terms."

6

The Golden Ball
– Halifax

JEREMY SAT ON A DAMP COIL OF ROPE with his back against a carronade carriage, one long leg extended, the other drawn up. A slash of light from the propped gun port illuminated the square of speckled paper balanced on his knee. He bent to the scrap, carefully scratching it with borrowed ink and stylus, squeezing four pages into one.

Ashore, paper is rare. At sea, it is precious. For previous letters, Jeremy had to exchange rations or extra sentry duties just to get a leaf or two. Merit managed to secure this single sheet from the quartermaster by way of his tooled pig's knuckles. Like most sailors, the quartermaster was a seasoned gambler and he couldn't resist a quick roll and wager. He was also a stout Royalist and always staked the crown, making him an easy mark for Merit and his anchor-heavy dice. Before handing the paper to Jeremy, he made his cousin promise to write something favourable about himself.

The sixth letter home.

Dearest Alice, Jeremy started. He wanted to address it *Mother* or even *Mum*, but couldn't bring himself to do it. First, the letter would be from both of them, Jeremy and Merit. Second, he wanted to convey to her a sense of maturity and self-assurance. And third, mostly, the very word

Mum evoked in him such warm memories of freshly steeped bohea, heavy slices of molasses bread toasted with butter and currant preserves, thick sweetness of birch and apple smoke in the hearth, and the lush lilac bunches that she would bring inside their modest cottage each spring, that fragrance that she seemed to exude with every embrace; it made his eyes sting.

Despite our earnest hopes to the contrary, we have to assume that none of our previous correspondence has crossed your blessed threshold. For all we know, and we pray it isn't so, you still await our arrival home and have no knowledge of our whereabouts.

Jeremy stretched his neck and peered from the porthole. The water was so vitreous it looked as though he could just step out and walk home to Cornwall. He looked across from the carronade and watched Merit as he shuffled a deck of cards, ready to deal the next round of whist. Beside him, at another porthole, sat Splinter, a fellow marine, leafing through the slim volume he was rarely without. Jeremy assumed it was a psalter and had asked to borrow it on several occasions. It would have been a balm to be able to re-read the gospels, at his leisure. Every Sunday, of course, the ship chaplain would recite to the men from his personal copy of the Oxford King James. But there weren't prayer books to go around. Too often they were used for mopping spills, propping tables, or lighting lamps, so they were no longer supplied. And Splinter would not give his up.

"My da' gave it me," he would say, as though that was sufficient justification not to lend. "He was a miner. But he 'spired."

This made no sense to Jeremy and he was determined to try again.

But first, the letter.

Merit and I have had the

He hesitated. Then he decided he didn't care whether his letter might be intercepted.

horrible misfortune to be impressed into the Royal Navy, fruit of our bad judgment and heedlessness of your wise counsel. We serve on board The Lancer out of Portsmouth, under the commission of Captain Rowton. I won't nettle you with the details of how we ended up here (I gave you some description in earlier letters). As I write, we are becalmed, somewhere north-west of the Azores, south-east of Newfoundland. Splinter Throckmorton, who just this moment sits next to me (I believe Thomas to be his given name), has told me we are bound for Halifax, Nova Scotia. He thinks we'll be there within the week. But not at this rate. Personally, I don't mind lying adrift a day or two (afterall, what are Merit and I, but adrift?). As you can imagine, we've seen some heavy seas, so a little listlessness is refreshing. I've been a-chunder four days out of five since we last saw Porthleven. Merit, on the other hand, is as fine as a pheasant. His legs, unlike mine, are as ever sea-worthy.

It has been terribly difficult to write you these last seven months. Usually, when not drilling, marching, and keeping watch, we are kept busy attending to chores of the most tedious nature (I spent yesterday in the orlop — I must have bilged half the Atlantic through that wretched pump). At night, I'm so exhausted I fall asleep before closing my eyes, which is no simple feat given my bed, a so-called 'hammock', a torture device worthy of Torquemada. But still, I sleep, so it can't be that bad. Please don't think we fare badly; both Merit and I are safe and sound, we get our four square and ~~rarely~~ never are put in harm's way.

We haven't seen much action. Our job is mostly patrol, enforce the embargo, impress more men. You'll be happy to know we haven't been in any real shooting matches, no broadsides, no crossing the T. Like the ancient mariner, we roam the seas.

"Chew some fat?"

Augie Gardiner had just arrived with a pouch of salt beef he'd pilfered from the pusser. Gardiner, originally from Boston, son of a whaler, had been impressed before the war had even started. He vowed to desert at the earliest opportunity. One had never arisen. Jeremy pulled a strip of beef from Gardiner's outstretched hand. It resembled a length of pigtail, the tobacco twist that all the jacks liked to gnaw: stiff, leathery, and tar-coloured.

Augie moved on to join the card game and offer the others a wad. Jeremy attempted to bite his in half and could not. He folded the entire plug into his mouth and continued writing.

We shouldn't complain. We should think upon Job, yes? Augustus Gardiner has just brought us vittles. A capital lad. If we weren't confined so, if we were back in Porthleven, I'd invite him home for tea, to meet you. He has had some education (Providence Grammar School), and is one of the few jacks I can discuss philosophy and literature with.

His favourite poet? Cowper! Do you remember reading to Merit and I before bed, Cowper's Odyssey and the Olney Hymns?

Splinter fidgeted with his book. He flipped to the middle, and then the end, and back to the middle, never lingering over a single page for more than a few moments. At one point, he appeared to be holding it upside down. Then he closed it, held it to his breast, shut his eyes, and sighed. Perhaps he's looking for particular passages of inspiration, Jeremy thought. He longed to help him with it, to hold the book and find favourite quotations together. A book, any book, in the confines of a warship: as welcome as fresh fruit.

"God moves in a mysterious way, His wonders to perform," as Cowper would say. Never before have these words rung truer. Poor Augie (as he's known hereabouts) has been aboard this stick of wormy wood for nigh on four years and not once has he been ashore. I'm made queasy by the thought. I feel that he can't possibly deserve such a fate. But ours is not to question, perhaps?

Still. Augie says Captain Rowton never lets him ashore because he knows with the merest brush of a toe against terra firma, he will leg it. He tells me he swims like a mud hook (though probably not worse than me), otherwise he'd swan over the side. I pray that Merit and I get ashore, back to Cornwall, well before such an eternity, but I suppose we'd better brace for the worst. Just know this: everything I do is with a mind to freedom and returning home.

Cowper's translation is excellent, but I don't think you get a real sense of what Odysseus had to contend with until you are actually wayward. At least he got to stop in at Aeolus and Helios. He spent a few years with Circe and then Calypso. Couldn't have been all bad.

I don't want to give you the wrong impression. Merit is kept occupied, working his first true frigate, furling her sails, making the lines sing. You should see him clamber the rigging, a regular sea monkey. In truth, I think Merit is often enjoying himself, but he would never admit it. He's got himself into difficulties a couple of times, in our rare moments of leisure, with enlisted men and even midshipmen. I've had to step in more than once.

Jeremy looked across at Merit, arranging and re-arranging a fan of frayed cards in his hand. Merit tapped a finger and harrumphed, impatient for his opponents to play a card. Jeremy recalled one occasion, early in their tour, when Merit had relieved the bosun's mate of amethyst cufflinks, spoils from an earlier *Lancer* victory over a French ship. The mate had questioned the impartiality of Merit's dice. Jeremy had offered to give him satisfaction through a cudgeling match, staking the cuff links and five guineas besides, if he won. In his high pique, the mate, a stout man himself, an ex-convict, jailed for involuntary manslaughter, had sized Jeremy up and had passed.

Jeremy didn't include these sorts of details.

I know you would disapprove, but all in all Mer's ledger is in the positive. Weekly he adds to an account in his purse which he calls his Penzance fund. Penance, I call it. He hopes one day to have enough to buy us out of our obligations and find passage home. It's a start and his motivation is a good one. He's got a lot of saving to do.

Jeremy pulled the morsel from his mouth and examined it. It was greyish and frayed. It resembled a strand of the oakum he'd spent so many hours in the past months picking, for caulking the ship's timber joints. The knot of gristle at its heart remained intact but all salt and flavour had leached out. He pushed it back between his lips with a finger and started grinding it with the other side of his pasty mouth.

Is there much mention of thirst in the Odyssey? I don't remember. It is the central, abiding fact of life here on the Lancer. We have nowt but cocoa for breakfast, grog (bilge) at dinner, and tea at supper. All served from a thimble of tin not larger than a baby's boot. No allowances made for stature or workload or length of exposure. If Beelzebub himself joined our ranks, with a notion to haggle, I'd be hard-pressed not to trade away for a pitcher of your elderberry cordial, or a cool jar of good, Cornish swanky.

I've run out of space. I suppose that is all for now. One other item: for reasons unbeknownst to me, I've been made corporal. I seem to be climbing the ranks here far faster than I ever did at St. Michael's.

Ever yours,
Jeremy and Merit

He folded the letter over on itself twice and then sealed the loose edge with a wodge of tar. He addressed the exposed fold: *Mrs. Alice Castor, Perenn Cottage, Green Lane, Porthleven, Cornwall* and then carefully placed it in his leather pouch. He would give it to Major Stokes and request that he include it in the next packet. They'd come alongside dozens of England-bound sloops and schooners, barques and brigs in their six months at sea. Each time Jeremy had watched the quartermaster exchange packages and papers with his counterpart. He could only hope that his letters were among them and at least one of them had reached their destination.

Splinter was mumbling. "My own mind." "My own church." Jeremy couldn't make it out. Splinter had the book open again, his index finger digging at the rows of words as though they were root vegetables.

"For the love of pudding, will you let me read it to you?" Jeremy said.

"I kin read it fine," Splinter said, alarmed at the sudden intrusion. "My da' gave it me."

Jeremy had to fight the sudden rage welling up within him, at the stupidity, the senselessness. He appraised Splinter, the pale, stick figure of a boy, runty son of a lead digger, his eyes as empty and dark as two abandoned mine shafts. He reckoned he could pick him up with one hand and snap him in two over his knee.

Instead, he moved abruptly from the carronade and joined the circle playing cards.

"Deal me in," he said,

"How's bout you deacon?"

"How's bout what?" Jeremy said.

"What you going to spend your shillings on?"

"What shillings?"

"Them that's owed you by the King. Augie here, not ashore once in four years, reckons he's got forty pounds in back pay, not to mention treasure share."

"Rumour is we get paid in Halifax. In full."

"With a furlough and time enough to spend it."

Jeremy allowed himself a moment to imagine what it would be like to have forty pounds, all at once. He tried to conjure something extravagant to spend it on: an Arabian bay, a polished Swiss pocket watch, silver and walnut Henry Nock dueling pistols. But he didn't ride or duel, and didn't own a waistcoat. More practical concerns came to mind: a comfortable pair of dry boots, a new roof for the cottage, or a skein of top quality worsted yarn. Then he realized it wasn't an object he most desired. It was time and space. For himself. How much would forty pounds buy? Not much.

"Homard!" Neven Tanguay, the Breton, said, clapping his hands together, scuddering his cards across the deck. "Lobster feast. I will demand the largest ever trapped. Un monstre! Avec beurre. Melted. Et champagne. Beaucoup de champagne."

"Broiled beef rib, impossibly rare, with roast tates and all the trims. A vat of brown ale for washing down and a bottle of cognac for afters," Finn Davies said.

"Millefeuille," Lilac, Finn's wife, added.

"Trifle."

"Plum pudding."

"Brandy, lots of it."

"A case of rum."

"A swish hotel, with down mattress, cotton linens, and a water closet," Augie said.

"Water closet?" asked Neven, "Qu'est-ce que c'est?"

"And new trousers, stockings, blouse, silk neck-cloth, and drawers. Several pairs of new drawers."

"You have the right idea, Augustus," Lilac said as she gathered the cards and began to shuffle. "A hot bath. That's the first thing I'll spend my money on."

"Finn's money you mean," Neven laughed.

"I've got me own resources," Lilac replied, fanning her raised chin with the cards flicking through her grimy hands, "you know I do because most of it was once yours, rashly gambled." She started to deal them out. "Which isn't to say I won't accept gifts, from Finn, or any of you gallants for that matter."

"We'll take up a collection Lil'," Augustus said, "and purchase you a good, long soak, Lord knows you need it. You've become more than just a little savoury lately."

"No more than the rest of you. Can't take water from the scuttlebutt for washing. What are we to do? Oh," she held her hand, sevens and twos, Queen high, tight to her chest and squeezed, "a hot bath, a scorching, scalding bath!"

"I'd purchase me one or two of them squaws," Neven continued, folding, "as plenty as sparrows they said to be."

"Depraved."

"We can only hope."

"How about you Tecumseh?" They called Merit after the Shawnee Chief, scourge of the Michigan and Indiana territories, due to the feather sown into his tunic.

"You'd prefer squaw, Chief? Beads? Wampum?"

"Freedom," Merit said as he collected and shuffled the cards. "To buy our way out of our obligations, and home, Jem and I."

"You'll need a bit more than the few pounds you two will get, I'm afraid."

"It's a pleasant thought though."

"Aye, 'tis."

"And you Deacon? Books?"

"Drink," Jeremy said. It was all he could think of.

The others laughed and Merit started to deal. Three hands later they heard the steady four-four beat of boot leather on the deck. Major Stokes materialized from the gloom, his extensive whiskers deforming his silhouette.

"Captain has asked me to inform you, and all on board."

The men looked up from their cards. Splinter put his book down and eyed the major.

"Snow."

Finn dropped his hand.

"You may go above decks."

The men scrambled, collected themselves, raced to their quarters to retrieve tin cups, wooden bowls, pewter mugs, and clay pots, anything watertight and hollow, and clambered topside. Before he joined them, Jeremy left his letter with Stokes, who promised to make sure it got added to the next packet.

When Jeremy arrived on the main deck he was met with what seemed like a swanky-induced dream. The men, some wearing woolen caps and fearnoughts, others in shirt sleeves, cavorted arm-in-arm across the slushy deck, hooting and singing. Snow accumulated on moustaches and brows making them look like grizzled, cabin-mad prospectors. The bank above Stokes' upper lip grew into an architectural impossibility. Men placed a receptacle of some kind, upturned and collecting each stray flake, on every available flat surface. They cupped their grails to the sky, as though to get the freshest snow, their cradling hands distilling the harvest into a sort of nectar, something more precious than just water and dust. And when they sipped, the melt rinsed a six month briny crust from their throats. They could not get enough. They let it drift into open mouths. They sucked it from woolen sleeves. They cooked it in raw, red palms. And finally, when the urgency of their need had been slaked, they packed it and pelted it at each other, while Rowton, and Stokes, and the rest of the officers watched from the quarterdeck, laughing.

The snow fell in fat, lazy clumps. Jeremy had seen snow before, back in Cornwall, but nothing like this. Cornish snow was diamond-like, rare and sharp. It cut across the Celtic Sea and bit into the face of anyone foolish enough to stray from their fire grate. This was something else. It was fresh and abundant. It coated every surface until it was nearly impossible to discern where the ship ended and the hoary atmosphere began. Even the lines and shrouds were frosted. It was as though the ship was made of crystal and her crew ivory and the whole tableau had been delicately unfolded into a bottle. This snow was warm and clean and so thoroughly blanketed the archaeological layers of sweat and tar, salt and blood on the *Lancer*'s decks that each man and woman, from smooth-faced cabin boy Teddy Wilkinson to the old man, Rowton himself, quietly harboured the thought that the ship, and its inhabitants, could be re-launched, could start over.

Jeremy scooped a mound of snow into the cavern of his big right hand and tamped it down with his left, making it tight and round. He spied Merit gliding gleefully back and forth one of the rails of oak, raising his leg behind like a ballerina. Jeremy cocked his arm, released, and the icy boulder exploded against Merit's head and neck, knocked his cap to the floor, and sprayed bystanders with debris. Merit swung round wildly, picking slush from his ear. He looked across to see Jeremy grinning, hands on hips. He responded in kind and before long there was a full-blown donnybrook. A stray missile knocked Lieutenant Coulson's bicorn from his head and officers began to mortar snowballs from the quarterdeck. No enlisted men dared fire back, but they didn't mind the intrusion. For twenty minutes, officers and recruits, marines and wives, young and old; everyone was once again twelve.

Like all in life that is pleasant, it did not last. A fresh wind scythed in from the north-east and began to push aside the snow.

"Weather's coming," Rowton said to the ship's master.

"Aye, best bring in some sail."

"Lieutenant Coulson, order the men to stations. Prepare ship for heavier seas."

Coulson began relaying instructions to the lieutenants and sub-lieutenants arrayed across the quarterdeck. They, in turn, began their bellowing to the men below on the main deck and there was a general scurrying up the rigging and a hurrying below. Hatches were battened, portholes fastened, loose items secured.

In their newfound exuberance and joie de vivre, the men were less exacting in their execution, the officers less stringent with their commands. Canvas was folded imprecisely, lines were coiled loosely. Some supplies weren't stowed at all.

That evening, gale winds topped fifty knots and the *Lancer* tumbled into swells twenty feet from crest to trough. Sleet cut across her decks and stripped off her newly acquired coat of snow. She had endured worse conditions through the summer but this was a sharp slap. Fortunately, for the captain and crew, it was a brief storm and was over by early morning. The ship, above and below decks, was a mess of torn sail, jumbled rigging, and strewn provisions. Bleary-eyed and sleep deprived, the men began cleanup.

Augustus Gardiner was the first to find Splinter. He was down the orlop deck, lying in a pool of blood and rum, his face smashed. A fifty gallon drum, its staves skewed and leaking, pinned down his mangled arm.

"He done us a good turn," Biscuit said, looking over the shoulders of the handful gathered around the fallen man. "Saved half a barrel. Propped up a dozen more. Hero's death."

Jeremy looked back to see Biscuit grinning. Biscuit tapped him, Merit, and a few others on the shoulder.

"You men. Tidy up. Save the bumbo."

~ ~ ~

Once more, all the men were topside. This time, the only thing to be heard above the luffing and timber creak were the words of the chaplain:

Unto almighty God we commend the soul of our brother departed, and we commit his body to the deep; in sure and certain hope of the Resurrection unto eternal life, through our Lord Jesus Christ; at whose coming in glorious majesty to judge the world, the sea shall give up her dead; and the corruptible bodies of those who sleep in him shall be changed, and made like unto his glorious body; according to the mighty working whereby he is able to subdue all things unto himself.

Thomas Throckmorton, straight and rigid like a harpoon, sewn up in a square of heavy sailcloth, was raised on a plank and tipped into the sea. All received two extra tots of rum, remnants of the barrel that extinguished their mate. The chaplain gestured and Augustus Gardiner drew a tin flute from an inner pocket of his fearnought. He played the tune to Cowper's hymn *Light Shining Out Of Darkness.*

Jeremy, quietly at first, then more confidently, in his tall man's baritone, sang:

God moves in a mysterious way,
His wonders to perform;
He plants his footsteps in the sea,
And rides upon the storm.

The chaplain nodded approvingly and added his tenor and encouraged the others, until all were singing, in time and harmony.

After the ceremony, as he returned to quarters, Jeremy was intercepted by Stokes.

"He didn't have much," the major said. "But he did have this, and the men agreed you should have it." Stokes handed him the slim volume, the testament Splinter was never seen without.

"Would you do the honour of writing his family?" Stokes asked, before Jeremy could thank him. "You knew him as well as anyone." Jeremy nodded and Stokes was gone.

Back in his hammock, Jeremy shifted, searching in vain for a position that would comfortably support his frame. Splinter's book lay on his stomach.

"Read to us Deacon," Lilac said. "Splinter never did."

Lilac had once asked Throckmorton to teach her to read. "Teaching a whore to read," he'd said, "is like dressing a sow in a frock. To what purpose?" Undaunted, she'd asked Jeremy, who agreed, when time allowed, and he wasn't dead tired, and they actually had a book at hand, to teach what he could.

The others looked out from the gloom expectantly.

"Go ahead Jem," Merit said. "Read something kindly."

Jeremy opened the book, squinting in the lamp light. He thought he might find something from the Book of John, something apt, like 15:13:

Greater love has no one than this, that he lay down his life for his friends.

Or, from Corinthians, maybe 4:16:

Therefore we do not lose heart. Though outwardly we are wasting away, yet inwardly we are being renewed day by day. For our light and momentary troubles are achieving for us an eternal glory that far outweighs them all. So we fix our eyes not on what is seen, but on what is unseen. For what is seen is temporary, but what is unseen is eternal.

But he couldn't find those passages. Instead, the recto title page read:

THE

A G E

OF

R E A S O N;

BEING

AN INVESTIGATION

OF

TRUE AND FABULOUS THEOLOGY.

He checked the next page. A list of chapters. With titles like:
Of The Theology Of The Christians; And The True Theology
and
Of The Means Employed In All Time, And Almost Universally, To Deceive The Peoples

It started off well enough:

I believe in one God, and no more; and I hope for happiness beyond this life. I believe in the equality of man; and I believe that religious duties consist in doing justice, loving mercy, and endeavouring to make our fellow-creatures happy.

But then:

I do not believe in the creed professed by the Jewish Church, by the Roman Church, by the Greek Church, by the Turkish Church, by the Protestant Church, nor by any church that I know of.

My own mind is my own church.

Jeremy closed the book and covered both his hands over it. He felt the same way he had when he'd been caught leafing through the curate's illustrated treatise on classical sculpture, lingering on the engraving of Aphrodite de Milos. How striking she must have been, in her prime, tastefully painted. No topic for an aspiring clergyman.

"Come on, Deacon, read us a fable. Or can't you neither."

"You know I can read," he said.

He preferred to read to them from a psalter Finn had pilfered from the ship's chaplain, or from the tattered copy of Defoe's *Colonel Jaque* that Merit had won from the bo's'un's mate in a card game. The tars loved the story of the orphan, a fellow Jack, who pulls himself up from poverty and obscurity to become a wealthy plantation owner who finds religion. He must have read it to them, in full, scores of times. They never tired of hearing it. Jeremy wasn't sure about reading this Tom Paine to them and, truthfully, they wouldn't have wanted to hear it. They wanted escapism, adventure, redemption, freedom; *Colonel Jaque*. Everything they thought their own lives would contain, but in fact lacked.

"Then?"

"It's not what I expected."

"What'd you spect?"

"Gospels. Matthew and John."

"And?"

"Something else. Rubbish. Someone named Thomas Paine."

"Read it anyway."

"Best not."

"Cracklings! Why not? Read it, for Splinter's sake."

"The captain might not approve."

"He ain't here."

Jeremy sighed. He began to read aloud from the beginning. And was shocked at the words he was speaking.

"How come you never read this Paine to me afore," Merit asked.

"I'd never heard of him afore," Jeremy said.

He was halfway through three, *Concerning The Character Of Jesus Christ, And His History,* when a tumult above decks interrupted.

"Land!" They could hear the men shouting. "Land! In the offing lads!"

Soon, everyone was again above board, this time to see the granite outcroppings and salt-stunted trees that made up Nova Scotia's south shore. Merit was busy in the rigging, helping to close haul the *Lancer* so she yawed the coast like a kite.

Jeremy stood with his arms on the gunwale, watching the numbing sameness sail by. Next to him, Augie Gardiner bounced from one foot to the other.

"I'm going to drink my weight in Kentucky straight. Then, vanish. You and Merit come too."

Four hours later, they were tied to a Halifax pier. Men watched from the gun decks as the sideboys hoisted Captain Rowton, Lieutenant Coulson, and the quartermaster over the side aboard a bosun's chair, rigged to a yardarm on the main deck. Stokes, Biscuit, and a number of other officers descended the Jacob's ladders to the dock. They were met by dignitaries and military men, who took them to The Golden Ball, a Halifax tavern at the south-west corner of Hollis and Sackville streets. There they received a dinner of roast squab and vats of claret, followed by brandy and cigars. They met with the Admiral. They discussed strategy. They got their orders.

On the *Lancer*, men waited. Just yards from their thirsty eyes, Halifax twinkled. There were bottles to drink, loaves to break, blackguards to challenge, women to coax. They could see it; a skinny girl of sixteen propping a flushed forwarder, moonlight dusting his rosy, hatless head, as he staggered uptown from the harbour. They could hear it; off-key shanties rising from the open doors of the Seahorse, green-tinted glass showered on the cobblestones, screeched oaths. They could smell it; jasmine and clove emanating from under the collar pins of the tawdries strolling the boardwalk, alone and in pairs, charcoal and duck fat wafting from the fusty kitchens of Gallagher's and The Golden Ball, yeasty vapours steaming from the waterfront brewery.

But they could neither taste nor touch it. They could only wait.

"Not even a bumboat," Augustus said, gesturing out one of the portholes, his voice unsteady as though he might begin to cry, "no over-ripe fruit, no stale pastries, no watered liquor at extortionate prices."

"No women," Neven added, "Rien."

"You forget me," Lilac said, "am I ship's cat?"

"You are lovely, maïs," Neven sniffed, "vive la difference."

"And the other wives?"

"They're actually married!"

Neven tramped to his hammock and flung himself into it, turning his back. Finn glared at his wife and did the same. Her face darkened a moment and she muttered into her hand.

Royal Navy regulations stated: *no women be ever permitted to be on board but such as are really the wives of the men they come to; and the ship not to be too much pestered even with them.* The Admiralty considered forbidding wives also. In practice though, at sea, captains used their discretion and most admitted women.

Captain Rowton would have preferred none on the *Lancer*. When he confined them to the surgeon's station they drank and squabbled and brawled. When he gave them free range, they raided fresh water from the scuttlebutt for their washing. He allowed some of the officer's wives on board, the carpenter's wife, the master's wife. For morale's sake, Rowton permitted some marine's wives, provided they shared their husband's rations and caused no fuss. For some, it was marginally better than being ashore, being closer to their husband's pay packet, getting a fraction of a regular meal rather than risking no meal at all.

Lilac continued to talk into her hand, as though it contained a tiny confidante.

"I'll be the next pretty cabin boy. One day, you'll see. The old man has his eye on me, I've seen him glancing."

Rowton never allowed his own wife on board. He preferred the company of Teddy Wilkinson, the *Lancer*'s pretty cabin boy and captain's servant. Everyone knew Wilkinson was actually Margaret Barton, of Cork, dressed in trousers, tunic and a cap. The pretense was kept.

"He'll tire of her, eventually," Lilac whispered to her hand.

In port, once Rowton and his top lieutenants had safely disembarked, as many women were permitted on the *Lancer* as the men could afford. Better to gratify the animal urges of the lower ranks while at anchor rather than at sea or in the heat of battle.

Lilac had come aboard two years earlier at Cardiff. She was one of eighty women: wives, daughters, lovers and whores. Selected only by their comeliness or ability to pay, they were rowed out to the *Lancer* on a pair of bumboats packed in alongside crates of produce, baked goods, tobacco, liquor, ready-made clothing, tools, canaries; anything the enterprising operator thought might fetch a price from lonesome, hungry sailors. With her long, mahogany-tinted tresses and clear skin

Lilac claimed the first spot. Finn Davies, a boy from her neighbourhood who'd been pressed into service only a couple of weeks previous, saw her amid the rubbish and rabble. He paid the three shillings.

A three-day debauch below decks followed with non-stop drinking, eating, singing, dancing, and fighting. Sailors and marines, wives and whores - all were sardined into one large room, copulating one on top of the other, side by side, in plain view, all of the rows of tiered hammocks just feet from one another writhing and grunting and swaying in on themselves.

Taking payment for sex had not been her first choice. Being a lady, a woman of means with a title, Princess of Wales perhaps – that would have been her first choice, had it been available. But, she had to admit quietly to herself, it hadn't been all bad. There were moments in those first three days aboard the *Lancer* that actually were fun. She'd made more money in three nights than she had in three months as a seamstress's apprentice. There was food, plenty of it. And rum. And music. Deliciously bawdy sing-alongs that never failed to make her laugh. The men, in fine fettle after long months at sea, were exuberant and cheerful and, for the most part, respectful. She knew the current Princess of Wales might not approve, but she could not deny that she even enjoyed her couplings with some of them, usually the older, more experienced ones, the ones that had cleaned themselves up. She liked their broad shoulders, ropy arms, tanned, weathered faces. She liked that they smelled of the surf.

Lilac decided that staying aboard held more allure than returning to penury on land. But she discovered that a night in port is far different from a day at sea. There was drudgery, worse than back home. Below decks it was hot and filthy and stinking. There was no privacy but plenty of sea-sickness. And the same pecking order that existed ashore thrived below decks. The officer's wives refused to associate with the other wives and gave them orders instead. A corporal's wife expected obedience from a regular marine's wife.

Within a week, Lilac's friend Olive was jettisoned for repeatedly drawing fresh water from the scuttlebutt. Lilac held on, making herself useful, mending the men's clothing, preparing extra meals when she had the materials. She assisted the surgeon, applying her sewing skills to binding wounds, becoming in the span of two years his most able nurse.

"I'll be the next Teddy Wilkinson," she'd say, to anyone who'd listen.

Of course, she shared the men's hammocks. In exchange, they shared their rations. Now, two years later, she was considered by the men more of a sister than Finn's wife. She was as disappointed as any of them that their stopover in Halifax hadn't resulted in a three-day long party of Cardiff proportions. Just like the men, she would have enjoyed meeting some different women, Canadian women.

Lilac became aware that Jeremy was watching her. She turned to him. A smile swept the darkness from her face like a lifted curtain.

"Come on Deacon," she said as she sidled toward him, "we can still have some fun."

Jeremy looked over his shoulder at Finn, lying in his hammock, staring glumly at Neven's back in the hammock above.

"Oh, don't worry about him," she said. "You know we're married in name only."

In Cardiff, Augustus had written up a fake marriage certificate to show Captain Rowton, joining Lilac to Finn. In truth, Finn had paid her fee and she bedded with him more often than any of the others. Everyone called her Finn's wife, though she wasn't exclusive. And still, she charged.

"Thank you Lil'," Jeremy said, not unkindly. "You're lovely, but I'll save my shilling for next time."

7

Ferguson's Tavern
– Barriefield
Early Autumn, 1814

ONLY ONCE DID THE CANADIANS STOP SINGING. From the moment they lay seasoned palms on the oars or bent pine poles into the silt, lifting the batteau up the frothy tangle of the *St. Lawrence*, they would erupt into their rounds. In their grey capotes and peaked hoods, there were four to a batteau, with *le conducteur* steering, calling tunes, keeping them on a measured beat. "Ha, ha, ha, frit à l'huile," they would sing, endlessly, "fritaine, friton, fritou, poilon," and fifty other chansons, each percussive note marking a stroke, each ruder, simpler, than the last, pipe after pipe, league after league, until the hypnotic cadence was no longer human; it was the harmonics of cogs and gears and steam.

> *Ha, ha, ha, frit à l'huile,*
> a stroke up and down
> *Ha, ha, ha, frit à l'huile,*
> paddles slicing the river
> *Ha, ha, ha, frit à l'huile,*
> hulls carving its tongue
> *Ha, ha, ha, frit à l'huile*

Whatever they were singing about, it was *fried in oil*. And they were enormously pleased. Jeremy had never before seen men endure such punishing toil so joyfully. Their good spirits were infectious and made their passengers, Jeremy, Merit, Augustus, Finn, Lilac, Neven, and the rest, momentarily forget the awful disappointment of their forfeited furlough.

They had waited all night. It was well after one in the morning when the sideboys finally hoisted a jolly Captain Rowton back aboard the *Lancer*, along with Stokes and the other officers. Back in his cabin, discussing with his lieutenants who should go and who should stay, the captain's jowls matched the blush of claret staining his waistcoat. None disembarked at Halifax.

It took two hundred shipwrights ten months to build *HMS St. Lawrence*, a first rate warship of one hundred and four guns. It had just been launched and sailors and marines were needed upriver to fully complement her crew of seven hundred. Admiral Yeo had given Rowton orders to contribute a detachment from the *Lancer* and then head to Bermuda to press for more recruits. Volunteers were promised that, upon reaching Kingston, at least half the wages owed them would be paid out by the Fort Frederick paymaster. Gardiner volunteered immediately. Finn volunteered himself and, by extension, his wife Lilac. Merit and a few dozen others were selected. Jeremy volunteered in order to stay close to his cousin. Stokes was sent as the senior officer. Biscuit was sent to discourage desertion. They had sailed up the river to Quebec where the detachment transferred to the batteaux that would carry them the rest of the way up the rapids. In Montreal, they were joined by a trio of itinerant thespians and a man wearing a sharp, thin beard and an empire, who introduced himself as Barnabas.

While the Canadians caroled and the players drank brandy, shouting their sodden soliloquys to the rushing applause of the chutes, Stokes' men were mostly quiet. Jeremy huddled into the batteaux, sinking deeper into his fearnought, trying to stay warm. He gaped at the impenetrable forest with its paint palette canopy. He wondered at the breadth of a country in which he'd been told that one could travel all day without seeing a single person. What lurked in the endless stretches of birch, maple, and tamarack that towered over each riverbank?

At this constriction of the river, on a clear day, upstate New York was so close that a Loyalist could make out the new spangled banner on the opposite shore, with its fifteen bars and fifteen stars, flying from the top of a church steeple. On this autumn day, the river retained some of its August heat and a thick miasma rose from the contrast with the cooling air. At times, neither riverbank had been visible. Somewhere between Prescott and Elizabethtown, where the river narrows, the singing stopped.

Two boats materialized from the grey fleece, going down-river, each carrying at least a dozen men.

It was difficult to discern the others through the dirty weather, despite being within anchor-throwing distance. They seemed to be just as surprised and they suspended their oars as they drifted by. The two companies sized each other up, as if staring into a trick mirror, their own shapes deformed. Jeremy stared at the man in the bow of the first gig sitting behind a long-barrelled, swivel-mounted gun. He wore a frayed, wool jersey and a lop-sided leather cap from which spilled a hank of oily hair, covering one eye. The skin of the man's lip and jaw on the right side was torn completely away, exposing saddle-brown teeth and mottled gums. Such was the man's surprise, he'd let the remains of his jaw drop, and a rivulet of tobacco tar dribbled a path through sparse chin whiskers. Like a ship of spectres from a feverish dream, they vanished as soon as they appeared, washed away with the current.

The batteauxmen paddled upstream, increasing their rate by a few strokes a minute. The noise of their exertion was muted. The three brandy-steeped actors quieted. Oars creaked in their locks. The blades slashed at the water's surface. A crow complained. It was a harsh silence after the cacophony of the previous eight hours.

In about the time it would have taken the voyageurs to sing another round of *En roulant ma boule* or *La belle Françoise* the prows of the other two gigs reappeared, nosing through the fog, astern and to port. The ghoul with the shattered mouth remained at the prow, the curtain of hair drawn from his eyes, folded under his cap. The barrel of the long gun was now concealed, a jacket thrown over. Their gigs were lighter, carried less cargo, and had more rowers. For now they tailed at a discreet distance, just inside their shroud of vapour.

It seemed an age that they travelled like that, a couple of boat lengths separating them, as though they were sculling a race on the Thames, not canoeing rapids through new world fog. A muffled voice, calm and firm, now came from the obscured second gig, issuing commands.

Jeremy wondered, *why won't someone say something? Hail them. Inquire to their intentions. Demand they back off.*

As corporal, Jeremy thought maybe he should speak. But Stokes was in one batteau and Biscuit in another, and several other higher-ranking officers besides.

Even just an 'Ahoy'.

Thibodeau, the head conducteur, remained quiet, tapping his elevated stroke count against the gunwale. The marines freed and adjusted their muskets and located their cartridges. Rowers rowed.

"Steady as she goes, lads," Major Stokes said, finally, in a low, matter-of-fact voice, as though he was discussing supply levels with the quartermaster. "Steady as she goes. About your business."

They rowed another hundred yards. The two phantom boats clung to them like duck grass.

"Mr. Gardiner," Stokes said again. "Would you be so kind as to play?"

Gardiner searched for the tin flute in his kit bag.

"Something stirring, if you please."

He began to pick out a tune.

"That will do nicely, Mr. Gardiner," Stokes said. Jeremy found it odd that Augie Gardiner, the Bostonian, chose *Heart of Oak*. He didn't know that Gardiner had the lyrics of the American *Liberty Song* in his head as he played.

Stokes began to sing in a baritone as deep as the river:

> *Come cheer up, my lads! 'tis to glory we steer,*
> *To add something more to this wonderful year;*
> *To honour we call you, not to treat you like slaves,*
> *For who are so free as the sons of the waves?*

"Join me," he said, his bass expanding, "you know it well." Voices joined the chorus,

> *Hearts of oak are our ships, hearts of oak are our men;*
> *We always are ready, steady, boys, steady!*
> *We'll fight and we'll conquer again and again.*

> *We ne'er see our foes but we wish them to stay,*
> *They never see us but they wish us away;*
> *If they run, why we follow, and run them ashore,*
> *For if they won't fight us, we cannot do more.*

By the time they had sung all the verses twice over and Augie was about to begin *Ye Gentlemen of England*, they noticed that the prows of the gigs had faded away. They rowed on in silence for another several minutes. And then, Thibodeau struck up, at a more reasonable forty five beats per minute, a giddy,

> *Ha, ha, ha, frit à l'huile,*
> *fritaine, friton, fritou, poilon,*

All the marines and other passengers joined in.

"William Johnston," Thibodeau said later, in his broken English, when they were well past Elizabethtown encamped safely along the riverbank. "He has grudge against the crown."

Thibodeau stuck a wooden spoon into his bowl of lobscoss, and fished the green paste for a clump of bread or a sliver of pork.

"Privateer. That's his mate Kelly in the bow, la demi bouche. Vilain."

One of the rowers poured another dollop of brandy into the cup in Thibodeau's gesturing hand.

"Aujourd'hui? Bonne chance. Monsieur Johnston n'aime pas les muskets, ou les chansons. Lost May shipment – Fort Frederick supplies, dispatch. Aujourd'hui? Non, merci!"

They sat on logs pulled close to the small fire beneath the tripod. One of the Canadians scooped lobscoss from the kettle into the wooden bowls and passed them around. Others swilled brandy or tamped their long clay pipes. The journey had been measured in pipefuls, with brief tobacco stops every hour or so. Thibodeau debated whether they should camp for the night. Stokes urged pressing on, hoping to make Fort Frederick before morning.

Merit stood, belched, stamped his feet near the fire and hugged his arms to his shoulders.

"Bloody cold," he said.

Barnabas, the man with the pointy beard and the empire hat stood from his stump. He held his case before him.

"An antiphogmatic, for the frigidity?" he asked Merit. "Only a shilling per."

Merit shook his head.

"Are you sure?" Barnabas called. "A most bewitching elixir. 'Twill set you free, I guarantee."

Biscuit called the man over and gave him a shilling. He got a small phial in return.

"Froid?" Thibodeau snorted. "C'est rien, English. Fevrier. Cette, c'est froid. Be 'appy not July – il fait tres chaud. Et mosquitos. Toujours."

The actors agreed with Merit and had been putting their extra costumes on over their regular clothes to fight the chill. One of them, a slender man with a sallow complexion and ginger beard, wore long blond tresses and a patterned sun dress over chemise and pantaloons. He approached the fire and draped his arm over Merit's shoulder.

"You know, sailor," the man falsettoed, pursing his rouged lips, "nothing keeps you warm like a good cuddle."

"I'd as soon gut you," Merit said, flinging the man's arm from his shoulder.

Lilac, wearing Finn's alternate blue trousers, stepped forward and extended her hand.

"I'd stand up with you, little lady," she said huskily, "if you'd do me the honour."

Ginger blushed and curtseyed, took her hand, and fell into her embrace. They separated again and, around the clearing, did a jerky impression of an English country dance, to the applause of the men.

Another of the players, wearing a bonnet and a long skirt, crossed to Jeremy.

"Heavens! What a man!" he said, hauling on Jeremy until he was standing, "Seven feet if he's an inch. A rare specimen indeed." The man put Jeremy's arm around his waist. "That's it, make a woman of me, but mind you don't snap my spine, you brute."

The third actor grabbed the Breton and soon they were reeling and galloping and twirling in some absurd mockery of a waltz. Augustus played a sprightly air on the flute and the Canadians laughed and clapped along.

"It's best we continued," Stokes said to Thibodeau.

"Ah, yes, you're right. We're almost there."

Pea sacks and cooking utensils were packed away, the fire snuffed, and the thespians bundled back into the batteaux. Within three more pipes, two beneath a grinning, harvest moon, they were just a few miles from Kingston.

"About twenty minutes now, Monsieur Stokes," Thibodeau said, between puffs.

"Is there a tavern nearby?"

"Mais oui, of course. Ferguson's, peut-être? Mile from the fort, seulement."

"Which direction?"

"Nord. You see road? Follow to town."

"Thank you. You are as fine a paddlesman as I've ever witnessed and a credit to your profession and country."

"Merci, monsieur."

"You've delivered us a half day early, I'm grateful. I intend to take our men to Ferguson's for a proper meal."

He glanced at back at the site of the fire where the lobscoss had simmered.

"No offence, of course."

Thibodeau shrugged and smiled.

"Perhaps also to find pillows a little softer than moss for their heads, at least tonight, before we all must report for duty."

"Je comprends."

"You are welcome to join us."

"Merci, monsieur, very kind. Mais, we stay with boats and supplies. We deliver to the fort. Le matin. Nous préférons le plein air."

Already the other Canadians were happily unloading the batteaux, tipping them, and spreading tarpaulins between them to create makeshift shelters. Stokes shook Thibodeau's hand and led his men in search of Ferguson's. Barnabas and the players followed.

"It's usually officers that honour us with their custom," Ferguson said, opening the heavily timbered door, when they arrived and rapped it with a musket butt. Ferguson peered at the bearded man in the sundress, the other with a bonnet and floral skirt, and Lilac in her trousers, her straight mahogany hair falling halfway down the back of her short white jacket. Jeremy, wearing his bell-top shako looked to be about eight feet tall, while next to him Neven Tanguay, wearing one of the tasseled, knitted caps favoured by the Canadians, resembled an elf.

"Enlisted men usually go down the road or into town," Ferguson added.

An intoxicating blend of maple smoke, toasted malt, tobacco, and browned pastry gusted from the opening into the crisp, autumn night.

"I'm Major Stokes, of the Royal Marines, previously of *HMS Lancer*, now of *HMS St. Lawrence*. We've travelled many difficult miles to be with you here in Kingston. I'd be obliged if you might find some space for the night at your hearth and table for a party of weary men."

The innkeeper sized up his clientele.

"And women," Stokes said.

Ginger waggled a finger.

"We have our own bedding," Stokes continued, "but a warm, dry stretch of floorboard would be a conspicuous luxury compared to the hollow logs and sodden moss we've lately had to endure."

Ferguson still seemed unsure.

"I'll be sure to mention your hospitality to the Commodore. You'll be paid handsomely."

"That's fine then, come inside. I'll tell Mrs. Ferguson to stretch the stew."

An hour later, Jeremy sat with his socked feet before the fire. Merit sat beside him, shaping a miniature hull from a chunk of cedar while Augie Gardiner played a plaintive air. Stokes sat at a table nearby, going through his orders and papers. They were full, made docile by the pounds of stew, dumplings, and black bread. Each of them sipped at a sherry cobbler, one of two they were allowed for the evening. Finn Davies, lying on his stomach, sucked at his through the clay tube of a broken pipe stem.

"These are delicious," he whispered to Jeremy. "But only two? Bloody torture."

"On the King's penny," Stokes said, overhearing, "everything must be rationed and accounted for. Be thankful for two. You'll soon be paid off and get your leave and you can spend every copper on drink. We can remit directly to the tavern-keeper of your choice, if it would expedite matters."

"Beg your pardon, major," Finn said.

"He'll not be doing that," Lilac said, hoisting Finn from the floor. "Not if I have any say. We need to be saving up for our family. And anyway, Finnsie can't hold his liquor the ways I can, not since he was a whippet and, in a duel, got clubbed by a sabre. More than two nips and he's ridiculous. I must keep a close eye on him."

"Most sensible, Mrs. Davies," Stokes said, not looking up from his papers.

Finn groaned and Lilac led him to a space and they spooned into a woolen blanket next to the actors who were already curled up by the fire, snoring.

Jeremy read through a copy of *The Kingston Gazette* broadsheet, left in the drawing room by Mr. Ferguson. His eye caught a notice describing in strict terms the punishments for aiding and abetting desertion. Alarmed, Jeremy folded the paper into a quarter and handed it to Augie. Augie held it up and read out loud.

"Theatrical Entertainment, Wednesday evening, at Mr. Poncet's large room, …much admired comic farce…*The Doctor's Courtship*."

Ginger woke briefly.

"That's our show!" he cried. "Not just Wednesday, Saturday too. You must come. Bring your friends."

"Not that!" Jeremy said. He thrust his finger to the notice below the theatrical announcement. "And," he whispered, looking behind him, "not out loud."

Ginger, disappointed, lay down again.

Augie read the notice of punishments for aiding desertion and shrugged.

"They have to say something, don't they?" he said. "Have you read Samuel Johnson? Do you know his opinion on the matter?"

Jeremy shook his head.

"'No man will be a sailor,'" Augie whispered, "'who has contrivance enough to get himself into a jail; for, being in a ship is being in a jail, with the chance of being drowned.... A man in a jail has more room, better food and commonly better company.'"

"This isn't jail," Jeremy whispered back, "this is a public whipping just for aiding and abetting."

Jeremy took the paper back and continued reading. Below the desertion bill there was an item entitled INFORMATION with a brief notice directly below:

If any subscriber may have information, it read, *as to the whereabouts of a Jeremy Castor or Merit Davey, who disappeared from the coast of Cornwall, March 1814, their mother who resides at Porthleven anxiously awaits word of their situation, not having heard from them since. Please contact Mrs. Alice Castor, Perenn Cottage, Green Lane, Porthleven, Cornwall.*

"Jesus," Jeremy breathed, wiping the spilled sherry cobbler from his trouser leg.

"Merit."

Merit grunted.

"Merit, look." He showed him the paper, forgetting Merit couldn't read.

"Mom," he said. "She's looking for us. She still doesn't know."

Major Stokes stood up from behind the table and adjusted the sculpted ends of his moustache. He stepped over to where Jeremy was sitting and handed him a bundle of papers secured with twine.

"Your letters home, corporal," he said. "None sent, I'm afraid."

Merit put his knife down and Augie stopped playing. Jeremy took the bundle, undid the twine, and flipped through six months of his writings to Alice, the early ones where he explained the awful circumstances and promised to be home soon, and the later ones where he described shipboard life, his mates, hunger, thirst, sickness, and the majesty of the Atlantic. All were there. Jeremy looked up at the major.

"The captain saw fit not to include them in the packets."

Merit extended his arm as far as he could around his cousin's broad shoulder, hugging him to his cheek.

"He discarded them to the pile of fire starter."

"Why?" Jeremy asked, simply. Nothing could make less sense.

"I cannot say."

Jeremy stared at the jumble in his lap.

"He moves in mysterious ways," Stokes added, not unkindly, "as Cowper, aptly, might put it."

Jeremy jerked his head away to look again into the major's perpetually impassive face. There was a slight creasing at the corner of his eyes.

"Captain Rowton is a barnacle on the ass of a whore," Merit said, plainly, as though he'd just stated he preferred ale to stout, "and King George is that whore."

Such an assertion made on board the *Lancer*, within earshot of an officer, could lead to a dance at the gratings. Biscuit, who'd been slumped in a corner, rubbing his temples, was already on his feet, eager to deal out one punishment or another.

"Thank you, Mr. Prout," Stokes said, waving him away, "I think we can dismiss that as a harmless bit of gun-decking. We aren't on the gangway now and it's been a rather long journey. I'm content to face tomorrow with the understanding that it never happened."

"He's no marine, major," Biscuit said.

"Aye, he's not. But I'm the ranking senior officer. At your ease."

Biscuit bristled into his corner.

"I retrieved them for you," Stokes continued, speaking again to Jeremy. "That you might post them from Kingston. Which, if all goes well, you'll be able to do tomorrow."

8

Old King's Head

JUST AFTER NOON, market square enjoyed the sun's gentle, autumn embrace. Inside the Old King's Head, twilight. The few windows fronting the building permitted little light through their richly tinted glass. To lift the gloom, Argand lamps were arrayed around the dining room doughtily burning their day-long reserves of whale oil. It was these little shows of ostentation that attracted Kingston's nascent squirearchy, the Family Compact. The port-wine paneling, dark, engraved tables, and fine bone china tea sets reminded patrons of their clubs back home. At the Old King's Head it wasn't necessary to bring your own glass.

Dorephus sat at one of the rosewood tables across from Noble Spafford. In front of him there was a dish of baked oysters, seven of eight remaining, trapped in congealing butter. Spafford had moved on, working his way through the beef head soup, the salmon mayonnaise, the boiled tongue with roasted brussel's sprouts, and the broiled pheasant with chestnut stuffing. He awaited syllabub.

"Do you realize what a rare treat this is, what an extravagance? You don't mind do you?" Spafford asked, spearing one of Dorephus' oysters, sucking it from the tines of his fork. "Milward doesn't get them very often, perhaps once, twice a year. Packed in ice, shipped all the way up from Malpeque to Montreal to here. We live in a wondrous age."

In the middle of the table, in a terra cotta sleeve of icy lake water, sat a bottle of Perrier-Jouët, 1808, two thirds empty. Dorephus' glass, a willowy flute of aquamarine, was full, minus a sip.

"That's an exquisite glass, is it not?" Spafford said, holding his own flute up to the lamp glow.

"True craftsmanship there. And appropriate. The beauty of the vessel accentuates the preciousness of its cargo. I don't understand these chaps who are content to swill a delicate vintage from any old mug."

Spafford wrenched a wing from the remains of the pheasant, cracking the bones apart with his teeth.

"Barbarity, if you ask me. Eh Barrett?"

Dorephus dipped his head.

"Of course. We're of the same mind. You're a decent egg Barrett. We all make mistakes, after all. I think we've arrived at a most acceptable reparation, don't you?"

Spafford drained his flute and brought it down sharply to the table, making it ring.

"Ah, le vin de Diable!" he sighed. "Divine. Do you know why they call it that, devil's wine?" He didn't wait. "It's because the spirit is so lively that it shoots its cork. Peasants. Superstitious and credulous. Why they'll never rise above their station. No offence meant."

Dorephus regarded the bottle and envied the champagne its devilish spirit, wishing he too could shoot the cork.

Milward's daughter came to the table. Spafford motioned the pheasant carcass away. She returned with the bowl of syllabub, a silver ladle thrust into its frothy entrails.

"It's telling. For a long time, only English glass makers could produce the ponies, demis, and magnums that could capture this magic and keep it confined. The French couldn't stand the pressure. Still can't. Take the Battle of Trafalgar. Or, the Hundred Years War. Sure, they can create some works of art, some masterpieces of the banquet, they've got the attitude, the arrogance, I'll give them that, they've got the, the *je ne sais quoi*, I suppose, but it takes good English know-how to bottle it and bring it to market."

He licked a dollop of cream from his thick thumb.

"You know," Spafford peered again at his glass, remembering something, "there used to be a glassmaker here in Kingston, that could produce this sort of quality. Can't remember his name now. Wanted to establish a glass manufactory here in town. We couldn't have that, of course. Had to put a stop to it. Gentlemen have glass interests in Montreal and at home. Mustn't take bread from the mouths of good, English craftsmen."

Spafford got halfway through the syllabub before he pulled a pocket watch from his waistcoat and realized with a gasp that he had to be somewhere else. As he rose abruptly, his paunch caught the edge of the table, tipping and shattering his champagne glass.

"Ah well," he said, looking back, "nothing lasts forever, beauty least of all." He had Milward put everything on his tab and he was out the door.

Outside, the market bustled, and if he'd been listening, Dorephus would have heard the billingsgate issuing from the mouths of mongers and the shouts of barkers:

"From the mystic Orient, the sultan's bazaar, an authentic panacea, the renowned Paregoric Elixir! There is nothing it can't cure. Sir, yes you sir, a minute of your time…"

"Available in Kingston for the first time, Dr. Bateman's celebrated Pectoral Drops!"

"Try Dr. Gilson's Female Pills! Excuse me madam, do you suffer from…"

Outside, the world lived on. Dorephus was deaf to all that. He stared at the tiny spheres in his flute, appearing near the bottom, clinging to the side a while before they detached themselves and rushed to the surface, expiring on arrival. He stared and stared at the endless procession of bubbles as if it was a matter of life and death.

Eventually, he became aware of the publican's daughter standing at his table, a hand on her thrust hip, her head cocked to one side. She looked to be Amelia's age.

"Oh, yes," he said, "I'm finished."

Dorephus collected his things, pushed the door, and stumbled into the noise and glare of the market.

"Sir, please, a moment. You're a strapping how do you do. Have you ever considered farming? This operation is for you. Ernesttown. You've not seen soil like this. Magic. See this beet? Prize winner. Nine and a half pounds, twenty three inches round. From this very farm. That's no flannelmouth. Just fifty pounds down."

Dorephus looked at the man, puzzled, and kept walking.

"Sir, do you have persistent itch? Wheaton's Itch Ointment, you'll be amazed..."

He needed escape. To be free of the market, the people. He walked north until he found Montreal Road. When he joined Montreal Road, he continued, one foot mechanically in front of the other for hours, until he arrived at Franklin's Tavern where he requested a jug of cider and a bag of popped corn.

"Going hunting," was all he would say when Joseph asked where he was headed or what was on his mind. Joseph had learned not to ask specifically about the work bee. He handed the supplies to Dorephus sadly, refusing to take the last of his shillings.

Dorephus continued his march, to Loughborough Road, to the guest house at Spafford's. There he picked up the old land pattern flintlock along with a pocketful of cartridges. The musket had been disassembled, cleaned, oiled, and reassembled. The trigger mechanism worked fine. He had tested it several times, shooting after grouse.

It was dusk now. He kept walking. He walked until the road ended and then pushed further through the tangled underbrush. Despite the cool air, the way was difficult and his back was wet with perspiration. He began to shed clothing, dropping his jacket here, his vest there.

Overnight, when the temperature would threaten to fall to freezing, he would need those layers, but it didn't occur to him. His arms and shoulders were made raw by the low, grasping branches of the cedars. Birch lances gouged his ribs. The flesh of his face was mortified by long needles of the pompous white pines, standing shoulder to shoulder, barring his way. He didn't mind the gantlet of trees. He welcomed it. He continued to push his way deeper into the woods, until finally, scraped and bloody, he arrived at the lake. The nearest Loyalist homestead was many miles away. The only person he might meet would be a trapper, a Yankee outlaw, or perhaps, a Mississauga. He could see the suggestion of a trail along the lake shore, outlined by the silvery light. Under different circumstances, he would have been afraid.

Dorephus uncorked the jug and took a long draught. He scooped a fistful of the salty corn, stuffed it in his mouth and looked up to the sky. As he located the various stars and constellations, Polaris, Cassiopeia, Ursa Minor and Major, he wondered how they looked from his native Yorkshire, whether they looked the same. He brought the jug to his tilted face and let the cider flow. He thought of his short but pleasant childhood growing up in the Dales and how his mom and dad, poor and hard-working though they were, always made sure he was warm, well-fed, and happy.

There was little opportunity there for a grown man. Not like Canada.

He gazed and drank, drank and gazed, until the pot was hollow. For the first time he noticed he was shivering. He hurled the empty earthenware deep into the bush and crossed his arms around himself, his hands upon his shoulders. He lifted his gaze again and marveled at how bright the sky was at nine o'clock in October. If the moon wasn't full, it was nearly so.

The Plough. That's what they call Ursa Major in Yorkshire. Not a dipper or a gourd. A Plough. He pictured an actual plough, carving up the sky, casting off the stars. He could see a ploughman behind the plough.

A grinning, leering, sweating ploughman.

Carmichael Jones.

Dorephus howled like a wounded animal, cinching his arms tighter, hugging them against his chest. The flood of anguish was so guttural, so primitive, it seemed to carry no words. *Moonie*, he seemed to cry.

At length, he subsided. He gathered himself up.

Dorephus picked up the musket and stared closely at the breech. He pulled a cartridge from his pocket and tore the top of it with his teeth. He primed the pan with a measure of powder. He stood the musket up and poured the rest of the powder down the barrel. He pulled the ramrod from its holder, pushed the envelope holding the ball into the muzzle and rammed it home.

He followed the trail along the lakeshore, shedding more clothes as he went, freeing himself of shoes and socks, trousers, chemise, until he was down to flannel shorts and shirt.

He followed the trail as it veered from the lake into the woods, about two hundred yards. He sat beneath a giant, centuries-old sugar maple and put the muzzle in his mouth and his toe on the trigger. In the forest it was perfectly silent; the birds were roosting, the crickets and cicadas had long finished their seasons, foragers and predators, voles and mice, foxes and fishers, had yet to start their nightly contest. There was the merest breeze in the very top of the canopy.

Dorephus bit hard on the barrel and shoved his toe down. Nothing. He squeezed his toe against the trigger again. Nothing. Jammed.

Dorephus leapt up from the roots, bawling. He picked up the musket and bashed it against the trunk of the maple. He drove it hard into the yielding soil made spongy by centuries of dying leaves. He picked it up by the barrel and lifted it high over his head and brought it down as though he drove a stubborn fence post, striking the butt hard against a limestone outcropping.

The hammer fell and ignited the flintlock's main charge, firing for the last time.

9

Walker's Hotel

THE CHATTER STOPPED when they drifted past the corpse.

Merit had been describing the fish dinner he would order and Finn, who'd convinced Lilac to go ahead and hire a room at Walker's, said he hoped the town's taverners had put a substantial stock of cognac aside because he aimed to empty every cask.

"I'm not coming back," Neven had been saying, "until I kiss a beautiful Upper Canadian girl. They can pack me into a gallows, I don't care. That'll be my pitch. 'Kiss me now pretty lady or I'm gallows bound.' Or maybe…" he tailed off.

Every man in the batteau, Jeremy, Merit, Augie, and the rest, going into town for their forty eight hour furlough; all were quiet now as they regarded the dead. The first corpse, with which they nearly collided, was chalky and tattered so that it blended into the slate grey of the lake and was so unexpected and out of place, it didn't register. The second was difficult to miss; obese in life, gargantuan in death, the blue and bloated torso of this more recent arrival fissured the fabric of her sodden petticoat. Saturated flesh at her ankle puffed up over the bowline that tethered her to shore.

"Bienvenue à Kingston," Thibodeau said. The men had hired him to ferry them across the channel from Fort Frederick into town.

"Disgrace, n'est-ce pas? Drunk, ou stupide, ou le même, they fall down the bank, dans le lac. Chaque semaine."

"There's your first Canadian girl Neven," Augie said, as the body passed astern, "I don't think you'd get too much resistance from her."

"Poor, alone," Thibodeau continued, "none to bury them. They bob for weeks."

Thibodeau brought them to the dock and they disembarked. Scores of people lined the wharf, some sitting on chests and trunks, others bundled together under filthy woolen blankets. One couple quarreled over a crescent of hard bread. A group of women washed soiled linens, cursing and heckling in their impenetrable brogue. A clutch of boys and girls, none older than ten, lengths of twine holding sackcloth breeches above their waists, gathered around a single switch of poplar which the eldest jigged up and down. Upstream, a man whose red eyes were barely visible beneath his thick beard and tattered, wide-brim hat, made his way unsteadily down the bank until he got to a bough of cedar overhanging the shore. Once there, he dropped his trousers, perched, and defecated noisily into the water below. "Sumtin t' catch," he cackled after he'd finished, re-hoisted his trousers, and made his way back up the slope.

"Tout le monde," Thibodeau said, as he cleated the batteau. "A better life. Ici. Ça, c'est désespérée, non?"

"Thibodeau," Jeremy said, as he was the last out of the batteau. "Why don't you and your paddlemen come with us?" His hand riffled the shillings and half-crowns ringing his pocket. "We'll buy you some supper and the brandy to go with it."

Thibodeau looked back toward Kingston and the crumbling warehouses and tenements of grey-weathered wood rising up from the shore. He watched as the carters filled their casks with lake water. One of the children, a cherub with a mud-smeared face and a robin's nest thatch of hair, squatted in the water, cupped his hands, and slurped.

"Non, merci," he said, with a smile, putting his fingers together into a peak, "merci beaucoup. We avoid roof. Nous préférons le plein air. Au revoir, Monsieur Jeremy."

Jeremy watched them leave, attaining the safety of Kingston harbour, the Cataraqui river, and out to open water, singing and rowing joyfully. Merit pulled at his arm.

"I know what's afore your mind cousin," he said, "I'm thinking the same. But, for tonight, let's make the town's acquaintance. Let's enjoy ourselves." Merit swirled the knuckle bones, making them do-si-do his palm. "I'm a wagering there's a whole population that's not yet played crown and anchor."

"Mer, it's not worth the risk. We've saved a little, let's preserve it."

"We need a hoard to buy out our commissions. Don't trouble yourself. I'll pick my marks carefully. Old men and imbeciles."

"No officers."

"Unless they're dead drunk."

"No-one carrying a firearm. No-one bigger than you."

"That's what you're for," Merit said.

Someone tugged at Jeremy's trouser hem. He looked down to see a black man sitting bent on a rotted crate, his prodigious white hair bulbous like a giant cotton blossom. His left eye was cloudy, the right was yellow and watery, and his two hands were turned in on themselves, like pincers.

"Scuse me misser," he said, "you seen my sons?"

Jeremy stared, puzzled.

"Roderick and Charles. You seen 'em?"

Jeremy mumbled, still confused.

"I ain't no slave, if that's what you thinkin. I be free. Was a slave, in Albany. But they made me free."

He held up useless hands to shield his eye.

"Why not, now?" He laughed; a short, phlegmy hack. "I come up here to find Roddy and Charles. They here? I'm sure they is. But I ain't got a farthing."

Merit pulled at Jeremy's arm again.

"Come on, they're already up the hill, we'll lose them."

"You got a farthing you could lend? Some vittles?"

Jeremy put his hand in his pocket. Merit took him by the belt and yanked.

"Jem, later."

They turned from the old man and sprinted up the muddy slope to join their mates at the corner of Front and Barrack. They scanned the intersection. Months of rain had dissolved the layers of slop. The streets ran like open sewers. A bony, doddering cow meandered down the centre of Barrack, toward the water, her brittle hooves squelching the muck with each uncertain step.

Further ahead, a man and a woman, her gloved hand gripping the crook of his tweedy elbow, picked their way along the sidewalk's wooden slats, most of which were either broken or loose. No pedestrians used the street. They all took their chances with turned ankles on the boardwalk. The couple ducked into a shop door when a bull terrier arrived from an adjoining street and cornered them with a low growl. The terrier became distracted by a pig snuffling scraps along Front. The dog chased it into a nearby carriageway to fight over a scavenged fish carcass and the street filled with the hog's desperate shrieking.

A pair of Canadian Fencibles passed, on their way to the Tête de Pont barracks.

"This is what land looks like, Jack" one of them said. "Maybe you ain't seen it in a while?"

"T'ain't Covent Garden, is it?" the other laughed over his shoulder.

"Go dig a trench, swaddy," Merit called.

The soldiers paused and turned.

"Perhaps we can discuss it further, tonight," one of them called back.

"If you feel it necessary."

"Bottle and Glass," the soldier shouted, from outside the entrance to the barracks.

~ ~ ~

Merit and Jeremy sat in the waiting room of the *Gazette*. Ahead of them, Noble Spafford was dictating his announcement to the clerk.

"Colonel Noble Spafford would like to announce his marriage to Miss Amelia Barrett, in this town, the 25th day of October, 1814, at St. George's Church, Rev. Official Stuart presiding."

The clerk scratched it down.

"The Colonel and Mrs. Spafford would like to thank all friends and family in attendance for joining us on this joyous day."

He waited for the clerk to finish.

"That should do it."

"Congratulations sir," Jeremy said, standing, as the Colonel turned to leave.

"Thank you," Spafford said, extending his hand. "Have we met?"

"Jeremy Castor, corporal, Royal Marines, *HMS St. Lawrence*. This is my cousin, Merit Davey, able seaman, also *HMS St. Lawrence*."

"Ah yes, the new men. Great to have you here. Do you know Major Stokes?"

"He's my commanding officer."

"Capital bloke. Capital."

"It's an honour to serve under him."

"I should say it is. Please give him my regards."

"Will do, sir."

Spafford was out the door. Merit stared at Jeremy.

"What?"

"What is wrong with you?"

"What's all this yes sir, yes sir, three bags full sir, 'swallop?"

"Friendliness."

"If I didn't know better I'd guess you were growing a little too comfortable into your scarlet coat."

"We're going to be here a while, I don't see how it can hurt to be decent."

The clerk cleared his throat. Jeremy showed him the announcement Alice posted in his paper and asked if he would be able to send his bundle of letters home to her at Perenn Cottage in Porthleven. After Jeremy had dropped some coins into his outstretched hand, the clerk said he was happy to do so and to receive replies on his behalf.

~~~

The men of the *Lancer* spent the afternoon at Walker's, lunching, loafing, sprucing themselves for the evening's festivities. They feasted on pheasant. They quaffed from the wassail bowl. They napped on sheets of pristine linen, free of lice and fleas. They took piping mugfuls of dark roasted American coffee with trimmings, real cream and cane sugar cut straight from the loaf. Lilac took a leisurely bath in scalding water free from fear of reprimand. They were renewed, full of promise. They would start at the Bottle and Glass, to take in *The Doctor's Courtship*, presented by the troupe from Montreal.

10

Violin, Bottle, and Glass

DESPITE THE CRISPNESS OF THE LATE OCTOBER AIR, the atmosphere was soupy inside Mr. Poncet's tavern, at the sign of the Violin, Bottle, and Glass, at the edge of Sir John's Park; thick with sweat, breath, and desire. You could taste the air, a complex mélange of sour tobacco, sweet liquor, and spicy bodies, with traces of sea-salt. It was Saturday night and it seemed as though all of Kingston was crammed into the two story clapboard roadhouse; soldiers and sailors, veterans and greenhorns, dockmen and dowagers, carters and bakers, bankers and beggars, aldermen and milkmaids. Each had their own private need. The farmer who'd spent all week alone desired company. The bos'n's mate looked to drink something other than lime-leavened rum and to think of home. The young seamstress hoped to meet a midshipman and to think of away.

The bored needed distraction.

The bottled; release.

"Three threads, mind you don't stint," Jeremy shouted to Alfred, Mr. Poncet's brother-in-law, behind the bar.

"The same," Merit said.

"A Robinson's lager, I've me own tankard."

"Rye."

"Rye and lager. Aye, just pour it right in."

"Splash some whiskey in my lager as well, Alfie."

"Scotch, neat."

"Brandy, warm."

"Robinson's Brown."

"Robinson's Pale."

"Applejack."

"Whiskey. I don't care, any kind. And water."

"A gill of your finest rum. No, keep her pure, just rum."

"A pot of chilled genever, half a lemon, and a dish of sugar."

"I'll take the whole crock."

"Vin rouge, s'il vous plait."

"What's she drinking? Metheglin? Three of those."

"A porter will be just fine."

"No negus? Just tea then. With a jigger of brandy."

"Gin with sugar and a touch of lime."

"Got any maple syrup? Do ye? A tumbler of rye and a spoon o syrup."

"Tuppenny. In me blackjack, if you please."

"Beef broth and bourbon."

"In the cauldron? Mulled wine? A cuppa that."

"Sherry with lemon and a drop of bitters."

"Rum toddy."

"Porter."

"Can ye fit a finger of whiskey in there? Can ye? Then fill 'er up."

"Porter."

"Porter."

"Porter."

"Straight up."

"Shaken."

"Same again."

On it went. Poncet's best night until Christmas Eve.

In the great room, a musical prelude to the main feature. Ginger, wearing his wig, gown, and large, rosy ovals painted over his powdered cheeks, sang a ballad while one of his associates poked out accompaniment on the battered upright in the corner. They were barely making themselves heard.

"All the Doctors are naughty," Ginger cried to the balcony, a manic smile on his face. The third member of the troupe was already in his doctor's costume of an over-sized frockcoat, false pointy beard, and monocle. He carried a leather valise and he darted around the ten foot square stage, leering at the front row.

The doctors now are all getting in fault,
Bolusem, Blisterem, Jollop and Salts—
They're naughty bricks now every day
Among the ladies the doctors play—

The doctor pulled a giant magnifying glass from his bag and proceeded to examine one of the women at a nearby table, running it from her lace up boots to her frilled collar. The balcony roared.

Oh ladies the doctors are comical chaps
They are naughty men it can't be denied,
And Godfrey's Cordial they do prescribe,
The people all say they are at fault,
By giving the females jollop and salts.

The doctor retrieved a jeroboam-sized apothecary's bottle from the bag and displayed it to the crowd, nodding. Ginger distributed song sheets.

He had them chanting:
Keep your wives and your daughters free from fault
And learn them to shun the jollop and salts.

Noble Spafford maneuvered his bulk toward the bar bouncing patrons from his way, a snifter in each hand. The path was blocked by Carmichael Jones, his back and elbows resting against the bar. He was watching the doctor chase Ginger around the stage, his jaw slack with amusement.

"Excuse me," Spafford said.
Cordial and Gin a trial had—
The, lawyers all did play;
Brandy lost! And Godfrey's Cordial—
Nobly gained the day.

"Way hey!" the ploughman shouted toward the stage, clapping his hands, sloshing his porter. "You make an appointment with Dr. Jones! I'll set you right."

"Excuse me!" Spafford said again.

"I haven't heard this one before, have you?" Carmichael asked young Sam and Cornelius Harris, standing at his elbow.

The damsel's father was a publican,

"Hooray for Poncet," the crowd called, "show us your daughter!"

"Here am I," Ginger said, hiking the hem of his dress and they cheered.

The girl was young and keen
She liked the Godfrey's Cordial
With that she found no fault,
But upon my word she didn't like
The doctor's jollop and salts.

The doctor now pulled from his bag an iron device with a screw and four metal blades, a cross between an ancient speculum and a pear of confession. The crowd hushed and Ginger's singing became dramatic. He put the back of his palm against his forehead. He put the other against his thrust hip.

He said he never blistered her—
He could do nothing Worse;
The doctor swore he never felt
The little maiden's pulse.

"Stand left!" Spafford barked, just as he used to do on the deck off the coast of Spain.
Carmichael became aware that he was being shouted at.
"Sir," he said. "Excuse me, sir."
Spafford stared.
"Sir," Carmichael repeated, patiently. "Tis a matter of respect."
"Cockfosters and twaddle."
"We's all sirs here, sir, in the Bottle and Glass."
"What's your ship? Are you of the *Lancer*?"
"*Lancer*? Nay. Of the plough."
Spafford frowned, trying to recall a frigate, sloop, even a packet, in his majesty's navy, named The Plough.
"Polyphemus?"
"Plough," Carmichael said, "I'm a ploughman. Now, excuse me, I'm enjoying the entertainments."
"A ploughman? A ploughman?" Spafford said, flushing the words from his mouth like a walrus clearing its throat. "Yankee?"
"I'm no Yankee, though I often wonder whether I'd be better off if I was."

And when the trial ended,
And Cordial knew his fate;
You could hear him sing from Ernesttown
Right down to Kingston Gate.

"Colonel."

Jeremy had been standing nearby with Merit, Augustus and the others. He stepped forward and extended his outsized hand.

"Ah, young Corporal...," Spafford said as he turned, showing Jeremy a snifter in each hand.

"Castor, sir."

"Yes, Castor. Excellent timing. I was just having the most appalling conversation with Brother Jonathan here."

Spafford turned. Seeing the arrival of the marines, Carmichael, Cornelius, and Sam slipped away, inching further into the great room.

"No matter," he said, "I can order now. Thank you lads."

He stepped to the bar with his snifters.

"Cognac," he said to Alfie, holding up two fingers. "I'm celebrating. I say, Cartwright!"

Spafford shouted toward Richard Cartwright leaning at the rail.

"You won't believe the riff-raff they allow into this place. Hold on, let me get Dunbar to take this drink. Dunbar!"

Dunbar was five places down the bar and couldn't hear.

"Castor," Spafford said, to Jeremy again, "would you be kind enough to take this glass to Mrs. Spafford? I need to have a word with Dickie here."

"Of course," Jeremy said.

"She's just over there," Spafford said, pointing to a table in the great room. "Let her know I'll be right with her. What're you having?"

"Porter."

"I'll buy when you're back. Oh, and this too."

Spafford pulled a small silver looking glass from his waistcoat.

"A wedding present. Silly girl wants me to hold on to it."

And the little girls did sing
Let us mix some Godfrey's Cordial
In a drop of Hollands gin.

Jeremy passed his own drink to Merit and took the item.

"Hot air balloon. Why do his bidding?"

"Decency."

Jeremy crossed the room slowly, his head and shoulders conspicuous over everyone else. He reached the crowded table and tried to get near the woman Spafford had pointed out. Half of her thin, greying hair had escaped the bun it was pulled into and it was wisping her red, greasy face. She had a whiskery mole just left of her dimpled chin and another one on her butcher's forearms. She watched the performers and guffawed.

So now the trial is over
And the doctor has got free

Someone craning his neck around Jeremy brayed.

"Thistle-grower! Siddown!"

Jeremy knelt next to the woman.

"Mrs. Spafford? Your husband asked me to bring you this."

The woman looked at him, gripped his shoulder, and brought her flushed, sweating face close, enveloping him in peppermint vapour.

"I ain't no Mrs. Spafford, though could be for the right price. I'll take the conyak, either way."

And the little maid has got a kid
To dance upon her knee—

"I'm Mrs. Spafford," a girl said. It was Amelia Barrett, sitting at the same table.

Jeremy looked at her. She didn't look older than sixteen. He'd assumed she was someone's daughter. She sat perfectly straight, hands folded in her lap, unsmiling. She wore a white gown with pearl buttons up the front, following her gentle contour. Clusters of auburn ringlets framed her pretty scowl. A sweltering multitude of bullet-headed men and bottom-heavy women pushed in around her. A columbine amid a field of cow parsnip.

"You're Mrs...."

"Spafford, yes. You can keep your liquor, I don't want it."

"I'll have it," the first woman said, eyeing Jeremy, "and the rest, besides."

"My apologies, ma'am," Jeremy said to Amelia, bowing slightly. "I didn't know. My name is Jeremy Castor, corporal, lately assigned to *HMS St. Lawrence*. I'm pleased to make your acquaintance."

Amelia had already shifted her attention and was looking into the middle distance.

Oh girls beware—or else I fear
As you through life goes on
If you take the Godfrey's Cordial
You may find it rather strong.

"Thank you very much, ladies and gentlemen," Ginger was saying, "please refresh your refreshments. In a few moments we will present to you *The Doctor's Courtship*, in full and without censure."

Jeremy now stood to his full height.

"Can I get you *anything*?" he asked Amelia. She didn't answer.

"Oh, I have your looking glass as well," Jeremy said, holding it out.

"Keep it," she said.

Jeremy hesitated, then put the glass into his pocket and retreated to the bar.

"My mother named me 'Noble'," Spafford was saying, expansively, to Merit, Augustus, and anyone in earshot, "after my great, great, great grand-father, Archibald Ponsonby, 2nd Earl of Meathfield. Neither my father nor I are part of the peerage, but I don't mind saying governor Drummond may be the only man in Upper Canada with bluer blood. We distinguished ourselves on the field of battle for King and country which, I warrant, is as worthwhile as being swaddled in ermine."

"Is that the same Earl of Meathfield who oversaw the forced famine of twenty thousand of its native, Catholic inhabitants, as part of the Tudor conquest?" Gardiner asked, imperfectly recalling a dusty nugget from his studies at Providence Grammar School in Boston.

"There's no better way to test one's mettle," Spafford continued, "than to stare down Bonaparte's eight-pounder Gribeauvals, without flinching, as we did at the Siege of Roses."

"You were at the Siege of Roses?" Merit asked, wiping ale froth from his furrowed lip.

"Merit is it? Of course lad, Royal Marines. It's the sort of thing that's impossible to forget. A bloody marvelous show. *HMS Excellent* was going great guns and we all held steady. Until we had no choice but to surrender the garrison. Still, I made Colonel that day."

"It was mostly Spanish and Portuguese levies that manned the garrison, wasn't it?" Gardiner asked. "The English kept mostly to their frigates."

"I went ashore, I assure you," Spafford puffed his cheeks. "Had French lead nipping my breeches every inch up the gangway. And where do you call home, I wonder?"

"Boston."

"Most edifying."

Jeremy returned, still holding the cognac.

"I'm sorry Colonel, she said she didn't want it."

"Poor dear. It's our wedding day. I thought she might like a little entertainment, she's been so overwrought. You know how flighty little doves get, especially on their big day. Keep it. On me. It's a Croizet."

"Bonaparte's favourite whistle wetter," Merit said to Augustus.

"You're not a Bonapartiste, are you?" Augie asked, with mock severity.

Spafford reached up to clap his hand on Jeremy's shoulder and turn him around.

"A word of warning boy. Lots of the Yankeefied here in Kingston. Airs. With the war and disruption it seems only to get worse. An erosion of decorum. You're best to stick to your own. Let me introduce you to Dickie Cartwright. Good Family Compact. Restoring the old order."

"Ladies and gentlemen," Ginger cried over the din, "we'd now like to present to you, a comic farce in three parts, *The Doctor's Courtship*. We request that you direct your gracious attention to our humble stage."

A boy retracted the wicks on some of the oil lamps along the wall and dimmed the light. The noise in the great room abated to a tolerable level. Ginger, still in frock and wig, entered through an imaginary door into an imaginary office where the doctor was sitting at a table. He opened his mouth to speak.

The front door of the Bottle and Glass burst open with such force that the posts and beams shook. Finn Davies clattered across the foyer and leapt onto the first table in his path.

"War is over!" he cried, filling the quieted tavern. "The treaty is signed and peace declared!"

The Bottle and Glass erupted in shouting and applause. Husbands kissed wives. Veterans embraced. Strangers clasped hands. Fathers trembled and mothers wept.

Spafford batted his fat palm dismissively at Finn, who by now had descended from the table and was being clapped on the back, a large glass of sherry cobler pressed into his hand.

"Once a week someone declares peace," Spafford said. "I won't believe it until I hear it uttered from the governor's lips."

"I've done that five times," Finn said, breathlessly, joining Augustus and Merit. "five different taverns. Free drinks everytime." He sucked up half the cobler through his broken clay pipe stem.

"Is it true?" Merit asked.

"Don't know. Heard someone else say it at the Rob Roy. Had about six pints shoved into his face. I've scooped him at every ale house up this way."

With much throat clearing, foot stomping and cane tapping, the doctor tried to renew his courtship of Ginger and gain just one person's attention, but they could not compete with the armistice. After their first few lines were absorbed and obliterated in the general clamour, the third player donned a shovel hat and white collar, sat at the upright, and began to punch out some syncopated profanity. Ginger and the doctor emptied their blackjacks and joined the nearest gallopade.

Now the din was ferocious and the Bottle and Glass shook. In every corner, at every table, patrons cackled and roared, quarreled and spat.

~ ~ ~

"None can drink more than Derry boys," Dunbar shouted at Gerry Kilpatrick at the end of the bar. "Two to one against you silk-skinned southerners, you Limerick choirmasters and Cork altarboys."

"A Limerick man will have already counted a half-dozen dead soldiers before a Derryman has even found a coaster for his glass."

"It's endurance I'm opinioning, not speed. Any daft sprat can swaller an ale or two quick. It's a grizzled trooper who can keep knocking 'em down until the crowing. That's a Derryman."

"Proves nothing. It's idlers that want to drink 'til morning. Unlike a Derryman, a Limerick man more often than not has an employment, an important one too, and so's early to bed, early to rise. But will still pack away the same measure of nectar, in half the time. Bloody efficient, he is."

Dunbar poked a finger into the pockets of his waistcoat and found only his watch and chain, the last vestige of his patrimony. He pulled it out, opened the glass, blew on the hands, shut the glass, tapped it, and put it back, as was his habit.

"Spring for a pair an' I'll prove it you."

"Spring for your own."

"I'm a bit skint just now." Dunbar looked down the bar at Spafford, who was chortling something to Cartwright. "My employer is in the thrall of marriage this month and slow with wages."

"'T'ain't my problem."

"Two to one, Gerry, two to one. Let me prove it."

"Half the time. Been proved."

"Lor and begorrah," Biscuit bellowed in a mock brogue from his stool at the corner. "I don't know about capacity fer drink, but you patlanders could blather the ears from an elephant. If there be prizes for talking big, yer both winners, no contest."

Gerry Kilpatrick put down his jar. Dunbar drew his sleeve across his slack mouth. A circle of silence spread out from Biscuit five people deep in all directions. Conversations were dampened and laughter hushed with the promise of impending violence. While Dunbar had made a career of artfully avoiding confrontation, Gerry Kilpatrick had been a prolific pugilist in his day. That day belonged to an earlier century. They appraised Biscuit's stare, seeing danger in the yellowed whites and lead-flecked irises.

"I've sat here listening to you two old hens cluck for an hour or more and I've never heard such fragrant blarney. I'm of Cornwall and on the moors we let our doings swagger fer us."

Jeremy believed that this was the most he'd heard Biscuit speak since he'd been on the receiving end of his boot heel six months earlier. On board the *Lancer*, there had been a handful of two or three word sentences, at most. Now, in the Bottle and Glass, Biscuit was loquacious. On his fifth pint of three threads, his migraine deadened, his rage stoked.

"A hero of the bogs without feats is nowt but a braggart," Biscuit continued. The trickle became a torrent. A valve had been opened.

"Now," he turned specifically to Dunbar, "I understand your valour is curbed only by your poverty. Here is what I propose. We'll request of the publican two gills of his finest bumbo, which I'll finance up front. Have you a pocket watch?" he asked, knowing the answer.

Dunbar nodded.

"Let's see it."

Dunbar hesitated.

"Impossible!" Biscuit clapped his hands. "Quailing already? You ain't heard no proposal yet. Sweet Mary and Joseph, you call yourself a Derryman? Do you?"

"Aye." Dunbar slowly pulled his watch from its fob pocket. He opened the glass, blew on the hands, shut the glass, and tapped it.

"It's a nice un," Biscuit said.

"Aye."

"Keeps good time?"

"Aye."

"Hear the rest. Bumbo on me. If you can neck it in five minutes, measured by your own reliable timepiece, with no spillage of any kind, bottle or glass, I'll give you my congratulations and this shiny yellowboy."

Biscuit held up between his thumb and forefinger a single guinea.

"In the improbable case that a thirsty Derryman such as yourself is unable to drain the tumbler in the allotted time, you surrender to me... your watch."

Dunbar smiled and shook his head.

"As I suspected," Biscuit said, "all talk."

Dunbar looked around at the audience that had gathered.

"Don't do it Dunbar," Kilpatrick said, "I'll buy. No conditions."

Dunbar saw Amelia's face amid the others. The moment he'd caught her gaze she looked away, to the ceiling, curling her lip.

"Fine," Dunbar said, finally, "you beggary whoreson, I'll take your tarnal wager."

Biscuit slid a couple of shillings across the counter.

"Alfie, two gills rumbustion, top shelf, any old goblet."

Alfie retrieved a pint-sized pewter from behind the bar, wiped it with a rag and measured into it two gills of rum from a bottle so black it was perfectly opaque. When he was finished Jeremy asked to see the bottle. He turned it around on its axis and saw the pontil mark, initials AB inside an acorn. He showed it to Merit. The same bottle maker. Likely the same batch of rum which Captain Rowton had foisted on them, their first day aboard the *Lancer*.

"Doubt its purity?" Alfie asked.

"No," Jeremy replied, "I…"

Alfie was already applying the test. He brought a small leather pouch from beneath the bar, poured a measure of black powder into a jigger, and then an ounce of the rum.

"Drink," he said.

Jeremy passed. Biscuit downed the shot. Alfie took a stick of kindling from beside the stove, poked it into the cylinder of a nearby oil lamp until it was well lit. He then brought the flame to the jigger with the residue in the bottom. The gunpowder erupted, cracking and fizzing like a firework.

"Satisfied?"

Jeremy nodded.

"Davey," Biscuit shouted. "You'll want in on this."

"I want nothing to do with it," Merit said, "nor you."

"Retract your wager Biscuit," Jeremy called, "the humour's gone out of it now."

"On the contrary, it's just got started."

Others clearly agreed with Biscuit, as they gathered round, arguing stakes and odds. Within minutes, a score of side bets had been placed, approaching fifteen pounds.

"Go ahead, Derryman," Biscuit said, smiling. "Pass me the collateral, I'll measure the time."

"Keep it," Kilpatrick said. "I'll pay the tab. Walk away."

Dunbar held up his hand. He wiped again at his mouth with a sleeve and swallowed. He could do it, couldn't he? It wasn't all embroidery. He'd led some epic sessions in his time. True, he'd been a whippet and he was no longer in the habit, but still. Old dogs. He unfastened the watch and chain from its fob and handed it over. Biscuit took the watch, held it to his ear, and pursed his lips.

"On the twelve," he said, showing the watch face to the investors gathered round.

"Go!"

Dunbar knew he was in trouble from the start. Burnt molasses bloomed from the mouth of the flagon, watering eyes and flattening nostril hair. The jet fluid, tarry and dense, scorched.

"Four and a half minutes," Biscuit said, rubbing the watch.

Dunbar drank, pinching his nose with his free hand, squeezing his eyes tight. His knees knit. His toes clenched and scraped at the leather of his boot soles.

"Three and a half."

The rum scalded at first and then his throat numbed. He gradually let the liquor flow. It was his stomach rebelling now. The rum pounced and bit and tussled with the three pints of porter already arrived. A nor'easter raged through him. He came up for air.

"Two."

He was panting heavily now. He'd another gill to go.

"Jesus, Dunbar," Kilpatrick said, looking away, "what is wrong with you?"

"Nothing," Biscuit said, enjoying himself immensely. "He's a champ. Derry be proud."

Dunbar's pulse crested and subsided. He looked up briefly from the black, bottomless well before him and again caught Amelia's gaze. Was that a flicker of concern in her otherwise fresh, expressionless face? He raised the chalice to his lips. And drank, and drank, and drank.

"Sixty seconds."

It was pandemonium inside Dunbar now, a fluttering, kicking tumult, as his internal organs bucked and recoiled, seeming as though they would burst from his abdomen. The entire Bottle and Glass heaved like a sloop in a trough. The awful din on all sides became distant, until all he could hear was his own laboured breathing. He thought that at any minute he might catch fire.

"Fifteen."

There could only be two ounces left. He tipped it back. It dribbled past his gums.

And then nothing.

Cool air on his tongue.

Dunbar slammed the empty tankard down, mouth-first.

He fell to the floor.

"No spillage!" Biscuit cried.

The syndicate crowded round the prostrate man, rapt. Those with money on Dunbar claimed their payouts. Those betting against demanded an observation period; they were sure eruption was imminent.

Dunbar got to his hands and knees and began to honk like a cob swan. The punters shouted and pointed. Dunbar coiled, convulsed, and shook. Gerry Kilpatrick elbowed his way through and knelt down to Dunbar's face so the stricken man could hear him.

"Jesus H," he said, "what is the matter with you? Don't be an ass. Let it out."

"Was my pap's watch," Dunbar managed to squeak, "and his before him. Heirloom."

"'Tis just a watch."

"'Tisn't. 'Tis pride. Family. History. Everything."

Dunbar turned crimson and fell once more to the floor. Bubbles foamed from his lips and a pool formed at his cheek.

"What's that?"

"Spillage?"

"Drool."

"Get him a beer," said one of the punters. The others stared.

"Small beer," the man added, "sober him up."

"I stand corrected," Biscuit declared, while the rest of the punters argued. "I didn't think it possible."

Gerry stood and faced him.

"Shall I give these to you," Biscuit snapped the watch shut and pulled out the guinea.

"He don't think he's breathing," Gerry said, quietly.

"Dead?"

One of the bettors called for a doctor.

"We need a professional opinion," he yelled.

"Death changes everything," Biscuit said, putting the guinea back in his pocket. "It goes without mention that the contender must live in order to collect."

"You're some kind of bastard," Gerry said. "What about the watch?"

"He ain't be needing it now."

"Maybe he's just passed out."

Amelia stood before Spafford. Cartwright gestured toward her with an index finger lifted from his glass so that Spafford, who was in the middle of telling a joke about a pygmy witchdoctor, noticed her presence.

"Ah," he said, "my darling. Delightful. Enjoying the farce? A side-splitter, yes?"

She didn't bother to tell him the play had ended before it got started.

"Your man, Dunbar," she said, flatly, "he's not well."

"Pish. He's fine, he likes a drink, that's all," Spafford said, turning back to Cartwright. "Lovely girl, vivid imagination."

"You misunderstand," Amelia tried again, "he's in a bad way."

"Let him have his fun. He'll be fine in the morning."

Amelia returned to the knot of people gathered around Dunbar. The actor dressed as a doctor was bent over him, checking for a pulse.

"I can do nothing for him, I'm afraid," he declared. His audience nodded gravely.

"He's an actor," Jeremy cried.

The punters argued. Biscuit ordered two porters. He passed one to Gerry Kilpatrick and downed the other. He flipped open the watch, snapped it shut, tapped it and tucked it into his pocket. He left the tavern, whistling.

"Remove him," Poncet said to Alfie and his son, gesturing toward Dunbar.

"To where?"

"Church, street, harbour. Anywhere. Out of the Bottle and Glass."

~ ~ ~

Carmichael's chin was within a whisker of the gluey bar top. He gripped the edge and thrust his face forward.

"Alfie," he said, "I'm good for it."

"No doing, Carm," Alfie said, dipping his head toward Poncet, "boss won't allow no tabs. Not tonight."

Jeremy suggested to Gerry Kilpatrick that he ought to check on his friend.

"He ain't my friend, really," Kilpatrick replied, shrugging. "We bend elbows together."

Carmichael looked up at Jeremy.

"Spare a bob, Samaritan?"

Jeremy shook his head.

Spafford wobbled into Carmichael from behind, driving his cheek into the bar. Carmichael whirled, his face crimson. He raised his index finger and opened his mouth, his lungs loaded with the grapeshot of a hundred imprecations. Then he saw Amelia directly behind Spafford, a woolen coat gathered neatly over her folded hands. Her eyes were locked on the tavern exit, intent on shepherding her husband out the door.

"Let me help you Mrs. Spafford," Richard Cartwright said, hoisting one of Spafford's elbows. "He's had a good night. Celebrating. You've made an old…, you've made him very happy."

Amelia held her gaze and said nothing.

"I'll call for your carriage. King's Arms is it?"

"Spafford?" Carmichael asked.

"Yes," Jeremy said, "she and Colonel Spafford are newly married."

"That bagpipe? Impossible. She can't be but sixteen. We had an understanding."

"You?" Jeremy asked. "And she?"

"Why not?"

Jeremy smiled.

"Corny!" Carmichael shouted across the room.

Cornelius Harris looked up from the biscuit skidding down the shovel board.

"How many shekels have you got?"

Cornelius put his thumb and forefinger together in an 'O'.

"Me as well. I'm drying out. Come. I knows how we can extend our evening by a few pints."

Cornelius left the board reluctantly and shuffled through to the bar.

"You see that cove who just left?"

Cornelius shook his head.

"Colonel Spafford. A lardy rasher if ever. Could out-jaw a preacher. He married my Amelia this day."

"Amelia? The perky dollop from the Barrett farm?"

"The same. You could divide her age into his four times and still get a remainder."

"Are you thinking…"

"Aye, charivari."

"Capital."

"Gather the fellas. We'll serenade the King's Arms, under the honeyed moon. Tis only a half mile."

Carmichael rubbed his hands together as he, Sam, Cornelius and a handful of others left the tavern, brushing past the returning Cartwright on their way out.

"What's a charivari," Jeremy asked Kilpatrick.

"Odious, my boy. Old French custom. Parleyvous for extortion. S'pose there are newlyweds who are unusual in their pairing, say by class or age, or some other reason. This upsets the refined sensibilities of some of the more delicate townsfolk. Typically it's the idlers and toughs that take greatest offense. Those who can't abide by any lapse of decorum. Carmichael Jones or Cornelius Harris, for instance. These self-appointed censors cumulate and if they don't receive a payment in silver or in kind, they proceed to raise the foulest racket you've ever laid an ear on. They'll 'waul all night if not bought off. They may even prank the house, or the groom."

"What sort of pranks?"

"Last February there was a charivari, I don't know if Carmichael was involved. A barber, escaped slave, mind, married a washerwoman, Maggie O' Shea. I knew her. Homely, but amiable. The pack of scoundrels were so affronted, they pulled the poor negro naked from the matrimonial bed. He offered to pay them, all he had, in fact. But they didn't want no money. It was about the principle, see? They rode him out to the edge of town on a devilishly sharp rail and delivered their verdict."

"What happened to him?"

"Died. If it wasn't the bleeding, he froze to death, I guess, or his old, black heart just gave out. Poor beggar. He gave a good haircut too."

"And what about the washerwoman?"

"None know what really happened that night. None speaks of it. She disappeared. Rather than die of shame, I suppose."

Jeremy crossed the tavern. He jammed his hand like a spade into one of Merit's pockets and began to pull him from the crown and anchor. Merit was barely able to reach across to palm his dice and shilling.

"Cousin," Merit said, a term he used only when irritated. "Now's not the time, I'm down by two. Laying groundwork. Nothing could possibly be so urgent."

"We need to go," Jeremy said, "I'm concerned for Spafford and the girl."

"What girl?"

"The girl I was talking to earlier. Who refused the cognac. The Colonel's wife."

"Pretty, young. Pretty young."

"She just left with the Colonel."

"What's it to us."

"They were followed by men of questionable character."

"None of our business, Jem. Remember what the provosts said before we left. We represent the Royal Navy. Don't interfere with the civvies. If they catch wind of us mixing it up, we could be lashed, thrown in the stocks, worse."

"You're the last one I'd expect to want to please the provosts. It's just to warn them, or warn the others away."

"Why such interest? She's just married, remember."

"Just want to make sure they're safe. The Colonel too. First friends we've made here.

"That skite is no friend of mine."

"Also," Jeremy pulled the looking glass from his pocket, "I have her looking glass. I should return it."

Merit clucked his tongue.

"Mer," Jeremy pulled him toward the door. "We can go to another pub after, a whole new coop."

"Haven't started plucking these."

They looked for Neven. He'd already left, accompanied by a fishmonger's daughter.

They found Finn, stretched across two chairs, a broken pipe stem tilting from his face like a derelict chimney.

"Useless," Jeremy said and they turned to leave. Finn stretched an arm and caught Merit's trouser leg.

"A groat?" he asked. "Fer night cap?"

"You just got paid."

"Bought some rounds."

"A half year's worth?"

"I'm skint."

"Sorry."

"A fuppence?"

They turned to leave.

"A tuppence?" he gurgled to their backs. "Don't tell Lilac I'm here."

Lilac sat with Augustus at a table near the door. They were talking closely to an older man dressed in a frilled shirt of crisp linen, a buff waistcoat and a snowy, silk cravat. He had long sideburns and his hair was trimmed, brushed forward into a Brutus.

Lilac held her hand up as Jeremy and Merit approached, sheepishly.

"Don't bother," she said. "I know he's spent it all. 'Twas inevitable. No matter, I've me own means. And no real claim to his anyway. This lovely Dr. Scriven has already found me a position with his tailor, Mr. Stevens. I'll not set foot on another ship for as long as I live."

"Jeremy," Augie said, "do you have that Paine book with you? I've just been having an interesting conversation with the doctor."

Jeremy patted at the inside pocket of his fearnought.

"Aye, I have it, why?"

"Can we see it a moment? Dr. Scriven is a Whig and a radical and a follower of Paine. In other words, one of us."

Jeremy demurred.

"We were trying to get straight his comment about landed gentry."

Augustus was, in all respects, lit. A nearly empty bottle of Elijah Pepper lay horizontally on the table. The light flickering from the oil lamp was redoubled in Augie's unblinking eyes and his damp forehead. From his bright expression it looked to Jeremy that if he suggested wrestling an alligator, or eating fire, Augustus would be first in line.

"I don't know Augie, I'm not sure this is the place. Besides, we need your help with something."

"Name it."

"We need to go to the King's Arms…"

"Lead the way. Let me just read that passage and we can go."

Jeremy looked at Augie's smiling face, with its rose patina. He passed him the book. Augie flipped to the end of *The Rights of Man*, and searched. Jeremy and Merit had just enough time to introduce themselves to Dr. Scriven before Augie leapt to the tabletop, hoofing the bourbon bottle to the floor where it shattered loudly. Those nearby turned their befogged heads. Augustus held the book before him as he used to at Providence Grammar School, declaiming before the professor of rhetoric and oratory.

"Were the aristocratic pillar to sink into the earth," he boomed, "the same landed property would continue, and the same ploughing, sowing, and reaping would go on."

Those close enough to hear, looked back at Augustus like a herd of great cattle, reposed beneath the shadow of a British oak. They chewed, and swallowed, and blinked.

Jeremy and Dr. Scriven pulled at Augie's leg.

"Get down and shut up, for God's sake," Jeremy said.

Augie slapped their hands away and continued.

"The aristocracy are not the farmers who work the land, and raise the produce, but are the mere consumers of the rent; and when compared with the active world are the drones, a seraglio of males, who neither collect the honey, nor form the hive, but exist only for lazy enjoyment."

Most of his audience turned back to their pints. He closed the book.

"FREE YOURSELVES! START OVER!" Augie cried.

Merit clapped and whistled. Augie bowed deeply and stepped down.

"What's wrong with you Augie," Jeremy said, grabbing Augie's elbow.

"I want to give my farewell," Augie said, grinning.

11

King's Arms Inn

AMELIA'S MOTHER, MILLIE BARRETT, sat on the porch, gathered in a woolen shawl, stone bottles strewn about her. Augustus tripped over her outstretched leg and tumbled from Jeremy's grasp into the street.

"Alms?" Millie slurred, extending an empty bonnet.

Jeremy pulled a penny from his pouch and dropped it in.

"Which way to the King's Arms ma'am?"

"Thank you. My daughter resides there. This road, that way, 'bout half mile."

They hoisted Augustus to his feet and began their march. He retrieved a flask from an inner pocket, swigged, and passed it to Merit.

"Why are we going to the King's Arms?" Augie asked.

Jeremy began to explain.

"Nevermind," Augie said, "I don't care. I'm just happy to be here."

Jeremy became aware of the fact he was walking alone. He looked back. Augustus had his hands on either side of Merit's head and was kissing him on the lips. Merit cuffed him and laughed.

"You're good mates," Augustus said, "I'll miss you both."

"Stop your nonsense," Jeremy said. "Walk."

They'd gone no more than a hundred yards when they saw a pair of silhouettes entangled in the moonlight. It was some grotesque dance that they performed, the one figure whirling, limbs cartwheeling through the air, meeting and covering the second. One of them cycled through the shadows like a dervish. The second remained rooted. They heard thuds and thumps, like the sound of flour sacks hitting the deck.

With a jolly full bottle

one sang

*Let each man be armed
we must be good subjects*

On the word subjects one brought his fist down on the other.

We must be good subjects

Again.

We must be good subjects

Again.

Hearts are thus warm'd we must be good

They crept closer.

Here's a health

The first brought his boot to bear on the other's ribs.

to old England, King, and Church

He brought the edge of his hand down like an axe head into the man's kidney. They could tell, from the braids, darker skin, and leather leggings that the victim was Indian.

May all plotting contrivers

The attacker brought his knee up into the bridge of the Indian's nose.

Be left in the lurch.

"Biscuit," Merit breathed.
"The poor devil is getting the worst of it," Augustus said. "I saw him earlier, he was so pissed he could barely stand."
"Biscuit too, he's three sheets, but more adroit with each swig," Jeremy said.
"We need to step in," Merit said. "Even the odds."
"It's Biscuit."
"We can't stand and watch."
"What'll happen?"
"He's killing him."
"Pull him off."
"Restrain him."
"At least that."
"It's dark. He can't see us."
"He's drunk. He won't know."

They advanced. Augie grabbed Biscuit's jersey with both hands and pulled him back. From behind, Jeremy wrapped his long arms around the press master's flailing limbs. Merit stepped between Biscuit and his victim. He bent to the ground and put his own face close to that of the Indian warrior. Moon shadow accentuated the damage to the man's otherwise handsome features. Thick, black blood streamed from his nostrils into his mouth and the space left behind by missing teeth. His breath sputtered through split lips. His left eye was completely closed over by its swollen lid. There was a strong smell of iron, as though the man was a slab of metal on an anvil; drawn, fired, and hammered.

Biscuit jerked and thrashed and snarled in Jeremy's embrace like a ferret in a trap. Augustus tried, and failed, to restrain his bucking legs.

"Can you move?" Merit said to the warrior, twitching two fingers back and forth like a pair of legs. "Can you walk?"

"Davey?" Biscuit shrieked. "I hear you Davey. I hear you."

Biscuit drove his elbow hard into Jeremy's ribs momentarily winding him. He flung his head back to meet Jeremy's face as it bent forward and flattened his nose. Jeremy let go, stunned, eyes watering.

The warrior opened his right eye. He studied Merit's outlined face and expression of concern. They regarded each other. If Merit didn't know better, it was though a moment of recognition passed between them, like old friends reunited after a long absence.

Biscuit could have cold cocked Jeremy if Augustus hadn't grappled his elbows from behind.

"Ambush!" Biscuit howled. "Treason! Treason!"

"Walk?" Merit asked again.

The warrior nodded slightly. Merit grasped him by his forearm and helped him gingerly to his feet.

"Know your way home?"

The man nodded again, looked briefly at Biscuit, struggling, and began walking in the opposite direction, cradling one arm in the other.

"Need help?" Merit asked the warrior.

The Indian shook his head and disappeared.

"Treason!" Biscuit cried again.

Jeremy drove his mallet-sized fist as hard as he could into Biscuit's face, as much to shut him up as to exact revenge. Biscuit wrenched free and groaned into abraded hands as they cupped his gushing nose.

Jeremy brought his fist up from his knees, twisted at the hip, parted Biscuits hands and broke his jaw. Augustus backed away. Biscuit fell to all fours and began crawling, slowly, toward the bush. *Treason*, he keened, the word distorted by the foam forming at his mouth. Jeremy ran three paces and kicked him hard in the throat.

"Jesus," Augustus whispered. "Jeremy."

Jeremy had never been in a proper fight. He'd never struck and had never been struck. Always much bigger than any other boy his age, with two older brothers just as hefty and twice as coarse, it had never come to that. He'd been free to follow other, gentler pursuits, encouraged by his mother, who'd always hoped for a daughter with her third. And, when not working the wharf, he'd been happy to spend long hours drinking tea with Alice, perfecting his stitch, reading to her from Cowper, the gospels, *The Lives of the Saints*.

Biscuit, through a year-long provocation, had awakened something in Jeremy, long suppressed. When Jeremy kicked at Biscuit's midsection, his boot toe probing for vital organs, he struck for the hobnail stomp at Chough Tor, many months ago. It was retribution for all the indignities that followed aboard *The Lancer*. But he didn't strike just for his own particular injustice, or Merit's. He kicked for the broken, drunk Indian dragging himself back to the woods. He kicked for Tecumseh, the Creeks and the Cherokee, bleeding into the new Thames, lead balls in their backs, used by all, supported by none. He kicked for the surrendered settlers and invalids slaughtered at Fort Mims by the Red Sticks. He kicked for the lady beggar they'd passed on the porch, surrounded by empty genever bottles. He kicked for Dunbar, the ass who drank himself senseless on a bet. And for the blind negro on the dock, seeking his kin. And for the bodies in the lake. And for poor smashed-in Splinter, victim of a careless, drunken shipmate and a storm. For everything.

It was anger, yes; vicious, appalling, bare-knuckled rage. It was white hot and righteous. But it was also release. A shattering of restraint. Undiluted freedom.

"Pick him up!" Jeremy cried, his fists balled so tightly that his nails lacerated his palms. "Damn you, pick him up. I'll strike him again."

Biscuit, a jumble in a wheel rut, struggled to breathe through his swelling trachea.

"Christ Jem, you're killing him."

Jeremy ran and jumped, landing with both feet on Biscuit's prone knee. The press master writhed and clutched, unable to do anything but sputter through his broken windpipe. Jeremy brought the tree-trunk of his right leg back, like it was an ancient and terrible siege weapon. Merit wrapped his arms around Jeremy and held him tight before he could deploy it. Jeremy moved toward Biscuit, dragging Merit with him. Augustus clinched Jeremy from the other side until he was immobile. At first, without forward motion, in the absence of an outlet, Jeremy's furious body trembled. Merit could feel it through his embrace, vibrating seismically through his arms and chest. Then came convulsions and Jeremy's face ran with tears. Merit and Augustus locked forearms and held on until the tremors subsided and Jeremy's breathing returned to normal.

Gradually they loosened their grip. Jeremy took from Augustus the offered flask and sucked at it until it was empty.

"Let's go," he said.

Biscuit continued rasping, from his rut, long after they were gone.

Davey. I hear you.

~ ~ ~

Life-long bachelor Bison Harris, proprietor of the King's Arms, thought long and hard about flourishes that might be appreciated by a new bride. For years Spafford, his friend and mentor, had urged him to capitalize on Kingston's designation as Upper Canada's honeymoon capital, to attract more newlyweds to his country inn. The master suite of the King's Arms, where Noble and Amelia Spafford had just arrived, featured heart-shaped pillows, rose-scented candles, two complimentary ponies of Tobermory, and a single loose, hand-rolled cigar.

Amelia examined the fistful of late-blooming asters stuffed artlessly into the water pitcher. They were wan and whiskery, looking as though they themselves wondered why they had bothered flowering this late in the year. Bison had hastily uprooted the whole bunch from the pasture with one yank of his big, clumsy hand, so other plants, crab grass and wild carrot, jostled the asters, like the louts of a common saloon, like the brutes of the Bottle and Glass.

The room itself was spacious but sparse, with little colour beyond the browns and tans of the unadorned furniture, dark paintings of fox hunts, wall mounted buffalo guns, disintegrating trophies of muskellunge, and the bearskin at their feet, sorrowful head still attached. It smelled of dust, leather, and lye. Amelia crossed the room and cracked open one of the heavy wood shutters. She pulled the crisp November air in through her nostrils and put her thumb between her teeth, biting back the rising tears.

More had happened to Amelia in the last year of her life than had happened in all of her previous sixteen. Recent events had elapsed with such speed that there'd been no time for reflection, only reaction, and even then, she'd only managed to bob up and down with the current. Now, in the honeymoon suite of the King's Arms, with her new-old husband, there was a brief moment for appraisal.

After the catastrophe of the work bee, Dorephus had met several times with Noble at the Old King's Head. He would arrive home from each meeting, slightly more ashen, slightly more worn. He would drink his cider, smoke his pipe, and stare mutely at the log in the grate, divulging nothing. It was much later at night, when Amelia was in bed, drifting into an uneasy sleep, she'd be aware of the hot whispers exchanged between him and Millie, always punctuated by an exasperated *Enough!* In the end, it was Millie who delivered the news, quietly, as she and Amelia strolled the neglected vegetable garden, picking through thistles and pigweed to find a few poxy tomatoes or a single, thin marrow.

"We think it must be for the best," Millie had said, unconvincingly.

Amelia had teetered and had barely made it to the stump to sit. She'd dropped the armful of stunted, perforated lettuce she'd carried.

"You'll be taken care of," Millie had continued, quickly, as if a torrent of hopeful words might fill the terrible void. "Far, far better than we ever could, or have. You'll be recognized as the lady we know you to be. Better than the workhouse. Better than a ploughman's wife. You can make a life for yourself."

"What about you," Amelia had said. "Dad?"

"Dad will help work Colonel Spafford's own lands. I'll help with Mrs. Simkins."

"A serf? A servant's servant?"

"Amelia, sweetheart, it's not that bad. It could be worse."

"I can hardly see how."

Dorephus never returned from his final meeting with Spafford. He fled. And as far as Amelia was concerned, he might as well be dead, because he was dead to her. Millie had reported to work under Mrs. Simkins three full days, but did not return on the fourth. She hadn't spoken to her daughter since the wedding ceremony. Dunbar had propped her up in a corner of the church, delivering to her a requested flask of gin. Through the entire service, she'd alternated between snoring and weeping softly.

"Dunbar! Where the blazes is Dunbar!"

Spafford's demand cut short Amelia's remembrances.

"At the Bottle and Glass," she said, in a low voice. "Remember? He's not well."

She was alarmed at Spafford's indifference. If he cared this little about the fate of his most faithful servant, how might he come to regard his spouse?

"Eh?" Spafford asked, his voice rising. He lay on the bed, trying unsuccessfully to loosen his corset. "I'm suffocating!" he cried.

"Bottle and Glass," Amelia said, loudly, as though to a grandparent.

"Damn him," Spafford cried. "Impertinent. Careless. I must have a word."

Amelia said nothing, watching him squirm, attempting to escape his buff trousers, silk-white blouse, and cream cravat. She imagined a fat moth emerging from its pupa.

"You'll have to do it," Spafford said.

Amelia didn't move. He stopped writhing and they regarded each other.

"Remove my boots!" he demanded, when it was clear she didn't understand. "That damned Irishman pulls my boots, loosens my whalebone. He's not here. You have to do it."

Amelia slowly approached the end of the bed. They appraised each other again. He shook his right boot at her. She took a corner of the blanket and put it over the mud encrusted heel and toe.

"Don't be prissy," he said, "it doesn't become you. Don't forget, I know your lineage."

She gripped, and pulled, and twisted. Just this once, she wished she were a man, brawny and brutish, like the giant Royal Marine from the Bottle and Glass, the one who offered her the cognac. She wanted to wrench Spafford's boot, sock, foot, and all, clean off his chubby leg, and bring an abrupt stop to his petulance. But she was a girl of seventeen. She held on as best she could as Spafford kicked and yanked and finally drew his foot free.

They repeated the process on the second boot.

"Trousers," he said, raising his feet again. She took hold of the cuffs and pulled. He lifted and held on to his undergarment until the trousers were clear, then he rolled to his side, facing the bedside table.

"Stays," he said. Amelia came round, and with one knee on the bed began to untie the corset.

Now facing the bedside table, Spafford ran a finger up and down one of the whisky tumblers.

"Perhaps I shouldn't have had quite so much myself, tonight," he said, more softly now. "Not sure I need this. You go ahead."

"No," Amelia said, bowing her head and backing away from the bed. She reversed all the way to the window.

"Do you like the candles? A pretty scent, yes?"

"Nice," she said.

Freed from his cocoon, Spafford was now standing beside the bed, unfastening the rest of the buttons of his blouse.

"It was a lovely ceremony," he continued. "Rev Stuart gives a good sermon. I'm sorry my mother wasn't here to witness it, to meet you. I'm sorry your mother missed it too."

Amelia was about to correct him, to remind him that Millie had been there. Then she detected the sarcasm.

Spafford removed the blouse and corset and folded them on a chair back. He pulled a nightshirt over his head, removed his undergarment, and stood facing Amelia with one hand on the bedknob, the other scratching at his hip. His penis dangled like a pendulum from below the hemline of the hiked nightshirt. She looked away and kept her eyes fixed on a pair of mounted antlers.

Spafford stood there a minute or two, scratching and swaying, studying Amelia. And then he was in the bed, the quilt pulled up to his paunch.

"Now you," he said, continuing to watch her. His eyes shone with anticipation, like a boy's before a pantomime.

"It is customary for a man and his wife to consummate the night of their wedding."

From the moment her mother informed her of the impending marriage she'd banished all consideration of this prospect. Now, confronted with the image of Spafford's antique apparatus, flopping between his legs like the neck and head of a plucked pheasant, she could no longer avoid it. She could not un-see it. She knew about sex, she couldn't have grown up on a farm without being aware of its mechanics, and she'd given some thought to how her own first time might unfold. She'd never imagined this.

Her gaze fled to the window, to the wagon path, to the sanctuary of the shadows, to the oblivion of the black woods beyond. To be a creature of sinew, feather or fur, zig-zagging the trees, taking flight or going to ground, with at least some chance of escape. But like a domesticate she'd been delivered from one cage to another.

"There's a nightgown in the trunk. From Montreal. Linen and lace. I bought it 'specially at Dick Smith's."

She looked at the trunk but did not move.

"Put it on."

She walked slowly to the open trunk and pulled out the ivory gown. She looked across the room at the three-panelled screen with the picture of a duck pond painted on it.

"Oh, if you must," Spafford said, sighing.

Amelia stepped haltingly behind the screen and for several minutes did nothing but breathe. She focused on each breath, in and out, staving tears. To cry was to admit defeat and she wasn't ready for that. At that moment, breathing was about the only thing within her control.

"Haven't all night," Spafford called. "Won't stay awake much longer."

Could she outwait him? Every night for the rest of their lives?

"Do you need help?"

Amelia could hear him getting up.

"No, stay!" she said, brusquely. "I'll be right there."

With leaden arms, she lifted her gauzy outer dress, also a gift from the Colonel, over her head and laid it carefully over the screen. She unfastened the ties of her petticoat and the short stays from the front of her corset, fumbling with each one, her fingers barely finding the strength. She wriggled free. Then, her chemise, slipping one elbow and then another, through the armholes. With cupped hands she splashed scented water from the nearby basin on her face, goose pimpled arms, and body. She toweled off, dabbed some of the supplied eau de cologne at her neck and chest and slipped on the nightgown.

"Ah!" Spafford cried, when she finally emerged. "Lovely. Come."

He patted the side of the bed. She shuffled across the room around the end of the bed and perched herself on its edge. Her breathing was jagged. She kept her gaze on the portrait of the King hanging on the wall above Spafford's head, focused on mad George's gleaming bug eyes and round, florid cheeks.

"Put your hand in mine," Spafford said, laying his arm in her lap, palm up. She placed her hand in the middle of his, so that it sat like a specimen pinned to a pillow. He wrapped his fingers around hers.

"Look at me," he said. She detached her gaze from the portrait and looked into Spafford's eager eyes. She began to sob.

"Dove," he said, "delicate dove. Please, no tears. It's not so bad. Look."

He pulled back the blanket to once again expose the slack length of his penis.

"No longer works. Hasn't done a damn thing in ten years, not since Gibraltar. Stumped every doctor. It's a damned old shooting iron, so not surprising really, jammed or rusted or some other."

Amelia caught a glimpse of the pale, pink twist and looked away sharply, eyes again locked on the face of King George. Spafford gripped her hand more firmly, preventing her from leaving his grasp.

"Amelia," he said, calling her by her name for the first time since the ceremony, "be at ease. That is not why I want you. I'll keep you in a fine fashion pet, I'll treat you well."

Still she refused his gaze and said nothing.

"Amelia," he said, "I'm a lonely man. I want only companionship."

She turned back to him and looked into his damp, pleading eyes.

"I'm sorry Mr. Spafford."

"Please. Call me Noble."

An empty bottle sailed through the opened shutters and showered the floor with glass. Amelia shrieked, jumped from the bed and backed toward the door, her hand over her mouth. A screeching and clanging erupted from the road below so deafening and sharply discordant that, for a moment, Spafford thought he was back at the Siege of Roses.

"Lieutenant Coverdale," he cried, calling for a subordinate he hadn't seen in a decade, who had died on Malta of yellow fever in 1802, "order a general retreat. Fall back to the *Excellent*."

Spafford fell out one side of the bed, ran its perimeter, and got into the other side, pulling the blanket up to his chin.

"What is going on?" he shouted to Amelia. She couldn't hear him, her hands were now over her ears.

"Where are they attacking from? How many are there?"

"Chareeeeeee," they wailed from the road, accompanied by pots clashing pans, tongs thumping tubs, stones rattling tins, "vareeeeeeee."

"Natives?" Spafford asked. "Have they come scalping? Where's Coverdale? Dunbar?"

"Chareeeeeee....vareeeeeeee."

Amelia jumped again when Bison burst through the door, nearly crushing her against the wall.

"It's a charivari, Noble," he shouted over the rising chorus of tuneless penny whistles, "they object to your pairing."

"Eh? Coverdale?" Spafford shouted back, made more confused by the fresh intrusion.

"No, Bison. Bison Harris. You've got to do something. Placate them."

"Bison?"

"It's a charivari. They don't approve of your match. We must do something, I fear for the inn."

"Don't approve?" Spafford was now out of the bed again and on his feet. "Impertinence! Hand me that buffalo gun and we'll address their concerns with hot lead."

"It's an old flintlock Noble," Bison said as he pulled it from the wall hooks and handed it to Spafford. "I'm not sure if it will fire. It may be dangerous."

Spafford advanced on the window.

"Bring me cartridges," he said.

"I haven't got any. I'm retired from the hunt. You know that."

Spafford was at the window, pointing the long barrel of the musket into the cool darkness. On the road he could see a half dozen figures, marching and dancing in figure eights. He couldn't make out their features with their white, wool caps worn low over their faces.

"Do you like our rough music?" one of them shouted up to him. Amelia immediately recognized Carmichael's voice. "'Tis our wedding march."

"Not him!" Amelia screamed, bringing her hands back to her ears.

Carmichael began to stamp and clap in place, singing.

Fork out, old pal,
The dough that you owe
We're your loyal subjects
And we want a good show.

"Cartridges!" Spafford shouted, gesturing with his outstretched palm.

"I haven't any, I told you," Bison said. "I'm an innkeeper now."

"Corny?" Carmichael yielded the floor to his colleague.

"Though we do find this union distasteful," Cornelius said, "and though the young woman was meant for someone else, namely my colleague Carmichael, we are reasonable men, we don't hold grudges. We understand that all's fair and that you, a man of the world used to the best life has to offer, could hardly help yourself. That is why, we will accept, on behalf of the greater community, a punitive fine of five pounds, or a crate of whisky, whichever might be easiest to procure tonight at this very hour. Plus, perhaps, one last glimpse of your lovely bride at the window. You will have our blessings and hear us no more."

We're wild as they come,
And out on a spree.
So, out with the coin,
Or, chareeeeeee – vareeeeeee!

The band took up the tune with renewed vigour.

"You must pay them," Amelia said, "make them go away."

"I haven't got five pounds. Bison, you'll have to give them a crate."

"I haven't got a crate. A few bottles. Not enough to give away."

Noble peeked again at the cacophonous mob.

One of the musicians, a scrawny, angular man, with ill-fitting clothes, fell to the ground like a tagged grouse, dropping his tin pot and ladle. A new figure, towering over the others, had clubbed him with a maple bough, still festooned with twigs and leaves. The rest of the band stopped their playing and turned to regard the newcomer. After the relentless noise of the charivari, the silence that now filled the road was complete and equally unbearable. Carmichael, Cornelius, young Sam, and the others brandished their pans, andirons and tongs. They spread out, holding out their cooking implements in front of them, phalanx-like. Though the interloper was a giant, they fancied their odds at five to one. But two more arrived, each swinging oak shillelaghs. The giant swung his cudgel again, catching one of the players full in the stomach so that he folded like a napkin. The remnants of the choir fled and melted into the safety of darkness.

"Jolly good show!" Noble said, dropping the musket and clapping his hands together. "You sir," he called to the large figure, "come closer, step nearer the lantern."

"I know you," he cried as the figure neared, "Corporal Castor of *HMS St. Lawrence*."

"Aye, Colonel, 'tis me."

"Please, come in Castor, let me buy you a drink."

Jeremy looked around at Merit and Augustus, who had dropped their clubs and were attending to the fallen musicians, the two Canadian Fencibles who had greeted them so much earlier in the day at the docks.

"Your friends too, of course."

Merit and Augustus waved him off.

"We're heading back to town," Merit said.

Augustus retrieved a woolen toque from the ground and handed it to the tin pot player so he could swab the blood pouring from his head.

"You'll join us, won't you Mr. Castor, for a nightcap? Please, let me express my gratitude."

Jeremy looked back up at Noble and saw Amelia's face looking back, over his shoulder.

"Certainly," he said.

Merit and Augustus turned to leave.

"We'll meet you back at Walker's," Merit said. "Be good."

"Take the rubbish with you," Spafford called down, gesturing at the Fencibles.

Augustus and Merit hoisted the prone Fencible from the ground, propped him, and pointed him toward town. The second's gasping had subsided enough that he too could stagger behind. The four of them disappeared into the darkness.

"It's twelve years old, aged in sherry cask," Spafford said, later, sitting at a table in the lounge of the King's Arms with Jeremy and Bison. He raised the glass to his lips with a trembling hand and sipped. "I keep telling old Bison here, scotch whisky will be as popular as brandy. This here's from Tobermory. I own shares."

Bison nodded and stoked his pipe.

Jeremy tipped back the tumbler. It tasted of peat, honey, and smoke, and it warmed every inch. Over top of the rim, over Spafford's shoulder and across the lounge, he could see Amelia standing at the foot of the stairs, a robe pulled tight over her new nightgown.

"You're a good lad," Spafford was saying, "you have immense potential. Stick with me and you could have a very bright future here in Canada. I was saying to Cartwright just this evening…"

He tailed off when he realized that he'd lost Jeremy's attention. Spafford turned and saw Amelia.

"To bed dove," he said, "excitement's over. Go. Close the shutters. You can sleep now. Let us talk. And drink."

Amelia lingered. Jeremy saw something indecipherable reflected in her eyes.

"To bed!" Spafford shouted.

She retreated silently up the stairs.

"As I was saying," Spafford continued, "you could be of great help to me. We'll be staying here a few days. I don't know what that damn Dunbar is playing at. Look in on us tomorrow. I may need your assistance. I'd pay you a retainer, naturally."

"Of course," Jeremy replied.

If it meant another opportunity to see Amelia, possibly to get closer, he was happy to oblige. He knew he shouldn't be thinking it, she was married, not even twenty four hours, and yet, he couldn't banish the thought. Despite having walked a mile to smash the charivari, and feeling no fellowship with its members, he now found himself agreeing with its intent and principle.

12

Mother Cook's

JEREMY'S LEGS WERE MARBLE PILLARS. He raised each in turn consciously, swung it forward and tramped it down, like a colossus escaped from its plinth. There was a clamour in his ears and a humming in his head, in part due to the scotch and the contents of Augie's flask, but also from the evening's accounting. Now, left alone with his thoughts on the silent walk back to town, images materialized and petitioned: floating bodies, sightless black beggars, torrents of porter, Ginger in his skirts, broken windpipes, legless Indians, Augustus kissing Merit, Mrs. Spafford in her nightgown. It had been only twelve hours that they'd disembarked to Kingston's sordid shore. It felt like a week.

The moon was on its downward descent when he reached town. Everything looked different in the dark. It was all he could do to keep his leaden feet moving, one in front of the other. He started on the sidewalk but his left foot fell through a gap where two slats were broken, jarring his knee. The fractured wood scraped his calf. He moved to the middle of the street. Two blocks later he turned his ankle through the skin of ice that had formed over one of the craters pocking the surface. His leather boot filled with achingly cold water and he inundated the street with such an opus of loud profanity that, at first, he failed to hear the low growl coming from the intersection ahead.

He could hear it, but he couldn't see it. He stopped his cursing and hopping. The snarling got louder. He began slowly to back away, stepping again into the icy basin, this time not noticing. He reached the crossroads, turned down an adjacent street, took several long strides, and then began a lop-sided sprint. Behind him, he could hear murderous barking and the scrabbling of claws on frozen mud. A wolf, maybe a bear, gaining on him; monstrous, rabid.

He ran as fast as he could, turning right at one street, left at the next. He rounded another corner, took a look over his shoulder for his pursuer, and in that moment collided with the warm, yielding flank of a shorthorn red. He fell flat on his back. The cow moaned and stamped. Jeremy caught his breath, scrambled to his hands and knees, brushed past her udder, and out the other side. He got to his feet and peered over her withers.

The beast chasing him scudded round the corner and slid to a stop, confused to find a cow. Jeremy could see now, in the different angle of moonlight, that it was a mongrel, part terrier, all bone and mange. The dog yapped with exasperation and made an occasional nip at the cow's fetlock. Someone shrieked from a nearby cottage. A bottle launched from retracted shutters. It narrowly missed Jeremy, struck the shorthorn in the neck, and fell to the street in pieces. The cow replied with a graceless kick that struck a hollow note against the mongrel's ribs. The dog crouched low and slunk from the street, whimpering.

Jeremy limped away in the opposite direction, walking two more streets before he realized he was lost. With the darkness, it was difficult to know which direction to take. Turning into the next street, he was surprised, and grateful, to find a figure backlit by a shop window.

"Excuse me," he said, in a low tone. "Am I far from Walker's Hotel?"

"Walker's?" the woman asked, turning to face him. She removed the cowl that protected her face and head from the cold, revealing hair of brittle grey, carelessly groomed, scored cheeks, and a faint, silvery moustache.

"Walker's?" she whistled through missing teeth, incredulous. "La di da. What's a swell from Walker's doing in these parts?"

What's a woman my mother's age doing, at this time of night, on the street alone…? The answer came as the question formed.

"Sailor is it? You don't need no Walker's," the woman continued, rolling the cloak from her shoulders and loosening the laces of her blouse until they were pulled free. "I know what a sailor wants. And it ain't fancy teas and cakes."

"Ye can stay here," she said, gesturing to the shack, "with me."

Inside, a single, blackened lamp threw an anemic circle of light over someone seated at a table, puffing a pipe. The smoker wore a tattered straw hat with its brim raked forward, a faded ribbon of silk tied beneath the chin, a single pale feather adorning it. The hat shaded a pair of eyes that looked out impassively at Jeremy.

"Nevermind her," she said, taking one of Jeremy's hands into both of hers. "Tis only my aunt. She won't make us no bovver."

"Come inside. It's warm," she said, thrusting Jeremy's hand through the neckline of her blouse until it rested on her slack breast. He withdrew immediately, despite its tempting heat.

"With respect, ma'am. Could you point me in the direction of Walker's Hotel?"

"You don't need no Walker's," she spat, "I'm telling you. All's you need is right here."

She leant forward and pulled her blouse open further, all the way to her navel, so that one of her breasts wobbled free. Her paunch was greyish in the moonlight. She began to hike the hem of her petticoat up her thigh.

"I'm sure I'll find it." Jeremy said, retreating. "Thanks all the same."

"Prat," she called after him.

Jeremy kept walking, each lethargic step a triumph. He found the buildings had thinned; he was in an area of coops, pens, and pastures. There was a small clutch of buildings at the next crossroads and, some activity along the wall of one of them. No voices, no barking. The night air was brittle and carried only indistinct sounds. The swish of milling bodies. Grunts and snuffles. Jostling. He didn't want to go back the way he came, to meet again the whore and her queer aunt. He continued, cautiously, thinking he could quickly escape the intersection without notice. As he neared, he realized with relief that what he heard was nothing but a passel of hogs mobbed against the clapboard.

He sidled through the intersection, hoping to escape notice. Midway, he stopped. What was it that poked out from the edge of the group, between hooves and snouts? Jeremy turned and crossed the street. A pair of boots. Parallel to one another, toes pointing upward, as though they still contained feet. From the porch of the nearest building he retrieved an abandoned corn broom, tassels worn to a nub. He waded in, swinging the ash rod, sweeping away infuriated swine. He cut and parried the bolder pigs until they backed off.

When he felt he could turn his back, he looked down to see what had their attention. It was a body next to the exterior wall, knees drawn up, hands clutched at the stomach, face set in a grimace. The nose, an ear, and part of the cheek had been chewed away. The pigs had ripped holes through the jersey and trousers and had bitten bruises into chest and thigh. He forced himself to kneel and look more closely.

Dunbar. The drunken boaster from the Bottle and Glass. Spafford's man.

Jeremy whirled, his eyes filled with hot, acidic tears. He wept not for the fallen Dunbar, who was a stranger to him, but for himself, that he should have to witness such an atrocity, such an outrage to his sense of decency, by himself, at this awful hour, in this hateful, unfamiliar place, three thousand miles from home.

Jeremy advanced on the hogs, thumping, clouting, and plunging until his stunted corn broom was nothing but a mass of splinters. Grudgingly, the bewildered pigs wandered away, snorting their disapproval. He threw the remnants of the broom after them and returned to Dunbar. The Derryman's eyes were cinched tight and his face tinged blue. He emanated rum vapour. Jeremy picked him up by his upper arms and pulled him to his feet. Dunbar remained crunched. Jeremy lifted him up over his shoulder, putting his arm behind locked knees. *I'll take him to the King's Arms*, he thought. *He is Spafford's man, he should take care of him, make sure he is treated decently. No man, regardless how stupid or drunk, should be left as slop.*

Jeremy trudged a hundred yards in what he thought was the direction of the King's Arms before he had to put Dunbar down. He rested him on the tilted porch of another clapboard shanty. He sat beside him and stared into the gloom. *Just a minute or two*, he thought. The mass of damp wool in his head caused it to loll irresistibly from his neck. His eyelids dropped like heavy stage curtains, as if closing on the evening's final tragic act. Despite his best efforts, he fell asleep, sitting at first, and then, slowly listing, his back met the porch and his ponderous head came to rest on Dunbar's hip.

He woke screaming. The shorthorn red loomed over him, her preposterous, pink tongue laving the sweat from his face.

"Don't eat me," he cried, seeing, in his delirium, a giant pig, "don't eat me."

He dug his heels into the rotted wood of the porch and tried to propel himself backwards, away from the beast. Dead Dunbar blocked him like a doorstop, his stiff arms embracing him. Jeremy had forgotten him. When he turned and looked into the man's lifeless, half open eyes, he screamed again.

"Geraldine!" Someone was on the porch, shouting. "Gitaway now!"

"No need for caterwauling fella," the man said to Jeremy. "Pay her no heed, she's friendly is all. I feed her scraps sometimes, she likes t' visit."

"Shut it!" a voice yelled from across the street. "Tis Sabbath. Peace, God damn you!"

The man disappeared a moment and then returned, whacking a huge wooden spoon against the cow's haunch.

"Geraldine! Gitaway, you daft bitch!"

Geraldine mooed loudly. In a nearby house, a baby cried.

"Jesus and Mary and Joseph!" bawled a woman. "Quiet! For Christ's sake!"

"Geraldine!" The man paddled her again. The cow stepped away.

"You and your mate best move along," he said to Jeremy. He glanced at Dunbar and noticed that the man hadn't moved. He observed that his nose was missing.

"Is he alright?" he said, looking back at Jeremy. "Oh."

"It's not what it looks like," Jeremy said, getting to his feet. "I need help, let me explain."

The man on the porch was backing up, fumbling with the latch of his skewed door.

"None of my business," he said and was back inside.

Jeremy could hear a heavy beam slide across. He thumped his fist against the door.

"Please," he cried, "let me explain. It's not how it looks. I need your help."

"I'll come over there and gut you, you son of a bitch," shouted a neighbour.

Jeremy charged across the street.

"Show yourself," he screamed at the window, spittle flying. "I'll twist your pocky head clean from your shoulders."

The shutters closed. Shrieking filled the space behind.

"Bar it," a woman said, hushed now, "he'll dash baby to pieces."

Jeremy returned to the porch.

"Let me explain," he said again, quieter now, through the door.

"Is he dead?" the man asked.

"Yes."

"Did you kill him?"

"No. He drank himself to death."

Silence.

"I barely know him."

Jeremy pressed his face closer to the door.

"I rescued him from pigs."

More silence.

"If I had killed him, do you think I would be toting him round?"

Jeremy thought maybe the man had retreated deeper into his house.

"'Tis fair point, I s'pose," the man said, finally. "But what do ye 'spect me to do about it?

"I don't know," Jeremy said, hanging his head.

"What're doing with him?"

"I don't know."

"Why are ye with him?" the man asked again.

"I was going to take him to the King's Arms."

"The Arms? That's a mile away!"

"His employer is staying there."

"Who are ye, anyway? Not from here. I dinnit recognize ye."

"Jeremy Castor, corporal, Royal Marines, *HMS St. Lawrence*," Jeremy said, sadly.

"Eh? I can barely hear ye." The man pulled the bar back and opened the door a crack.

"Jeremy Castor, from Porthleven, Cornwall. I don't belong here."

"Aye, you've got that right. Nor do I. Porthleven, ye say? I'm of Plymouth."

Jeremy stood mutely at the threshold and stared at the mud caked on his boots. The man opened the door a foot.

"You didn't kill him?" he asked.

"No!" Jeremy roared.

"Good, good." The man looked Jeremy down and up, from the filth spattered boots, to the torn knees of his woolen trousers, the raw knuckles, the missing buttons, the dried blood beneath his nose, the cow spit slicking his hair.

"Castration! You're a sight. Ye could use a restorative, I warrant. Come in a minute."

Jeremy turned and regarded Dunbar, folded in on himself like a giant insect caught in a web.

"He'll keep a while longer," the man flicked at a bottle sitting on a shelf outside the shack, a third full of ice. "It's plenty cold."

The shack had no windows. Inside it was as pitch as a blacksmith's and just as humid. He could taste the air; it was sweet. Jeremy felt as though he was being coated with thin layers of melted toffee. Moments earlier he'd been trembling with cold. Now he felt a drop of perspiration roll down the back of his neck. He removed his jacket.

"My apologies," the man said, opening the door of the wood stove. "I have few visitors. Please, here, take a seat. Warm yourself by the fire." He cleared rubbish from a crate with the back of his hand and pulled it over to Jeremy.

Jeremy sat, feeling faint.

"You're in luck, I just happen to have a pot of tea on. Excuse me a minute."

The man left the shack with a small glass ewer.

"Geraldine!" He was shouting. "Geraldine!"

Jeremy closed his eyes and let his forehead fall into the cradle of his hands. There was a scraping outside the door. He squeezed his eyes tight and tried to conjure the inside of his mother's cottage. The details were slipping away, becoming indistinct. Why couldn't he picture her pen and ink drawing, the one she'd hung over the armchair, the one he'd glanced at a thousand times. Of Chough Tor? Of The Pelican? The Rode and Shackle? Why couldn't he remember? His head snapped back. He'd slept. Jeremy stood up and was about to find the door when the man returned, with a jug full of milk.

"There is one advantage to a wandering cow," he said.

Jeremy's eyes grew accustomed to the light thrown by the fire. The stove stood in the middle of the room, hissing and popping. It had a vast, blackened cauldron and kettle on top. The liquid in the cauldron pitched and rolled, sending up sheets of gauzy steam that didn't dissipate. It hung in the air and draped itself over the rest of the room's contents: the stained pouch of straw in the corner, the jumble of pots and paddles, the sculptures that looked as though extrusions of lava, now cooled, arrayed on every available surface.

The man poured tea from the kettle into two glass mugs and then some milk from the jug. He picked up one of the lava sculptures and broke an edge from it.

"Sugar?" he asked, before he took a large bite. Jeremy shook his head.

"Scum," the man said as he gestured to the cauldron and handed a mug to Jeremy. He took another bite from the fragment and then put the rest of the black shard into his mug. It listed and dissolved like some infernal iceberg in a sea of warm milk and the debris of twice-steeped tea leaves. "When they make bastards, lowest grade sugar, they filter out the scum. They would throw it out. But I take it. I boil it again. I scrape out another grade lower. I sell it to Mother Cook next door. She bakes with it. Sometimes I get a bread loaf or sugar pie out of it."

He lit two lamps, each sitting on a different crate.

"Sorry, 'tis smudgy. For light, I leave the door ajar, but not in winter. Oil's dear."

The man's soiled rags hung sharply from his scarecrow frame. His head, in contrast to his spindle limbs, was bulbous, long greasy hair falling from it in patches. His sunken face was pitted and pocked and a plum coloured boil poked like a poll from his forehead. It was as though a carved pumpkin had been impaled onto the sharp stalk of his neck and it had been left to rot.

He smiled and sucked the treacle from his mug through a pair of blackened teeth.

"I don't get many visitors," he repeated.

Jeremy looked away. He lifted his eyes up. Around the perimeter of the room, on a pair of shelves, stood the most extensive menagerie of bottles and glass that Jeremy had ever seen. They were in every shape and size, every tint and design: stubby jars of russet and amber, hefty brown jugs and delicate, silvery carafes, petal-figured bowls of coral balanced atop impossibly slender stems, phials and flasks of aquamarine with globular stoppers, jade canteens trapping shafts of light as pond-water suspends rays of sun. There must have been hundreds, each of them refracting the lamp light, twinkling through the caramel haze. He felt as though he was trapped inside a kaleidoscope.

"Wasn't always a scumboiler," the man said, shrugging.

On one shelf, Jeremy spied a black, lanky bottle. He stood, crossed the room, and picked it up. He looked at the pontil mark at the base. Initials AB inside an acorn. He pulled the cork and put his nose to it. Burnt molasses bloomed from the neck and seared his nostrils. He knew the volatile bouquet. He'd tasted it on the *Lancer*. He'd smelt it on Dunbar's breath.

"Ah yes, devil's blood, secret recipe," the scumboiler said. He was tipping an amethyst-tinted ampoule over Jeremy's mug. "Tea is fine as far as it goes, but this? This restores."

Combustion from the open wood stove sucked the oxygen from the upper levels of the syrupy air. Jeremy felt light-headed. He worried he might fall over. The scumboiler was looking back at him, smiling and winking, waggling a black lump over his mug of tea. "A bit o' sugar for the medicine?" he asked, scratching at his hip with the other hand. Jeremy thought he might be sick.

"Mr. Castor!" the scumboiler called after him as he bolted through the door and back out on to the porch. He held up the mug. "You haven't even sipped it."

Jeremy was outside, eyes rolled back, bridling like a jittery horse.

The dead man was no longer on the porch.

"Where is he?" he cried. "Where's Dunbar?"

Jeremy ran into the street. He looked into the open window of the low, flat hut adjacent to the scumboiler's. Just above the door and below the roof of mottled, marsh hay a hand-painted sign read *Mother Cook's – Est. 1780.* An old black man sat at a table with his head flat on its surface, unconscious, his hand gripping a stone bottle. Another man sat in a corner dipping crust into a bowl. A pair of women, one older, the other ancient, dropped bloody joints of meat into a stewpot.

"Mr. Castor," the scumboiler called. He had the broomstick of his arm angled through Jeremy's and was trying to lead him away.

The first woman looked up and recognized Jeremy. It was the whore and her aunt, Mother Cook. In the confusion and dark of the night he had retraced his steps and returned.

"You," the whore squawked. "You'd rather spend the night with Scratch? The scumboiler?"

Mother Cook tipped back her ribboned, feathered hat, pulled the pipe from her gums and wheezed.

"Mr. Castor," the scumboiler called again. He was next to a small door between the two buildings. "When I went for milk," he yelled, "I decided you were right, we shouldn't leave your Mr. Dunbar out front. 'Twasn't decent."

"Mr. Williams and Mr. Foster next door," he continued, gesturing to the two men in Mother Cook's, "helped me move him into the cold cellar. Until we can call next of kin, and the undertaker, of course." He gestured next door with his bony thumb. "Mother said that would be jus' fine."

The scumboiler opened the door and gestured inside. Jeremy could see triangular shanks of meat and sausage coils hanging from the rafters. Mother Cook's horsy laugh continued as she shook her head and plunged a cleaver the size of her wizened head into cartilage and bone.

"Where is he?" The scumboiler was asking, poking his head into the cellar gloom. "He was right here."

He turned back to the street. "Mr. Castor?"

Jeremy was already two blocks away, tramping his legs of marble as fast as they could go.

13

The Britannia Inn

NEVEN AND MERIT, FINN AND LILAC breakfasted on toasted bread, butter and preserves, tea and brandy.

"Hallelujah," Finn cried, clapping his hands when he saw Jeremy stride past. "I told you Augie would be last back. Shillings please."

Neven and Merit dropped a shilling each into his outstretched hand. Lilac picked them out and put them in her pouch before Finn could close his fist.

"Just in time, deacon," she said, "Bishop Stuart gives his sermon in thirty minutes."

"You look like a swill bucket," Finn said.

"Sit down and twist the yarn," Merit said. "I'll pour."

"Must sleep," Jeremy said and he went straight upstairs. Merit stood from the table and followed.

"Jem?"

Jeremy was already under the quilt, having removed only his encrusted boots.

"What happened?"

"This is a filthy, miserable place," Jeremy said, into the pillow.

"Aye."

"I want to go home."

"Aye. Me as well." Merit put his hand on his cousin's hulking shoulder. "We'll get there, mark me."

"It's a Goddamn barnyard, full of slop and shit and feral pigs."

"What happened?"

"Got to sleep," Jeremy said, burrowing deeper into the mattress.

He'd have slept right through supper if Merit hadn't punched his shoulder again mid-afternoon.

"What?" Jeremy's voice was low and gravelly. It felt as though a boot pressed his head against the pillow.

"Augie," Merit whispered. "He's still not returned."

"What time is it?"

"Almost tea."

"The Spaffords!"

Jeremy twisted from the bed, rubbed his face, and looked for his coat.

"Did you hear me?"

"I told them I would look in."

"Augustus."

"I must tell them about Dunbar."

"We need to return to our billets. The provosts will be looking for us."

"Back soon."

~ ~ ~

It was an hour before sun up that Spafford finally came to bed, redolent of whisky and smoke. Mercifully, he hadn't balked when Amelia chose the chaise lounge as a place to sleep, far from the four-poster. She'd been kept awake by his discordant symphony: rumbling moans, girlish whimpers, ratcheting teeth, tympanic snores, brassy flatulence. *Is this what it will be like*, she wondered, *for the rest of our lives? She made macabre calculations. How long will it be? Fifteen years? Twenty?*

Amelia broke a piece from the corner of a fruitcake and nibbled, watching Spafford as he tossed and murmured. The charivari had interrupted the sleep of all the guests at the King's Arms and Amelia had refused to descend to the dining room, unwilling to bear their low whispers and censorious looks. Bison had relented and brought tea and dinner upstairs.

"Dunbar!" Spafford falsettoed, lurching to his elbow.

"He's not here," Amelia said, from the little table by the window.

"He must be! I need him!"

"He's not."

Spafford rubbed his eyes with a clumsy fist and looked back at Amelia from his envelope of blankets. Thin hair wisped from the top of his fleshy head, colour rose to his fat cheeks, and his bottom lip jutted. He looked as though he might start to cry.

Nursemaid, she thought. *That is what I am to be.*

"What about the big lad? Castor."

"We've had no visitors."

"He promised."

She shrugged.

"Fetch me the chamber pot."

Amelia looked back out the window.

"Please!" he cried and his stridency startled her. She crossed the room, retrieved the pot from underneath the bed and handed it to him.

"Thank you."

Spafford pulled the covers back, swung his legs out and stood stiffly. He lifted the front of his nightgown over the pot and held it to his crotch. Amelia, already back at her seat, looked out the window, resting her ear on her hand to muffle the sound of urine spattering porcelain.

"Pass me the black valise on top of the wardrobe. Please."

He was back in bed, fidgeting. She pulled a chair to the wardrobe, stepped on it, pulled down the valise, and handed it to him. He rifled through it, rattling the glass phials inside, digging and ripping. Amelia noticed his face was flushed. He was sweating. Finally, he pulled an amethyst-tinted ampoule from the confusion of bottles. He held it up in the direction of the window, peering through its body. He shook it next to his ear.

"Empty!" he cried, flinging the delicate vessel against the wall so it shattered. "I need more. For my nerves. I told him."

Bed linen was bunched up in his pudgy fists.

"I'll go," Amelia said.

Out the window, she watched as a female cardinal hopped through the branches of a cedar and then flew away. The brighter, showier male remained absent.

"I could use some fresh air anyway," she said, looking back at Spafford stewing in the rumpled bed like a giant ham hock.

"No," he said flatly. "You can't wander about town unaccompanied."

She turned back to the window. Jeremy Castor now stood in front of the cedar, unmistakable in his scarlet coat. They gazed a minute as though seeing each other for the first time, taking a moment to get acquainted. Finally, Jeremy raised a mittened hand. In it he held her looking glass. She raised her hand and they smiled. Spafford was saying something, but she couldn't hear the words. All she heard were cardinals, sparrows, and chickadees, projecting their coupled conversations.

"He's here," she said, quietly.

"...you must learn this," Spafford was saying, "decorum. As the wife of an officer...eh?"

"He's here," she repeated. "Mr. Castor."

"Is he? Good show!" Spafford was out of bed again pulling up his flannels. "Corporal. Corporal Castor."

He stuck his head out the window.

"Ah, Castor! Very good to see you. We've been waiting. Please come up!"

Seconds later Jeremy was knocking on the door. Amelia let him in. He doffed his hat and smiled.

"Come in, come in," Spafford said, ushering Amelia out. "Just give us a moment dove, we've some business to discuss. Tell Bison to make you a tea."

Jeremy stepped in sideways past Amelia, his thigh brushing her petticoat. Spafford closed the door and now she was out on the balcony, while Jeremy and her husband were inside. A pair of elderly women ascended the stairs, returning to their rooms from the lounge. When they reached the balcony, they stopped and stared at Amelia, whispering. She thrust her face toward them and widened her eyes. They turned the other way, chattering, and disappeared into a bedroom. Amelia cupped her hand against the door of her room and put her ear to it.

"Dunbar is dead," Jeremy said.

"Blast him!" Spafford cried. "Drippy patlander. As reliable as Irish weather. Where did you see him last?"

"Mother Cook's. It's a low tavern on the outskirts of town."

"I know Cook's. Refuge of the depraved. Clubhouse for rapists and Yankees. He must have been truly desperate for more drink to end up there."

"He didn't arrive there of his own volition," Jeremy said, trying hard not to remember too vividly the details of the night before, "he was brought there. I'm not sure he's still there."

He banished from his mind an image of Mother Cook with her bloodied cleaver.

"Never mind. Thanks for bringing it to my attention. I'll have Bison send a courier to inquire about him and to inform the gravedigger."

Spafford stared at the painting of the buffalo hunt.

"He hasn't any family, as far as I know," he said, tapping his lip with a finger, "so I don't think there is anyone to notify. I suppose I'll have to pay the fees myself. Damn inconsiderate of him, really, saddling me with this. Thankfully he was owed wages; they'll cover the undertaking fee. He'd have pissed those into the gutter too, if I hadn't held them back."

"Sorry," he said, returning to Jeremy. "I need your assistance."

"I'll do what I can."

"Good lad. We gave Boney what-for on the Peninsula but I should tell you that I didn't get out of Spain unscathed. Had a terrible fall during the show, thought my back was broken. To this day, I get terrible headaches and find it difficult to sleep. I don't mind admitting that my nerves are a bit dodgy at times."

Jeremy nodded but his expression betrayed confusion. Spafford paused.

"My apologies," he said, "I'm rattled."

"I understand."

"Still, no excuse for lack of hospitality."

Spafford pointed to the bottle of Tobermory on the table.

"Let's have a dram. To our health."

Before Jeremy could object Spafford put a tumbler of whisky into his hand.

"That's a start," Spafford said, sipping from his own glass and exhaling loudly. "You see this?"

He lowered his voice and held up the glass stopper from the empty amethyst ampoule that lay in pieces next to the wainscot.

"Paregoric Elixir. Very difficult to obtain. Most of the so-called medicine men of our little Arcadia haven't even heard of it. Few prescribe it. None can procure it. It's the only thing that works."

Spafford handed the stopper to Jeremy.

"There is a man from Montreal. Barnabas I think it is. He often has the stuff. He's said to have returned to Kingston two days ago."

"I think I know him."

"You do?"

"Aye. He shared our batteau from Montreal to Kingston. Peculiar man."

"I've never met him. Dunbar is..., was..., my agent in this matter. You have to understand. I'm an important man. A town father. I have a reputation to uphold. Interests to upkeep. I can't have idlers in pubs and pews murmuring about old, dotty Noble."

Spafford affected a nasally, high-pitched voice.

"'He's got neuralgia, don't you know.' 'One foot in bedlam, he has.' 'Devoted to the elixir, he is.'"

He swigged, as if to wash away the voices of his critics, and wiped his mouth with the back of his hand.

"It is vital that I project an air of propriety to Kingston yeomen. Of confidence and strength. Especially in this time of war. Cartwright, Stuart, Strachan, myself; we provide a foundation upon which this young outpost of British civilization can grow and thrive. A limestone footing, if you like. You can imagine how my banner might start to fade if I was seen loitering common saloons, fraternizing with moonrakers, dealing in illicit goods, can't you?"

Spafford slapped Jeremy's knee before he could answer.

"You're a Loyalist and a gentleman, I'm sure of it. That's why I feel like I can trust you to be discreet, just as Dunbar was."

"Of course."

"When this Barnabas is in town, he stays at the Britannia. I suspect he is there now. You'd be doing me a great favour if you would seek him out and obtain a measure of this medicine."

"Where?"

"The Britannia. Run by a garlicky frog's leg called St. Charles, if you can believe it, another reason I'd rather not go myself."

Jeremy sipped his whisky. His head throbbed. He would have preferred to be back at Walker's with Merit, Finn, and the rest. What did Merit say as he was leaving? He became aware of the fact he was ravenous. And light-headed. The scotch had seeped directly into his bloodstream through his empty stomach.

He would have preferred that Amelia was in the room with them. If he was honest, it was the only reason he was there, that he might see her again, to return her looking glass. Instead, he sat in the strangely masculine bridal suite, with its hunting accoutrements and its leathery fug, and Noble Spafford, who still reeked of the night before. A whiff of ammonia billowed from beneath the four-poster. Jeremy imagined, with distaste, that they likely consummated on that bed, less than twelve hours ago, the sheet and quilt still a mangled, sweaty mess. And now this unseemly request to meet with a witch doctor and secure a mysterious potion.

"We are already in your debt," Spafford said quickly, detecting Jeremy's hesitance, "make no mistake. And I intend to remedy that forthwith." He pulled a guinea from his vest pocket and slapped it onto the table. "Please, take this as a partial reward for your gallantry last night."

Jeremy looked at the coin and then at Spafford and then back to the coin.

"May I have some cake," he asked, finally.

Spafford frowned. He looked over his shoulder at the table by the window.

"Cake?" he repeated. "Oh, yes of course! I think you'll find bread and cheese and pickle as well. Please, help yourself."

Jeremy rose from his chair unsteadily and moved to the one by the window. He tore a chunk from the loaf of bread and folded it over a thick slice of cheddar and some pickle and stuffed as much of it into his mouth as he could.

"As I mentioned to you last night, your commanding officer Stokes and I are old friends. I could ask of him a favour. I'm officially on half-pay but I still have ceremonial duties and I could use a personal assistant. I could have Stokes assign you to me, to free you from the drudgery of drill."

Jeremy chewed.

"What can I do for you?" Spafford asked.

"Sir," Jeremy said, swallowing noisily, "I would very much like for my cousin and I to go home."

"Home?"

"Yes sir."

"To Cornwall?"

"Yes sir. We were driven from the Rode and Shackle in Porthleven, assaulted and pressed aboard the *Lancer*. My mum still doesn't know where we are, six months later. I didn't even get to say good-bye."

Spafford was quiet, thinking.

"To go home, that's my dearest wish."

"That's no insignificant request."

"I know it."

"It's not something that could be done quickly. There are many official channels that would need traversing."

"I suppose, yes."

"And I would want the benefit of your service for a month or two at least, until I can find a permanent replacement for Dunbar."

"Aye."

"I'll talk to Stokes, see what I can do. Provided you go to the Britannia immediately and return today with Paregoric Elixir."

Jeremy jumped to his feet. The cheese and bread and fruitcake sopped the scotch in his stomach and steadied him.

"Be back shortly," he said, and was out the door and down through the lounge, not noticing Amelia as he sprinted past.

She peered at him over the spine of a copy of Plutarch's Lives, borrowed from the small library of classics, purchased by Bison Harris to add class to the King's Arms.

~ ~ ~

A boy stood outside the Britannia, leaning on a barrow, chewing a wodge of tar.

"Kid," Jeremy said, holding a groat between his thumb and forefinger. "Can you take a message to a Mr. Merit Davey at Walker's Hotel?"

The boy nodded.

"Who?" Jeremy asked.

"Mr. Merit Davey."

"Where?"

"Walker's."

"Good. Tell him to meet Jeremy at…" He paused. "What's a hand's pub? Where do the carpenters, turners, and curriers go for a drink? Where would you go?"

"Dunno. Royce's, maybe, Royce Inn?"

"Tell Mr. Merit Davey at Walker's to meet Jeremy at the Royce Inn this evening for a late supper. Got it?"

The boy nodded again. Jeremy handed him the groat and the boy scampered away, pushing the cart before him.

Jeremy entered the Britannia and he had the strange sensation he had, in one step, left one continent and entered another.

From the outside, it was a single story log building chinked with oakum and moss. The sign hanging over the door, with its faded union jack, was barely legible. Inside, it echoed, faintly, the halls of Versailles, minus the marble, gilt edges, and priceless art. There was a secretaire of dented tulipwood in the foyer, where Quetton St. Charles greeted guests and signed them in. On a tiered guéridon by the window in the lounge, a trio of lemon-scented, regal pelargonia, leant their ear-shaped leaves toward the diminishing light as though they were hard of hearing. Jeremy had never seen plants inside a house before. At the end of the bar there was a plaster bust of Louis Seize, minus the nose. The articles of furniture in the Britannia, the ones yet to be sold, represented all that St. Charles had been able to bring with him when he fled Republican France. He couldn't afford to have a new sign painted. Everyone knew the place as the Britannia.

At Sunday tea time, the lounge and dining room appeared to be empty. Motes of dust drifted leisurely along the architrave of late autumn afternoon sun slanting from the window.

"Bonjour, monsieur!" Quetton said, meeting Jeremy at the door. "'ere for tea? Une chambre, peut-être?"

"I'm looking for a Mister Barnabas," Jeremy said.

"Ah, Monsieur Barnabas." Quetton said sadly, leafing through the empty pages of his register. "Oui. 'E is 'ere. Là." He pointed to a corner of the lounge.

He sat in a red velvet chair at one of the round, marble-topped, mahogany tables, reading. From his sharp, thin beard and the empire top hat sitting next to him, Jeremy recognized him as the eccentric who had shared the batteau with them from Montreal.

"Mister Barnabas?"

The man looked up from his book. He took the burnt cedar strip used to light the lamp, put it between the pages and laid the book on the table.

"It is he. Mister Castor?"

"Aye."

"I recognize you from the batteau. Welcome to my phrontistery. Please."

Jeremy pulled a second chair and sat opposite. Barnabas watched him carefully, stroking his heavily oiled moustache.

"You'll take some tonic? You could use some, I hazard."

Pale green fluid twinkled from the slender flute of crystal on the table.

"It's most hygeian, Dr. Ordinaire's miraculous panacea."

"Thank you, no."

"I'm most grateful to you and your tarhood, staving off those river picaroons. They'd have arrogated my entire stock."

Barnabas motioned Quetton over. The innkeeper brought a second flute.

Jeremy waved him off.

"Please, favour returned."

Barnabas poured from a pear-shaped bottle into the glass.

"'Tis as effective as any of Dr. Hofstaeder's Cathartic Drops or Parker's Liverwort Compound."

Jeremy raised the glass to his nose and inhaled the licorice sting of anise, fennel, and wormwood. He let fluid lap his tongue. Bitter. Medicinal. He was reminded of Thackeray's Tar and Naptha Syrup, the nastiness Alice prescribed when he'd contracted catarrh.

"Supernaculum, yes?"

Jeremy returned the glass to the table.

"Not my cup of tea, I'm afraid, thank you. I have a favour to ask."

"Go ahead." Barnabas cupped his ear and beckoned. "Impetrate."

"You know a man named Dunbar?"

"The Hibernian? Manifestly."

"He's dead, I regret to inform."

"No!"

"Yes. He was in the habit of procuring from you, on behalf of his employer, a medicine called Paregoric Elixir."

"Of course. Dunbar was my best customer in all this Regiopolis."

"At this difficult time, his employer, who is ailing, finds his supply of the elixir has gone dry. As a favour to him, and his wife, I've come to you to obtain some more."

Barnabas took a sip of absinthe and regarded Jeremy. He smiled and twisted the tip of his beard.

"Haven't got any."

Jeremy started. He was expecting to quickly make the transaction and return to the King's Arms.

"Are you sure?" he asked. "None at all? This man, an important man, has a great need."

"Good, good. You have specie?"

"Yes, two guineas."

"Excellent. Give me one now. The other later."

Jeremy handed him a coin. Barnabas was up from the table. He emptied his flute and tipped the hat to his head. He lifted his large square valise from the floor.

"Don't despair," he said. "I have most components. I know a man in town who has the rest. Come."

In ten minutes they'd traversed eight blocks, each getting progressively familiar. Finally, they turned a corner and stopped outside of Mother Cook's.

"Voila," Barnabas said, gesturing. "The scumboiler. He can despumate anything."

14

The Royce Inn

WARM STICKINESS GUSTED from the scumboiler's opened door.

"Barnabas," he said. "And Mr. Castor. Again. I've not had this many visitors in a month."

"May we irrupt?" Barnabas said, smiling, removing his empire and pointing it inside.

"Yes, please. Mr. Castor, come in, I'm a-feared we started off wrong."

The two men entered the damp darkness and the scumboiler retrieved a pair of crates.

"You know each other?" Barnabas asked.

"We met this morning," the scumboiler replied. "Didn't we Mr. Castor?"

"Aye, we did."

"You'll be pleased to know that your misplaced Mr. Dunbar was found. The undertaker was here not more than fifteen minutes ago to retrieve him."

"Thank you, I'm grateful for your assistance."

"Poor Mr. Dunbar," Barnabas said. "If you don't mind my indelicacy, what brought the ferry man to the Derryman?"

Jeremy turned to him, ready to once more recount the evening. Barnabas raised his hand before Jeremy could speak.

"Bind it, gag it, drown it in the Lethe," he said. "Matters not. We wish to be expeditious, yes?"

Jeremy took a deep breath of the syrupy air and regarded Barnabas twisting his moustache tip. He was winking and grinning. Across from him, shadow eclipsed the scumboiler's pumpkin head so that he was all hairline and brow ridge, his caved-in mouth made apparent only by the sugar shard wedged into its corner, slowly dissolving.

"Affirmative?" Barnabas asked again.

"Yes," Jeremy said.

"Quite." Barnabas turned back to the scumboiler, holding out a guinea. "We require a minim of your best turpentine, a fluidrachm of your most mephitic rumbustion, and an amethyst ampoule with which to steeve our cargo."

He cupped his long fingers at the side of his mouth and directed it toward Jeremy as though he were disclosing a state secret.

"I'm not sure you fully appreciate the genius of our associate. Yes, he can despumate. He can coax the aqua vitae, distill the spirit, boil the scum; but as you can see," he swept his arm around the dingy, airless room at the bottles arrayed along the shelves, "more than anything he is a master of blowing glass."

The scumboiler took the guinea.

"There is more to Paregoric Elixir than its container, I warrant. It's that special extract you carry in your valise."

"Laudanum. Most active. But you underestimate the power of your own work."

"I have only one ampoule left. My own quantity of the Paregoric. It's me last, but you're welcome to it. I'll siphon off the elixir to another vessel."

"Excellent. And I will mix you some more besides. Fetch it and I'll mix a batch right here so Mr. Castor can rush it to this Mr., Mr…"

"Spafford," Jeremy said.

"Spafford?" The scumboiler asked, his scarecrow frame frozen. "Noble Spafford?"

"Yes."

"I'll supply no ampoule for Noble Spafford," the scumboiler said. "Nor turpentine, nor rumbustion, neither."

"Dear chap," Barnabas said.

"Not for the man who put the Family Compact against me, who blackballed my glassworks."

"Steady."

"You can't ask me," the scarecrow said, standing and turning his back to them, his voice quavering. "He ruined me Barnabas, you know it. 'Tis why I live and labour here now, in this hovel, boiling bastards and scum. My battledores and borsellas, my kilns and clappers, my crucible and glory hole; everything I had, all gone, sold to satisfy creditors. Spafford bought up most of it. At a criminal price too. The Yankees, just a hundred miles south, they are rolling thousands of pieces over their marvers. We could compete…"

He waved at the collection of bottles winking and glinting from the shelf around the perimeter of the shack.

"This is all I have left, my pension. Each month I lose a couple more. I'll be damned if I'll give Spafford another."

He threw the guinea back at Barnabas.

"Please," Jeremy said, seeing his opportunity slipping away. "I beg of you. I'm no friend of Colonel Spafford. But he is in a position to do a great favour for my cousin and me. He could get us home."

The scumboiler crossed the room to the wood stove, opened it and added a few green sticks which sparked and hissed. He stirred the cauldron.

Barnabas cocked his head to the side and drum rolled his knees.

"I beat out a chamade. Truce. Let us parley." he said.

The boiler remained silent.

"You can't force a man to trade," Barnabas said.

"Must it be an amethyst ampoule?" Jeremy asked. "Why not any old green bottle?"

"You're clearly unversed in the Hippocratic art." Barnabas replied. "The ampoule's importance is utmost. It is the vessel's pulchritude that imbues its magic, convinces the patient of its efficacy, and that is more than half the struggle. We healers, we *pharmacologists*, we deal in essences and extracts, tonics and tinctures, but mostly we deal in faith. And to maintain faith, to maintain the *integrity* of faith, we must present the patient with a consistent show of refinement. Every lapse lets in a chink of doubt. Doubt torments. We traffic in the prelapsarian; pill-sized portions of paradise. Analgesics, for body *and* soul. Would you accept a homily from a sackcloth bishop with a kerchief for a mitre?"

Jeremy thought a moment. He had a memory of studying scripture in the curate's parlour at Helston, on a cloudless February afternoon, sunlight steeping the room with lazy warmth, infusing it with the aroma of orange pekoe, honey, and currant buns. The curate lectured on nineteen of the book of Matthew. *It is easier for a camel to go through the eye of a needle…*

"Of course you wouldn't," Barnabas continued. "Noble Spafford is a man of means and expectation. He will expect the next bottle of Paregoric Elixir to look exactly like the last one, and the dozen previous. Otherwise he'll suspect fraud. Trust me, I have some experience in these matters. Dunbar returned a bottle on several occasions because it wasn't the *right* one, presumably on behalf of the Colonel."

Jeremy held his head in the basin of his hands. He tried to conjure again the cozy memory of the curate's parlour, but it was prevented by the turbidity of the air, the sweatiness of the boiler's shack, and the irate clank of his spoon against the cauldron.

Barnabas regarded him and tutted.

"Perhaps you could obtain the previous, empty ampoule from Mr. Spafford himself?"

Jeremy held up the glass stopper; all that remained of Spafford's elixir.

"I see. The man's a Philistine."

The boiler said nothing. He continued to stir the foaming broth, occasionally ladling a spoonful of scum from its surface.

"Please," Jeremy said to him, as he got to his feet, "Mr., Mr., ...I'm sorry I don't even know your name."

"Nor will you," the man said into the vat.

Jeremy stepped outside. Barnabas followed with hat and valise.

"Mr. Barnabas. Is there anything we can do? Somewhere else we can find an ampoule? This really could be my best chance at getting home. I know of no other way."

Barnabas rubbed two bony fingers together, as though they were the appendages of some monstrous insect, a giant locust signaling his mates.

"Money?" Jeremy asked. Barnabas nodded, tilting his head back toward the scumboiler's shack.

"I don't have much." He pulled his coin purse from behind his coat. "A few more guineas, six pounds worth. All I own. My cousin and I are saving to buy out our terms of service."

Jeremy considered the few coins in the leather pocket. He looked up. Barnabas appraised the purse.

"It will take forever," Jeremy concluded. "The Colonel could make it happen much sooner."

"Give me all six and let me try again," Barnabas said.

"Six pounds! For an ampoule, some turpentine and rum?"

"It is a simple matter of supply and demand. Pass the expenses on to Spafford."

Jeremy dropped the coins into Barnabas cupped hand and he deposited them into a deep recess of his coat.

"Wait here," he said and was back inside.

"It's fine," the scumboiler said when Barnabas re-entered. "I've changed my mind, I shouldn't be churlish, not with the young lad anyway. I'd go home too, to Plymouth, if I had the opportunity. Here's the ampoule. I'll measure out the turp and rum."

Barnabas smiled.

"It's clear who the true gentleman is. Here's your guinea." He flipped a single guinea into the scumboiler's empty tea cup. "Magnanimity begets magnanimity. Let me brew you a potent batch, something with whiskers on."

"Is the lad still outside? I'd like to apologize."

"Ah. No. He's gone on. I'll take it to him, with your compliments."

"Warn him 'bout Spafford. Not to be trusted."

Fifteen minutes later, Barnabas stepped sprightly from slanting porch and handed Jeremy a full amethyst ampoule. The additional five guineas never left his pocket.

"In good health," he said, beaming.

Jeremy shook his hand and rushed for the King's Arms.

~~~

It was well past seven when Jeremy stepped through the front door of the Royce Inn, a small, single-story saloon in the north end of town, the town's first stone house, with three rooms — a kitchen, a back room where proprietor Mrs. Kidd slept, and a single front room. Half a dozen men sat at tables, singly and in pairs, drinking beer from wooden mugs, speaking in whispers, if at all.

"Late supper?" Merit asked from one of the tables. "'Tis perhaps our last. We should have returned to our billets."

"Merit, you got my message."

Jeremy pulled a chair to the table and sat down.

"Aye. The others have returned. Where have you been? Why we here?"

"The same," Jeremy said when Mrs. Kidd arrived at their table.

"Slumgullion, as well?" she asked.

"Please," Jeremy said. "Have you eaten?" he asked, and Merit shook his head.

"Can you pay?" he asked Merit.

"Aye," Merit replied, narrowing his eyes.

"Two please," Jeremy said.

Mrs. Kidd returned shortly with another mug of Dalton's and two wooden bowls in which it was difficult to distinguish the mutton from the dumpling.

Merit's face darkened.

"What happened to yer savings Jem?"

"Invested," Jeremy replied.

"Twas s'posed to be me we had to worry about. I doubled me crowns at the Bottle and Glass. You're skint?"

"It's been an eventful spell."

As they fished with carved spoons through the stew bowls for arcs of chopped carrot and grey strands of scrag, Jeremy recounted his discovery of Dunbar, his meeting with Spafford, his negotiations with Barnabas and the boiler. He explained how Spafford had offered to take him on as an interim officer's servant in place of Dunbar and how, if he delivered the Paregoric Elixir, he promised to speak to Major Stokes about a discharge for Merit and himself, in as soon as two months.

"And the six pounds?" Merit asked.

"It's what I had to pay to get the elixir."

"Reimbursed?"

"He has expensive repairs on his house, Willowpath. Renovations for Amelia..., Mrs. Spafford, ... so she is comfortable. He said he will repay, with interest. When he is liquid."

Merit shook his head.

"You're the last one, I'd've wagered," he said, "to be done in by a pretty face."

"Mollath Dew," Jeremy replied, reverting to Cornish. "I'm trying to get us back, best I can. We're here because of you, don't forget."

"Augie's still missing," Merit said, stonily.

The shrill of a bosun's whistle sounded outside the front door, fading as its bearer ran down the street.

"Curfew," Jeremy said.

"Last I saw him, he asked me to give you this."

Merit passed him the Paine book. Jeremy stuffed it into a jacket pocket.

"We've got to go."

The two stood up abruptly from the table and drained their mugs. Jeremy slipped the book into an inside pocket. Mrs. Kidd returned, looking askance at the two bowls, both half-full.

"Twas lovely," Merit said. "What do we owe?"

"Shilling per. Ye pay whether ye like it or no."

Merit left two shillings and six pence on the table and they exited, each to their separate billets.

15

The Black Bull

LENORE STOKES SWISHED THE BOILING WATER through the belly of the teapot, round and round, until the liquid held together as a ghostly flash, haunting the vessel's recesses. Her mind wandered outside the four walls of the summer kitchen, to the call of the bosun's whistle, up and down adjoining streets, and the clipping of hard leather against cobbles as those outside hurried to their assignments, to their stations. She had a sudden yearning for somewhere to rush.

In the study, Peregrine cleared his throat.

She poured the water from the pot back into the heavy cauldron which heated water for her husband's bath. She measured three teaspoons of Assam black tea from the porcelain tea caddy into the pot, and then refilled it with water from the kettle. She replaced the pot's lid over the billowing steam, jacketed it with a knit cozy, and put it on the tray along with a tea towel, a strainer, and two porcelain cups, one with a dollop of milk and sugar. Ordinarily, she'd have had Abigail make the tea, but she sent her home early. It had been over a year he'd been at sea. This night was the first they'd had alone since he'd returned. She carried the tray into the next room where he sat at a desk, wrangling paper.

"I spoke to Eliza at lunch today," she said as she placed the tray on the edge of the desk.

"Mmm," Stokes replied, not looking up from the sheet of accounts.

"She was at the Bottle and Glass last night."

"Oh yes?"

"Said she saw a lot of your boys there. The new lads, from the *Lancer*."

"I heard they might go."

"Quite wild they were, she said, everyone was."

"I'm their major, not their father."

"Of course, of course, I'm not judging, though Eliza may have been. Some of the stories she told me!"

Lenore watched Peregrine. He made no reaction. He still hadn't looked up.

"I suppose they were a tad pent, cooped up on that ship. Such a long time since they've been ashore."

"'Tis true."

"Never seen it that lively, she said, what with the troupers. Mr. Poncet has many entertainments planned, she says."

"Mmm."

"Sounded like fun."

"You should have gone. You could have accompanied Eliza. A pair of naturalists, taking notes."

Lenore pushed a ringlet from her face.

"Perry," she said and waited. She poured the tea, hers into the cup with milk and sugar, his into the dry cup.

"I thought we might have gone," she said, finally.

"Darling, thank you," he said, raising his tea and winking. "You know it isn't my cuppa. A quiet evening home is what I like. It's lovely to be here again, with you. Why would I want to spend my first evening home with them I've had to live with all these many months, cheek by jowl, when I could spend it with you?"

"They can't all be so bad, or you wouldn't choose to spend your life at sea."

"Darling."

"The one that's staying with us?"

"Jeremy Castor of Cornwall. He's a good lad. Best of the bunch. Otherwise I wouldn't have brought him home to you. It's only temporary, until the *St. Lawrence* returns."

"I don't mind at all. Nice to have men in the house again, even for a little while."

Stokes regarded his wife. She'd somehow managed to become more attractive in his time away. He wanted to tell her that he would resign his commission when the war was over, soon, and that they might retire somewhere sunny, like south of France or Gibraltar. But he couldn't bring himself to do it. Not while she was pressing.

"Lenore," he said. "You knew the life. Your father, your brothers. There's a war on. I'm needed. It's my job."

"Yes, of course."

"You could come with me next time. Look after me. There are lots of wives aboard."

"No."

"Well."

Stokes pulled his watch from its pocket and checked the time.

"He's late?"

Stokes nodded.

"Still at the pub? Perhaps not such a chorister after all?"

"He studied for a deaconship before we pressed him."

"Oh. Boring then."

"You'd prefer I'd brought home one of the convicts? The cutpurse? Rodney? Or, Thomas? The rapist?"

Lenore shrugged and sipped noisily.

"It's lonely here Perry," she said, looking at the stack of papers on the desk. "You're home, finally. But you're not."

"I need to get this done. We have drill first thing tomorrow and Commodore's review."

"Early to bed, early to rise, back on the boat."

"It's not due for another week. Let me finish this tonight. Tomorrow we'll go for a nice roast beef dinner at the Black Bull."

"At lunch, Eliza brought by young Isaac. Little cherub. Pudgy forearms like his father. That makes three they've got, fourth on the way."

"Lenore!" Stokes brought his cup down sharply on its saucer. "We've discussed this. We've not been blessed."

"How do we know!"

"We'd've had one by now."

"How can we know the Lord's will if we never test it? You're never here with me to petition Him. Joe and Eliza give the Lord something to think about nightly."

"He's a brewer! What else does he have to do besides malt and mash, swill and sparge?"

"Oh Peregrine."

"I'm a Royal Marine. I was when you met me and I always will be. I sail and fight and keep the seas safe for British interests. It takes me away."

"Yes I, of all people, know that much. But while you're here, we could at least try, roll the dice."

"Of course, we will. But it's too late."

"Tonight? With the boy coming?"

Stokes laughed. "Yes, certainly tonight. But in general too. It's a young woman's game. I wouldn't gamble if the stake was losing you."

Lenore reddened.

"I'm not too old! Eliza is only a few years younger."

"Darling, please," Stokes left the desk and joined her on the love seat. He put his arm around her. "It doesn't matter."

He smelled of soap and leather. His blue eyes sparkled and Lenore was reminded of the skinny nineteen year old she first met, in Brighton, when he'd been assigned to her father's command, crisp and eager, looking capable of anything. She wanted to kiss him, but the vast, elaborately landscaped moustache that spanned his face seemed insurmountable.

"It doesn't matter," he said again, smiling, as though he could read her thoughts, "because I just don't think you're capable. God, in his providence, hasn't ordained it. But, I don't care, I love you forever and always, regardless. With you, I want for nothing else."

She reddened further.

"Not capable? Me? It's not true."

"Darling, please don't get excited, it must be true or it would have happened by now."

She pushed him away and stood up.

"I'm capable. I know it. I know it for a fact."

She wanted to continue. She wanted to say *it's you. You must be impotent. You don't know what I've been through. I have proof.* But she stopped short. Stokes looked up at her from the sofa, frowning, confused by her vehemence. She moved back to the desk and poured more tea.

Before Stokes could ask *how so? What makes you so sure? What proof?* there was a knock at the door. Lenore looked at her husband and he studied her face. In over twenty years aboard the ships of the line, marshaling his troops, he was an expert in reading the faces of men and boys. His wife was inscrutable.

He nodded toward the door. Lenore skipped across the room, lifted the latch, and opened it to a towering marine.

"You must be Jeremy," she said, relief flooding her voice. "Please come in."

She extended her hand and Jeremy held it, gently.

"Thank you. Mrs. Stokes?"

"Please call me Lenore."

"Thank you."

Jeremy ducked his head beneath the lintel, took the ditty bag from his shoulder, and stepped into the lamplight of the foyer.

"Goodness," Lenore said, appraising Jeremy's full length. "They sprout 'em big in Cornwall, don't they? I shall have to ask Abigail to bring in more food, I see. And prepare her for extra laundry. Some night you must have had, judging from your trousers."

Jeremy looked down at his mud-stained knees and the tear at his thigh.

"Bottle and Glass?" she asked. "Story's all over town."

"Lenore."

She smiled and walked to the desk.

"Some tea?" she asked. But Stokes didn't let him answer.

"Bit late Castor," he said.

"Yes sir, sorry sir. Late supper with Mr. Davey."

"We have review in the morning."

"Yes sir."

"You have an extra pair of trousers?"

"No sir."

"Mrs. Stokes can find you a pair to use until you mend those."

"Yes sir."

"I'm not sure I'll find any that fit," Lenore said. Stokes ignored her.

"Your trunk is in the spare room."

"Thank you sir."

"Everyone home? Accounted for?"

"I believe so, sir."

"Darling," Lenore said, "is it necessary to be so formal under our own roof."

"If we slip here, we slip on the square."

Lenore sighed and her head tilted.

"Best get some sleep," Stokes said. "Looks like you could use it."

"Aye sir, 'tis true."

"A bath first, perhaps?" Lenore asked. "A nice hot one?"

"Yes ma'am, that would be lovely. Thank you."

"Water's ready. Peregrine will pour it for you."

Jeremy glanced at the major. Stokes glared at his wife. It was the first Jeremy had heard Stokes' given name in the six months that he'd known him.

"Go ahead," Lenore said. "The tub is just in there. Get those filthies off. I'll look for some trousers. I'll leave them at the end of the bed for you. Nice to meet you Mr. Castor."

She extended her hand and Jeremy took it again, engulfing it in his own. His grip was firm and gentle, *as though he cupped an egg*. Stokes said nothing as he emptied two cauldrons into the tub, one hot, one not.

"Alright?" he said, when he was done. Jeremy nodded. Stokes closed the door behind him.

"Don't forget behind your ears," Jeremy heard Lenore say from the other room, laughing.

Jeremy stripped off his trousers, drawers, and wool socks. He took off his jacket and shirt and folded them over the back of chair. When he did so the Paine book slid from an inside pocket to the floor. He scooped it up and stuffed it into the rucksack. A quick knock and the door opened. Lenore stepped in. Jeremy held the sack awkwardly at his crotch.

"Oh, Mr. Castor," she said, "you're not the first billet. You're part of the ship's company and the company is family. No bashfulness between family. It's been a while, but I've seen a marine's buttock before."

"Lenore!" Stokes called from the other room. "Let him bathe."

"Here's a towel," she said. "Let me take your clothes and Abby can launder them first thing tomorrow."

He handed her the clothing with one hand, holding the bag in place with the other.

"Your sack? Are you going to bathe with it?"

"I'll keep it, if it's all the same."

"As you like."

When he was sure she was gone he slipped into the bath. It was shaped like a mining cart and Jeremy had to bring his knees nearly to his chin to fit. He leant his long arm down and retrieved the book, held it near the lamp and opened it to the first page. Someone had scrawled the frontispiece with a quill:

Jem

If I have any measure of luck in this accursed life, I will be safely returned to the confines of the Commonwealth of Massachusetts by the time you read this note. I warned you of my vanishing trick! I'd have taken you and Merit with me, but I didn't think you were ready. Read this book. Let it seep. Old Thom speaks much sense, for a Brit. When you've had your fill of monarchy and loyalism, finally, come to Boston. Look me up at the Athenaeum or the Green Dragon Tavern, I'll be at one or the other. The Republic yearns for good men like you.

Tell Mer farewell. Will miss you both.

Yours,

Augustus T. Gardiner

P.S. I'll tell Ma you're coming. Wait 'til you try her chowder. Best in the Union.

~ ~ ~

The next evening, Stokes sat at his usual table at the Black Bull, close to the hearth and its lively fire. A serving girl placed a large wooden platter in front of him, laden with the house specialty: standing rib roast. The cut itself was plate-sized, surrounded by a palisade of roasted potatoes, carrots, parsnips, and pudding. An earthenware pot of pickled horseradish formed a redoubt in the corner. Stokes had dreamed of the meal before him the day after his last visit, almost a year previous. He looked down at the slab of pink, with its concentric circles, awash in a pool of hot, dark juice and he found, with dismay, he'd lost his appetite. He emptied his baluster of Warre's 10 year old port-wine.

"Lovely isn't it?" asked the Commodore, Sir James Yeo, his dining partner. "Much as ourselves, it just gets better with age. Don't think you'd find a finer vintage in Oporto itself. And old Chestnut claims to have the only hogshead of the stuff in town. Pour yourself another."

Stokes filled his baluster.

"Good of you to meet me Peregrine," Yeo said. "You had a nice time with the missus yesterday? Re-acquainted?"

Stokes nodded and put a forkful of prime rib into his mouth.

"You're a lucky mongrel, to have snagged a woman as handsome and charming as Lenore, if you don't mind me saying. Still, eh?"

Yeo winked but Stokes wasn't sure what he meant.

I'd rather I dined with her, is what Stokes wanted to say.

"I don't mind, you're quite right to say so, thank you sir," he said, instead.

"My wife adores her," Yeo said.

"It is most requited," Stokes replied.

"Well, I wanted to give you a proper welcome back and brief you on how things fare on the lakes. As I'm sure you know, Governor Prévost has made a complete hash of the attack on Plattsburgh."

"Mmm."

The Commodore refilled his own baluster.

"You were short by two this morning," he said, "so the post captain tells me."

"Yes sir. A midshipman and a marine. Biscuit, the first, is aboard the hospital ship."

"Biscuit?"

"Mr. Prout, sir, everyone knows him as Biscuit."

"Fight?"

"Most likely. Claims he fell down a ravine."

"And the other?"

"Augustus Gardiner. Hasn't returned to billet."

"Two. Not bad, considering. Still, we must hook this Gardiner. If he went south, he'll be gone by now. But, more likely, he went north or west. He probably passed out somewhere north of Loughborough and has lost his way. The Indians will find him, if he's to be found."

"Is it necessary? He'd been on the *Lancer* four years, never once stepped off. He's given good service."

"You know the answer to that."

"Kid's not even British. He's from Boston."

"I don't care if he's from Timbuktu. Precedent."

"He should stumble in today or tomorrow. I'll have him flogged when he does."

"We take our boot off their necks for one minute they'll scarper, the lot of them. It will be just us two left to face brother Jonathan."

"He's well liked. Morale. I worry..."

Yeo pronged his steak knife into the oak of the tabletop so that it stood on its own, wobbling.

"Christ Peregrine! You aren't listening. You know as well as I do that we must prosecute every desertion to the fullest. We must be seen to be doing everything, and a little more, or the whole enterprise dissolves like horseshit in a storm. You aren't at sea anymore. You don't have a thousand mile moat keeping potential deserters below decks. Not here. The enemy is just a couple of miles across the lake. Everyday smugglers, privateers, and traitors are trafficking back and forth, up and down the river from Hickory Island to Sackett's to Prescott. In the city itself, the *King's* town for Christ sakes, every third man is an American, a republican, or a sympathizer. If I had my way, I'd never let the men across the river. I'd rebuild Fort Henry so that it's five times the size, with Martello towers and barracks, and I wouldn't let a single soldier step past the ramparts until Napoleon himself charged the slopes ahead of the Republican Guard."

Stokes put his baluster down and tamped the corners of his moustache with a napkin.

"You're right, of course," he said. "I'll arrange for a search party. A shame Biscuit's in the infirmary. He'd be the man for it."

"Already done. Shortly after parade. A party of Mississaugas. They put the best press master to shame. If this Gardiner is still one hundred miles of here in any direction, either side of the border, they'll find him."

"Very good sir."

"Welcome back to the show, old son," Yeo said, smiling now, pouring the last of the port into their glasses. "You'll love the *St. Lawrence*, she's as brash and buxom as the *Royal George* or any of the first-rates. There are a hundred carpenters over in Sackett's right now scratching their heads – wondering how they'll top her. She'll win us the war."

"Glad to hear it sir, looking forward to seeing her."

Yeo was just about finished his meal. Stokes had finished only half of his own, but it was as much as he could stomach. He wondered if he might be able to draw the dinner to a close, excuse himself, and take Lenore to The Old King's Head. They'd started early, there was still time.

"Gentlemen." Noble Spafford stood next to the table. "May I?"

"Noble!" the Commodore cried. "you scabby albatross! Of course. Chestnut," he called, swiveling in his chair, "another bottle of the Warre's."

Stokes stood as Spafford sat.

"Evening Noble," he said. "I should be going."

"Nonsense!" Yeo said. "Sit and drink with us."

"Yes, Stokes," Spafford said. "Do stay. It's you I have come to speak with. About your corporal. Jeremy Castor."

16

Old Sam's

JEREMY DREW THE NEEDLE through the coarse fabric and pulled the thread taut. It was two forward through the underside of the patch, one back through the trouser front, each penetration being met by one of the thimble's divots. When he finished backstitching the patch, he started a French seam on the trouser crotch, which had begun to separate. In and out, rhythmically, the needle, curved slightly from use, parting the fabric and lacing it with linen strand. With each pass, the fibres would re-gather and enclose the thread, embrace it. The needle went under, nudged through, and crossed over. It danced, it seemed, a sliver of light freed from the prison of Jeremy's grip, tracing the same arcs and trajectories, over and over. It ran and lapped and spiraled and looped, hundreds, thousands of times, until it was purest meditation and Jeremy's brain no longer had to issue commands.

In a mild ecstasy, he rose above the mechanism of his body and its repetitions. His mind roamed, through the woods, to the King's Arms, across the foyer and the library with its dusty, untouched copies of Plutarch and Cicero, past the elderly patrons in the dining room and their reproving looks, up the creaking staircase, along the papered hallway to the room with the hunting trophies, over the threshold and through to the boudoir. Amelia sat at the vanity. She brushed her hair, the lace and muslin of her careless nightgown in flimsy disarray, the sweeps and contours of her body straining the delicate seams, the front drawing open majestically, like a seraphic curtain, hinting at a paradise that lay beyond. Unhindered by corporeality, his mind became the mirror, the brush, the frill, the filaments of silk curling round her thigh. It became the merest prints of her fingers; smoothing, caressing, stroking. He relished the leisurely mind's eye tour of her topography, visiting many locations more than once.

"Braaa!"

The spectre of Spafford entered, braying for his dinner, spectacles, medicine. Jeremy plummeted back to the chesterfield and to his own body.

The quadrille of his fingers never faltered; they stepped on with precision, unperturbed.

Returned to himself, it occurred to Jeremy that he had no right to be so happy, with Augustus gone and hunted. He couldn't help it. Outside, sleet knifed the windows. Inside, the woodstove snapped and popped, radiating jolly warmth. The night before, he'd had the best sleep in half a year, on a chaff mattress with flock topper and sheets of cool, clean linen. Being reminded again of a proper bed, he wondered whether he'd actually slept at all in seven months of the *Lancer*'s saggy hammock. Earlier, Abigail had prepared an excellent meal of pan-fried trout with boiled, buttered potatoes and dried parsley followed by tea and biscuits. Before leaving, she'd delivered Jeremy's clothing, washed and ironed, in a neat stack. She'd apologized for not having time to darn them, with the extra chores and time spent at market. Jeremy refused her apology, glad to have the opportunity to do it himself.

Mrs. Stokes, Lenore, had anticipated dinner at the Black Bull with the major. When it became clear that her husband would not be returning from the fort after all, she had dismissed Abigail for the evening and retired to her room. Jeremy had several quiet hours to himself, in the rich glow of the cottage, stitching and mending.

He threaded and plaited and before long the spell was rewoven. He was at his family cottage in Porthleven. Christmas Eve. Outside, a north Atlantic gale raged at the lath and plaster. Inside, on the table, there was a pot of bohea and a plate of mince tarts. Charles, his father, rocked in the cane chair next to the hearth and smoked his briar, humming quietly. His brothers William and Thomas argued over cards at the dining table. In the corner, Merit worked some bone with an awl. Alice, with a heap of knitting on her lap, looked up every few minutes to assess and to smile and crinkle her eyes before returning to her clacking needles. Jeremy sat under the hurricane lamp with a volume of Coleridge, occasionally wriggling further into the sofa.

"'Twill be Christmas soon."

Again, a voice broke his reverie, but this time it was real, a woman's voice, gently mocking. He stopped sewing and turned to see Lenore enter the room, holding the translucent white muslin of her high-waisted dress in front of her as she walked. She crossed the floor noiselessly in silk slippers and alighted on the armchair before Jeremy could stand. His eyes rested briefly on her décolleté until she brought a corner of her burgundy, lawn shawl abreast of the gown's low neckline.

"You needn't stop," she continued, "just thought you might get new ones. If you've been good."

"Thank you," Jeremy smiled, resuming his stitch. "I'm nearly done."

They sat in silence as he sewed and she watched, returning his smile.

"I think Abigail left supper in the oven," he said.

"That's kind," she said. "I'm not hungry. Not for trout."

They were quiet again.

"You had a good night Saturday?" she asked. "Acquainted yourself with town?"

"It was interesting. Much more contending with livestock than I expected."

"Yes. Beastly."

She pinched a pleat of the curtain and parted it so she could peer out the window.

"A big barnyard," she said. "Not much to recommend it, really. You mind the Canadian girls though. Only one thing they're after."

Jeremy lifted his head and imagined Amelia, alone in her room at the King's Arms. He increased his sewing rate. Lenore stood from the chair and crossed the room, unhurriedly, to the rosewood armoire. She opened one of the cabinet doors, retrieved two crystal schooners and a bottle and placed them on the drinks tray.

"Sherry, Mr. Castor?"

He met her gaze, unsure of what to say.

"It would be ungallant to refuse."

"Then yes, of course."

She poured, generously, and brought one glass of the coppery liquor to Jeremy placing it gently in his open hand. He brought it to his face and it smelled of carnations, baked clay, and concentrated Spanish sunshine.

"Cute as chickadees, chirpy," she said. "Provincial, but they know what they want. An officer's wedding ring and passage out. Little do they know. Trading one lonely burg for another. Worse, possibly. Gibraltar, Port Royal, or down the lake to Little York maybe."

She returned to the armchair with the other glass and descended with a sigh.

"And you see him once or twice a year, spending the rest of your time with garrison wives."

"Well, I'm no officer, so I suppose that puts me out of danger."

"Peregrine says you have all the makings."

"It's decent of him to say so," Jeremy hesitated. "And doubly gratifying because he so carefully measures his words."

"He's fond of you. And you him. I can tell."

"I'm very grateful to be billeted with you and Major Stokes. At least until the *St. Lawrence* returns."

"Please. Not so formal. You have permission to speak freely between these four walls, especially when Perry is away. It's just we two."

"Thank you ma'am."

"Lenore."

"Lenore."

"You love him the way so many other young, devout men have before you; the way a philosopher loves a principle. The way I love him."

He looked up and frowned. She stared at his lap where his right hand lunged and swept and fluttered at his left like a bird, displaying.

"Jeremy...,"

"Yes, Lenore?"

She smiled and paused, shaking her head.

"Where did you learn to sew so well?"

"Every sailor must know it."

Jeremy recalled how, aboard the *Lancer*, he had traded for the sewing kit. Splinter stitched fabric as well as he read books and he agreed to give up the collection of needles, threads, and thimbles in exchange for free mending.

"Almost every sailor," he added.

"I doubt Perry does. He always has a bale of rags for Abigail when he returns."

"You'd be surprised."

"I've seen some of the tatty pantaloons you tars wear, flapped and jagged and perforated. But you're more able seamstress than able seaman."

Jeremy laughed.

"My mother taught me. I'm the youngest of three boys, plus my cousin Merit and his brother, and my dad. By the time I arrived, she needed help with all the darning. At first, I resented it, wishing I could go fishing or play ball. But I grew to love it. It's contemplative. A balm."

"My mother forbade me," Lenore said. "That's what the helps are for, she said. I was to learn to play piano, to become fluent in the arts of conversation, to laugh graciously at men's jokes."

"I suppose if I'd been a daughter…"

"She raised you well, that's clear. What's her name?"

"Alice."

"Alice must be a fine woman."

"She is," Jeremy agreed.

"You miss her."

"Very much."

"Perhaps I'll get to meet her one day."

"I wasn't able to say goodbye. She doesn't know where I am."

"It's a barbaric practice, impressment."

"Aye, 'tis."

Jeremy's hands slowed their frantic dance. Lenore drank the last of her schooner.

"Done," he said, tying off the thread and reversing the pant leg so it was no longer inside out. He held them up.

"Bravo," she said, "you'll have steady work as a bespoke tailor when this wretched war is over."

"What I miss most are my knitting needles. I haven't done any knitting since we were pressed."

Lenore stood abruptly and went to her bedroom. When she returned, a minute later, she dropped a large canvas bag at Jeremy's feet. She refilled his schooner and then her own and retook her seat. Made warm by the sherry and the fire, she no longer wore her shawl.

"A wedding gift from my mother-in-law. A demonstration of how well she knows me. Open it."

Jeremy opened the broad opening of the bag to scores of hanks and skeins of fine Saxon Merino wool, of every possible colour. Jabbed into the balls of yarn were pairs of needles, straight, cable, and circular, of every weight, diameter and taper.

"It's Macarthur wool, all the way from New South Wales in Australia. The place is infested with sheep, apparently."

Jeremy looked across at her, his face illuminated, not just from the sherry and lamplight but as though it really was Christmas morning.

"Go ahead," she cried, playfully, "it's all yours. I have no use for it."

"Winter's coming," he said.

She looked back out the window.

"Already here."

"What do you need? Warm socks? Toque? How about a cardigan? Let me knit you something."

"You're lovely."

"I'm serious. Name the article."

"Oh, fine then, a sock."

The sherry percolated and they both felt a giddy warmth seeping through.

"A single sock?"

"Make it a big one," she said, holding her hands up opposite each other.

"I'll start with a scarf," he said, laughing. "Something basic. To remember how it's done."

He dove eagerly into the bag, fishing twists of yarn from it, holding them to his face, running his hands up and down their spun lengths. Lenore watched with delight.

"These," he said, choosing two skeins, one royal blue and the other corn-silk. He held them up and she nodded. He yanked pairs of needles from their woolen sheaths and tested them, balancing them on his fingers, looking down their lengths judging their truth, like a duelist measuring a shank of Toledo steel. Finally, he spied two shafts of flawless ivory with golden inlay and just the right heft. He pulled them from their hank like Arthur releasing Excalibur and he hoisted them triumphantly above his head.

Lenore laughed and clapped. She watched as he wound the wool round the delicate wands that looked like matchsticks in his fists, measuring out the casts, and it was her turn to be mesmerized. His hands, parts of him that in other circumstances, she imagined, could crush a nut, a neck, a bottle, just by squeezing, were engaged now in a ballet of such grace she could scarcely credit it. The batons, glinting in the light of the Argand lamps, leapt and pirouetted. They came together urgently and rhythmically, grazing each other, again and again. With each meeting they snicked; the sound of a noisy kiss. They met and curled, swept and entwined and in the time it took to look again, something else had materialized: a length of patterned fabric, produce of their coupling, straight and symmetrical and fine, surpassing its progenitors, taking shape and growing with each contact. Something from nothing. Repudiation of the ancients, of Parmenides, of common sense. She forced her eyes from his hands and studied the whole of him. This David rising up from the end of her chesterfield, his face lowered, rapt at the magic at work in his lap, was, at once, both a boy and a god, and she didn't know whether she wanted to cradle him or bed him.

Jeremy cast and looped and purled. The glass, the sherry, Lenore; they all began to recede until nothing existed beyond pins and yarn. He loved this singular act of creation – bringing together millions of otherwise inconsequential fibres, not much more than motes of dust, spun into thread, knitted into something so much stronger than their parts. It was, in every literal sense, divine. He inhaled deeply of the mild, lanolin must. His fingers arched, teasing the wool, testing its elasticity, and he rolled the shaft of the needle between his thumb and finger mid-stitch and noted with satisfaction the appropriateness of the diameter to the desired gauge. The wool rubbed against the tapered end of the needle and sent minute vibrations down its length. He'd never knitted with ivory before. It didn't clutch as well as wood, but it wasn't as slick as steel. Ideal for a good, fast garter. It had been so long; he was hesitant at first, slightly awkward, but he warmed, adjusted to the needle's grip, and soon hit a steady pace, with no stitches dropped. At this rate, it wouldn't be long before he could bind off.

"Jeremy."

Lenore broke the spell a second time. He raised his eyes and looked at her as if she'd just been lowered into the room on a wire. The needles in his hands continued their congress.

"Would you teach me?"

He stared, not understanding the question, forgetting for a moment who she was.

"Yes," he said after a moment, remembering. "Yes, of course. I'd be delighted."

He stood, crossed the room, and placed the knitting in her lap, kneeling before her. She looked down at him and he returned her smile.

"This one is most straightforward," he said. "I've stitched and purled, but we can just stitch, it's easiest. Hold the yarn in your right hand, that's it. Hold this needle, the one with the stitches on it, in your left. Make sure you keep the tip pointing to the right. That first stitch shouldn't be further than a thumb's width from the end. Good. Take the tip of the empty one, the one on the right and slide it into that loop of the first stitch on the other one. No, no, not that one."

Lenore cast her eyes and tilted her head. Only her brows were knitted.

"Not to worry, we can start again," he laughed, "it takes time and practice."

"I hope you're a patient teacher," she said, waggling her free fingers. "These hands haven't seen much employment, besides holding cards, poking out sonatas, pouring from bottles of Amontillado, and, other such things."

"It's difficult to show you in reverse like this."

"Maybe you could come around?"

"Let me try."

Jeremy got to his feet and stepped behind the armchair. He leant over and placed his hands over hers, frozen as they were at the precipice of committing their first stitch. She hadn't exaggerated: they were the softest he'd ever touched, unblemished by chafing, calluses, or the etching of soap lye. Each slender finger was elegant in its own right; indistinguishable from the impeccably crafted strands of ivory and gold they so artlessly held. They were cool and pliant and he was surprised at his desire to clasp them. He'd forgotten the needles. His chin brushed against the Apollo's knots spilling from her forehead. His gaze tumbled down the slope of her upturned nose, into the lush valley below, its extent barely bounded by the square hem of her neckline. Entanglements of lavender and jasmine caught in the thermal updraughts filled his nostrils and made him light-headed. He felt like he could let go and descend the zephyr gently, like a late Autumn leaf, zig-zagging into warm, scented oblivion.

Keys rattled the door.

Jeremy stood at attention, as though on parade. He marched back to the chesterfield and reached it just as Stokes bustled through the door. Jeremy's cheeks were rosier than the major's.

"Jeremy's been teaching me to knit," Lenore said, girlishly.

"Ah yes," Stokes said absently as he removed his boots and fearnought. "At ease, Castor."

"Yes sir," Jeremy said, re-taking his place on the chesterfield. "I've mended my trousers."

"Very good. Drilling on the square first thing tomorrow morning."

"Yes sir."

"A glass of sherry, dear?" Lenore asked.

"Not tonight I'm afraid. I'm shattered. Busy day tomorrow. I think I may just turn in."

"Yes, of course."

"You as well Castor."

"Yes sir."

"But we've just started my lesson."

"Lenore."

Jeremy stepped to the spare room.

"Lenore," Stokes said again, now at the bedroom doorway. "I'm sorry about tonight. The commander kept me for hours. And then Spafford joined us. Tomorrow night. Or, the next. I promise."

Lenore smiled and nodded and held the burgeoning scarf to her bare neck.

~ ~ ~

The wind ceased and the sleet became snow. Damp lashes tumbling from the grey above were so heavy they looked as though they might make a sound when they touched down. They accumulated on heads and shoulders, slowly disintegrated, and soaked through. For a moment, Jeremy was reminded of the deck of the *Lancer*, when it snowed and everyone, from cabin boy to ship's mate, frolicked, threw snowballs, and shared an hour of unadulterated joy.

Marines and sailors were formed up on the decks of the *St. Lawrence* and the other ships in port. The Canadian Fencibles, garrison soldiers, and members of other regiments were arrayed along the shore. Beyond them, half the town, many of them idlers, others lured from their duties by the promise of spectacle. Only the drummer boy's lento beat could be heard; all else was baffled by the snow.

The Commodore came through first, on his bay, eyes straight, unsmiling. He was followed by a quartet of provosts on foot. Behind them, Mississauga braves, in their furs and deerskins, holding aloft their trophy. One of them limped. Beneath his fur cap, his face was swollen and purple ringed one of his eyes, the other was patched. Jeremy recognized him as the man they had rescued from Biscuit, two nights earlier.

"Sing," Stokes said, as the cavalcade neared, "you men of the *Lancer*."

The major began to sing *Heart of Oak*. Jeremy heard Augie's *Liberty Song* in his head.

"Mr. Castor, lend us your baritone," Stokes thundered.

Jeremy looked across at Merit. His cousin stared at the shoreline, once perfectly white, churned to mire from boots and hooves. His lips were fixed and his face was wet. Jeremy began to sing and soon most of the Lancers and some of the Fencibles joined in. Their chorus was out of tune, discordant, muted by the snow. They lacked Augustus Gardiner's accompaniment.

The pole went up in front of the barracks. From his horse, the Commodore addressed the rank and file, but Jeremy didn't hear a word. He looked at Augie's head on the pike and he tried, unsuccessfully, to reconcile the wrongness of it, to make sense of the incongruity. His friend, the closest friend he'd made aboard ship, perhaps his closest ever, had an expression full of light, animation, and eager smiles, regardless of what troubles they had faced. His head, with its nest of dark whorls, was attached to a well-proportioned body boasting fine limbs and athletic grace. He loved to dance.

The protuberance at the top of the pole was something else. It was made fast yet disconnected. It was sallow and tinged blue. The mouth grimaced with teeth permanently bared. The nose was flat and blood caked the thin moustache. The dull eyes wandered. Blood blackened the fringe of the neck and the shaft of the pike. The hair, normally kept so neatly parted, was flattened on one side, in disarray on the other. It had lost its curl.

"Traitor!" someone cried, and a snowball, speckled liberally with the mire of the street, struck Augie's forehead and shattered.

The Commodore said a few more words about duty and loyalty and then dismissed the assembly for the afternoon, ordering everyone to disperse.

"I'm going to get drunk," Finn said to Jeremy, by way of invitation. Jeremy stared across at his cousin staring at Augie's battered face as he was jostled by those around him.

"Nearest tavern," Finn said. "The Royce?"

"You go ahead," Jeremy said, "we'll catch up."

He crossed the deck and put his arm around Merit. Merit looked up at him, his eyes saturated.

"It aint' right Jem," he said.

"I know it."

"They done wrong by him."

"'Tis true. By God, I wish he hadn't run."

"I loved him," Merit said, and he began to sob. Jeremy hugged him to his fearnought, staring away the gawkers.

"I know, Mer, I did too."

"I really loved him."

"Come on, let's get out of here. Let's go for a walk, clear our heads. Remember Augustus how we knew him, not like this."

Merit nodded and Jeremy led him from Barrack Street up Store Street. They walked silently through town, block after block, past Walker's and the White Bear and the Black Bull and the Old King's Head. The snow continued to fall. All they could hear were their own footsteps. Soon, they were past Mother Cook's and they were on the outskirts. They might have kept walking, past the Violin, Bottle, and Glass, Badgley's and Metcalf's, and Olcott's, one of the new stops on the stagecoach's route, until they found themselves on the Kingston Road, winding it's lonely way through the dense forest along the Bay of Quinte, to Adolphustown, across the water to Prince Edward Country and onward finally to York. And then? Maybe they could just keep walking.

"Mr. Castor?" Someone was calling Jeremy from the doorway of a nearby cottage. "Excuse me, Mr. Castor?"

Jeremy was nudged from his reverie and he turned to the voice. He recognized the older man in the doorway but he couldn't place him. He had a buff waistcoat and a white cravat. His sideburns were long and he had a Brutus cut, with his grey hair brushed forward. Jeremy had seen him two nights earlier at the Bottle and Glass, introduced by Augustus, just before he had jumped to the table and recited Thomas Paine.

"Doctor Scriven," the man said, extending his hand. "Please, come in a minute, the both of you."

"We're not really...," Jeremy said.

"I know what happened today. I'm sorry for your loss."

Jeremy nodded.

"Please, let me buy you both a drink," the doctor said.

They entered the pub and Jeremy followed. Dr. Scriven waved at the bartender and raised four fingers and led them to a rough oak table in the corner.

They regarded each other and the interior of the non-descript cottage. Old Sam's was similar to the Royce in size, appearance, and clientele. It was rustic, not much more than two rooms in the front, joined by a sliding door, a bar and a wood stove. No food was served. The patrons were tinkers and waggoners, cobblers and staymakers; all labourers. Unlike the proletarian Royce, there was a din to the place, as the groups of men shouted and argued.

Old Sam arrived with a tray and three earthenware mugs, each spouting a column of steam.

"They make a superlative toddy here," Scriven said, as he sipped from his mug. "Perfect for a day like today. Drink some life back into you."

Jeremy tested the heat of the brew with his bottom lip. The fragrance of cloves and honey and brandy cleared his nose. He puffed at the vapour and swigged.

"He was a good man," Scriven said,

"You hardly knew him," Jeremy said.

"We talked a great deal Saturday night."

"We spent every day together for six months, crammed into a crate, barely afloat."

"You get to know someone that way too, I wager."

"I can confirm it."

"He spoke a lot about you Saturday night. Said you were a Tom Paine acolyte."

"We was mates," Merit said.

"I think I may have been the last to see him," Scriven replied.

Jeremy frowned.

"I thought you saw him last," he said to Merit.

"I thought so too. After the King's Arms, he said he was going for a final night cap. I went back to Walker's."

"He came here, to Old Sam's, that's where I saw him last," Scriven said. "One more for the road he said. And he was off."

"Did he tell you he was deserting?" Jeremy asked.

"Yes."

"Why didn't you dissuade him? Tell him to sleep it off?"

"Why would I? He had every right to desert."

Jeremy was quiet. He drank his toddy and eyed the smiling doctor. He wondered if he had in fact encouraged Augie.

"That's a matter of dispute," Jeremy said, "but either way, he was in no shape."

"I'll grant you that, he'd have done better if he'd sobered. I think he felt there wasn't time. It was his best opportunity."

Jeremy regarded him again. There was something about the man's tone that irritated him. He sat there in his smug attire, the uniform of the elegant extracts, the established order, and pronounced on the rights of man as if he were above it all.

"You're right, I wish he'd waited," Scriven added, as if reading Jeremy's thoughts.

Jeremy recalled Augustus talking on the *Lancer* about how he would bolt the moment his feet touched dry land. How he had said his "farewells" at the Bottle and Glass. How he hadn't heard Merit's insistent *Augie's missing*. He began to feel the weight of his own responsibility and was doubly irritated.

"I'll be going," he said, standing, "thank you for your hospitality."

"Jeremy," Scriven said, "you needn't run. Tell me more about Augustus."

"Mer?" Jeremy asked.

"I'll stay awhile," Merit said, as he gripped his mug and stared into it.

"Please come again," Scriven said to Jeremy's back. "The Headstrong Club meets here every Wednesday evening and we discuss the latest pamphlets. We have lectures on Voltaire, Jefferson, Cobbett. And Paine, of course."

Scriven cupped the side of his mouth with his hand.

"This week one of our members is bringing in Robert Gourlay's latest," he shouted.

Jeremy was already out the door.

~ ~ ~

He stood just past the threshold, snow melting from the black thatch of his head, to the eaves of his coat shoulders, to the jute carpet below. His lowered face stared at his boots, his right foot pointed inward. He looked as though he'd been caught poaching.

"Tea is hot," Lenore said, gesturing inside to the chesterfield. "And I've brought out the yarn."

Jeremy looked at the rainbow of wool arcing the low coffee table. Fragrant bohea filled and agitated his senses, already raw. He pushed his tongue against the point of one of his incisors and nodded.

"I thought you might teach me some more," she said, eager to fill the heavy silence, sensing his unease. "I tried another stitch, but it was nothing doing, all pinkies and toes. I didn't want to ruin what we've started. And I need a good scarf. Afterall," she said, looking toward the window, "it's miserable out there."

Jeremy looked out the window.

"Isn't it?" she asked, tilting her head.

He nodded again.

"I'll need something doughty, something that can stand the weather. I need you. To help me knit it."

"Terrible," she continued, when he still hadn't spoken or moved, "I'm prattling and you're standing there wet as an otter. Come," she said, pulling at the lapel of his fearnought, "let me take your coat. You'll want to warm yourself by the stove."

She peeled the burdened overcoat from his shoulders and hung it on a cast iron hook on the back of the door.

"You're very kind," he said, finally.

She put her hand on the camber of his upper arm. He turned slowly and looked directly into the balm of her coppery eyes.

"I heard what happened today," she said quietly, "Eliza told me all about it. Too much really, more than I needed to know. She loves to share detail, particularly if it is news to me."

Jeremy's eyes were burning and despite every effort he couldn't prevent the quiver undermining his chin. He had to look away, to refuse her obliging gaze. He looked up and studied the stylized lilies of the crown moulding. An image of Augie's misshapen face appeared, disembodied and hoisted, striated with snow and manure.

"Sweetheart," she said, steadying the tremors at his cheek with her perfumed palm. "It's horrid. I'm so sorry."

He swiveled slowly, still averting his blurring gaze. She took his other elbow and put his arm around her back. He wrapped himself around her.

"He was a beautiful boy," Jeremy shuddered, "they brought his head, left his body. They defiled him."

Jeremy let the year's torments howl from him. The storm was as brief as it was violent and it soon subsided into shallower breath. His body became lax and lank. They maintained their embrace for several minutes. An observer would say that he encompassed her; they both knew it was she who held him.

"Castor," Stokes said, as he came through the door.

"Sir!" Jeremy cried, bolting upright, taking a giant step back. He wiped at his eyes with the backs of his hands. The major stared at him with a look of contempt and disappointment. Jeremy had seen that look before, aboard the *Lancer*, leveled at a seaman, drunk, asleep at the watch. It had never been directed his way.

"You've been re-assigned," Stokes said. "Spafford's servant. Report to him, nine am, King's Arms."

"Yes sir," Jeremy said, continuing to back way, bowing, "my apologies sir. I was just retiring for the night."

Jeremy continued all the way to the guest room.

Stokes said nothing. Lenore glowered at him as he took his cap from his head and smacked it against the heel of his hand, knocking it clean of snow. He hung it on one of the wooden pegs along the wall by the door. She watched him take off his overcoat and slap its length and hang it next to the cap. Returning her stare, he kicked his boots against the door jamb and placed them side by side on the mat.

"You killed the Gardiner boy," she said.

"Lenore," he said, as he entered the sitting room. He crossed to the armoire and poured himself a schooner of sherry before returning to the chesterfield. He held open one end of the canvas bag and brushed the yarn array into it, a bramble of tangles and pins. As he did, he dropped a stitch on the budding scarf.

"Knitting?" he asked, putting his socked feet on the table, holes showing through the wool at both heels. "It softens him. And you can't. Never could. Leave it for Abigail."

In that moment, with breathless clarity, she realized something essential about her husband. Peregrine Stokes was a model marine. He could puncture hulls and shatter masts with nine pound shot. He could perforate bodies and scatter limbs with canister. He could lead a platoon of boys up a jagged escarpment through leaden enfilades, not hesitating to look back to see where they fell.

He can destroy, she thought. He can't create.

17

Tête-du-Pont
– Officer's Quarters

The previous year, Commodore James Yeo, master shipwright William Bell, and a squadron of toppers and fellers had gathered around an immense white pine near Loughborough Lake. They hadn't needed to hack through the bush to reach it. Its canopy was so lofty the other trees could not compete. Only a coterie of bowing saplings and quaking aspens circled its base. Looking back toward Kingston, Yeo could see a swath of fallen timber a mile-wide. Thinking always in terms of bayonets and broadsides he couldn't help but see a defeated army, fighting for their general to the last. He shaded his eyes with his hand and looked up the trunk, as smooth and straight as the barrel of a carronade. The pine's first branches gestured across the valley of toppled trees, as though ordering a last-ditch defensive maneuver, aloof to the threat at its foot. Yeo thought, for a moment, he should offer parole.

"You'll not find a tree like that in all Europe," Yeo said to Bell as they appraised the giant.

"Aye, I warrant. Finer candidate for a main I'll never see."

"God bless England that she can call upon such resources."

"No knot nor whorl nor even twig for at least one hundred feet."

"There's an entire navy in these woods."

"As though 'twas born a titan and never once was a seedling. Fated for service in a flagship."

The men stood another minute contemplating the pine.

"Cut it," Yeo said, finally, before marching back down the hill toward Fort Frederick.

Yeo arrived in Kingston in the spring of 1813. He brought with him approval to build another warship, one in line with the largest of the American ships, something that could match the 58 gun frigate *USS Superior* that blockaded Kingston through the summer of 1814. He ordered his shipwrights to draw up plans that doubled the size of the approved ship. The result comprised nearly six thousand trees, an acre of oak for every cannon, and several massive pines for the masts. *HMS St. Lawrence*, a first-rate, 104-gun warship, launched on Sept. 10, 1814, the first and only ship of the line to sail the great lakes. On her maiden voyage to the Niagara River, a month later, she was struck by lightning. It was the only time she would take fire. On her return trip to Kingston all American ships stayed close to harbour and the cover of their shore batteries.

~ ~ ~

Merit lingered by the main mast, taking a moment to size up the full extent of the Olympian column rising seventy feet from deck to sky. Men rushed on every side. They carried oakum and hot pitch, coiled and uncoiled lines, scraped the quarterdeck, and clambered the rigging. On *St. Lawrence*, a floating castle with the lake for a moat, he was only one of eight hundred and thirty. Despite this, or because of it, he couldn't help admiring the ship's immensity, its overwhelming brawn, its confident slouch in the water as it took up the entire length of the quay. He looked up through the acres of canvas and leagues of hemp above his head and longed to dance through the lines like a spider through a web.

He struck his knuckles against the mast's rough arc, hoping the resulting pain might remind him of his hatred for the Navy. His hand came away sticky. He looked at the scuff marks and noticed they were spotted with resin. Rubbing his palm along the mast, he found it oozing sap. Looking down to where the timber penetrated the deck all the way to the keel, he could see remnants of bark and green cambium all around its circumference. He looked up, half expecting to see needles and branches. Below, he imagined the tree's roots intact, spreading across the full expanse of the orlop deck, like long, tentative toes searching in vain for dry land. *St. Lawrence* was burly and thickset, hastily dressed.

"You," shouted a midshipman, pouring his orders directly into Merit's ear. "Ain't no sight-seein' jaunt. Take the oakum below."

Merit hoisted his wooden bucket, descended the scuttle and navigated the warren of decks below, pushing past knots of cooks and canvas-workers, coopers and carpenters, until he reached the hold. The oak planking, young and unscuffed, gripped at the soles of his boots. The hold was filled with barrels and crates, cylinders of hemp rope, stacks of folded sail, pyramids of heavy iron shot. Merit brought his load of oakum to the hull where ordinaries were chinking seams. He noticed a contraption next to the chinkers, something he didn't recognize. It consisted of barrels and spiraled glass tubes and large glass alembics.

"What's the mechanism?" he asked the sailor closest to him.

The sailor paused and turned.

"Oh. Fancy somethin'. Desellator, desistor, or some such."

"Desalinator bosun said," his mate said.

"Aye, that's it. Makes salt water fresh, they says."

"Comes all th' way from Southhampton. Hundreds of pounds dear."

Merit looked at the machine, to the men, and back to the machine.

"We're on a lake. Fresh water all around. 'Tis what you're chinking out."

The two sailors shrugged and continued their work.

"Bloody typical ain't it," Merit said. "Admirals. Port-stewed with sponge for brains. Can't pay the lifeblood more than a shilling day, but will drown a hundred pounds on swank apparatus we can't use. Next, they'll give us inward-shooting cannon. Cretins."

"I'd like to think you misspoke Mr. Davey."

The new voice, hoarse and raspy, as though someone had their hands around the speaker's throat, came from behind a stack of barrels.

"But we both know that to be false."

Biscuit limped from behind the barrels, swinging his splinted knee forward, leaning on the cane in his right hand. A strained whisper had replaced his stentorian boom. The ordinaries stopped their chinking, excited to know what punishment the press master might inflict on the topsman who'd brought them oakum.

"Consistent lack of respect for superiors and colleagues. Same on *Lancer*. Seditious, republican, mutinous, trouble-making talk. I'll have you up on charges, Mr. Davey."

"Biscuit," Merit said, his hands raised. "Be reasonable, 'twas just idle chatter. I meant nothing by it."

"These lads heard you."

The sailors nodded.

"Come with me, Mr. Davey. I've a pair of iron garters for you."

"Biscuit," Merit pleaded.

The press master struck him hard against the back of the head with his cane.

"Sir!" Merit cried, cowering. "Sir, please, forgive my error."

Biscuit grabbed Merit's ear lobe in his fist and yanked it to his mouth.

"I heard you Davey," he breathed, filling Merit's ear with heat and moisture. "'Twas you that near crippled me, near muted me. I heard you."

"'Twasn't me."

"I'll repay you with interest, count on it."

"I swear it, it was…" He stopped before calling his cousin's name. "'Twasn't me."

Biscuit flung Merit's head away from him in disgust.

"Save your squawking for the cat. March for the upper deck and we'll get you fitted for bilboes."

Merit slumped toward the scuttle, rubbing the side of his head. Biscuit's cane split his ear.

"Double quick," he said, "or I'll beat you to powder right here on the orlop."

~ ~ ~

Lake ice stretched from Point Frederick across Navy Bay to Point Henry and beyond to Garden and Wolfe islands.

"Never mind the fleet. Brother Jonathan will just march over from Sackett's," the Commodore said.

"'It will be so cold he won't bear to leave his hearth," Major Stokes replied.

The first day of 1815 was achingly cold but, mercifully, windless. Celebrants were wrapped in many layers of wools and furs, mittens and toques. Even the horses were clad in brightly-coloured blankets and hoods. All morning the bay had grumbled as the ice tightened and thickened. It groaned like some colossal hawser tethering the fort to the city as the freeze pushed them apart.

Jeremy held the reins lightly in his hands. He'd never been mistaken for an equestrian. He'd driven horses before, back in Cornwall, from a hay cart, never a sleigh. Spafford had asked him if he would drive his sleigh in the annual New Year's Day sleigh race. "I'm too old for that nonsense," he had said, "but Mrs. Spafford might like it. And it will give me a chance to show her off."

Farriers had fitted the horses with special single-picked shoes. Each sleigh represented different regiments or ship's companies and sported their colours and emblems accordingly. The course ran north of the city, along the shoreline, out on to the bay and back in a large oval. Townsfolk and country folk, officers and enlisted men lined the route, cheering, wagering, sipping from flasks. Jeremy and Amelia were bundled into the front of Spafford's sleigh, beneath a pair of buffalo robes to keep them warm. He focused on staying the course and allowing the mare her own pace through the snow and ice. They brought up the rear of the seven sleighs.

"You drive as well as you sail, Mr. Castor," Major Stokes said, without turning, as his sleigh, bearing the colours of the marine regiment, slid past.

Lenore, peeking out from an envelope of fur next to him, looked over and smiled.

"Mrs. Spafford," she said.

The other teams were almost out of sight. As Jeremy's sleigh shushed by, the crowd's applause faded and spectators made their way to the finish line to see which of the contenders would triumph. To someone of a competitive nature it would have been galling to garner so little interest. But to Jeremy and Amelia it was exhilarating. The louche shouts and bloodshot stares receded steadily until, picking their way through a trail in the forest, they were alone. Only the sibilance of the sleigh runners could be heard. Snow muted the mare's clopping. Chickadees chased each other through the thickets of cedar. Maple smoke from a nearby wood stove hung sweetly in the air. His ears stung and his eyes watered, his nose ran and his toes ached, but Jeremy was again surprised at his happiness. Forgetting the race, he let the mare slow from a trot to a walk.

Jeremy nearly dropped the reins when he felt the outside of Amelia's skirted thigh touch his own. He swiveled his knee away. It could have been accidental. It seemed to linger. They drifted another twenty yards and Jeremy regained his breath. Tentatively, beneath the buffalo robe, he brought his thigh back, until they were once again touching. They kept their legs perfectly parallel, with just the slightest pressure between them, each of them gently pushing outwards. Neither of them took their eyes from the path ahead.

Minutes later they emerged from the woods, coasted down a slight embankment, and were out on the ice. The sleigh sped up, pushed the mare, and she began to trot again. Steam now rose from her flanks, curled out from the edges of the blanket, dampened with the sweat of her exertions. The cooler air above the bay slapped at their faces as they picked up speed and they once again saw and heard the crowd in the distance. Jeremy felt Amelia's petite, mittened hand squeeze his leg, just above the knee.

"Mr. Castor," she said, her voice barely audible over the sound of the sleigh's runners. "I'm glad you agreed to drive for Mr. Spafford."

Jeremy's face was frozen. He kept his eyes on the trail.

"And," she continued, "I'm glad you agreed to take this position."

The hooves of the horses thumped at the skin of ice stretching across the bay as though it was the head of a side drum. Tympani rolled from shore to shore as though beating out a quick march, vibrating into the numb feet of the spectators. The tremors infiltrated the frame of the sleigh, jangled the seat, and thudded Jeremy's ribcage.

"Me too," he said. He slowed the mare to a walk again and held the reins in his left hand. He plunged his right hand beneath the buffalo robe and put it over hers. He turned to face her. "Please call me Jeremy."

"Jeremy," she said and smiled.

He turned back to the track. They were on a stretch where the wind had pushed the snow aside and the mare stumbled slightly on the bare ice. The crowd was still a hundred yards ahead. He watched carefully to make sure she wasn't going too fast.

They passed over a body, stuck just below the surface of the ice, like a specimen in a display case, hands upraised, bronze coat buttons glinting. It was headless.

"Mollath Dew," Jeremy said, jerking his hand from under the robe to grip the reins again. "Did you see that?" he asked, looking to the side and back where from they had come.

"No," Amelia said, startled. "What was it?"

Jeremy looked again but they were well past. Now he wasn't sure.

"What?" Amelia asked again, her grip insistent on his knee. "What is it?"

"Nothing," Jeremy said, "eyes playing tricks."

They continued along the course, Jeremy flicking the reins now to pick up the pace. In the face of the onlookers; past the laughing urchins throwing snow, the ruddy matrons waving their scarves, the shouting tradesmen already drunk at midday, the mocking farmers who, blindfolded, could drive a better sleigh, the stony faces of Finn and Lilac, Neven and Merit, glaring up at them from the enlisted mob, past the waiting Stokes, proud Spafford bragging to Cartwright; in the face of them all, safe in its warm pocket beneath the robe, Amelia's hand never left Jeremy's.

~ ~ ~

The officer's common area at the Tête-du-Pont barracks could have been mistaken for a hunting lodge. Lieutenant Cochrane and his committee had gone to great lengths to adorn it, to make it fit for the ladies, with yards of bunting, freshly cut wreaths of fir and cedar, and the regimental silver and trophies arrayed conspicuously along the head table.

Cochrane himself mixed the first round of juleps in the silver chalice. He'd managed to muster a small brigade of receptacles in which to serve them. He kept the best glasses, the elite troops, along the flanks. There was some cut crystal, mostly lead glass; elegant bowls with air twist stems. These were kept back for the Commodore, the Brigadier-General, the Colonels, the Majors, and their wives. The balusters, tumblers, and rummers, made of cloudy soda glass, the brigade's mainstay, the chipped and scuffed infantrymen, these went to the lieutenants, captains, and ensigns. The disparate earthware and porcelain reserves, trained for other duties, pressed into service out of desperation, those were for everyone else.

"Vandemonia," the Commodore said as he assessed the table. "This is the motliest parade of irregulars I've ever laid eyes on."

"Aye, 'tis," Cochrane replied. "My apologies sir, tis all we could rustle from the ranks. We've lost more than a few over the year. Heavy casualties Christmas Eve in particular."

"We need reinforcements. You've spoken to quartermaster?"

"Aye. Many times. They're dear, he says. Just one supplier in town and he just raised his prices."

"Who has the contract?"

"Colonel Spafford."

"The old gouger. Who's side is he on anyway?"

Cochrane began to ladle juleps into the waiting vessels.

"It's unacceptable," the Commodore continued. "How can we defeat the Yanks if we can't even field enough glasses for a New Year's fête?"

"It hardly projects a position of strength, sir."

"Precisely what I'm saying."

Cochrane handed the Commodore a graceful cordial glass with a long, twirled stem, the regiment's motto engraved on one side, their coat of arms on the other. Inside, shards of ice and a liquid the colour of winter sunset, sprigged with spearmint.

"Why do we always have an iced drink on this glacial, first day of the year? Why not something mulled? Something hot?"

"We have plenty of ice," Cochrane said, shrugging.

"I'll talk to Spafford. Appeal to his love of king and country. Who's the pilchard in scarlet standing next to him?"

"Corporal Jeremy Castor, I believe it is."

"Corporal? Since when do we admit rankers?"

"Spafford's guest. His new servant."

"Oh yes, that's right. What does he need a servant for? He's on half-pay."

Cochrane continued with his ladling until the chalice was empty. Other members of the committee had ushered over important guests and all the glass had been distributed. Cochrane opened another bottle of cognac and began to mix the next batch.

"Good show Cochrane," the Commodore said, sipping his cordial, moving away, "carry on."

When everyone had a julep, the Commodore gave a toast. He led them in *Auld Lang's Syne* and the dancing began. An ensign started on the piano and another took up a violin. A third did the calling. The Commodore made his way toward where Spafford was sitting. He was talking to Richard Cartwright sitting on his left, smoking a pipe. Amelia sat to his right and he had his hand over her hand on her lap. She was watching the uniformed officers and the ladies in their gowns leaping into a quadrille. Jeremy towered behind them, sipping a julep from a cracked saucier.

"Happy new year Spafford, you outstrapalous warthog."

"Eh?" Spafford said. "Oh, and to you, James, you…you brindled whoreson."

Spafford turned to Amelia. "Pardon, darling," he said. She kept her gaze on the dancers.

"Noble," the Commodore said, sliding a chair over. "We need to talk business."

"Yes, of course. What kind?"

"Bottles and glass."

"Amelia, dove," Spafford said, "why don't you dance?"

Amelia ignored him.

"Look," the Commodore said, "just look at the state of the regiment's service. You can see it. Mint juleps served in teacups and wooden mugs. That fellow is making do with a cruet. Your man there," he nodded toward Jeremy, "slurps from a gravy boat."

"It's shameful, I grant."

"'Tis worse in town. You're the only supplier. Glass is scarce."

"Across the colonies, it's dear. Nothing can be done."

"Surely you can order in some shipments, from your contacts in Montreal, from your interests in England. At a price that won't cripple the war effort. You do want us to win?"

"Mr. Castor," Spafford said, "would you kindly escort Mrs. Spafford to the quadrille and stand in as her partner? I'm held captive."

Jeremy stepped out from behind the chairs and offered his elbow to Amelia. She stood and accepted and they advanced on the quadrille, waiting to join.

"Have the quartermaster see me James," Spafford said. "I'll see what we can do."

"What do you need a servant for Noble?" the Commodore asked, once Jeremy was out of earshot. "You're no longer in active service."

"You insult me James. I may not be on deck, but you know I still have duties. No man in Upper Canada cares more about whether we win or lose, of that I'm certain. I'm big enough to let the younger bucks their fair share of glory."

They watched as Jeremy and Amelia tentatively entered the fray.

"I've seen ostriches move with more grace," the Commodore said, pointing his cordial glass at Jeremy.

On the third cycle of the round, Jeremy hooked arms with Lenore Stokes.

"Canadian girls," she said, winking, before making a small balletic hop past him into the arms of the next officer.

18

Richmond Hotel
– Near Point Henry

ON NAVY BAY, TWO HOURS OF HOCKEY CONCLUDED with the picked men of the *St. Lawrence* beating the best of the *Wolfe, Prince Regent,* and *Princess Charlotte* by a score of thirty four to twelve. In the nearby Richmond Hotel, a tilting January sun lit up the shields, helmets, and crossed hurling sticks on the walls of the great room. Players peeled off sodden gear. The rafters resounded with their boasts and profanities. Spilled ale, soaked leather, and tobacco mixed with the aromas coming from Richmond's roasting pans.

Merit sat in the midst of the celebrations, rolling and re-rolling his dice on a table across from Jeremy. He looked over his shoulder, as if expecting it to be tapped.

"I got your note from the carter," Jeremy said. "What is it? I'm supposed to be helping with Spafford's move to the country house."

"Haven't long," Merit said. "'bout an hour. Neven's covering. Biscuit's back at the infirmary, laid out with headache. They'll give him Paregoric. He'll be back and more nettled."

"C'mon Mer. Can't be all that bad."

Merit brought his fist down on the table hard enough to topple his mug of Robinson's Pale.

"Abarth Dúw," Jeremy cried, standing suddenly to avoid the spill. "What's wrong with you?"

"Don't say it Jem, 'cause you don't know. No idea."

Jeremy huffed, mopped his seat with a nearby scarf, and ordered another round.

"We endured Biscuit afore," he said, as he retook his chair. "Six months."

"'Tis worse than afore."

"How worse?"

"Much, hang me! That," he pointed at the ale dripping from the table edge, "is the first brew I've had in two weeks. First refreshment other'n bread or water. I ain't hardly been out of those Goddamn upper deck shackles more than an hour or two since I saw you last, afore Christmas. Ordinaries mocking me, mates gobbing."

"What? Why? You never were in them once on the *Lancer*."

"Smallest things. Coiling halyards to the left, not the right. Stacking sailcloth six-high, not five. Trousers not creased. Hair too long. Braid too loose."

Jeremy shook his head.

"'Tis true. And every time I open me mouth."

"Keep it shut."

"Chatting with Finn, on the gun deck mind, I referred to one of the nobs as Lieutenant Lickfinger."

"Merit."

"Biscuit collared me for insubordination. Seemed to spring from a vent hole."

"But we used to sling all sorts of slop on the *Lancer*'s gun deck."

"Ain't the *Lancer* Jem," Merit said, lowering his face and his voice. "That's what I'm telling you. Captain Rowton favoured me, but I've never met this new one, don't even know his name. Just Cap'n."

They drank deeply from newly delivered drinks.

"At sea, we was busy. A whole week goes by, I don't see Biscuit.

Now I see him every minute, day or night, awake or nightmare. This *St. Lawrence*, 'tis a different soup kettle. I put one foot wrong, I muddle a P, I misplace a Q, I've got my legs in iron garters. Or, I'm scouring the quarterdeck with a hairbrush."

"You'd think in port, laid up for the winter, he'd relax."

"I can't take it any longer," Merit said quietly, into his mug.

"Surely he'll give up eventually, he'll shift his attentions to some ordinary, some landsman."

"You don't understand Jem. There's more to it."

Merit searched his cousin's face for some reminder of the awkward kid from his childhood that he knew and loved. How was it that they had changed and aged so much in such a short time?

"What? What is it?"

Merit drank again, peering into the darkness at the bottom of his mug, wishing he could dive in, swim out the other side. Or perhaps, to dive, and not to emerge.

"Jeremy..." he started, but then raised the mug again, this time to drain it.

"Jesus," Jeremy said. "How can I help if you don't level with me."

Merit motioned for another Robinson's and rubbed his face vigorously with both hands. He crossed his arms one over the other on the top of the table and looked again at Jeremy, his face red and weary.

"I've never told anyone this. Not even Alice. Dúw, what am I saying, especially Alice."

A hockey player, clad only in his one-piece unmentionable, fell into him, shoved playfully by a team-mate.

"Old chap," the man said, laughing. Jeremy hoisted him and flung him back.

"Do you remember when I was fourteen," Merit said, "and I went to serve on the *Spartan*."

"I do," Jeremy replied. "I remember pleading to go with you. I missed you terribly. Luckily, you were back within the year."

"'Tis true. Didn't you ever wonder why so soon?"

"I don't know, I was ten, didn't think about it then I guess. Does seem like a short tour." Jeremy looked to the rafters as he tried to remember. "You were honourably discharged. You went to work for Mr. Pringle on the *Pelican*, he secured your release. That's how it was told."

"I wish he had, bless him. On the *Spartan* I first met Biscuit. An ornery stoat even then. As a fellow Cornishman, he said he'd look after me, show me the ropes. Made me his own special ship's boy."

Jeremy frowned. Such an image of Biscuit could not be reconciled.

"He kept me well. Pet-like, almost. Brought me choice scraps from mess. And little gewgaws he whittled. Paid as much attention as he does today. But…, differently."

Merit leaned in and lowered his voice to a whisper, pushing the wooden tankard next to his cheek, so it was between him and the roaring players.

"Too much attention, Jeremy. Too much."

Jeremy leaned in similarly.

"I asked him to stop, to leave me alone. Seemed only to interest him more. He would run his hand through my hair, like a comb, like I was a poodle. I would push his arm away. He would bring it back, forcefully. Afore long, we was grappling."

Jeremy narrowed his eyes.

"Please, for Christ's sake, don't make me explain. He arranged it we would be alone. He let me nap in his cabin on his comfortable straw mattress. But he didn't let me nap. I slept very little."

Jeremy's unknit his brows and brought his face away from the table.

"Mollath Dew," he whispered, now stretching back in his chair.

Merit nodded and looked away, searching for the serving girl with his order. He was irretrievably parched. They said nothing for several moments until the ale arrived.

"It was intolerable," Merit said, slowly. "I didn't know what to do, where to turn. I thought I might throw myself overboard. Or, swallow a few ounces of lye and black powder."

"Oh Merit," Jeremy said. "I'm so sorry. All these years…"

Merit held up his hand.

"Now I've started, let me finish. I knew none of the nobs would believe me. So I arranged it, that the top lieutenants would visit Biscuit's cabin at an appointed time. I told them there was to be a juicy dice game or some such. Wasn't, of course. They arrived, shocked to find a game of an altogether different nature. Just Biscuit, myself, and a trio of appalled officers."

As Merit gulped at his tankard, Jeremy looked around him. Now he expected a tap on the shoulder. None of the rejoicing horde paid them any attention.

"That ended it, of course," Merit continued. "Biscuit was flogged and thrown into the brig. At the next port of call, we were disembarked. Biscuit court-martialled, sentenced to jail and hard labour in the mines. I was," he made a wry smile, "honourably discharged home to Porthleven where Mr. Pringle was good enough to hire me on. I never saw Biscuit again until he pressed us at the Rode and Shackle. I'm sorry Jeremy."

"Sorry? Why?"

"He came specifically for us. Me."

"Why didn't you tell me? Mom?"

"They made it a condition of my discharge that never a word be breathed. Appearances sake. Of course, they seemed to have forgotten all about it, enough that Rowton would recruit him again."

They drank and were quiet.

"I should get back," Merit said, finally.

"You need to be patient. There are rumours. That the war is already over."

"What good is that to me. I have no seniority, no rank. It could be years before I'm discharged."

"Spafford has promised. He's well connected, he's got the Commodore's ear. He'll get us free. Just a few more months. And home again to Cornwall."

"Jem," Merit said, reaching across the table to grip Jeremy by the wrist, hard enough to mark the skin. "He knows. He knows 'twas us that put him in the infirmary that night at the Bottle and Glass. He means to break me."

Merit released him and stood from the table.

"You should have finished it," Merit whispered hotly. "Broken his neck proper. You should have killed him."

He began to put on his jacket.

"Merit, what are you going to do? Nothing foolish."

"I can't take it," Merit said as he leaned over for the last of his ale.

Jeremy stood and came around the table to crush his cousin in an embrace.

"Christ," he breathed. "I think I saw Augustus. Frozen in the ice. Our sleigh passed right over him. Looking up out of the ice. Except not looking, because…"

He clinched Merit tighter.

"Don't run, please don't run," he said, "you're all I have."

Merit freed himself and straightened his jacket. He started to make for the exit, deking the confusion of skaters and their supporters. Jeremy followed.

"Fine words from the servant to Colonel Noble Spafford," he said over his shoulder. "You have no idea. Understand this. I can take it no longer."

"I'll go to Spafford directly, I'll press for action. Just wait."

Merit was at the door. He stopped and turned.

"I talked to that Dr. Scriven, at Old Sam's, for a long time after Augie went up the pole. We discussed how Augie went about it, where he went wrong, what could be done better. In an unjust, uncivil society, he said, it's a man's duty to disobey."

"Don't," Jeremy said, to Merit's back, as he exited into the crisp twilight. "Let me keep one promise to Mum."

~ ~ ~

Jeremy strode past the two old women sitting in the lounge of the King's Arms. Their chattering stopped and they put down their brandy-laced tea. They watched him ascend the stairs and rap on the door to Spafford's room.

"Come in," Amelia said.

Jeremy stepped in and saw her across the room, reclined on the chaise lounge, one leg propped on its arm, the other angled to the floor. On a side table next to her sat the amethyst ampoule containing the Paregoric Elixir, an earthenware jug, and a clay goblet.

"Is the Colonel not here?" he asked, pique draining from his voice.

"He went to see about the house."

Jeremy thrust his hands into his pockets and looked at his boots, unsure what to do next.

"I'm here," she said, smiling.

"Yes, of course," he said, returning the smile. "I'm sorry. I'm preoccupied."

"Sit with me and talk a while. I've had no company all morning."

She sat up and swung her leg around, wincing as she did. Jeremy now noticed the bandage at her ankle. And the bruise, above her wrist, just below her diaphanous sleeve.

"I'm fine. Clumsy, but fine. Turned my ankle, is all."

It was a hollow way that she said it, as though she'd been told it by someone else, not experienced it first-hand.

"Please," she said, "tell me. What troubles *you*."

Jeremy regarded her a moment, one hand on a book she was reading, the other on her knee. That knee that not long ago had been pressed against his own, exchanging warmth beneath the buffalo robe. He couldn't involve her in his worry. Wouldn't be fair. Or proper.

"*Please*," she insisted, leaning forward so her arms ran along her thighs and the book dangled from her slender fingers.

"What do you read?" he asked.

"Bison Harris has an enviable library of classics downstairs. All of them untouched by the biddies in the lounge. Since they refuse my society and my husband is always away, I've little else to do."

"I'm sorry to hear it. I wouldn't stay away, if I were he," Jeremy said.

Amelia smoothed the skirt of her dress.

"I'm happy for it," she said, gesturing to a cane chair next to the chaise lounge.

"Will he be back soon?"

"Not till late."

"And the biddies? Won't they talk?"

"That's all they do. Let's be generous and give them material for their embroidery."

Jeremy took the curved back of the chair and brought it around so that it was facing her. He sat in it gingerly as though it might crumble beneath him. He felt he had crossed a Rubicon.

"Would you like some cider?" She ran her hand down the side of the jug. "Please help yourself."

Jeremy poured himself a goblet.

"Have you read Plutarch," Amelia asked, "or Tacitus?"

"Some. I studied a few years with the curate in Helston. Mostly gospels. But also, some classics. Virtuous pagans."

Jeremy stole a quick glance of her entirety, comparing her in real life to his imaginings.

"I mean no offence," he said, "but I'm surprised to find you reading... those books."

"Empty-headed milk maid?"

"No, no," Jeremy said, stammering. "I meant..."

"My dad taught me to read," she said. "We weren't meant to be farmers. His father, my grand-dad, was a failed printer. In York, the original, in England. There were always books around when I was little. But when the shop failed and there was no work, dad brought us here, to farm."

"Where is your father? Your mother?"

"Dad ran away. Haven't seen mom since the wedding. In and out of gin shops, the Colonel says."

"Amelia, 'tis unkind."

"Aye, 'tis. So's the truth. I still can't believe what they have arranged for me."

"You should seek her out. So important, family."

She nodded and picked up the amethyst ampoule from the side table and rolled it in her fingers, examining it absently. Jeremy blanched.

"He doesn't need more already, does he?"

"No," she laughed. "Look, still half full. Was it so difficult to obtain?"

"Somewhat. Unusual men that procure it."

"Tell me about them," she said, sliding forward attentively.

Jeremy described his encounter with the loquacious Barnabas and the poxy scum boiler, the steam and boil of the sugar shack, the reek of body odour and turpentine. He told her about the menagerie of glass and how the scum boiler, in an earlier life, had been a master craftsman, until Spafford had put him under. How the little scarecrow had vowed to go hungry rather than manufacture anything for the Colonel. How Barnabas, with his quicksilver tongue, had convinced him otherwise, with the help of Jeremy's life savings.

Amelia was quiet several minutes as she spun the ampoule and held it to the light. Jeremy was worried he had bored her and wondered if he should leave.

"I should like to meet him one day," she said, finally.

"Who?" Jeremy asked, startled.

"The scum boiler. Our stories aren't so different."

"I couldn't imagine two more dissimilar people."

She put the ampoule back on the table and retrieved the Tacitus.

"You know," she said, leafing through the book. "I was never that interested in history before. I find this fascinating."

"Yes," Jeremy said, "ancient Rome. Emperors and gladiators and triumphs."

"Not so much that," she said, with a wave of her hand. "It's the women. I had no idea."

"Oh?"

"Power. And ambition. And brass. Have you heard of Livilla?"

"No."

"She was married to her cousin, Drusus Caesar, heir to the throne. She had him poisoned so she could be with her lover. Agrippina?"

Jeremy shook his head.

"She poisoned Claudius to make sure he was succeeded by her son Nero. Or, what about Augustus, the greatest emperor of them all. Some say Livia staged it so that he took poisoned figs, to make sure her son Tiberius became emperor instead of the emperor's adopted son Postumus."

"Augustus," Jeremy said, suddenly faraway.

"I'm sorry," Amelia said, "you distracted me and I've prattled. I was asking you about your troubles."

"Merit!" Jeremy cried, remembering. He told Amelia quickly the less prurient details of his meeting with his cousin and of Spafford's promise to intervene on their behalf.

"He'll likely be at the St. George and Dragon," she said, as Jeremy got to his feet and grabbed his coat and stepped into his boots. "I'd be wary of any promise made by Noble Spafford, but I wish you the best of luck."

As he left, she returned to Tacitus and Livia, rolling the ampoule around in her hands.

19

St. George and Dragon

SPAFFORD WAVED THE CARPENTERS AWAY when he saw Jeremy walk in the door. He thumped his tankard against the table and a gill of flip splashed from it.

"Where in blazes!" Spafford cried. "I've had to spend hours in this spider's nest, wheedling masons, prodding upholsterers, jollying joiners. Where the hell have you been?"

"I'm sorry sir," he said, "I had to meet with my cousin."

"Who?"

"My cousin, Merit. I've mentioned him. The sailor that I hope you can get discharged."

"Discharged? Look here Castor. I took you on as my servant as a favour to you, since you helped us out of that," the Colonel cleared his throat, "unpleasantness at the King's Arms. You seem like a decent, loyal chap."

"I'm grateful sir…"

"Take a chair for God's sake, you look like a beggar standing there with your cap in hand. The redlegs are staring and snickering. Have some dignity man."

Jeremy sat.

"Applejack?"

"No, thank you."

"Most wise," Spafford said, as he topped his glass. "It's atrocious. Other lads would sell their mothers to be my servant. But you have to be there when I need you. You're my agent with these rustics. That's what I pay you for."

"You haven't paid me anything, yet," Jeremy said, swallowing hard. "In fact, 'tis you that owes me six pounds, for the elixir I obtained."

"Christ's pajamas," Spafford said, pushing his hands downward, as though he was trying to tamp out a fire. "Not so loud. Discretion. Yes, six pounds, it's true. As you know, I'm not in a position to repay it just now. You should consider it an investment for future services."

"Sir, I'm sorry, but my cousin is in a bad state. He has an enemy on the *St. Lawrence* who is making life very hard. I fear he is about to bolt."

"Desert? What kind of a low mongrel is this cousin of yours?"

"Sir, please. I think he fears for his life."

"Listen to me Castor. These things take time. You, and your cousin…, you need to be patient. I'm not sure if you've noticed but there's a war on. The Commodore has more than a few distractions. I will talk to him, mark my words."

Jeremy nodded.

"In the meantime, your cousin will need to stiffen a little. And you, you're my right hand. I'll need you at Willowpath first thing tomorrow. We'll go over what's left to do. Eventually we'll have a room set aside for you. Mrs. Stokes has kindly agreed to continue billeting you until we do."

He nodded again.

"My carriage will be by at eight."

~ ~ ~

Spectators again crowded the bay on Shrove Tuesday, for football between army and navy. At noon, two massive teams arrayed themselves on the ice and spent the next few hours pummeling each other as they kicked, pitched, and carried a leather ball back and forth between the shores. The contest was followed by acres of griddled cakes and maple sugar served with tea and rum.

HMS St. Lawrence was mostly empty. Deep in the hold, two midshipmen escorted Merit to the storeroom where the pig iron and shot was stacked.

"What's he done?" asked one, over his shoulder.

"Last down from the yards," Biscuit said, his voice more air than vibration.

The men looked at each other. They knew Merit to be one of the ship's best topsmen.

"Also," Biscuit added, "absent without leave. Was seen at hockey, 'spite strict orders not to leave ship."

Merit maundered into the thong of leather gagging his mouth, shaking his head.

"And he's to be punished down here?"

"Captain's given leave to me to minister," Biscuit replied, forcing the words through his broken vocal cords. "Strap 'im to cannon."

"And what about the others? Don't you want an audience, for deterrence sake?"

Biscuit struck the man across the shoulder blades with his cane.

"Strap 'im and hold yer peace, or I'll have you in iron garters too."

The man let go of Merit, contorted, rubbing at his back.

"This isn't a formal," Biscuit whispered, "'tis a summary. A warning. Snap to."

The two midshipmen led Merit to an old cracked eighteen pounder stowed for ballast. They looked back at Biscuit.

"Kissing the gunner's daughter?" one of them asked.

"Aye."

They turned Merit so he faced the cascabel at the other end of the cannon's muzzle. They bent his trembling body at the waist, hoisted his shirt, pulled his arms down so he hugged the bore and bound his wrists underneath. His toes strained to touch the green pine of the deck.

"Trousers," Biscuit said, limping forward.

"What? Like a ship's boy? A topsman?"

Biscuit raised his cane and snarled. The two sailors moved quickly, loosening the belt at Merit's waist and yanking them to his ankles. Cast iron burned cold against the skin of his thighs. The bulb of the cascabel dug into his groin.

"Good enough," Biscuit breathed. "Dismissed. Join the match."

The two men hesitated.

"You're goin to cane 'im?" one of them asked.

"Ain't going to tickle 'im. Go. Eat pancakes."

The two midshipmen shuffled into the gloom. Biscuit followed and drew the heavy canvas partition across and fastened it to the ship's rib. He pulled it aside a crack and saw the two men still standing there, five feet away.

"Git! Or, you'll be next for flogging. And take yer lights, I got me own."

The men dissolved into the shadow and Biscuit listened to their footsteps as they crossed the hold. When he could no longer hear them, he turned back, grinning.

The ever present ache behind and above his eyes was dulled by the many doses of Paregoric he had indulged that morning. He knew this would be his opportunity; he wouldn't miss it for a migraine. He gazed at Merit, hunched absurdly over the monstrous, iron phallus, embracing it, a ball of leather in his drooling mouth. The lantern emphasized the relief of lash marks on his back. It made his shivering gooseflesh glow.

Biscuit hobbled close and brought his mouth low.

"Alone again," he whispered as he ran a hand along the barrel of the cannon.

Merit shouted imprecations through his gag. Biscuit stood and brought his cane sharply down on his buttocks. Merit emitted a strangled cry and squirmed around the diameter of the cannon. When the pain had subsided and the only movement he made was the heaving of his ribs, Biscuit leaned in again.

"I knowed it was you on the road, that done me. You fancy the red men, do ye?"

He rubbed his temple.

"One day, the steam drill scraping at the seam in my head will hit bottom and I'll no longer trouble you, nor anyone. But until then Davey, until then… each hour is borrowed and I intend to die a debtor."

His breath was hot on Merit's neck. It smelled of brandy and bitter herb.

"Uncomfortable? Chilled? Ashamed? Tell you this…"

Biscuit scuttled to the edge of the curtain. He pulled it back slightly and peered into the darkness. Nothing. He twirled.

"So's you feel less alone," he said, breathlessly, giddily, his hand at his belt. "I'll remove my mine too."

The two midshipmen lingered at the stairs to the upper decks and listened. They heard the rhythmic crack of cane on flesh and wood and iron. They heard Merit's anguished muffles. They heard something else. Something guttural. Husky ejaculations that could only be associated with pleasure.

"Biscuit," one said to the other.

"Aye. He's hard."

"'Tis true. Best keep on his right side."

They ascended the stairs, through the decks and gratefully out into the strengthening February sun, to follow the beckoning scent of batter fried in oil.

20

Olcott's Tavern

MERIT WALKED NORTH UNTIL HE FOUND MONTREAL ROAD. He joined it and continued, darting culverts, tramping brush, until he arrived at Franklin's Tavern. It was dark; barely discernible in the gloaming, not a single lit candle in any window. He longed to enter, order a bowl of stew and black bread. A tot of rum. To sit by the smouldering fire. He walked on.

Jumping the *St. Lawrence* had been relatively easy. Stars aligned, the moon agreed to look the other way. Biscuit was confined to quarters, nursing the ache in his head. Finn had the middle watch of the larboard division, next to the dock. He, Neven, and Merit pooled their rations of rum and small beer and offered them to the other members of the watch. Midway through the watch, two hours past midnight, Finn offered to look out while the others dozed or played cards. It was then, hearing Finn whistle the tune to *Heart of Oak,* Merit emerged from the scuttle, dressed as black as a Jesuit's frock, his face smeared with tar, a rucksack over his shoulder. He vaulted the gunwale and shimmied the thick, forward hawser to the pier. He paused a moment, crouched behind the squat bollard, catching his breath and then, dissolved into the moonless night.

Still, the escape was more spontaneous than he would have liked.

He'd paid little attention to what should happen next. The night after Augie's death, Merit had discussed desertion at length with Dr. Scriven at Old Sam's; the right way to go about it and the wrong. Scriven had said it was important to pre-arrange passage south, across the lake or river to New York, with one of the batteauxmen, Thibodeau perhaps, as soon as possible. Merit hadn't the opportunity to do that, trapped as he was on the *St. Lawrence*. When the situation became intolerable, he could wait no longer. He hadn't even got word to Jeremy, hadn't been able to properly say goodbye. He hoped that Finn or Neven would be able to do that for him.

Merit spat on the path's crust of snow. *Not that Jem had been listening*, he thought, *not really*.

His toes had begun to ache in the shells of his hard, unlined leather boots. Soon they would be numb. He tried to keep to the road as much as possible but even then there was a foot of snow and he was often ankle deep. On occasion, when he thought he detected another traveler: a carriage, a drunken farmer, or worse, military police, he would be forced into the bush. More than once his foot plunged through the deeper snow into the creek or marsh below, drenching it with freezing water. He thrust his raw, red hands into the pockets of his fearnought. He untied the bedroll from the top of the sack and draped it over his head and shivering shoulders.

Impenetrable darkness had been ideal for ghosting from the ship; now it was an obstacle. He found himself sprawling over deadfall, nearly blinding himself on low branches, twisting his ankles on the pits that pocked the road. He was only a few leagues out of town and already lost. His plan, improvised while he walked, was to head north a little and then east, toward Montreal, then dip down toward the river. He knew that Thibodeau and his batteaumen plied the river between Prescott and Kingston. If he could find one of their stopping points, where they refreshed themselves on brandy and pipes, perhaps he could wait for them and negotiate passage across to the American side. But without the stars or the moon to guide, Merit found himself stumbling through the countryside, not even knowing his current heading. *Completely at sea*, he thought. *If only.*

He patted at the dice in his pocket and the guineas in his purse. He stroked the eagle feather, the one his mother gave him so many years ago, hanging from the loop of leather around his neck. It's dark, it's cold, *I'm lost*, he thought, *but I'm free. Intact. 'Tis a bargain I'd make again.*

He came to a clearing; three acres of fallen trees, their stumps protruding through the snow like broken teeth. He passed the charred bones of a barn frame. There was an enormous potash kettle, overturned, with a stack of limbs scattered before it, like the remains of a giant, drawn and quartered. A burnt-out cottage stood at the edge of the clearing, most of its cedar shakes roof reduced to ash scattered across the floor. Merit shivered. He noticed two wooden chairs on the cottage's front porch and he pulled one aside and sat. *So tired*, he thought, *just five minutes.* He pulled the blanket over his body tight against his chest and looked up, into the region of the sky where Dorephus and Amelia, from the same vantage point, had tracked the harvest moon, a year and a half earlier. Merit saw nothing but void; the moon had turned its back.

The shivering wouldn't stop. He considered lighting a fire. *Homesteaders nearby, likely. Could raise suspicion. Anyway, 'twouldn't banish the chill of this place. Must keep walking.*

He walked until the road ended and then pushed further through the tangled underbrush. He began to find clothing, picking up a jacket here, a vest there. At first, he was unsettled. Then, shaking the snow from the clothes, he began to put them on, extra layers to fight the cold. It was if a scout had gone ahead, leaving cached supplies. He continued to push, stamp, and tumble his way deeper into the woods, through the lances of birch, the low, grasping cedars, the patrician pines. *If the trunks were masts and the branches lines, I could swing away.* Scraped and bloody, he arrived at the lake.

Merit followed the shore trail and found more clothes as he went, donning what he could: chemise, trousers, shoes and socks. The trail veered from the lake back into the woods, about two hundred yards. Following the limestone outcropping he tripped over an ancient musket that leaned against it. He sprawled forward, landing beneath a giant, centuries-old sugar maple. In the dim light he could just make out a half-decomposed corpse, face shattered, scalp eaten, a blanket of snow pulled to its chest, shards of white sticking through the red flannel and blackened flesh at his collar.

Merit stood and ran, back the way he came, through the woods, back to the trail, along the shore. He was made breathless again when he fell through the ice where a stream drained into the lake.

Mollath Dew. Mollath Dew.

He followed his steps, retracing and doubling back several times, eventually returning to the cottage. He scavenged kindling from the gaping structure and formed it up as a teepee in the cavity of the stove. He ripped the wool from his claw-stiffened hands, thumbs no longer opposable, and he struggled to extricate the tinderbox from his pack. His hands shook violently as he unraveled the jute into a nest and snugged a pinch of char cloth into its centre. On his knees, he struck the flint against the steel, barely able to hold it steady. On the second strike, the steel twisted from his grip and the sharp edge of the flint gouged his thumb.

Mollath Dew!

On the third strike, a spark landed in the middle of the tinder and the char cloth began to glow. Merit blew at it, gently, insistently, until it grew and spread. The jute bundle took fire and soon sprouted fluttering flames. Merit put the delicate, fleeting construction into the centre of the kindling latticework like a bird into a cage. The fire took hold and cast a warm, orange glow several feet into the murk. Merit watched carefully for a while as though, if he turned his back, it might fly from the stove. He added more sticks, judiciously larger, encouraging the blaze but fearing it might snuff itself under the weight of his expectations. Finally, he added a split log, a half cylinder of hard maple. The stove radiated a sphere of protective heat into the space and steam began to rise from the front of Merit's trousers. He retrieved a chair from the porch, put it next to the stove, and sat, head in hands.

Intact, he said to himself, repeatedly, as though it were a mantra, *and free*.

After stacking a pyramid of wood next to the stove, Merit began to peel the wet clothing from the lower half of his body. His feet were dappled red and, where the flesh had frozen, white. He cried out as the blood pressed painfully back into fingers and toes. The clothes, hung above, dripped to the hissing stovetop. He wrapped himself in the blanket and sat again in the chair.

Just an hour or two, he thought, *until the clothes are dry*.

It was that time of night, just an hour or two before dawn, when sleep is most insistent. Having been so perilously cold, Merit had pulled his chair as close to the fire as he could bear and now he was overwarm, made drowsy by the heat and the toll of the night's exertions. He pinched his arm, rubbed his face, stamped his feet. Nothing could stop the inexorable fall of his eyelids.

Just five minutes.

Merit woke to an embrace. He stared into a chestnut eye a half foot from his own. The other eye was patched. He jerked his head back. It was a braid-framed, cinnamon-coloured face looking at him, so close he could kiss the full, grinning lips.

Mississauga.

"Fire out," the man said, nodding toward the clutch of embers winking from the open door of the wood stove. He looked up at the wisp dawdling from the broken flue pipe, unfurling like a flag, marking Merit's location.

Merit looked over his shoulder and saw three more braves standing nearby. He wriggled free of the clinch and sprinted for the ruined doorway, forgetting the blanket around his legs. When he toppled, like a fallen tree, the Mississaugas laughed and clapped. He rolled to his back and the warrior advanced, limping, the ten-inch hunting knife glinting in his hand.

"You woke me to kill me?"

One of the other braves took Merit's hands, pulled them over his head and pinned them. A second pinned his feet, still bound in the blanket. The third forced a thong of leather into Merit's mouth like a bit and secured it behind his head.

The warrior with the limp and the patch removed Merit's wool cap and ripped open his shirt. He saw the eagle feather, dagger-like against his chest. He flipped it with his knife and looked at his comrades, gauging their expressions.

Merit recognized him. It was the Indian they had saved outside the Bottle and Glass.

The warrior's knife swooped in like a talon, reflecting the brilliance of the dawn.

~ ~ ~

Biscuit sat near the hearth at Burnside's, nursing a nor'wester. The pain in his head surged and receded, surged and receded, as surf erodes a breakwater. From an inside pocket he pulled an amethyst ampoule, examined it, found it three quarters empty, and put it back. The other men of his hunting party sat at a nearby table and played high low jack, keeping their distance. When they'd finished their supper break, they would continue, searching the roads and homesteads north of town for the deserter.

Biscuit was about to give the order to re-assemble when a carter entered the tavern.

"Mississaugas sir," the young man said, "claim to have caught him."

Biscuit followed him from the tavern, along the road, into the forest. Four Mississaugas stood in front of their horses, waiting. The one with the eye patch limped forward, raising a pole before him, the tip affixed with a bloody scalp. Biscuit came to meet him, propping himself with his cane. He eyed the Indian. Found him familiar. He stood before the scalp, appraising its lustrous blondness. He ran his fingers through the sweep of its buttery curl, supple like gosling down.

"There's no mistaking it," he whispered, caressing the pelt as though it was still attached to the head of a boy.

"Jackals!" he cried, savagely. "Alive. You were to bring him alive!"

21

The Rob Roy

JEREMY STOOD IN FRONT OF THE TÊTE-DU-PONT. Barrack Street fizzed and flowed. Drunks promenaded its length, arm in arm. They passed bottles, flasks, and jars. They danced singly, and in pairs, spasmodically, as though they'd contracted St. Vitus. A makeshift band got up: a powder monkey shrilled a tin whistle, a fishmonger, twanged at a jew's harp chocked between uneven teeth, a colour sergeant puffed on the neck of a jug. The din of the street was louder than the lower deck of a ship crossing the T.

Jeremy didn't notice. He didn't notice the delirious rioters stumbling into him, falling to the street, laughing hysterically. He missed the ensign next to him, doubled over, spattering the cobbles with half-digested pie. He didn't see the same boy wipe his mouth with the back of his hand, shake his head, shudder, and swig from another pot of porter. He didn't hear the marine burble:

"Ship's cat! Deacon, ye made a stone? Have a nip o' bilgewater, set you to rights. You ain't heard? We won! Brother Jonathan signed the dotted line. War is over!"

Jeremy stared at the blond shock that had replaced Augie's head atop the pole. He was aware of nothing else. "It can't be him," he kept saying, "it can't be."

Lenore was at his elbow. "Lamb," she pleaded, "come home. 'Tis no place for you."

He turned to look at her, his eyes red, streaming. "Mrs. Stokes," he said, mechanically, "ma'am. I told him not to run. Why did he run? He saw what they did to Augustus. Why?"

She patted his arm. "Jeremy, please come home."

"I'm alone," he said.

A voltigeur, stinking of brandy, lurched and gathered them into his arms so the three were locked in an embrace.

"Keees 'er," he slurred, his breath and accent impossibly strong. "Eeef you don', I weeel."

Jeremy stared at the winking, drooling soldier.

"Keees 'er. Don' wase la belle laydeee."

Lenore could see visions of murder and rage reflected in Jeremy's hot gaze.

"Leave him," she begged, "he's just drunk, happy."

"Why," Jeremy asked, darkly. He put the basin of his cupped hand over the man's face and shoved. The voltigeur fell heavily to the street.

"Tabernac," the man spat. "Connard!" He picked himself up and moved on.

A bottle smashed against the wall. Lenore jumped, returning to Jeremy arms.

"Please let's go," she said. "A letter came for you today. Perry brought it. It's from Cornwall."

Jeremy looked at her, his face trembling. "Lamb," she said, tilting his head down into the crook of her bare neck. "You're not alone."

She took his hand and led him from Barrack Street. They wound through the revelers packing market square and picked their way through the streets until they were back at Stoke cottage. Lenore sat Jeremy down at the dining table and retrieved the letter for him. She set about reinvigorating the fire, putting a kettle on, and preparing tea.

The return address read: *Mrs. Alice Castor, Perenn Cottage, Green Lane, Porthleven, Cornwall.*

He opened the small, square envelope and plucked the folded paper inside.

Jeremy!

Oh, Jeremy, my beautiful boy. Damn the Royal Navy that they should take away my last born and I don't care what admiral reads this. Damn the RN! You can't know what a balm it was to receive your letters, (six of them all at once!), to know that you and Merit are alive.

Don't misunderstand. Joy. Then livid, red-faced rage. Slammed doors. Thrown crockery. How could you two pilchards be so foolish? After all my pleading? Stay out of the taverns, that's all I asked. Merit wasn't it? Dicing. Rode and Shackle. That's the rumour.

You never could refuse him. He's older, but you're bigger. Use your size, give him a braining now and then, would do him good.

Joy again. My pilchards. At least you're together, looking after one another.

Jeremy sniffed.

"Good news, I hope," Lenore said from the kitchen, as she pulled cups and saucers from the shelves and poured milk into a creamer.

I'm sorry to give you this news in a letter, but I think it's better that you know. Shortly after you and Merit disappeared I received a letter from the war office. You truly are my last born, now, my last kin. Last spring, William and Thomas died in France, at Bayonne. Papa too. Letter says they showed uncommon valour, charging an embankment, that ultimately was won.

I'm so sorry Jem. Sorry that you are so far away and we can't grieve together.

I'm having difficulty wringing Papa's pension from the army. No income for close to a year. I may need to sell the cottage, see if I can stay with Aunt Gladys in Helston. The curate has little room there, but he's a good man.

Continue to send letters (please!) to Perenn Cottage. The postmaster will forward them, if need be.

It's difficult to admit this, but I've rather enjoyed reading about your adventures. I'm so proud of you both, Merit a topsman, and you a corporal, already! And, I suppose it's been good for you to get out of Porthleven and see a bit of the world. Give your fins a stretch.

And this Augustus Gardiner. He sounds like a lovely boy. I do hope I get to meet him one day.

Still, I'd prefer you here, safe and sound. Give Merit a hug, look after one another. Love to you both, I pray you'll be home someday soon. Looking forward to your next correspondence.

Love Alice (Mum)

Lenore entered the dining room with a tray of hot tea, sandwiches, and biscuits.

"So," she said, looking up from the tray, "what did it say?"

The room was empty. The door to the guest room was shut. She put the tray down on the table, stepped quietly to the door, and cupped her ear to it. Nothing. *Asleep*, she thought hopefully.

Jeremy had slipped out of Stoke Cottage and was already headed north on the Montreal Road. Just before leaving the city he stopped at the Rob Roy where he bought an earthenware jar of genever, cut with lime and sugar. He marched toward the Barrett farm and the backcountry around Loughborough Lake, in the direction he was told that the Mississaugas had killed Merit. If it was true, there must be evidence, signs of a struggle. A body.

22

Burnside's Tavern

AMELIA POKED A PIECE OF SHARPENED TOAST into the egg's closed eye. She worked it around, breaking the yolk, as she surveyed her new room from the vantage point of her four poster. It had been her first night at Willowpath and she had to admit, grudgingly, it wasn't so bad. Most blessedly, it was her room, and hers alone; Noble was down the hall. Morning light, redistributed through the crowns of two large, sash windows, cast the newly papered walls in bright yellow and illuminated the mahogany bookcase housing the library of classics acquired from Bison Harris. Sunshine twinkled and refracted through the perfume phials, essential oils, and cruets of scented water formed up on her vanity table. The faded fragrance of lilac, milkweed, and phlox exhaled from an urn of dried flowers and made a welcome change from the whisky and tobacco residue of the King's Arms. Her coral-coloured bed linen, crisp and cool, smelled faintly of fresh snow. She shifted beneath the breakfast tray to feel again the caress of it against her skin.

She finished the eggs and toast, put the tray aside, hopped from bed, and slid into a robe and slippers. She wanted to see the rest of the house but, more importantly, she wanted to see Millie, her mother. They hadn't met since the wedding, over two months, and even then, Amelia hadn't acknowledged Millie's presence. She knew that Spafford had offered to take her on as a domestic, an assistant to Mrs. Simkins, but they'd been living at the King's Arms through the renovations, and Millie had never been invited to visit, so she wasn't sure. She never spoke about her mother and that had been fine with Spafford. But after her conversation with Jeremy, at the King's Arms, she had decided that when they moved in to Willowpath, it was time to reconcile. There had been something in Jeremy's sad expression when she had told him of their estrangement that had blunted her anger. She descended the stairs, quietly, in search of the kitchen.

It was easy to find; every room in the house was quiet save one, from which she heard laughter and the clinking of cup against saucer. Four people rose from their seats around a rough oak table when she entered: Mrs. Simkins, an Irishwoman shaped like an aubergine, a thick set man in a checked, linen shirt and overalls, a slight woman with head scarf and gingham apron, and a boy of ten or eleven, in dungarees and suspenders. The fifth, Millie, turned from the stove and the pot she'd been stirring to see what had interrupted the conversation.

Amelia stared. Millie was thinner but her face was puffy and sallow, her blue eyes, ringed red, were pale; as though she'd aged years, not months, since they'd last seen each other. The wooden spoon she held, gravy droplets inching downward, trembled in her fist.

"Mum," Amelia said, quietly.

Millie looked at her feet and a patina of colour rose to her ashen cheeks. The floor boards of thick, white pine rattled as Amelia crossed to her. She put her arms around her and cinched her tight.

"Amelia," Millie sobbed, dropping the spoon, returning the hug, "our little Moonie. How I've missed you."

They stood, clinging and swaying, until Mrs. Simkins finally spoke.

"We'd best be going," she said to the others.

"No," Amelia said, over Millie's shoulder. "No, stay, please. I want to meet you all. Go on doing what you were doing, I don't want to interrupt."

"Mrs. Simkins," Millie sniffed, allowing Amelia to separate from her, "was telling us a funny story about her first boss."

"Please," Amelia said, leading Millie to the table, "continue. Sit. I'm Amelia."

"I'm Mrs. Simkins, as you know. This is Joseph, Sarah, and their son, Nat."

As Amelia helped Millie into one of the wooden chairs and took one herself, the rest retook their seats.

"Tea, Moonie?" Millie asked, patting Amelia's knee. Amelia nodded and smiled. Millie took a flask from a hidden pocket behind her apron, unstopped it, and poured one of the cups half full.

"A spot of brandy," she said, smiling weakly, shaking the flask over a second cup, "for the chill?"

Amelia glanced at the others and noted their forgiving looks.

"No, thank you," she said.

Millie pulled the cozy from the pot and lifted it with a tremulous hand, securing the lid with the other. She held it suspended over the cup, but could not steady it enough to pour. The lid rattled. Tea sploshed from the lip. Amelia put her hand over her mother's.

"Shall I pour?" she asked. Millie nodded and fresh tears crested her eyes.

"Please," Amelia said to Mrs. Simkins, as she took the teapot and poured, "continue."

Mrs. Simkins, after a *now where was I...* and a *did I already say...*, resumed the yarn.

"Simkins!" someone yelled, from a different part of the house. "Simkins!"

Noble Spafford gusted through the kitchen door, shirt unbuttoned, suspenders at his knees. He shoved the ampoule in his pudgy fist, still half-full, into a trouser pocket.

"Mrs. Simkins," he bawled, "there you are, have you seen my..."

Wife, is what he intended to say. But then, he saw her, sitting at the rough-hewn table, next to her mother, drinking tea.

"Ah, dove," he said, "there you are. Lost?" He drifted a slight smile toward Mrs. Simkins. "First night in a new house. A little disorientation is perfectly understandable." He turned back to Amelia. "We're upstairs. If there is anything you want, just ring for it."

"No," she said, shaking her head. "There's nothing I want."

"Come along then. Busy day."

"Thank you, no." She pointed to her cup. "Just poured a cup of tea."

Spafford stamped his feet and puffed his cheeks.

"Amelia," he said, affecting a tone of sufferance, as though she were seven, not seventeen. "'Tisn't proper. You belong upstairs. Come with me and we'll discuss it, civilly. There is much you need to learn about Willowpath. Life here is different from what you're used to."

"I am learning. I'm starting by meeting fellow residents. Mrs. Simkins. And Joseph, and Sarah, and Nat."

The others looked out the window, to the orchard. Spafford drove his fist into the fleshy palm of his hand.

"You can't fraternize with the helps!" he cried. "Your place is upstairs."

"Why not?" Amelia was standing now. She put her hand on Millie's shoulder. "I can't speak to my own mother? Am I prisoner?"

"No," Spafford said, flatly. "Just now she is Mrs. Barrett, Mrs. Simkin's assistant, not your mother. I fished her from the dram shop gutter and took her on as a favour to you. We're not running a charity here. If you must speak to her, do it in her free time."

Millie brought a handkerchief up to her face and sobbed gently. Amelia shook her head scarcely able to believe what she was hearing. It was as though she'd stepped into the pages of Tacitus and it was Caligula that stood before her.

"I enjoy their company," she said, fiercely. "I prefer it."

Spafford coughed. "The helps? Negroes?"

"Yes," Amelia said, "I have more in common with them."

"Are you getting this Meriky nonsense from books? I'll take them away. Don't you know how brother Jonathan treats his Negroes?"

Spafford walked toward Nat, raised his hand, and feinted striking the back of his head.

"Devil's children," he said, turning to Amelia. "Come."

"No."

"The rest of you. Leave."

No-one moved.

"Leave the house, attend to your outside duties," he cried, "or I'll give you such a lashing you'll wish you were dead!"

Millie, Simkins, and the others stood and began to leave. Amelia started to go with them.

"Not you," Spafford said, blocking her way. He stooped to pick up the dropped wooden spoon, clotted with congealed gravy. Millie paused at the door and looked back.

"Leave, damn you! If I find out one of you has remained, I'll thrash you all."

Amelia nodded her ahead.

"In need of domestication," Spafford said, after the others had left. "It's been a decade since I've broken a filly. Don't worry, I remember."

~ ~ ~

I'll resign Jeremy repeated to himself as he walked south on the Montreal Road. He'd spent the night at the Barrett farm, having found no evidence of his cousin. *It's too late for Merit. I'll demand my six guineas and get them home to Mum so she can stay at Penrenn. I'll speak to Stokes, request the soonest possible discharge, and wait it out.*

Jeremy arrived at Willowpath mid-morning, just missing Spafford.

He struck the front door's lion-head knocker. Struck it again. On the third strike, the door cracked open. Millie's face appeared in the gloom behind, her eyes strained red.

"Morning missus," Jeremy said, "Jeremy Castor. Is the Colonel in?"

"Not in," she said, moving to close the door.

Jeremy pushed at it.

"I'm his servant."

"He's already in town. Lunching at Burnside's."

"Mrs. Spafford?"

Millie said nothing. She looked away.

"Not taking visitors."

Jeremy frowned.

"Is she well?"

He could see now that Millie had been crying. He put his boot against the door and forced it open.

"What's happened?" he asked. "I insist on knowing, on speaking to her."

He stepped into the foyer. A glass cabinet held souvenirs of a life spent on the continent: medals, a French bayonet, a republican's cigarette case, a pair of dueling pistols, a pouch of powder, lead balls.

Millie shuffled to the kitchen holding a handkerchief to her face. Jeremy went upstairs. He called out Amelia's name and got no reply. He knocked on the only door that was shut. Again. And again.

He put his hand on the door knob. *I can't enter a woman's bedroom uninvited.* His mind raced with what might be inside.

"Go away," Amelia said from the other side.

"Amelia!" Jeremy said, with relief. "It's me, Jeremy."

"Go away," she said, gentler now. "I'm seeing no-one."

"Please," Jeremy said, softly insistent. "It may be a long time before I see you again. Maybe never."

It was quiet for what felt like a very long time.

"Please. I won't leave until you see me."

The knob turned and the door drifted open half a foot. He waited in vain for her to open it fully before pushing it carefully and stepping inside. Amelia was seated on the chaise lounge by the window, looking out. She was barefoot, but otherwise covered, dressed in a flowing empire dress, her knees brought up to her chest. From where he stood, her face was completely obscured by the scarf over her head.

"I had to see you one last time," Jeremy said, advancing no further than the middle of the room, holding his cap in his hand. "I'm resigning my post with the Colonel."

"Good."

"Returning to my unit."

"Mm."

"Requesting an immediate discharge. With the war over, I hope to return home."

"You should."

Colder than she'd been when he first met her at the Bottle and Glass.

"Can I see you one last time?"

"No."

"I'll miss you. About the only thing I'll miss. I'd like to see your face one last time, so I can remember it."

"Jeremy?"

"Yes?"

"You must promise something. Don't be rash."

"I don't understand."

"I'm not made of crystal. I may seem it, but I'm not. Rock glass more like. I can withstand it. And I have a plan."

"What is it Amelia? I'm not following."

She turned to him and removed the scarf, gingerly. She smiled, crookedly, accommodating a puffed bottom lip. Her left eye was a half-moon of swollen indigo. A plug of crimson cotton protruded from her nostril.

Jeremy rushed to her and put his hand against her cheek, cupping the whole side of her face.

"Abarth Dúw," he breathed, "what happened? Who did this to you?"

She looked away.

"Spafford?"

"He's more Caligulan than I realized," she said.

Jeremy shook his head.

"I'll be fine," she said, smiling again. "Mother is looking after me."

"She's here? You've seen her?"

"Yes, you were right. We'll take care of each other."

Jeremy kissed her forehead.

"I'll see you again," he said.

"Where are you going?"

"Burnside's."

"Jeremy. You promised. Don't make it worse."

~ ~ ~

David Burnside poured cider and brandy into a ceramic tureen, spooned in honey, stirred, and dusted with nutmeg. He handed the tureen to his wife who took it outside to the adjacent stable. She placed it under Midge's udder and with a dozen brisk tugs on her teats, filled the tureen. She brought it back into the tavern and put it in front of Noble Spafford, where he sat with Cartwright and other retired officers.

"That's the stuff!" he said, rubbing his hands together. "No-one makes a syllabub like you Mrs. Burnside, and Midge, of course. Gentlemen?"

Spafford dipped the ladle into the froth, still steaming with bestial heat, and poured out four portions.

"Tell me lads, how do you stop a Canadian girl from having sex?"

"Jesus, Noble, we've heard it a hundred times."

"What about you McNeil?"

McNeil shook his head.

"Marry her."

Spafford called to the bar where Major Stokes sat with Captain Carlyle.

"Stokes! Stokes, you'll like this one. Why do the Royal Marines exclude Jews from their officer ranks?"

Stokes glanced over but otherwise made no other form of acknowledgement.

"Because they accept only uncircumcised – complete pricks."

Spafford laughed and tipped his cup back. When he brought his head back down, he saw Jeremy striding toward him.

"There you are! How come you're never around when I need you? I'm of a mind to find a new servant."

Jeremy threw a glove on to the table.

"You're welcome to, though you may no longer have a need."

Spafford put his cup down. The brown-speckled froth lining his upper lip wobbled. Jeremy leaned in with his left hand on the table and nudged McNeil aside. With his right, so there would be no ambiguity, he slapped Spafford, leaving a florid, hand-shaped mark on his cheek. The others pushed their chairs back from the table, unable to make sense of it.

Syllabub flecked from Spafford's mouth.

"What's wrong with you boy?" he sputtered.

All that Jeremy knew of duels was what he had read in books.

"Satisfaction," he said, "I demand it."

Burnside's clientele of Napoleonic and Peninsular war veterans stopped their reminiscing. They had seen this scenario play out many times in their decades of service. All eyes were on Spafford and the tavern was as quiet as Sunday morning. Spafford laughed, rubbing at his enflamed cheek, scanning his drinking companions to see if they also saw the humour. They didn't so much as smile. Either he had just been insulted and his honour needed defending, or, more likely, knowing Spafford as they did, he had something to answer for, a grievance to be redressed. There was no joking it off.

"Come lad, you can't be serious," Spafford said, through a forced chuckle. He picked up the ladle. "Tell you what, have a seat with us, let me pour you a silky cupful. I'm big enough to forget this incident for what it is – a bit of youthful high spirits, eh?"

Jeremy said nothing. He stared at Spafford as if he might lift the tureen and jam it on the Colonel's head.

"Castor," Spafford said, stretching his arms, palms out. "Is it the six pounds? I told you I'm good for it. Look," he dug into his purse, "here you go, six guineas. No, seven. Interest. Fifteen percent return, not bad."

Jeremy took the coins and put them into his pocket but otherwise didn't move.

"That's not it," he said.

"The discharge? Is that it? For you and that cousin of yours. Martin? Merit? Merit. I haven't forgotten."

"Merit's dead."

"Eh?"

"Executed by a Mississauga tracking party yesterday."

"I see. Unfortunate. Still, not much to be done for a deserter. Even so, you remain. I'll speak to the Commodore this evening, on your behalf."

"That's not it."

"What is it then, damn you!"

"You know what it is!" Jeremy thundered, bringing his fist down onto the table like a gavel, upsetting the bowl, causing the remains of the syllabub to bloom across.

Spafford looked around the room, giggling, bringing his fingertips back to his chest.

"Do I? Do I?"

"I was up at the house today. At Willowpath."

"Yes?"

"I spoke to Mrs. Spafford. Saw her."

A broad smile crossed Spafford's face as understanding dawned.

"That's what this is? Oh my, how quaint. Fancy yourself a gallant?"

"I fancy myself humane."

"Tell me, did she bite her lip? Cry a little? Curl a ringlet round one of those little, grasping fingers? Trust me boy, you have much to learn about women. Like dogs and horses, or any moving chattel, they require training, or they'll be ruined, useless to you and themselves. One day, she'll thank me."

"I doubt that very much. I don't think Amelia sees it that way at all."

"Amelia? First name basis? It's becoming clear to me. Perhaps, it is I who should be taking offence. Improprieties?"

"There have been none," Jeremy said, hotly.

"Move along son. Consider yourself terminated. I'm sorry it didn't work out."

"I'll not go anywhere. Not without satisfaction."

"This is no cause for a duel. First of all, it is a private matter. Isn't your place."

"I don't accept that."

"Second, more importantly, you're a mere corporal. I won't duel below my station."

Spafford motioned to Burnside, rapt like everyone else, for another syllabub. He crossed his arms and smiled at Jeremy. A steady drip drip drip to the floor from the sweet mess pooled on the table marked out heavy seconds of silence. Jeremy didn't know how to proceed. He knew he wouldn't move until Spafford accepted his challenge. But this last objection seemed insurmountable. He thought he might stand over him for an eternity, a monument to his disgrace.

Stokes stepped across from his place at the bar. He tweezered Jeremy's glove from the table between his thumb and forefinger and slapped it, dripping with milk and brandy, on to Jeremy's chest.

"Go home," he said. Jeremy opened his mouth to protest but Stokes continued. "As you know, dueling is against the law. If you persist, I'll have no option but to clap you into irons."

"Go deacon," Spafford said, "Consider yourself lucky, having avoided a duel with a Peninsular veteran and hero of the Siege of Roses."

"Be at the *St. Lawrence*, first thing tomorrow, to report for duty," Stokes said. Jeremy paused. He scanned the Major's eyes, judging whether he could resist him as well. Finally, he sighed and slunk out Burnside's front door.

Stokes turned back to Spafford.

"You're the fortunate one, Noble," he said, pouring a cup from the newly delivered tureen. "I trained him myself. He's no deacon."

~ ~ ~

The road leading to Willowpath was cratered worse than any continental battlefield. Spafford thought the brougham carriage might dash him to pieces. The hogshead of syllabub in his belly thundered and crashed. At any minute, he thought, it might break its levee. He stuck his head out the window.

"For mercy's sake," he shouted up to the driver. "Slow down!"

The brougham slowed. Then it stopped. They must have been only a hundred yards from Willowpath, just out of the woods and at the front lawns. Home was achingly close; he longed to be ensconced in the goose feather of his bed.

"Slow," Spafford cried, "not stop! Why are we stopped!"

"Can't go no further, sir, 'tis blocked."

"Blocked? Then, get out and clear it!"

"Can't sir."

"Tallow and sluts! I'll do it. 'Tis a scandal, the quality of helps in this brambled Arcadia."

Spafford trickled from the brougham and staggered forward to look for the obstruction. Ten paces ahead, silhouetted by the brougham's lanterns, towered a figure, rooted to the centre of the road, like an oak the road-builders neglected to cut. A pair of pistols were leveled back at Spafford, extended, held steady by the man's broad limbs.

"Dick Turpin," the driver breathed.

Spafford ignored him.

"Don't be a child, Castor," Spafford called. "Put the guns away and go home. 'Tis the last free pass I shall give you."

Jeremy walked toward him, pistols trained.

"Not till I have satisfaction," he said, "I demand it."

"And you're just going to shoot me down, like a common highwayman?"

Spafford turned and faced the carriage.

"Perhaps you'd prefer to shoot me in the back."

"'Tis a duel," Jeremy said, now directly in front of Spafford.

"A duel? At this hour? Without seconds?"

"We don't need seconds." Jeremy flipped the pistols so the handles faced the Colonel. "Recognize them? Your shooting irons, so you'll suspect no funny business. Powdered and primed, one ball each."

"Antiques! They'll likely blow our hands from our wrists."

Jeremy shrugged.

"Didn't you hear Stokes? You'll go to jail. More likely, I'll shoot you dead."

"Or, I'll shoot you dead."

"Then, you'll hang."

"Take a pistol."

Spafford shook his head.

"Take one or I'll empty them both into you."

Spafford searched Jeremy's face, looking for some switch, some safety catch, that he could flip to defuse the situation. He'd thrown up as much cover as he could conjure. His foaming stomach performed cartwheels. He pulled the amethyst ampoule from his fob pocket. Spafford lifted the stopper and put the neck to his lips.

"I'm not well," he said, after swigging its entirety, tilting his head beseechingly to the side.

"Matters not. Take one."

Spafford made a high-pitched bleat, exasperated, and took one of the pistols. He examined it and confirmed that it was, in fact, loaded.

"I'm a crack shot. Killed five French in one hour at Roses alone."

Jeremy strode away from the carriage, twelve paces, to the extent of the lantern's thrust into the shadow.

"'Tis suicide," Spafford shouted at him. "You'll go to hell."

Jeremy turned. His musket, pointed back at Spafford, suspended motionless in the dusk as though it was grafted to his arm.

"Raise it," he said, evenly.

Spafford raised his pistol and it shimmied in his hand like freshly caught salmon.

"Ain't right, damn you," he said, "I'm a Colonel. A Goddamn Colonel!"

"On the count of three. Ready?" Jeremy asked.

Spafford squeezed his trigger.

Both were wide-eyed as the powder in the breach fizzed and smouldered and then, nothing. Jeremy lowered his pistol and stared, astonished, for the last time, at the Colonel's lack of scruple. He raised his own pistol once more.

"Please, I beg of you, show some mercy," Spafford blubbered, on his knees, his spent musket dropped to the ground. He clutched at his head and then his chest.

"You vandemonian scoundrel!" he shrieked.

The Colonel was now on his side, in the foetal position, tearing at the cravat around his crimson neck. He sputtered and coughed and foamed. He ripped at his buttons as though he was trying to free a spirit from his chest. Jeremy, with a sigh, lowered his pistol again. He couldn't shoot such a man. He shuffled toward Spafford, slowly, warily, expecting a rouse.

By the time he reached him, Spafford had quieted. His eyes were cinched tight and his breathing was ragged. At times, a wet gurgle. And then, nothing. A string of specked froth trailed down his cheek from the corner of his mouth.

Jeremy stared at him. If it was an act, it was convincing. A man can't vomit bile on command. He can't turn himself a different colour. He can't hold his breath longer than five minutes.

Jeremy hurled his pistol as far as he could into the woods. He picked up Spafford's from the ground and did the same.

"Best take him to a doctor," he said to the driver, helping him bundle the Colonel back into the brougham. "You might try Old Sam's. Dr. Scriven."

23

Jim Beach's
Easter 1815

NOBLE SPAFFORD ARRIVED at Old Sam's later that evening and Dr. Scriven pronounced him dead of indeterminate cause. Symptoms, he concluded, were consistent with heart congestion or dropsy but he couldn't rule out complications arising from a perforated ulcer, over-consumption, or tainted food. Certainly not death by duel, as the agitated carriage driver insisted. There was no bullet wound, no loss of blood. Despite the many witnesses to Jeremy's challenge, his involvement was never seriously considered. Spafford's death was put down to an unfortunate natural occurrence. He was put to rest at St. George's cemetery, with most of the city's elegant extracts in attendance.

In the following weeks, whenever Jeremy had a half day or more of leave, he headed north of town, toward Loughborough Lake, to follow the footpaths of the Mississauga. At Easter, he was given a three-day leave. He convinced Neven and Finn and Lilac to accompany him, to take a room at John Size's Inn, to help him search. Mid-way through the second day, they found a badly decomposed body beneath the giant maple, its blanket of snow melted, the scalp missing and much else fallen away. The forest was like a cathedral; vast, somber, cavernous.

They spent several hours collecting fragments of limestone, which they built up into a cairn around the corpse. They marked it with a cross and urged Jeremy to say a few words. He began to recite the 23rd Psalm:

The Lord is my Shepherd; I shall not want.
He maketh me to lie down in green pastures;
He leadeth me beside the still waters.
He restoreth my soul;
He leadeth me in the paths of righteousness for His name's sake.
Yea, though I walk through the valley of the shadow of death...

He stopped. He pulled his copy of Tom Paine from the pocket of his fearnought. Once he had found two particular lines Augustus had circled, he continued:

I speak an open and disinterested language, dictated by no passion but that of humanity. To me, who have not only refused offers, because I thought them improper, but have declined rewards I might with reputation have accepted, it is no wonder that meanness and imposition appear disgustful. Independence is my happiness, and I view things as they are, without regard to place or person; my country is the world, and my religion is to do good.

and

I trouble not myself about the manner of future existence. I content myself with believing, even to positive conviction, that the power that gave me existence is able to continue it in any form and manner he pleases, either with or without this body.

"Independence is my happiness," Jeremy repeated.

They stood a few minutes, without speaking. They listened to the returning birds, resounding the woods with their flirtatious greetings. They breathed in the musk shaken free from stamens and buds. They looked out on to the winking surface of the lake, as it caressed the shore. Then, back to John Size's for a few quiet pints of Robinson's

Pale, before packing up and returning to town, cutting their holiday short by a day.

~ ~ ~

As they floated down-river in the skiff, the single sail catching a westerly breeze, there was no need for rowing. The platoon of eight marines and two sailors chatted in whispers as the endless carousel of tamarack, birch, and pine spun by.

"Sir," Jeremy said to Stokes, seated next to him. "A word?"

Hardly loquacious, Stokes had barely spoken to Jeremy since the confrontation at Burnside's. He nodded.

"I want to offer an apology. I've been a fool these past months, getting entangled with the Colonel, seeking the easy way out. Lost my bearings. I'm sorry for any dishonour I've brought upon you, the unit, myself."

"Square and cricket. No dishonour, Castor, but I accept. I also should apologize. When I first met you, on the *Lancer*, I thought to myself, here's a jolly lump of clay. But, I admit, I was wrong. A sculptor doesn't shape, he just frees what's already there."

There was no recrimination in the Major's tone, just a simple statement of fact. For a moment, Jeremy felt ashamed.

"Chin up," Stokes said, "it isn't to say you don't have potential, you most certainly do. I expect great things. Just not with His Majesty's Royal Marines. As you know, forces are being drawn down, with the war's end. We're demobilizing. I intend to recommend you for a discharge immediately after today's patrols."

Jeremy looked up, the morning sun lighting up his face. Stokes met his eye and nodded, nearly smiling.

"Sir!" one of the marines shouted. "Ahead!"

Downstream, about half a league, two gigs crossed the river. By early April, the St. Lawrence River had been completely free of ice and traffic had resumed, bringing much needed supplies from Lower to Upper Canada. But it had also thawed out the privateers on either side of the river, malcontents that would smuggle and confiscate any cargo. Chief among them was the disaffected Loyalist, Bill Johnson, a man who believed himself wronged by Richard Cartwright and who vowed revenge against the King and his colonies. Peace had been declared; war had gone underground.

It would be a prize to collar Johnson and his crew, especially if caught ferrying contraband from one shore to the other.

"All hands to the oars, men. Row!"

They gained another quarter league before they were noticed. Distant shouting could be heard as the gigs picked up their pace. They got just close enough to see the long-barrelled, swivel-mounted gun on the first gig and the man in the bow behind it, with his lop-sided leather cap. Jeremy had seen him before, on his first journey up the river, the previous year.

The gigs disappeared around a headland. By the time Stokes and his men reached the cove there was no sign of the privateers or their boats. Either they had them carefully hidden, or they had paddled them inland up one of several creeks that spilled into the river.

"'Tis the American side," one of the marines said.

"Aye," Stokes said.

"They're likely long gone."

"Aye. We'll sniff around anyway. Land her."

They pulled their skiff up onto a sliver of beach, wedged it between two cedars, and tied it off. Stokes had them break off into pairs to scout the immediate area, looking for stashed goods, concealed boats, temporary structures; any evidence of privateering.

Jeremy, and another marine, set off from the most westerly point and began to hack their way through the bush. Stokes had ordered that they not go any further than two hundred yards in any direction, and that they return within the hour. It was an easy command to keep; the way was thick with alder, dogwood, and buckthorn. Finally, after twenty minutes, not having gone inland from the river's edge more than a stone's throw and no further than one hundred yards west, they found a rough trail running parallel to the water. Sweating heavily now, and panting, they took up the trail and continued west. Though narrow and slight, it appeared that the trail was regularly used. Jeremy put his hand on the hilt of his scabbarded dirk. If they came upon a privateer's nest now, in these close quarters, there would be no time or space for muskets.

"At the ready McNaughton," he whispered over his shoulder.

"Halt." A voice came from behind, crisp and even. Jeremy's first instinct was to turn, as difficult as it was in the narrow defile with a pack and a rifle over the shoulder.

"Eyes ahead, lads. No curiosity. No lurching about."

They heard the unmistakable click of a musket hammer being cocked. And another.

"I can't miss from here. And I've one for each."

They stood sweating, short of breath, wondering if it might be their last, their nostrils full of pine, and cedar, and the thawing, spongy humus underfoot. Jeremy tried to formulate something he might be able to say to gain their freedom.

"You, the short one, closer to me," the voice continued. "I want you to back up, slowly. That's it. Watch it, there's a root, there you go. I'm going to step aside and let you pass. Mind the branch. You're free to go. It's the hulk, here, I want. Turn now. No peeking! Head straight back, heel toe, heel toe, no running, take your time. I've got a pistol on each of you. Overgrown one. March. Double-quick."

Jeremy began to walk forward down the path. He glanced quickly over his shoulder to see a man with a lop-sided leather cap and kerchief over his face aiming two pistols at him.

"Eyes forward!" the man cried. "March. Faster!"

Jeremy turned back to the path and walked as fast as he could. For hours, it seemed, they blundered through the bush, Jeremy's face and neck and hands, streaked red by the raking of sharp branches; his jacket torn, his boots muddy, his feet cold. They hurdled deadfall, forded streams, and scaled escarpments. He'd done little drilling in the past few months and was unused to such exertion. Several times he crested a ridge, winded, light-headed, and thought he might collapse. Finally, they came to a lowland, where the forest thinned. Jeremy could see the river's edge again. He could smell wood smoke.

"Stop," the voice called. Jeremy did, gladly. "Turn."

Jeremy turned slowly, panting. With his hands on his knees he looked across at his captor, a man of medium build, wearing a frayed, wool jersey, leather trousers and cap. Still the kerchief, now darkened with sweat, covered his face.

"Is this it?" Jeremy asked, breathlessly. "You're going to shoot me here? 'Tis a long way to march someone just to kill them."

Jeremy was so tired he wasn't sure he cared either way.

"No," the man said, removing the kerchief. "Of course I ain't."

"Merit?" Jeremy cried, when he saw the face. "Merit!"

Jeremy sprinted the twenty feet between them, picked him up, and shook him. Merit laughed, holding his arms straight out from his body, aiming the pistols away.

"Careful cousin! These cannon still be loaded."

Jeremy set him down and stared, his hands on his hips. As though he still wasn't sure whether he was a figment.

"I knew it," he said, finally, shaking his head. "I knew you couldn't be."

"Nearly, but not quite."

Jeremy punched him hard in the shoulder.

"Why didn't you reveal yourself sooner? Why march me all over creation?"

"To put enough distance between us and the others. And your partner will report back an abduction, not a desertion. You're free."

Jeremy hugged Merit again.

"Must keep proving your reality," he said, smiling.

"Thirsty?"

"I could drain a hogshead."

"Come. I know of a tavern."

"Here?" Jeremy laughed. "In the middle of the woods?"

"Jimmy Beach's. Doff your scarlet, don't want to give 'em a fright."

Merit led Jeremy another twenty yards down a slope to the river's edge, where there was a clapboard structure, not much bigger in size or scope than an ice-fishing hut. It was on the inner arc of a bay that cut deeply into the shore. Evergreen branches had been laid over its roof and walls so it was invisible from the water. As they approached, Jeremy could see a number of skiffs and canoes, pulled up from the water, also covered.

Inside, it was dark, forest gloom barely able to penetrate the single grimy window.

"Best damp the fire," Merit said, as they entered. "Navy patrols are nosing this side."

"What can I get ye?" Beach asked, as he shuttered the flue.

"Beer and bourbon, two each," Merit said, "the first for thirst, the second for effect."

"A penny extra for the vessel. No fresh beer just now. Bourbon's good, tho'"

"Water?" Jeremy asked. The last time he'd been this thirsty was aboard the *Lancer*.

Beach laughed. "There's a whole river of it out t' door. Help self, but wouldn't trust it. Got some rattle-skull. Bit sour."

"'Tis fine."

They sat at a table made from a cross cut disk of raw wood, the surface rough with concentric circles, held up, tentatively, by three crooked sticks of birch. There were six other customers in the confines of the hut, four hunters and a pair of Indians. Beach brought by a beaker of bourbon and four tin cups, two filled with the sour beer, mixed with brandy, wine, nutmeg and lime.

They clinked tin, drank, ordered another round. Jeremy leaned his back against the wall of the hut, careful not to rest so much weight that it collapsed around them.

"Tell me what happened," he said.

Merit sipped.

"I could have planned it better," he said. "less spontaneous, better laid out. But there wasn't time. Biscuit took it away."

Merit looked thoughtfully at his cup and continued.

"I made it further than Augie, anyway. I thought maybe I could go north and then east and circle around to hitch a ride on a batteau, with Thibodeau maybe. But the Indians caught me up. And well they did, because I'd prob'ly been done in by the cold, otherwise."

He pulled the feather from inside the chest of his tunic and rolled the quill between his thumb and forefinger so it pirouetted.

"This, Jem, what ma gave me, 'tis what saved my life, gave me my freedom. But I'm no longer completely intact."

Merit ripped the leather cap from his head. It was like the surface of a cow's tongue, damp, pink, hairless, and grooved. There were deep scars above his ears and around his skull, and above his neck. They looked tender and scabbed. Tufts of hair demarked the line where the scalp had been torn from his head. Merit leaned in so Jeremy could get a good look, but Jeremy turned away.

"Freedom costs Jem," Merit said with an intense whisper that rose to a shout, "those bastard Indians took my scalp. My bleddy scalp!"

Jeremy looked across the room at the two Indians, quietly drinking. They seemed not to notice.

"But here it is," Merit continued, draining the bourbon and signaling for another round. "They saved my life. The disfigured one, the one we saved out front of the Bottle and Glass that night, with his one good eye he recognized me, I swear it. He knew 'twas me. And he saw me feather. He knew I didn't deserve to die. He cut the locks clean from me head and you've never felt such excruciation, nor do I hope you ever will, bless you. It was as though a white hot blade cleaved my brain in two. I passed out. But those cunning bastards, they held coals to my gushing skull, cleaned it, and wrapped it in clean linen, packed with snow. They took me to the river, changing the bandages regular along the way. They brought me here, left me, and returned with their trophy. At that time, Beach's was across the river."

Jeremy drank, wishing Merit would replace his cap.

"It was built upon the ice," Merit continued, "on the Northern side, to capitalize on frozen river traffic; fishers, loggers, rumrunners. A few of these roughnecks, body smugglers, filled me full of rum spiked with cloves and laudanum, took all my coin, and said they would take me across to the American side that night, undercover of dark. But, before they could, the whole tavern lifted up from the shore, sailed downriver and landed on the American side. Easiest smuggling operation ever known. Beach's went from being a Canadian tavern to an American ordinary in a matter of minutes."

"You're drunk."

"'Tis true! And not uncommon, I hear. Beach, like others before him, wanted to squeeze a few more weeks out on the ice, to wring every groat from thirsty river travelers. He chained the hut to trees along the shore, but the current swole and calved the floe, snapping the cables, taking the tavern with it. Lucky for Jimmy, it had a gentle landing in New York State. As did I. I demanded my money back from the smugglers since they'd done no work on my behalf, and they tossed me back a guinea. Since they were three, and I was one, there was no debating. Here, I convalesced a while, till the money ran out, and the headache dimmed, then I looked for work. Found out Bill Johnson is in need of qualified sailors."

Jeremy shook his head.

"I wish it were made up, but it ain't. What about you Jem, what's happened to you?"

Jeremy told him what had happened after Merit ran, how his scalp was displayed, how everyone thought he was dead. He told him that Stokes was going to put in for his discharge, possibly as soon as the next day. He described, to Merit's delight, how he'd challenged Spafford, and how Spafford had dropped dead without a single shot.

"Clears the way, then, don't it?" Merit said.

"What do you mean?"

"You can begin courting the young widow."

"Merit."

Merit laughed and clasped Jeremy's hand.

"Merit, some bad news as well."

He told him of the letter from Porthleven.

"Poor Alice," Merit said, staring into his tin cup. "She must bear me some grudge."

"Aye, she does a little, both of us, but overall forgives."

Merit now clenched his fists and pounded the table. He looked fiercely at Jeremy, pointing at his scalp.

"Haven't I paid for my mistake," he cried, "my gamble at the Rode and Shackle? You have it made: Stokes' protection, a discharge, the lady's attentions. What have I got? On the run, half-skinned."

Merit stood and pulled his tattered wool jersey and cotton chemise over his head and turned. A latticework of welts scored his back.

"Look!" he cried. "Each inflicted by Biscuit, and so much more besides. So much has been taken! What is left? What is left?"

Jeremy stood from the table, gently bringing the jersey down, enveloping his cousin, staring away the looks from the other patrons.

"And Augustus," Merit mumbled, into Jeremy's chest. "Poor, sweet, Augustus. Dead."

Jeremy held him a while until Merit pushed him away and retook his chair. He wiped his face with the back of his hand and settled.

"I'm fine," he said "I'm fine. I'm free. That's enough. Sorry Jim," he called, "another round please, and one for the house."

Jeremy sat.

"What will you do?" he asked.

"Freelance with these brigands a while, until I tire of it. Then, west, I think."

"Will we ever see each other again?"

"I'm sure you'll see me again," Merit said, smiling, "when you least expect it. I'll have to be careful, of course, for the next little while, until I'm forgotten. When will you leave for home?"

Jeremy peered out the fogged window.

"I've decided to stay."

"Stay? After everything?" Merit sniffed. "Ah. The girl."

Jeremy returned his smile but said nothing.

"I'm sorry I got you into this whole mess Jem."

"I'm sorry not to get you out."

24

Violin, Bottle, and Glass

More were shoehorned into the Bottle and Glass than in October, at the grand opening. The magistrate and sheriff, seated at one of the tables near the front, might have worried that the town was ripe for looting with the streets deserted and most citizens folded into the inn on the park, were it not for the fact that most of the criminal element also attended. John Poncet eyed the posts and beams hoping they would bear up under the crowd on the balconies. He turned none away. Proceeds for the night had already surpassed all of the previous month's takings.

Ginger, wearing a wig of long, powdered curls and a faux-ermine robe, addressed the crowd while one of his colleagues rattled a spinet and another trilled a flute.

"Welcome back!" he cried. "I hope you have your blackstraps and bombos and whistle bellies! I hope you've drunk your settlers and stiffeners and you've braced yourself for more astonishment! We continue on, for your perverse pleasure, the last of our two hundred curiosities and unimaginable feats, never before seen in these parts, guaranteed to baffle and amaze. Next... our collection of relics."

Ginger went across the stage to a chest, opened it, and retrieved a small object.

"First!" he shouted. "We give you… the Pharoah's finger!"

He held aloft a length of blackened material, the shape and colour of a tobacco twist. Where the knuckle might be there was a gold-coloured ring set with a garish, red stone. He placed it on velvet cushion and handed it to one of his associates.

"Index finger of Ramses the third, three thousand years old. Taken from his mummified corpse by unscrupulous antiquarians and brought directly here, to Kingston, for your edification. We will pass it around for closer inspection. No touching please!"

One of the performers waded into the crowd with the cushion, bending and holding it before the drinkers pushing together, craning their necks. Neven, Finn, Lilac, and the rest of the poorer folk made do with squinting from the balcony.

Ginger went back to the chest and pulled a bundle from it.

"A two-headed baby, carefully preserved!"

He handed the tiny body to his assistant and dipped back into the chest.

"Unicorn horn, taken from the last to walk the earth!"

Ginger presented an endless procession of oddities and relics, from mermaid skins to dragon teeth to a lock of Marie Antoinette's hair.

"I don't know how you talked me into this," Stokes said to Lenore, seated beside him. "Pure bunkum. We could be enjoying a quiet meal at the Black Bull."

"Perry. Don't sulk, it's fun. At least we're together."

"I have something important to tell you."

"Go ahead."

"This hardly seems the place."

He watched her as she examined the two-headed baby, thinking she would have taken it home if it were alive and hers to hold.

"Lenore," he said. "Lenore."

"Yes," she said, absently, her eyes locked on the shriveled figure.

"I've decided to return to the continent. They're gathering men for the seventh coalition, to defeat Napoleon for good. This is my chance. It shouldn't be for long, I expect we'll win a quick and decisive victory. But there's little time. I plan to leave this weekend."

It was his turn to appraise the relic. Lenore stared at her husband, digesting his words. She fought threatened tears and looked away, across the room to where Jeremy sat, talking and grinning. She watched him gesturing and clapping with his big hands and she imagined them covering hers again, guiding them through loops and patterns. She yearned to bring him his tea, to tuck him in.

He sensed her and met her gaze.

"There are others that I'd like you to meet," Jeremy said to his mother, seated next to him, as he smiled back at Lenore.

"Give her a minute," Amelia laughed, winking at Alice, "she just got in today and you've dragged her to an exhibition. I'm sure she'd like to sit a while."

"How was your passage over, Mrs. Castor?" Millie asked, scrutinizing a swatch of navy blue cloth no bigger than a sovereign; an artifact Ginger had introduced as a scrap of Nelson's death shroud.

"Please, call me Alice. Bearable, just. And then the paddle upriver, carted around like so much baggage. I hope never to travel anywhere again."

"Better than being shaken to pieces via stagecoach."

"Aye, 'tis what they say and I suppose they're right. The paddlers were as chivalrous and polite as I've ever met, I don't deny it. I nattered with one called Thibodeau the whole way. Told me about his father and his mother and his nine brothers and sisters - his whole family history. Splendid chap. I'm rather surprised he isn't here — it seems everyone else is."

"Thibodeau prefers the outdoors Mum, he never sets foot in a tavern."

"You could learn something from him. If only you and Merit…"

"Mum."

Alice turned back to Millie.

"'Twas a tolerable trip, thanks for asking. It's good to be here, finally, and to see my Jeremy. Thought I might never see him again. You may know what it's like to lose a child. I only wish I could see my nephew again."

"You will before long, I suspect," Jeremy said.

Ginger and his troupe had moved on to their feats section, walking tight ropes and slack ropes, juggling sabres, spinning crockery, throwing knives.

"And, you Amelia," Alice said, "Jeremy informed me of your loss. I'm sorry to hear it."

Amelia evinced an air of grief and showed just enough.

"So young to be a widow. How will you manage?"

"I hope," Amelia said, smiling, "Mr. Castor will continue on as my advisor and agent."

Jeremy smiled and nodded.

"My late husband left a badly mismanaged estate. I intend, with Mr. Castor's help, to rectify that. We already have some investment ideas."

"My, my," Alice said, "investment ideas? Such a young woman, speaking like a captain of industry. Different generation, eh Mrs. Barrett?"

"'Tis true," Millie said, proudly.

The crowd gasped as one of the performers spat a plume of fire from his mouth.

"Look at them," grumbled Carmichael to Sam and Cornelius, over a jar of rye and water. "Like a pair of pigeons in May. Old Spafford's been in the ground less than a month. 'Tis unseemly. Woe be to them if they think to wed within the year, mark me."

"Charivari?"

"What else."

"He's the blister what boxed our ears the last time."

"No matter. We'll be ready for him the next."

Ginger built up to his show-stopping finale.

"Feat number one hundred and ninety-nine!" he cried. "For this, I need a volunteer."

A thicket of hands rose from the rows of tables. Ginger wove in and out, cajoling and teasing, seeking his volunteer.

"I need someone of a particular stature," he said. "You sir!" He pointed at a man in a tattered wool jersey with his back pressed firmly to the wall. He wore a leather cap that darkened his face, casting shadows across his thick, blond moustache and beard.

Jeremy recognized the cap and the jersey and the eyes peering from beneath thatched brows. He looked around at Stokes, and Biscuit a few tables away, and Neven and Finn in the balcony. None showed any signs of recognition.

Ginger took Merit by the elbow and led him to the stage. Merit allowed himself to be led to a coffin-shaped contraption without a lid, standing on its end, with a painted bulls-eye at head height. Ginger positioned him on the base so he faced the crowd, as though it was a wake and he was on display.

"Do I know you from somewhere?" Ginger shouted. "Have we ever met before?"

Merit looked stricken. *We haven't*, Ginger whispered, *say we haven't*.

"No," Merit said, his voice unnaturally low.

"Of course we haven't! We're complete strangers to each other. Now! For this feat you must doff your topper."

Ginger tugged at Merit's cap

"No!" Merit barked and looked as though he might snap Ginger's arm from his shoulder.

"That's fine, we can work around it. Folks! I, your humble guide and narrator, will use this musket," he showed a loaded pistol to the audience, "from twenty paces, to shoot a bottle from the top of this brave gentleman's head."

As the crowd murmured, and Ginger took his place, one of his assistants produced an empty gin bottle and put it atop Merit's cap, dripping with sweat. He fidgeted, wondering whether he should flee and risk discovery.

"For God's sake," Ginger cried, "do not move sir. This feat requires me to concentrate deeply and for you to be perfectly still."

"Aren't you glad I didn't pick you afterall," he said to a lady in the front row.

"Don't worry, I'm a professional. A professional actor. And I must have completed this feat oh, I don't know, three or four times before. Not always successfully, of course."

The crowd laughed nervously as Ginger planted his feet.

"Quiet please! Are you ready sir?"

Merit said nothing.

Ginger squeezed the trigger and the flint struck the frizzen and ignited the powder with a sharp crack, filling the great room with smoke and sulphur. At that exact moment, one of the performers released a latch at the back of the contraption that caused a small hammer to spring from the centre of the bullseye. The shattered bottle fell to the floor in pieces. The house erupted.

"Thank you! Thank you! Thank you sir, you may take your seat, you've been a good sport."

Merit stepped shakily from the stage and he slunk out the back.

"Now, to soothe your savage hearts, feat number two hundred, and the conclusion of our little exhibition."

Ginger crossed to a cloth-covered table on casters. He rolled it until he was centre stage and he pulled the cover. Underneath, a crystal choir numbering more than one hundred, of varying shapes, sizes, and hues. Each glass held a quantity of liquid. The light from the Argand lamps arrayed around the great room was refracted and redoubled through the prisms so that the observers looked into a kaleidoscope of exploding light, radiating every colour of the spectrum, as though they were looking back into the beginnings of the universe. The performers gathered around the table and wet their fingers in the bowls. They began to rub, exciting the edges of the glasses until the most extraordinary curtain of angelic sound descended, trilling and humming into every crevice of the great room. It surged and swelled, drowning all conversation until, at last, no-one spoke, and every last soul packed into the tavern was bound together into one penetrating, harmonic communion that seemed as though it might last forever, ending in an ecstasy of ringing glass.

Ginger's audience leapt from their chairs, clapping and shouting *bravo*.

Jeremy took that moment to put his hand on Amelia's knee. He leaned in close to her, close enough to breathe in the lavender and rosewater.

"Tell me, what investment ideas do *we* have?"

"Manufacturing," she said, enclosing his hand in both of hers. "Much needed items, built and sold right here in Upper Canada."

"What sort?"

The ordinary din of the tavern had taken over, chasing the symphony's last echoes from the rafters. Amelia looked at Scratch, the scumboiler, her guest, sitting with Barnabas at another table, looking up at the stage. A rapturous grin spanned his jack'o'lantern face as though it had been carved with a knife.

"Glass, of course," she whispered into Jeremy's ear, after kissing his cheek, "bottles and glass."

Epilogue

BENNET'S FIRST ATTEMPT ended in tears.

A diet consisting mainly of low grade sugar had, over the years, rotted all the teeth from the front of his mouth. Without teeth, he couldn't find the purchase to purse his lips against the end of the blowpipe and create the pressure that would force his breath down its four foot length into the gather. He tried and tried, holding it at different angles, adding another attachment, putting the tube inside his flimsy lips. Either the molten glass didn't expand, or it expanded too fast and collapsed, or it was irretrievably lopsided and he had to start again. Salty beads formed at the corners of his eyes. He threw the blowpipe back into the furnace and he ran from the heat of the shop.

They persuaded him to try again. Jeremy obtained for him a set of polished oak teeth, carved by an American craftsman from across the river. Bennet applied the dentures and re-tried the blowpipe. It looked promising.

Dignitaries, friends, and family were re-assembled. Amelia had found, in Willowpath's cellar, a case of Perrier-Jouët, 1808. Four bottles sat in a tub of ice. She swung a fifth, attached by a sash to the ceiling, against the side of the roaring kiln.

Bennet thrust the pipe into the liquid incandescence beyond the furnace doors. He swirled and twisted and spun. He withdrew and re-engaged. He plumbed the depths of the crucible, rolling it over on itself like a dipper in a honey pot, until he had gathered a glowing bundle that radiated heat and light. Bennet rolled the orb on the marver, giving it shape. The mass of energy and matter, forcibly retrieved from the destructive boil of the cauldron, began to take form.

A gust of heat drenched the spectators and they stepped back. None of those in attendance could guess what the first piece might be. That was part of the captivation. To witness this act of creation first-hand was magical; to feel the heat, to smell the potash and charcoal, to be hypnotized by the volcanic glow.

Bennet blew, carefully at first, but he was excited, his old life returning to him. His breathing was uncontrolled, feverish. He spun too much one way, not enough the other. The first piece had a bulge. It shattered when it started to cool. He plunged it back into the furnace. Nerves, he explained to the gallery with a grin. Jeremy and Amelia exchanged looks, worried that after all these years the glassblower had lost his craft. He'd just got started. The old feeling returned.

The second piece made it as far as the glory hole. There he reheated it, after tweezing it, paddling it, adding coloured bits of broken glass. It entered the glory hole a few more times before it was abandoned and Bennet started again. He giggled. His audience had melted away. He was alone with his shears, blocks, and jacks. He blew and rolled. He peered into the cleansing boil of the furnace. *If I ever have to give this up again*, he thought, *I'll throw myself in*.

The third also seemed a mistake. The vessel was impossibly delicate, it couldn't succeed. Two stems going nowhere. Bennet entwined them, deftly, so they supported each other, grounding each other to the base. He cut the elegant sleeve from his pontil and melded it to the blended stem, conditioning it, galvanizing it again in the binding heat of the glory hole. Then, finally, he etched his pontil mark, AB inside an acorn. Remembering himself, finally, he turned with the finished product, a double-stem champagne flute with ivy decorating the base, and presented it to Jeremy and Amelia, who waited breathlessly. Amelia reached out to accept the glass but Bennet pulled it away.

"Too hot," he said. "Into the annealer to cool gradually, to temper and strengthen. With care, 'twill last a lifetime."

Jeremy popped one of the champagne bottles and the guests cheered when he accidentally knocked one of the imported glasses to the floor, a sacrifice to the altar of their fledgling glassworks.

Another had already begun to take shape at the end of Bennet's blowpipe.

Author Bio Note:

Morgan Wade's first novel, The Last Stoic, made the 2012 ReLit Awards long list. His short stories and poems have been published in Canadian literary journals and anthologies, including, The New Quarterly and The Nashwaak Review. He attended the Humber School of Writing and worked with novelist Michael Helm. He lives and writes in Kingston, Ontario.

For more information about Morgan Wade and Bottle and Glass please visit: http://www.morganwade.ca

Author's Notes

The chapters of *Bottle and Glass* (except for the first two) take their titles from actual, early 19th century Kingston inns and taverns (plus one in Halifax, Nova Scotia). Additional information on each drinking establishment follows. Establishment dates, where not exact, are based on first known mention. Proprietor is left empty where unknown. Locations, where known, are marked on the map at the beginning of the book.

1 – The Rode and Shackle

The Rode and Shackle is based on *The Bush Inn*, a 13th century free house located in Morwenstow, next to the Cornish coastal path between Bude and Hartland, overlooking the Cornish sea.

More info: http://www.bushinn-morwenstow.co.uk/welcome/

Swanky is a sweet, bottle conditioned beer spiced with ginger and raisins, specific to Cornwall.

2 – *HMS Lancer* – Captain's Cabin

The *Lancer* is modeled on *HMS Leopard*, the British ship involved in the *Chesapeake-Leopard* affair. The Leopard, under Captain Salusbury Pryce Humphreys, boarded *USS Chesapeake* in 1807 looking for British deserters, seizing four, three Americans and one Briton, Jenkin Ratford. Ratford was hanged for desertion. The Americans were sentenced to 500 lashes though the punishment was never carried out. The American public was outraged and the incident was one of the contributing factors leading to the War of 1812.

3 – Franklin's Tavern – Montreal Road

Established: 1805

Proprietor: Joseph Franklin and family

4 – White Bear Tavern

Established: 1808

The Kingston Gazette reported in 1817 that an Academy was opened across from the White Bear Tavern on Store Street with sciences being taught.

Bittered Sling – rye whisky, bitters, sugar, water, ice.

5 – Badgley's and Metcalf's, Blake's and Brown's

Established: before 1830

6 – The Golden Ball - Halifax

Established: before 1780

Proprietor: John O'Brien II. John O'Brien Senior, took the tavern over from Edward Phelan in 1780, looks to have died in 1808, after passing the business down to his son.

7 – Ferguson's Tavern - Barriefield
Established: before 1838

Proprietor: John Ferguson

Sherry Cobbler - sherry, lemon juice and rind, with shaved ice in a wine glass.

8 – Old King's Head (orig. King's Arms)
Established: before 1823

Proprietor: Owned by Mrs. Patrick, widow of Jermyn Patrick, run by George Millward.

9 – Walker's Hotel
Established: As early as 1810

Proprietor: Robert Walker

Wassail – hot cider mulled with brandy, sugar, cinnamon, ginger, and nutmeg, with a crescent of fried dough

10 – Violin, Bottle, and Glass

> **New Tavern.**
>
> THE subscriber respectfully informs his friends and the public, that he has opened a House of
>
> *Public Entertainment*
>
> directly opposite Sir John's Park, at the Sign of the *Violin, Bottle & Glass*; where those who may please to favor him with their custom, may be assured that every attention will be paid in the house both to Board and Lodging, and the best of Stabling for the accommodation of Horses.
>
> JOHN PONCET.
>
> *Kingston, January,* 1812.   11

Established: January 28, 1812, at Sir John's Park

Proprietor: John Poncet

Three Threads – 1/3 pint each of Robinson's Brown Ale, Pale Ale, and Tuppenny, Robinson's strongest. Also known as Robinson's Porter. Also known as *Entire*, combining the flavor of three threads. James Robinson, a local brewer, opened Kingston's first brewery in 1793.

The Bottle and Glass was evidently a going concern, with a number of advertisements posted in the papers for sensational entertainments.

> **NEW EXHIBITION.**
> *Theatrical Entertainment.*
> ON Wednesday Evening, at Mr. Poncet's large Room, which is fitted up for the purpose, with new arrangements, the celebrated and much admired Comic Farce in three acts will be acted, never performed in Kingston before, called 'The Doctor's Courtship; to be interspersed with Vocal and Instrumental Music.—To commence at half past 7 o'clock. N. B. Particulars in the bills of the day.

> **GOOD NEWS!!!**
> THE Ladies and Gentlemen of Kingston and its vicinity are most respectfully informed, that a variety of surprising Performances will be exhibited on Tuesday Evening, April 28, at Poncet's Inn, when a grand display of new curiosities will be exhibited, which has never failed in giving general satisfaction to all competent judges. There will be upwards of 200 extraordinary feats performed, never parallelled in Upper Canada.—Price of Front Seats 2/6 —Gallery 1/3. —Tickets to be had at Mr. Walker's Hotel, and at the place of performance.
> N. B. Good Music is procured.—Performance to begin at half past 7 o'clock.

11 – King's Arms Inn
Established: Before 1818
Bison Harris was an actual taverner of the era - it is unclear of which tavern.

12 – Mother Cook's
Established: Before 1818
Proprietor: Mother Cook
Common gin was sometimes flavoured with turpentine, in this case obtained from Loughborough Red Pine.

Daniel Cole, one of the members of that first U.E.L. Band, in his old age thus described his remembrance of Kingston, as the party passed through it on their way up the bay in 1784. He said: "Old Mother Cook then kept tavern in Kingston, in a low flat house with two rooms. There were only four or five other houses in the place. Some of our earlier log shanties were deeply covered with marsh hay or flags, carefully laid on lengthways, which seemed to keep out the rain and snow very well."

[From the remembrances of Dr. Allen Ruttan, written by T.W. Casey, published in the Napanee Beaver, Jan. 29, 1897]

13 – The Britannia Inn
Established: Early 1800s

Quetton St. Charles is based upon Quetton St. George, French Royalist emigre, who established a chain of stores in Upper Canada.

The Pernod Fils distillery was established in 1797. It produced an all-purpose elixir called absinthe, originally created by Dr. Pierre Ordinaire.

14 – The O.K. (Owen Kennedy) Tavern
Established: Before 1822
Proprietor: Owen Kennedy

Dalton was another early brewer and founder of the Kingston Brewery.

15 – The Black Bull
Established: Before 1822
Proprietor: Mr. Chestnut

William Warre's 10-year old tawny port was a popular tipple throughout the colonies.

16 – Old Sam's
Established: Early 1800s

Toddy – hot bohea with brandy, honey, cloves, lemon, and stick of cinnamon

17 – Tête-du-Pont – Officer's Quarters
Established: 1783 (on the site of the ruined Fort Frontenac, built 1673) – The actual Officer's Mess building was not built until after 1821, but there would have been a mess near the officer's quarters.

Julep – Cognac, simple syrup, spearmint, ice.

18 – Richmond Hotel – Near Point Henry
Established: Before 1820 (work began in 1812)
Proprietor: John Martin
Collins was a popular cocktail, made with Old Tom Gin

19 – St. George and Dragon
Established: Early 1800s
Ale Flip (or, One Yard of Flannel) – One quart of Robinson's Ale, heated, four egg whites, beaten, half cup sugar, four ounces rum, grated ginger, nutmeg and dried lemon peel, stirred with a red-hot poker.

20 – Olcott's Tavern
Established: Before 1816
Proprietor: Benjamin Olcott
Nor'wester – Tumbler, half water, half dark rum

21 – The Rob Roy
Established: Before 1817
Oude Genever - distilled from malt wine spirits, infused with juniper, anise, caraway, coriander

22 – Burnside's Tavern
Established: Before 1817
Proprietor: David Burnside
Syllabub – cider, brandy, honey, nutmeg, warm milk pulled directly from the udder of a dairy shorthorn

23 – Jim Beach's
Established: Early 1800's
Proprietor: Jim Beach

Books in the North Shore Series
Find full information at
– http://www.HiddenBrookPress.com/b-NShore.html

2 Anthologies

Changing Ways is a book of prose by Cobourg area authors including: Jean Edgar Benitz, Patricia Calder, Fran O'Hara Campbell, Leonard D'Agostino, Shane Joseph, Brian Mullally. Editor: Jacob Hogeterp
   – Prose – ISBN – 978-1-897475-22-5

That Not Forgotten - Editor – Bruce Kauffman with 118 authors from the North Shore geographic area.
   – Prose and Poetry – ISBN – 978-1-897475-89-8

First set of five books

— M.E. Csamer – Kingston – *A Month Without Snow*
   – Prose – ISBN – 978-1-897475-87-2
— Elizabeth Greene – Kingston – *The Iron Shoes*
   – Poetry – ISBN – 978-1-897475-76-6
— Richard Grove – Brighton – *A Family Reunion*
   – Prose – ISBN – 978-1-897475-90-2
— R.D. Roy – Trenton – *A Pre emptive Kindness*
   – Prose – ISBN – 978-1-897475-80-3
— Eric Winter – Cobourg – *The Man In The Hat*
   – Poetry – ISBN – 978-1-897475-77-3

Second set of five books

— Janet Richards – Belleville – *Glass Skin*
   – Poetry – ISBN – 978-1-897475-01-0
— R.D. Roy – Trenton – *Three Cities*
   – Poetry – ISBN – 978-1-897475-96-4
— Wayne Schlepp – Cobourg – *The Darker Edges of the Sky*
   – Poetry – ISBN – 978-1-897475-99-5
— Benjamin Sheedy – Kingston – *A Centre in Which They Breed*
   – Poetry – ISBN – 978-1-897475-98-8
— Patricia Stone – Peterborough – *All Things Considered*
   – Prose – ISBN – 978-1-897475-04-1

Third set of five books

— Mark Clement – Cobourg – *Island In the Shadow*
  – Poetry – ISBN – 978-1-897475-08-9
— Anthony Donnelly – Brighton – *Fishbowl Fridays*
  – Prose – ISBN – 978-1-897475-02-7
— Chris Faiers – Marmora – *ZenRiver Poems & Haibun*
  – Poetry – ISBN – 978-1-897475-25-6
— Shane Joseph – Cobourg – *Fringe Dwellers* Second Edition
  – Prose – ISBN – 978-1-897475-44-7
— Deborah Panko – Cobourg – *Somewhat Elsewhere*
  – Poetry – ISBN – 978-1-897475-13-3

Forth set of five books

— Diane Dawber – Bath – *Driving, Braking and Getting out to Walk*
  – Poetry – ISBN – 978-1-897475-40-9
— Patrick Gray – Port Hope – *This Grace of Light*
  – Poetry – ISBN – 978-1-897475-34-8
— John Pigeau – Kingston – *The Nothing Waltz*
  – Prose – ISBN – 978-1-897475-37-9
— Mike Johnston – Cobourg – *Reflections Around the Sun*
  – Poetry – ISBN – 978-1-897475-38-6
— Kathryn MacDonald – Shannonville – *Calla & Édourd*
  – Prose – ISBN – 978-1-897475-39-3

Fifth set of three books

— Tara Kainer – Kingston – *When I Think On Your Lives*
  – Poetry– ISBN – 978-1-897475-68-3
— Morgan Wade – Kingston – *The Last Stoic*
  – Novel – ISBN – 978-1-897475-63-8
— Kathryn MacDonald – Shannonville – *A Breeze You Whisper*
  – Poetry – ISBN – 978-1-897475-66-9

Sixth set of three books

— Bruce Kauffman – Kingston – *The Texture of Days, in Ash and Leaf*
  – Poetry – ISBN - 978-1-897475-86-7
— Chris Faiers – Marmora – *Eel Pie Island Dharma: A hippie memoir/haibun*
  – A memoir in haibun form – ISBN - 978-1-897475-92-8
— Theodore Michael Christou – Kingston – *an overbearing eye*
  – Poetry – ISBN – 978-1-897475-93-5

Seventh set of four books

— Alyssa Cooper – Kingston – *Cold Breath of Life*
  – Poetry – ISBN – 978-1-927725-02-3
— Bruce Kauffman – Kingston – *The Silence Before the Whisper Comes*
  – Poetry – ISBN – 978-1-897475-98-0
— S.E. Richardson – Kingston – *Before I Lose Light*
  – Poetry – ISBN – 978-1-927725-05-4
— G. W. Rasberry – Kingston – *More Naked Than Ever*
  – Poetry – ISBN – 978-1-927725-04-7

Eighth set of six books

— Brian Way – Carrying Place – *redirection*
  – Poetry – ISBN - 978-1-927725-20-7
— David Pratt – Kingston – *Apprehensions of Van Gogh*
  – Poetry – ISBN - 978-1-927725-21-4
— Felicity Sidnell Reid – Colborne – *Alone*
  – Young Adult Novel – ISBN - 978-1-927725-18-4
— James Ronson – Port Hope – *Power and Possessions*
  – Novel – ISBN - 978-1-927725-22-1
— Morgan Wade – Kingston – *Bottle and Glass*
  – Novel – ISBN - 978-1-9227-19-1
— Jim Christy – Belleville – *Bad Day for Ralphie*
  – Short Stories – ISBN - 978-1-927725-23-8

Date: 03.04.23/ Return to Albania

We are back in Sarande, Albania, and even with the drizzles and rain that greeted us, it was nice to be "home." It's not official, but for NOW, this is as close as it gets to home, anywhere.

Though the distance between Egypt and here is not great, it took us three days to get back due to the timing of layovers and flights. After our overnight train trip from Aswan to Cairo Wednesday night (3 hours late I might add...), we to "kill the day" in Cairo since our flight left the following morning at 0440. We mostly chilled in our room, which was surprisingly nice, took a nap or two, and headed to the airport just after midnight.

Our Cairo to Athens flight was a quick two hours, but we had to kill time THERE again, and we got to Corfu midafternoon on Friday. Unfortunately, there is only ONE daily ferry from Corfu each day, and stayed in a cute little apartment (more rain...), and returned this morning to finally get to our new flat for the next three months. Which we love, and is easily the BEST place we've stayed in four years—at the best price to boot. We are mostly unpacked and stocked on food and such, and now we can relax for a bit until we hit the road again in June.

This is our view from our new apartment in Sarande, so NOW you may understand why we love it here and decided to stay for the next three months. At $500 USD per month.

Now it is time to "catch up" on our travels, and for me to work on a revised web site for Travel Younger, as well as a new version of my Traveling the World for Six Weeks books, which will be condensed into one book, updated, and have more extra content.

THE END (for now)

March, 2023

For more information visit us at www.TravelYounger.com or email to: asknormb@gmail.com.

Manufactured by Amazon.ca
Acheson, AB